A GRAVE ABOVE GROUND

the total eclipse of a heart

A Beggar's Tale

DIANA HUTTON

BOOK PUBLISHING

HPEditions

Australia

A Grave above Ground: A Beggar's Tale
© Diana Hutton and HPEditions 2017

Categories: *Literary Fiction, Social Issues, Biography, Mental Health*

Printed by IngramSpark
Digital edition also available from Amazon and elsewhere

ISBN-13   978 0 98752 12 5 5
ISBN-10   0 9875212 5 X

Length: 106,800 words

Published by HPEditions
Australia

Mara's Story

This is a beggar's tale. It is the story of how easily life can change. An unwanted pregnancy brings a happy young university student with a bright future face to face with harsh reality, much worsened by the soulless poverty crushing Romania at the time of Ceausescu's cruel dictatorship. Family rejection is followed by a sordid kidnapping of the baby she had come to love and adore, a frantic search for the infant in the hellish confines of the many government orphanages, flight from persecution as a refugee, oppression as an illegal immigrant and even rape, abuse and eventual psychological collapse, all leading her to a life of squalor, discrimination and begging on the streets of Madrid.

While she inspires hatred in some people who look on her as refugee trash, others whose lives she touches see some good in her, offer love, care, a taste of normal life and even find inspiration in her humble self-possession. But is hers a fate that can be escaped from or is there no possible recovery from the total eclipse of a heart?

ABOUT THE AUTHOR

Diana Hutton lives in Madrid, Spain and has spent most of her career as a professional translator but has devoted the last few years to writing full-time. She has written two novels, "A Grave above Ground" and "Don't Call Me Lebohang" which is also available on Amazon.

She is currently revising another novel written some years ago and entitled "Sisterly Love". It delves into the intricacies of the sister relationship in old age, treating the subject with remarkable humour and sensitivity. She is also in the process of working on a new novel.

Although born in Southampton, in the United Kingdom at the end of the Second World War, Diana spent the first ten years of her life in London, then moved with her family to Sydney, Australia. She was educated there and dabbled in acting and contemporary ballet in Sydney on leaving school, then worked at the Australian Broadcasting Commission. As a young woman, she returned to London, but shortly afterwards moved to live in Paris where she met her Spanish husband-to-be whilst working in the Australian Permanent Delegation to UNESCO. She married in Madrid and has two grown up children. She has lived there on and off since 1970 and has found life in Spain to be a deeply enriching experience.

To the beggars on our streets

Times are to us like places: we live in both;
they touch us, and always, more or less,
make their mark upon us. Unwholesome places
and corrupt times infect us with their contagion.

Pensées of Joubert

Contents

Cast of Characters

Ana   a travel agent who offered Mara a cleaning job that turned sour

Andreea   woman with whom Mara escaped from Italy and a prostitute

Andrei   a drunk, homeless man who had a brief affair with Mara in Madrid

Ceausescu   the *Conducator*, Nicolae, communist dictator of Romania from 1965 to 1989 and wife Elena, both of whom presided over years of poverty and hardship for the people

Celia   Julia's sister, owner of an art gallery in Venezuela

David   a colleague of Jorge who sympathizes with immigrants

Emilia   cousin to Raimundo and manager of the Nursing Home where Mara works

Eva   the daughter of Ana, whose interaction with Mara caused her to run away

Federico   Florencia's ex-boyfriend

Florencia   young cleaning woman at the Clinic, who Mara likes

Franco   Francisco Franco, fascist dictator who ruled Spain from 1939 until 1975

Jorge   bank worker, follower of Franco and supporter of fascism

Julia   an old lady who wanted to befriend Mara but could not

Lola   or Dolores, patient at Nursing Home who empathises with Mara

Manuela	one of Mara's nurses at the Clinic, a kindly young woman
Mara	Romanian refugee and later beggar in Madrid, the main character
Marciano	an unpleasant, dictatorial patient in the Nursing Home
Marta	patient at Nursing Home who reminds Mara of her mother, Roxana
Mihaita	Roxana's husband who eventually left her, but was the only father that Mara had known
Paca	or Francisca, a kind young woman who was inspired by Mara to work with refugees
Petre	Mara's long-term boyfriend as a student and probable father of Tatiana, but who deserted Mara after her affair with Radu
Radu	student with Mara and with whom she had a brief affair
Raimundo	Mara's psychiatrist in the Clinic
Rogelio	Raimundo's father, killed in a terrorist attack
Rosa	one of Mara's nurses at the Clinic, rather unpleasant and mean-spirited
Roxana	mother of Mara and Viorica and a disagreeable woman
Simona	mother of Roxana and kind grandmother of Mara and Viorica
Tatiana	daughter of Mara, kidnapped when a baby
Viorica	Mara's young sister, possibly from a different father

1

Life at Ankle Level

Where do I start? Why not with what has occupied me for most of my life? Ankles.

Slender, bony ankles. They are the fine prolongation of a long shin. Hefty and thick ankles are like a lengthening of the calf muscle. Ankles can be smooth with brown skin. They can be wrinkled, motley and white with purple blotches, or crossed with minute red veins. I see them all. If they belong to a man, a few hairs might grow from them. If the man has hairy muscle on his leg, the hair thins out considerably at ankle level. I am observant, you see. Some ankles are clad in socks, sports socks with sports shoes on the feet. The sandal-wearers don't wear socks. Their ankles are bare and many of them are beautiful. If they are beautiful, they belong to handsome young women who walk haughtily by me not deigning to notice the huddled abject human heap at their feet. There are the old ankles too, old ankles with prominent veins, blue worms under a pallid skin. Old fat ankles with their folds of blubber. Old thin ankles with their creases of dry withered skin. Old ankles of old people that look as though they can barely support the bodies above them. With age, bones drain of their marrow and turn to fragile sticks that can snap, like a chicken bone, at the slightest wrong move.

Careful! Don't trip up old girl, or you'll be in a wheel chair for the rest of your days, a problem for your husband, a pain in the neck for your children. Careful there! Of course, I wouldn't dare to say that to them. If they fall, I won't be the one to have warned them. I'll only

1

have watched them. I wouldn't even feel sorry for them. Even with broken fragile old bones, their plight wouldn't be as bad as mine. Although, being older, they are closer to the grave than I am. Perhaps, however, death would be better than life, than this life, anyway. But, who knows?

Sometimes the frail bones are disguised in rolls of fat, fat ankles, yet frail. Outsize humans who can only lug themselves along, whose every step is an effort, a panting effort. Their legs are like elephants' legs, thick, shapeless, leathery, scaled and heavy … so heavy to put into motion. Their lives are a tragedy too, like mine. I mean, when every step is an effort … The bones on some ankles, the inner bone and the outer bone supporting the ankle, are prominent. On others, they are almost non-existent. Some ankles stomp. They are not flexible. It is as though they are stuck to the shin bone, no spring in them, unaware as their owners are, that their purpose in life is to serve as a hinge between leg and foot.

What is my purpose in life?

Of course, I only notice people's ankles because I cannot avoid seeing them, sitting as I am at ankle level. I stare at my own ankles protruding from the hem of my long skirt. Peering at my ankles occupies part of my time. It gives me something to do, helps my begging day to pass. I stare hard at them and don't always recognize them. That depends on the light. In the fierce sunlight of these interminable summer days in the hell-fire of Madrid, my skin looks almost translucent, but the grime pushes through the translucence, embedded as it is in the wrinkles at the base of my ankles, at the top of my feet. It's not always easy to wash properly. I would need a wire brush to scrape the grime from my skin. It is strange, this translucent grime. I peer at it, trying to associate it with me, with my Romanian soul, with my ruddy, gypsy-like face, with my thick-fingered hands, like my mother Roxana's hands, a washer-woman's hands. Yes, I suppose that the grime suits me, that it fits in with the general appearance. Living outside is a grimy business, Doctor, a lonely business, with no-one to talk to and only your ankles to look at. Although, true, there are other people's ankles to look at. My ankles

2

seem to have thinned with the years. When I was a young Romanian lass, they were sturdy appendages, strong, healthy, active. Now that I sit so much they seem to be frailer. Sometimes, when I get up, when I begin to walk after a whole day sitting in my street den, they crack as though groaning at me, protesting,

These ankles have been mine for the last fifty years or so. Attached as they are to my feet, they have trod many a path, inside Spain, outside Spain, inside Romania, outside Romania. That used to be my home. One day, when the glare of the sun, the heat rising from the furnace pavement, the sweat on my brow ... one day, when all that has subsided, I shall talk of Romania. But now I must concentrate on the people and their ankles, because sitting at ground level like this means that my first contact with any person is their ankles. The ankles are the first part of the human anatomy that I see, ensconced as I am on this hot granite pathway.

Many are the nights when I dream about ankles.

Some people pass by quickly. They pass by my indigence as if running away from me. They run away from what they don't want to see. Or perhaps they don't even see me. They? I am speaking about the human bodies with ankles, of course. Some come towards me. They don't know that I am watching them. My eyes squint. They are barely open, slits in my face, slit to protect them from the sun's fierce rays. Some passers-by jog or jolt, up and down, along the pavement. Others drag their feet, lazy, languid. Some trip on the paving stones. Others hesitate. If they slow down as they approach me, I think that they might drop a coin onto the small raffia mat which I have spread out in front of me. But that is rare. I forget. They don't want to see me, do they? They don't want my eyes to meet their eyes. I am a disturbance in their society, an ugly protuberance, a tumour on the edge of their lives, oozing out onto the broiling slabs of this pavement. I am an embarrassment, a stone weighing on their consciences, roasting as I am in the oven of my street existence.

Studying people's ankles and feet and toe nails is a pass-time for me during the summer months, although I think I prefer the winter months when they cover it all up in heavy shoes and thick socks - the

3

all is mostly ugly.   Feet have corns and calluses and bunions and leathery heels and hammer toes and ingrown toe nails and warts and red patches and splitting skin and flat feet and blisters and they smell. All this passes by me, day after day ... part of the human machine, the world's physical matter.

2

Observations and Memories

How did I come to be here, ensconced in my rags on this pavement, on my cardboard throne? Of course, it's a long story, Doctor. I don't know if I can tell it all just now, perspiring as I am, gasping as I am, of thirst. The heat beats against my brow and my brain throbs to bursting. Perhaps another time I shall talk of how I came to be here. When I am cooler, when the weather isn't so extreme. In Madrid, the extreme cold in the winter and the extreme heat in the summer make it hard for the brain to function. Instead of talking about how I came to be here, bundled together with my rags on this street corner, I can talk about what I can see from my look-out at ankle level. A description of my surroundings is easier than exhuming my life story. This is my street corner. No other beggar will come here. No other beggar would try to take it away from me. We all have our own street corners. We build up our own particular clientele. We respect each other's ground – mostly, anyway – each other's property, albeit not private property. There is more solidarity between beggars than there is between any other strata of the human race; although true, they are sometimes drunk and disorderly, but they are all in the same boat. And that is a very strong feeling. A bond.

I prop my aching back against a piece of street furniture – a used battery disposal unit. *Street furniture* is the name they have given to these ugly brown plastic receptacles for rubbish, for publicity, for used paper, for used bottles, for used batteries, for bus stops also with brown plastic benches and glass panels to protect the people in the bus queue from the wind, not from the sun because sun through glass and plastic makes you sweat. Street furniture. Not that I have ever seen anyone putting a used battery inside my battery disposal unit. It sits there empty, useless, behind me, underneath an advertising board. People sometimes stop right in front of me, without seeing me, to stare at the publicity on the board, publicity for a new film, publicity for a new play, publicity for a new car, publicity for women's make-up, publicity for men's after-shave, publicity for men's underwear with photos of a male deity sporting rounded, soft, female breasts, his attributes tucked neatly, suggestively, into Calvin Klein underpants, publicity for a football match, publicity for a tennis tournament, publicity for ice skating, publicity for a new commercial centre, publicity for holidays in Turkey, in Morocco, in Vienna, in Florence, in the USA, in an igloo at the North Pole, even in Transylvania – I could never return there, soon you will know why, even if I had the money – publicity for a cycling marathon, publicity for a running marathon, publicity for a cat show, publicity for publicity's sake. There is even an outsize board in the gardens in the centre of the street, where each publicity spot moves on to reveal another one after a couple of minutes. There is, in short, publicity for everything this capitalist society offers, publicity for everyone, for old and young alike. Maybe it's like this now in Romania. When I lived there, there was no publicity – it was a communist state.

The people stare at it. I stare at their ankles, those hinges between the leg and foot. I study their toe nails. Toe nails are uglier than ankles. Thank goodness they are smaller and generally less visible. Some of the toe nails that I see are broken and unkempt, to say nothing of the line of dirt beneath them. Some toe nails have fungus growths on them, yellow and lumpy and repulsive. Some toe nails are too long, curling round over the tip of the toes. Some of them are unevenly cut with sharp, jagged edges on one side and embedded into the skin of the toe on the other side. Some are black or dark purple in colour from a blow. Of course, they aren't all ugly. Young toe nails are better than old ones. They can be cut more neatly and painted with pretty colours in the summer. Smart young women, the ones who walk past me unaware of my presence, generally care for their toe nails, making a feature of them to add to their other allures. You can tell someone's life history from his or her toe nails.

*   *   *

The bright colours of their clothes, the baubles jingling on the women's wrists as they raise their arms in time to the music, the swirling skirts, the merry laughter, the dark seductive eyes. I close my eyes to protect them from the intense sunlight in Madrid and I see a myriad of colour, beautiful colour that takes me way back to the feasting of my youth. I often dream of those Romanian feasts, the feasts in my Transylvanian village near the town of Lugoj where we would dance into the early hours of the morning, happy, carefree, not blighted by consumer worries, unconcerned by adult problems. The whole village together, young and old, children and animals – the donkeys' ears and the cows' horns bedecked with bright flowers, the tails of the mules and horses threaded through with vine leaves and ivy leaves – all of us moving to the strains of the pan pipes and violins. We children danced in a frenzy and when we tired of dancing we raced around, pulling the dogs' tails, pushing in between the legs of the swirling adult couples, pulling at a ribbon here, tweaking the hem of a skirt there, treading on a man's shoes, laughing at ourselves, joyful, happy, free, full of life, escaping from smacked bottoms, splitting our sides with laughter, stuffing ourselves with the leftovers from the long trestle tables, sipping at the wine dregs in the glasses, pretending to be drunk and tipsy.

We used to light candles and run with them through the night, when your candle blew out you had to stop and light it again and so you fell behind the others and then had to try and catch them up. Some of the children shrieked when they burnt their fingers as the candle wax dripped right down, consumed by flame. I remember that my grandmother, old and laughing and wrinkled and always with a story on the tip of her tongue, told me that whenever I lit a candle I should make a good wish and think hard about that wish all the time the candle burned, then when I blew it out I should imagine that I was blowing something bad out of my life, away from me. She told me that candles were sacred and important in our churches. She told me that I should think of the good things in life every time I lit a candle on entering the church, or when the electric light went out at home and we had to use candles, which often happened, and she told me to think of the bad things about myself every time I blew the candle out.

7

Afterwards, at night before going to sleep, she said that I should remember those bad things and try never to do them again. Simona was my grandmother, old and laughing and wrinkled.

On feast days we wore our best clothes. The older women wore bodices heavily embroidered with pretty flowers. Their skirts were white and their bodices black in contrast, and some of them wore a coloured apron. Head dresses covered their hair, a round, white bonnet with silver trinkets falling daintily from the edges of it and starched lace trimmings. Or they wore a black bonnet. They all looked pretty, so pretty, so full of life. Wanting to live.

3

Just Sitting

Now I am half dead. Half dead in this grave. My grave above ground.

When I remember our Romanian feast days, Doctor, I see that my life today is only half full. Half? Maybe only a quarter full. Can this be called life, sitting in the same spot day after day on a pavement so far from my village in the Transylvanian hills and vales, Romanian dales, and with no desire to do anything else? The laughter has gone from my days. I no longer wear pretty clothes. I am dirty. My hair is greying and thinning. I am old, not young. A quarter of a life sitting in front of the white marble slabs of the building opposite me only three metres away. Dogs pee against those slabs and the piddle dribbles down in a yellow stream making a dark patch on the pavement. In the heat I can smell it. Dogs' urine. They come, one after the other, sniff, sniffing at the corner of the building, the bank, for the building is a bank. Money inside it, piddle on the pavement outside it. The dogs raise their legs, an automatic reflex after sniffing, and the urine spurts out against the bank wall, right in front of my eyes. Sometimes the dogs sniff at me, sniff around me, dig their muzzles into my long skirt. They stare at me with their sad eyes. If I talk to them, they wag their tails. Perhaps a dog would be a companion for me. Perhaps I wouldn't be so lonely if I had a dog. Occasionally, very occasionally, I dare to say a few words to a dog on a lead. I don't look at its master or mistress. I am not talking to him or to her, I am talking only to the dog. The dog understands me better than its master. Mostly, the moment I utter a word to the dog, it is pulled away vehemently, quickly, called to heel, told to keep

9

away from life's debris. If I had a dog I would have a faithful, golden dog with soft fur and soulful eyes. I have seen those dogs with their wonderful tails like banners, with fur that you could bury your sorrows in. It would lie beside me, touching me, nuzzling me, all day long. We would talk to each other, me with my words, the dog with its eyes. It would sit up, panting, staring around it, eyes glistening, tongue hanging sensually out of its mouth. It would lick my hand. It would fall asleep with its heavy head against my thigh. Yes, it would be company. ... Perhaps it would pee against the marble slabs of the bank too. Perhaps more people would notice me, talk to me, if I had a dog. These well-off people prefer dogs to humans. But how would I bring it to and from my place of work, to and from my slab of pavement? Dogs aren't allowed on public transport. And how would I feed it? I don't have the money to feed myself properly. It wouldn't be fair to the animal. People shouldn't have animals if they can't look after them. I have enough to do taking care of myself. I couldn't even take care of Tatiana. Tatiana ... my baby daughter. They took her away from me several weeks after I had pushed her out into the world. They left me a lonely mother. What is a mother without her daughter? Nothing. Nothing. Good enough only to sit begging on a pavement. Would Tatiana have helped me to beg? Perhaps she wouldn't have loved me. One day I shall talk to you about how Tatiana came to be born. There was Petre. Or was it Radu?

I sit in front of this bank, the bank with the white marble slabs on its wall, with the used battery disposal unit behind me. My place – my work – is on the corner of two busy streets where the buses go up and down, where cars and motorbikes never cease their whining, grinding of gears, their exhaust fumes, their screeching of brakes, where ambulances race past, sirens to the wind, where the rumbling buses stop at the traffic lights. Both streets have plenty of banks, a lot of shops – fruit shops, meat shops, herb shops, clothes shops, flower shops, gift shops, a stationery shop, a supermarket, a Chinese bazaar, a work centre, an iron-monger's, a shoe mender's, a haberdasher's, a newspaper kiosk, a hairdresser's, a travel agent's, a chemist - and several restaurants – Chinese, Asian, Spanish, Italian, American. Nobody here goes hungry. Only me. And sometimes I can smell the food when youngsters eat a hamburger, or their sandwiches, in the street. And I wish they would break a piece off for me. My stomach rumbles, like the buses. The streets are busy. The pavements are busy with old men, old women, young men, young women, children big and small, dogs on leads – you already know that – aunts, uncles, cousins, friends, parents, working companions, nuns, priests, black men begging, white men begging, drug addicts.

This place is a cross section of society. There are even mad people. Well, slightly mad because they wander alone up and down, talking to themselves, clutching their bags, muttering in their beards, counting from one to one hundred, one to one hundred repetitively, counting on their fingers, asking people the time of day, asking for a coin. ... I don't ask anybody. I just sit, watching the world go by, watching the ankles go by, hoping, hoping that one coin, two coins, might drop onto my raffia mat. Only occasionally do I let out a cry for help, a long-drawn-out *pooooooor favooooooor*. When I hear my voice resounding against the paving stones, resounding in this foreign language against the walls of the bank, when I hear that plea for help curdling the blood of the passers-by, I don't recognise myself. There are days when this plea becomes a habit, but really it is no more than an expression of my desperation. It comes from the very depths of my soul. I know that few will respond to it, and even though I don't recognise myself in it, it soothes me, it relieves the tension pent up inside me. That is why I cry out for help. And yes, sometimes it does work. Sometimes a woman will stop because she feels sorry for me, because she imagines what her own life might be if she had to sit out in the street begging. She stops, briefly, no intention of staying to chat, she bids me the time of day and drops a coin onto my mat or into my grubby hand. She smiles, but not at me. She smiles sideways. I look at her, trying to force a smile, *muuuchas graacias*. Our eyes meet only fleetingly. She smiles at her own act of benevolence and she leaves as quickly as she came.

One day, an old lady stopped and asked me why I didn't try to get some work instead of sitting here all-day long. Why don't I try to get some work? Perhaps because there is no work to be had. Perhaps because I know that it is useless to make the effort of searching even before I start. Remember, I am Romanian. My people are the most resigned people on this earth. They accept mishap. Our capacity for suffering is limitless. Suffering is heroic to us. One of our writers, Cioran, exalted his people for chaining themselves to misfortune. He said we suffered in silence. I remember his words when I was at university. And another Romanian poet, whose name I can't remember, wrote a song about the way we accept shame and ruin as though they were fate. We are peaceful people. We have a soft nature. We have no desire to dominate others. We live and let live, except for the dictator. I shall talk about him one day, how he robbed and tortured his own people. Yet I am proud in my resignation. I studied literature at Timisoara University. I used to read. I used to write. I dreamed through books. Now I have no intention of sweeping the floors and changing babies' nappies for Spanish civil servants and bankers. I prefer to do nothing, just to dream under this sun that beats into my brain with its vibrancy. And my Spanish isn't good enough to look for a job to match my studies. Why don't I learn Spanish? It isn't only the money I would need. I just don't have the will anymore to learn.

*　　　*　　　*

I was speaking about my surroundings, what I see from my place on earth on this noisy street corner, apart from the ankles and toenails, apart from the dogs' urine. In the middle of the street there are gardens. I could sit in the gardens, on a bench, but they are normally empty. People only go there when the children come out of school and play on the swings. Tatiana would have enjoyed those swings. No, I prefer to sit on the pavement. I no longer even have the will to get up and cart my body over the zebra crossing into the gardens. I am tired. In the centre of the gardens, where the two main streets meet, someone has erected a statue. It is a bronze statue of a deer and a mountain goat. It looks peaceful and bucolic. When I stare at it, I remember my village in Transylvania with the trees, the animals, the fields sloping down from the mountain peaks. When my life was healthy. When I belonged to society, before I became a disturbance on the edge of society.

For that is what I am now. A tumour.

There are days when the slightly insane people emerge from the residences where they are cared for, residences, homes for the mentally deficient run by nuns. They wander aimlessly over to the gardens. They stand by the bronze deer, staring at it, laughing, pointing at each other, dribbling, drinking from gigantic plastic coca cola bottles, singing in jagged tones that grate against the fine, keen air of Madrid, laughing in coarse, rasping sounds that tumble uncontrolled from their dribbling mouths. That laughter is hair-raising. I hear it at night when I lie down to sleep and I fear it.

I fear it in the way that many people fear me, those who avoid me.

Sometimes the mad people gather in the small square in front of the newspaper kiosk. They sit under the trees there, perched haphazardly and untidily on the wall on one side of the square. And there they continue with their drinking, their dribbling, their laughing, their pointing, their singing. They are happier than I am. Their minds have gone off, as if on an excursion somewhere else outside their present reality, and they don't realise how sad, how bad their lives are. Yes, I would be happier if I were mad.

Because my life is sad and bad now.

That square is on the other side of the street where I sit. I don't go there, although I could go there to find shade, but I don't because it belongs to another beggar. The steps just outside an all-purpose store beside the square are his territory. I respect that. We have never met. We have never spoken to each other, but I respect his territory, as he respects my territory in front of the bank. He has his few clients. I have mine. Of course, he never goes inside that store. There is a security guard at the door. He wouldn't dare to try to enter it. Neither would I. The store is for people who have money to spend on flowers, CDs, chocolates, biscuits, books, toys, games, newspapers and glossy magazines, the unnecessary things that make life more pleasant. There is a restaurant too at the back of the store. If Tatiana were with me, I would take her to eat in that restaurant, because if Tatiana were with me, my whole life would have been different, Doctor, and I would have made more effort to do something with it. Or I would get her to run inside the store to buy some chocolates. I wouldn't be so bored if she were here with me. But I don't even know her, do I?

13

She was a tiny baby when they took her from me.

I can hear her screams in my imagination. And my screams. The screams that chill my blood at night when I cannot sleep, when I hear them in my miserable abode. Screams that shriek at me through the wooden slats and the corrugated iron roofing of my slum home. They burst in on the wind. They shriek at me in accusation. They accuse me of having abandoned my baby daughter. I live on the outskirts of this city, this dry crust of a land. I live in a dusty road lined with hovels, off one of the main roads out of the city.

Where are my Transylvanian mountains? In my dreams. Only in my dreams.

The police come from time to time to pick up the drug addicts, the drug traffickers, the prostitutes. Things are bad for me but I have never lent my body to prostitution. Although my mother said that I had, that she had sent me to university to study, not to sleep around with boys.

4

The Clinic and Raimundo

She talked ceaselessly, deliriously of Petre, day in, day out, for seven whole days, Petre this, Petre that. Of course, we couldn't understand her then. And then there was Tatiana. Whenever she mentioned the name Tatiana she would sigh, sigh with a heavy groan, change her posture and her eyes would turn to lost pools. These were her first mutterings, her first sign of consciousness, of life, after thirty-five and a half days in coma. Thirty-five and a half days when those of us in the clinic who attended her – Carlos and Jaime her doctors, Manuela and Rosa her nurses, I, Raimundo, her psychiatrist, and others – were all sure that she would never surface from the depths of her unconsciousness.

For thirty-five and a half days she lay as still as death, utterly motionless on her back, her breathing imperceptible, her liquid food drip dripping through the transparent tubes into her veins. We thought that she had hit her head on something hard when she had fallen because when the ambulance brought her to the clinic she was badly bruised over her right eye. We didn't know whether she had tripped and fallen, and fainted because of the fall, or whether she had fallen because she had lost consciousness. She was in a terrible state physically. It wasn't until later that I was able to determine how much her brain had been affected.

Although she had a hefty frame, her body was wasted, her skin was dry and rough and hung in old folds around her thighs and stomach, under her chin and on her upper arms. On her legs, she had several

15

suppurating ulcers, ulcers caused from under-nourishment, although we realised that she had picked up some epidemic. Her body was filthy, as were the clothes the nurses removed from it. Her toenails and fingernails were jagged, broken, split, and dirty of course. She had years of grime engrained into her pores. She smelt unpleasant. The first job was to bath her, to wash her matted locks of hair and to cut them. This the nurses did after an initial examination by the doctors, before they could decide in more detail on her physical state.

*   *   *

Manuela screwed up her face in disgust. 'Washing her hair was terrible, Rosa! Those smelly strands, all stuck together! After lathering the soap and rinsing her hair thoroughly, I tried to comb through it, but it was like pulling a rake across thick grass. I had to put some softener on. I wish you'd been there to help me. I could have done it in half the time if you'd been there to hold her head up. You have more experience than the young assistant nurse who was with me. Because, of course, the patient was unconscious, wasn't she? It was like washing a dead person, a corpse and her head was heavy. I managed to wrap her hair in a towel and after it had stopped dripping, I combed through it again, all those strands, some of them white, others dark grey, and still a few brown ones. It was easier the second time with the softener. That was when I called on the assistant nurse to help me hold her head while I cut all those straggly bits of long, wet hair. Admittedly, I didn't cut it very well. After all, I'm not a hairdresser, am I! I'm only a nurse.

As I was doing her hair, I wondered if she would ever come out of her coma. Perhaps she would. Perhaps she would even call out to me - Manuela, Manuela! I know she was smelly and grubby. I know she was unconscious, not a spark of life in her face. All the same, there was something in her that I liked, something that was calling out to me for help ...'

'That's only your imagination, Manuela! You're always getting tangled up emotionally with your patients. You've been a nurse long enough to know that you should try and keep them at a distance.'

16

'But I'm only human, aren't I? If you like the look of a patient, Rosa, for whatever reason, then I think it's quite normal to want to help them, the way you'd want to help anyone else you like the look of who happens to turn up in your life. And don't forget, one of our commitments as nurses is to comfort the patients. Besides, I'm not the only one who wants to help her. Look at Jaime and Carlos. They're her doctors. And then the psychiatrist who's taken on her case. Raimundo, I think it is. All of them seem to like her. I've told you Rosa, I'm not the only one. Even Florencia, the girl who cleans for us on this floor, said to me one day when we were both by her bed: What a lovely, peaceful face that patient has ... Mind you, that was when she was in her coma. But now I find her crying a lot. Often when I go in to check her out, I see that she is crying quietly to herself, sort of lost in her own world.'

Manuela and Rosa were no longer young, but were two of the most experienced nurses at the clinic. As they sat enjoying a cup of morning coffee they discussed the Romanian patient. The small, nondescript table where they sat was placed beside the filing cabinets in the reception area of the neurological ward of the clinic. Manuela was glad to be on a day shift, but Rosa had always maintained that she preferred night duty. She said she could work better in the silence of the nights, only broken by a toilet being flushed, the occasional snore or somnolent muttering. Moreover, she could sleep most of the following day and didn't have to be worried by contact and stupid conversations with people. She lived alone, a confirmed spinster and quite determined never to give her body or soul to any man who snooped around her.

Rosa was quite impatient. Her face showed a grimace of irritation. She'd been fighting with the coffee machine, as she often fought with difficult patients. It hadn't only been her struggle with the coffee machine where the milk wasn't coming out properly. She'd also been reprimanded by one of the doctors because she'd mislaid the clinical history of one of her patients.

'By the way, Manuela', she said, her resentment rising to the surface, 'I'm fed up with Doctor fat-arse Jaime. He told me off this morning because I'd lost old Enrique's papers. You know, Enrique, the old boy in 207 with dementia?'

Embarrassed at her own outburst, Rosa turned away a little flustered, a redness rising up from her throat into her cheeks. She decided to turn the topic of conversation back to the Romanian patient-and said:

'Well, she's a foreigner, isn't she Manuela? She's obviously going to feel lonely here.'

'But she does speak quite a bit of Spanish. If you speak slowly to her she seems to understand. She must have been here quite a long time. If you ask me, it isn't so much that she doesn't understand Spanish. Her problem is that she's been alone for too long, no friends, I'm sure of that. There are times when she seems almost scared of people. One morning when I went into her room I saw that she had her hand out and she was stuttering *Poor favoor, poor favoor... Muuuchas gracias, muuuchas gracias.* It was as though she was begging.'

Manuela's eyes widened and she drew back involuntarily as Rosa spoke. Her chubby cheeks seemed to swell with compassion for the old woman and the tears that should have escaped from her eyes. She was such a bright, optimistic person. It wasn't that she was pretty, but she was round and joyful and jolly and fun to be with. The patients loved her, an absolute contrast to Rosa with her dry, breastless personality.

Both sat now in silence, lost in their own thoughts.

*   *   *

Down the hall, two doctors were seated in the otherwise empty conference room. They too discussed the Romanian woman. The younger one, Carlos looked quizzically at his colleague. 'Jaime, Raimundo told me the other day that he's planning to try and get her to jot down some things about her life. She'd muttered something about a university in Timisoara. That's in Romania, isn't it?'

'That's right, Carlos. But he's got a job on his hands if he thinks he'll make any sense out of her mutterings. I wouldn't take that on. A couple of days ago when I visited her, she was furious, shouting out

18

Radu, Radu, whatever that is, a man I suppose, *no me toques, no me toques, te odio, keep away from me, don't touch me, I hate you, soy de Petre, I'm Petre's.* She went on and on, wouldn't let me touch her body. I tried to get close to her with the stethoscope, but she started pulling at its cords and swiping me in the face. When I tried to make her calm down, she screamed hysterically, tears bursting from her eyes and she buried her face into the pillow, *Radu, no, no, no!* ... I'll tell you, that was quite enough for me that morning, especially after I'd had to tell that Rosa off for losing that mad fellow's papers. Stupid woman! How can we do our rounds efficiently if she doesn't do her bit. We're all pressed for time, as it is.'

Jaime was sweating. He mopped his brow with a crisp, white handkerchief. A large man, he often broke out in perspiration after any minor exertion or anything that got in his way during his daily rounds at the clinic.

'Don't worry about Rosa', Carlos said quietly. She's a good nurse generally speaking ... efficient, I mean, but a difficult character. As to our stroppy patient, perhaps she imagines that you're her Radu, Jaime! Maybe you even look like him.' He laughed. 'Obviously, it's someone from her past, some guy who tried to get his hands on her when she was with Petre, another man. To look at her now, you can't imagine how any boy would want her!'

'Well, that's now, Carlos. When she was younger, she might have been better. She's put on a lot of weight. I have too. A lot of people get bigger in middle age. But yes, she's too heavy and her face is ugly and lined, and, judging by the clothes she was wearing when they brought her in, she's had an awful life. Manuela told me she had a terrible job cleaning her up before we were asked to see her. I suppose that the only thing we can do for the time being is to keep her calm, at least until she starts eating properly and we can see that she's making some sense when she speaks.'

'The other day when I saw her,' Carlos replied, 'she kept on pulling at her clothes, almost tearing them, trying to get free of them. She muttered something about a prison, an orphanage, frightening children. She seems to have a hell of a mess in her mind. Really, I wouldn't be surprised if she is on the verge of a mental breakdown. It

19

might have been better if she'd never come out of her coma. Patients who spend more than a few days in coma are often affected badly and it takes them ages to come around, if indeed they ever do. This Mara even shows signs of violence and aggressiveness sometimes. Also, she mixes her words and concepts. Some Spanish here, Romanian there. I find it really quite hard to understand her. She stutters something about a university, then someone called Simona and she starts crossing herself furiously as though she's trying to break through some sort of religious taboo. Obviously, it has to do with someone else in her life. Then she jumps to Bucharest and to orphanages.'

'Well, that's all her life coming out, isn't it? The problem is trying to piece it altogether, trying to make some sense out of it so that we can help her, or at least pass on what we understand to Raimundo, so that he has something more tangible to work on.'

Carlos seemed fascinated with the Romanian woman, as if being a foreigner automatically made her more interesting. He was a good, serious doctor and collaborated well with his colleagues; always making time for everyone, particularly for his patients. He was convinced that *attitude* was half the battle. If you could win over a patient's confidence, that was half-way towards curing them. Drugs were important, of course, knowing exactly what and how much to prescribe, but in his heart of hearts he believed that they had to be helped along by a positive attitude. He felt that many patients didn't seem to understand what being positive was. They lay moaning in their beds, expecting the doctors to perform miracles on them.

Jaime stopped mopping his brow and said: 'Carlos, I just don't have your patience for all this! Let me work on her body and you can stick to her mind and help the psychiatrist if you like.'

'Well, I don't have his knowledge in that area, do I?' Carlos admitted. 'There isn't much I could assess about her, only, as I say, pass on these things she keeps talking about to Raimundo.'

'I think that she's really more of a mental case' Jaime replied, 'because even if she needs some attention physically, her organs seem to be functioning alright. The problem was obviously that epidemic that I read about. It occurred in some of the hovels on the edge of the city and I imagine that that's where she picked it up. It actually put paid to quite a few people. But the poor don't have the same resistance as those who are better off. I mean, it wasn't really that serious - a flu blight that attacked their lungs, made them sweat and shiver and cough, made their body temperature shoot up all of a sudden, hallucinations, that sort of thing, but once they came through the crisis they could recuperate. They were weakened, obviously. And of course, had they had access to medicines, none of them would've died like that. This Romanian woman obviously tried to get up and go off somewhere and then just collapsed on her way. She was found, wasn't she, at the entrance to a metro station, so she must have been going somewhere.'

'But why the coma, Jaime?' Carlos seemed to have a certain faith in Jaime's better judgement. Although he sometimes thought it was just his own innate modesty. Not that Jaime had a better bedside manner, he was in too much of a hurry, but he read up a lot about his patients' afflictions, kept abreast of the latest developments, attended as many medical congresses as he could.

'Well, she probably hit her head very hard against a stone or railings or something. You remember that she was badly bruised over one eye when they brought her in. We both saw that. … That would have given her concussion, brain haemorrhage, slight brain damage possibly and this injury threw her into coma. We shall have to work on those broken blood vessels. Apart from this, there doesn't seem to be much wrong with her.'

*   *   *

A pretty young woman in hospital staff attire was speaking to one of the nurses. 'I was busy, Manuela, not much time because I'd got behind with my cleaning. I had to mop the floor of her room before the nurses came to change her bedding. She was mumbling all the time as I worked around her bed. She went on and on about Tatiana, said how pretty she was, dark-haired just like me.

You're just like Tatiana, she told me. Come here, hold my hand, she said.

21

But my name isn't Tatiana, it's Florencia, I answered her.

Her voice grated a bit, then she cleared her throat. Suddenly, she let out a piercing shriek that made me jump out of my wits! And then it was No, no, no Tatiana, that's not you! You're not like that! Don't kill me, please don't kill me. I'm your mother. I love you! Come back to me. That was when she looked at me and pleaded with me to hold her hand. I'll teach you how to beg. I have a good place in a nice street. You'll love it. We can sit together and watch all the passers-by. She said all this in halting Spanish. She held my hand tightly, wouldn't let me go. I told her I was just the cleaner at the hospital. No you aren't, she retorted. You are Tatiana, my daughter. Kiss me, Tatiana, kiss me. Don't go away again! I bent over her and kissed her on the forehead. That was when you came in, Manuela. You saw me kissing her and you smiled. She needs lots of love, lots of affection, you said. Then you asked me what she had told me. Always tell me, you said. We need to know everything she talks about, everything that is going through her brain. Tell me. Tell the doctors - you know that Carlos and Jaime are her doctors. Anything at all will help us to help her, you said. So here I am, telling you this. You are a very good nurse, Manuela. Rosa doesn't seem to take the same interest in her.'

*   *   *

A few days later, Raimundo is staring intently at the papers on the table in front of him. It is his report on Mara's progress. He reads over it again. Little by little we are discovering the pieces of the jigsaw puzzle, he thought. I even held a meeting with all the staff who attended her, including Florencia the cleaning girl, her nurses, Manuela and Rosa, Carlos and Jaime, her doctors. I asked them to tell me everything she said to them. As her psychiatrist, I wanted to know as much as possible about her. Amongst us all, we were beginning to notice who she spoke about most, beginning to be familiar with the people in her past, to the point where we could judge her reactions to some of them. For example, there was no doubt that Tatiana was her daughter and, judging from her references to the orphanages and Bucharest, we guessed that the child had been taken away from her and flung into an orphanage. That sort of thing happened during Ceausescu's era in Romania. It's hard to know if she ever saw her daughter again because she mixes things up when she talks about her, as though she was sometimes real and sometimes a ghostly figure, perhaps even a figment of her imagination. I am not so sure who Simona is. Obviously, someone she was fond of because whenever she mentions her name, a shadow of a smile flits across her face, a feeling of calm that seems to smooth out the lines of tension on her forehead.

This morning, however, it seems she's almost fallen back into a coma. Closed-up like a clam inside its sharp, grey shell. There are now days like this, days when I have to admit that I feel like giving up on her. I call her gently by her name, Mara. There is no reaction, not so much as a flicker of her eyelids. I ask her how she has slept, how she is feeling. Still there is no reaction. She merely lies there, solidly, a heavy bundle beneath the sheets, her body quite motionless. Her eyes are open, staring up at the ceiling. I take her wrist to check her pulse because to all accounts she could be dead. Yes, she is alive, but not a muscle of her body moves, her breathing is imperceptible. It is as though she is lying in wait, but for what? I know that she can hear me and so I feel that there is something stubborn in her attitude. Why doesn't she answer me? She does speak Spanish, badly and hesitantly, but it is possible most of the time to understand her.

This poor, stray woman with her broken body and broken soul, her mind in a mess. Life has dealt her many bitter blows, of that I am sure. She is obviously quite alone. Nobody ever comes to visit her. She doesn't seem to have any friends at all. She must be very lonely.

Of course, her brain has been affected by her fall, by the thirty-five and a half days in coma. We can't expect her to react to our words when we want her to. She needs gentle coaxing, not pushing and pulling. She needs the correct medication, nothing too strong, just enough to nudge her mind towards us, outwards, away from her inner suffering.

The following morning, Raimundo looks in on Mara.

She is awake and seems alert. 'Today I have brought you a pen and notebook, Mara. I want you to write all about your life. There are things I need to know about you if I am to help you. You realise who I am, don't you? I am Raimundo, your psychiatrist. Do that for me. You have plenty of time in hospital and now that they've taken away all the tubes for your intravenous feeding you can hold a pen and sit up to write. Try to eat well. You will feel better with solid food inside you. You can write in Romanian. I know that is your language. You spoke to me about Timisoara University. Did you go there?'

No reply. I turn my eyes towards the window, wondering, wondering as I gazed out across to the snow-capped mountains, across the dry Madrid earth darkened here and there with splodges of growth and trees, wondering what had happened to this woman for her to have turned her back on a university education, on her country and to have come here to live what had obviously been such a miserable life. And I would go on wondering as long as she withheld her past from me.

I was beginning to recognise the old feeling of obsession with a patient. This had happened to me with other patients, not many of them, but as my obsession grew, it ate away at my time, my thoughts, my meals, my sleep. It always stemmed from a sort of fascination for the patient, the feeling that they had been sent into my care for a purpose, that I was doing something really worthwhile by helping. So often my work is routine and even boring. I don't always feel the need to delve so deeply into a patient's past. Mostly, I can see it in front of me just by judging the symptoms and by following a routine approach. But Mara is different. She has presented me with a challenge and I am determined to get to the bottom of her case.

5

Petre

I had known Petre from my childhood. We spent our tender years exploring the fields, the hills, the dales, the woods near our village. We ran together, we read stories together, we laughed together, we kissed together, innocent infantile hugs and kisses, no more. We giggled together in the classroom of our village school.

But the years made us serious and responsible. Petre wanted to be a lawyer. I wanted to be a writer. We would both go on to university to achieve our dreams. And for two and a half years this is what we did. We would travel together on the train from our village to Timisoara. On those journeys, I would study Petre, his dark skin, his black, wavy hair, the mole near his wrist bone, his lithe muscular body, but above all, his smile. When he smiled at me my world grew into a vast field of happiness, an expanse of golden, limitless time. I thought then that happiness was never-ending, that nothing could spoil it. But I knew you had to work at happiness to make it last. So it was on one of those train journeys that I made up my mind I would give myself, my whole self, to Petre. That way, I would be happy and I would make him happy. What would my grandmother, Simona, think about that? I felt intuitively that, despite her old wrinkled life, she would understand my quest for happiness. She would have told me to think about it when I lit the flame of a candle, and she would have told me to brush away my sadness when I blew out the candle. That is what I thought, before she died.

After she died, I lit a candle but no good thought came to me. All I could do was to sob and sob. I fear that she died because she thought that I had taken my quest for happiness too far. Remember, she was old and wrinkled, a woman from another age. Her daughter Roxana, my mother, crushed my happiness in her disappointment. She was disappointed in me, she said. Her life had been hard. She was a strict woman, hair brushed harshly and tightly back off her forehead into a bun, sturdy arms and hands made even sturdier from hours of washing clothes by hand at the village pump. She was a strict mother too. I think I was scared of her. I think I had always been scared of her. She stood no nonsense. She never laughed like Simona. She hadn't learned how to laugh from her own mother. She even called Simona irresponsible when the old lady would spend hours playing with me, laughing with me, talking to me. My mother would burst in on us, commanding me to help her to clean, to wash, to cook or to return to my studies. I think she was jealous. Life was no joke, she said, life was hard. It was hard, inside her embittered crust.

So when I returned home one day and I knew I had Tatiana's embryo clinging to me, when my mother set eyes on my gently swollen womb, my expanding hips, she stared at me, speechless at first, as though I was a despicable thing, a slut. When she came to, she raised her strong arm and heavy hand and slapped me several times across the face, backwards, forwards. She didn't ask immediately who my man was. She just said that I was a disgrace, a failure, a disaster, that I was dirty, irresponsible, that no-one would ever want me as a wife after this. Then she asked me who had done it to me. When I told her that it was Petre, she threatened to talk to his parents, to make us get married. We hadn't even thought of marriage and I didn't want to marry. I was too young. Too irresponsible, according to my mother. And in those early days I didn't want to have the baby either. At that time, there weren't many abortions in Romania. There were programmes, State programmes, to encourage women to have children. They told us that the Romanian population was dwindling, that it was a crime to have an abortion, that we had to fill the country with children. Ceausescu, the robber, the torturer, lowered the age for marriage to fifteen. He taxed any childless woman over twenty-five. He had us watched over closely and all pregnancies were monitored to ensure that they were brought to fruition. If you tried to have an abortion you could be flung into gaol for a year and the doctor who had practised the abortion could be imprisoned for five years. If you did it clandestinely you might die, hundreds of women died after clandestine abortions, died of infection, of the brutal use of instruments, of incessant bleeding, of weakness and abandonment.

In the 1980s, my country, Romania, was third-world. If you didn't study, if you were a woman, you had to work in industry, you had to marry, you had to give birth to child after child and you grew old and wrinkled before your time, old and wrinkled like Simona, my grandmother, but without her laughter on your lips. ... Yes, life was hard, but not only for my mother, for all of us in Romania. We were all desperate, not only Roxana. Food was rationed, shops were short of everything, even babies' nappies. People lived badly in small, cramped apartment blocks, or in villages without modern amenities. It was as though life had come to a standstill in those villages, as if they had jumped off the train of progress. There was no money. No-one could afford heating in the depths of winter. How could I bring a child into a country like that, Doctor? How could I let a child interfere with my studies?

But it wasn't Tatiana who interfered with my studies. It was my mother. She was determined to punish me and in her blind determination she forced me to leave the university, to return home to help her in the house. She would no longer pay for my train journeys to Timisoara, for my books and study material, for my lodging away from home during the weekdays. She kept on telling me I was irresponsible, that my studying days were over, my dreams about books and writing, that I had thrown away the opportunity she had given me, that this baby would spoil my life, her life. Little did she realise the truth behind those words ... she made me go through with my pregnancy, watching over me as an eagle watches over its prey. She watched my every movement. She was obsessed with the baby being born. She didn't leave me alone for a minute. Only at night could I find solitude; I would go to my mattress in the room I shared with my younger sister Viorica and there I would cry quietly into my pillow, hiding my sobs under the bed clothes, Viorica snoring on her mattress close by me. My whole life was crumbling apart. Petre wouldn't speak to me after I told him about the baby, after I left university. He said that maybe he was not the child's father because of Radu.

But Radu is another story. I shall tell you that story one day.

*   *   *

Now I am drowsing in the hot sun. Its rays hammer against my eyeballs, against my forehead. Why don't I move? I can't bring myself to move. I am hungry, but I don't have the strength or the will to get up and look for food. When I return to my hovel this evening, I can eat some of the potato soup that I made last night. Potato with cabbage. Then I shall feel stronger.

Through my half-closed eyes, I watch two tiny birds fighting on the pavement in front of me. They are sparrows, sparring with one another over a crumb, a crumb of chocolate-coated bun dropped by a child. They tweet furiously at each other, they peck, they hop away, they hop back, they flutter their wings, they move their heads incessantly. They are so small in this immense universe. They are a small expression of life. But not of my life, as I sit and wait for crumbs to fall into my hands. Yet they are my friends. Small friends to me in my abject condition.

Look at that mad man. He is singing, croaking stupidly into the afternoon air. He is surrounded by the others, by his mad companions, and they laugh at him and try to sing with him. Their group makes me feel lonely. Maybe I could join them, but I don't think they would want me. Nobody wants a lonely person. Lonely people shun others unconsciously. Unconsciously they put a wall, a barrier, between them and other people and nobody tries to break through the barrier. Lonely people make others question their lives, their stupidity, and that is the last thing people want to do. They want to go on living in a cocoon of unquestioned stupidity. A lonely person finds it hard to communicate with others. A lonely person communicates with the movements of others, not with them or their words, with the branches of trees waving in the wind, with the sunlight glinting through the leaves, with the woolly clouds in the high sky, and at night with the stars and the moon and the black firmament. All of nature is a friend to the lonely person. Did you know that, Doctor? The dogs peeing against the bank building, against the car wheels, against the lamp-posts, the birds flying, wheeling across the sky, the birds perched on the branches and chirping on the twigs of trees, the birds fighting in front of me over their crumb, the cats, proud and knowing, furtively doing their rounds, pacing in silence.

There is a little cat that comes to visit me some evenings. She scratches at my wooden door, she *miaows* to be let in. I let her in and she purrs, winding her slim body around my ankles, in and out around my ankles. She leaps lightly up onto the table and licks the remains of my potato supper from the plate. Then she licks her lips and cleans her whiskers. She is clean and neat, unlike me. I am grubby, with only a tap of cold water in the street to wash at. On some days, I take a plastic bowl, fill it with this bland, tepid water and carry it back to my hovel – the water in the hills of Transylvania was crystal clear and cold and fast-running. In the bowl I wash my hair, my body, as best I can. I have no perfumed shampoo, no delicate soap. Just the water. It is better than nothing. But my skin is drying, drying with the hot Madrid sun, drying the way it would in a desert with no water, drying with the years.

My soul is drying. My soul is dying.

The afternoon is dying. The light becomes heavier. It weighs against me as the sun dips its rays, lengthening shadows, immersing the world in a heavy, orange light. Soon it will be time for me to raise my weary body, push, pull it up out of my street trappings, gather these few trappings together, gather myself together and work my way slowly to the entrance of the underground train. I am old and I am not yet fifty. Fifty is young in this old people's world, a world where the old are meant to feel young for ever. The late afternoon summer light in this city is a gift, a golden halo through which we pass to meet the black night. A furnace halo. If I were happy, I would venerate that light.

But my day, this summer day, is not over yet. People emerge from the entrances to their blocks of flats, their voices slice the golden light into shreds, they jabber non-stop, parents with children, grandparents, friends, boyfriends, girlfriends, men, women, students. And I feel lonely. They jabber almost as much as the mad people in the square. They laugh raucous laughs as well. Perhaps there isn't much difference between them and the mad ones. How they love life!

How I hate life!

They go from one shop to another, from one appointment to another, from one restaurant to another. They guzzle at their drinks, they stuff themselves with unpalatable food, unhealthy morsels of bread and sweet cakes. They are always consuming, the children guzzling sticky drinks through straws out of small cartons, the adults sipping coffee or tea or coca cola or soft drinks. They are always filling their guts with lumps of food, un-nourishing nourishment because the food they eat, their between-meal snacks, is rubbishy food. My potato soup is more nourishing. But I eat only once a day.

And I am hungry.

The mass of late afternoon walkers. Some emerge from their flats after a siesta, some enter the hairdressing salon just down the road from where I am and they appear with their dyes and their perms, some are clad in sportswear and they run and jog, sweating in the hot air. Some push babies' prams.

Tatiana would have loved a pram like that.

And the babies shriek in discomfort or gurgle for joy, and their mothers shriek and gurgle with them. Some push shopping carts, others are laden down with plastic bags containing their purchases. An old woman makes her way towards me. She has a stumbling gait and leans on her walking stick. Her hair is white and thinning on her sunburnt scalp. Her bare legs are thin in her summer dress, her face emaciated. She is blown along the pavement amidst the surging mass of bodies, blown without the wind. Her eyes are faded and brown, lost in other worlds. I try to stare into her eyes, to meet them, as she approaches me. She looks at me and, for just one second, I think she has a glint of recognition in her eyes, that she will say something to me, acknowledge my presence, but the next second the glint has gone. She has moved on to another world, to another place, to another era, dragging her thin legs behind her. Is she a mother, a grandmother? Or is she alone, like me?

I am a mother, but I am alone.

The people come and go. Four of them have dropped coins onto my raffia mat. Four of them this afternoon, another five this morning. Today has been a good day for me. Now I know that I can eat tomorrow and the next day. All my earnings go on food and the metro fare. I need nothing else. I have a bowl for washing, a plastic bowl that I found on a rubbish heap near my place, a camping gas for cooking, one medium-sized saucepan that I also found on a rubbish heap with a small round piece of metal fixed to cover a hole in it so that the liquid doesn't leak from it, a big box for a table, a small box for a chair and a mattress for sleeping. I have some clothes. They are old, but sometimes people give me a skirt, a jumper, some sandals. And I have a brush to brush my hair and a rubber band to draw it back off my face.

6

A Bank Clerk

I make no bones at all about my feelings concerning these wretched immigrants smothering our streets in poverty. Time and again I talk to my friends about them. Some tease me. They say I am a fascist. So what? We all have our own ideas. And one of my ideas is that poverty and lack of effort infuriate me … and most of my friends agree with me. Why the hell do they have to come here, pretending to look for work, when all they are is lazy good-for-nothings? I see her every morning through the window of the bank where I work. She is dirty and smells unpleasant. As I walk into the bank I feel I have to dust the smell of her off my suit jacket, for fear of frightening away our clients. Several of us have discussed ways of getting rid of her. No, I'm not talking about murder, obviously. I just mean that our lives would be easier if she went off further down the street and we didn't have to sit at our desks watching her as we deal with our telephone calls and clients sitting on the opposite side of the desk. There are times when I am so irate to see her slumped there in her disgusting clothing, her fingernails filthy, that I can't concentrate on my work and I lose my temper with my colleagues.

Don't think, though, that I feel guilty about having a good job myself, a job climbing up to the top rungs of the ladder in this branch office of the bank. I just feel that no-one should be allowed into Spain without the appropriate papers, without a job to go to, without speaking Spanish. They should learn the language before they come. They should sort out all their papers, find a job from some agency in their own countries before leaving. Why should we have to do all that for them? Their children fill up our schools and require extra coaching to learn Spanish. That's money and effort on our part. What do we get from them? What do they give us? This country was better before they came, filling up our streets, clamouring for a tip at our traffic lights, their youngsters rowdy and even threatening in some districts. I don't want my children to have to grow up beside them - black, yellow, dark brown skins they are. Just as Spain was getting ahead, as well, they have to come and pull us all down into crisis. I hate them. In Franco's time, they wouldn't have been allowed here.

I have an idea. Perhaps we can get rid of her. When we leave the bank in the evening we could put some bags full of rubbish - old, unwanted papers and files, any old muck, on the pavement where she sits. The rubbish van doesn't come until later in the morning and even when the rubbish collectors come they probably wouldn't move those bags if they were really heavy. We could do it every evening anyway, if they do move them. So when the old tart comes in the early morning, if she wants to sit there, she would have to move the bags. We could fill them to the brim so she can't lift them. I don't think she speaks Spanish, so we could put a large sign with a drawing of her and a large red cross painted on it. She'd have to be completely daft not to get the message. I must ask the others what they think.

Time passed and of course we didn't fill her space on the pavement with any bags full of files and papers and rubbish from the office. We didn't make any signboards to frighten her off. My friends in the bank were too cowardly to contemplate doing anything of the sort. Now I regret having confided in them. Had I acted alone, no-one would have suspected me, but as I had told them about my ideas, they would have accused me if they had seen anything untoward on the pavement outside our bank. Cowardly, that's what they are. They all hate that dirty old gypsy woman. They all stick their noses in the air as they walk past her, or look the other way. They all agree with me that we shouldn't be letting all these miserable beggars into our country. But David, the man who shares my office, even said that how could they learn Spanish before coming here when they didn't have the money to buy a crust of bread, how could they afford that,

Jorge, he asked me. Pay money out for classes to learn a language when they probably don't even speak their own language correctly? You can't expect that of them, he said. His attitude annoyed me. He almost seemed to be in favour of their coming here to better their lives. But David, can't you see, I retorted, that they don't have better lives and, on top of that, they dirty our pavements.

No, I'm not the only person who thinks like this. What about that case recently of some neo-Nazis who beat up a beggar, leaving him blind and crippled. He must have deserved it, I would say. The lawyer who defended the offenders actually said that these beggars are a cancer in society and ought to be extirpated. I couldn't agree more. Vagabonds are simply not human beings. They are parasites sucking the decency from society. We would all be better off without them. Just the way we would if there were no more terrorists with their bombs, demanding huge sums of money from company directors in the Basque country. Fortunately, it seems that little by little they are coming to their senses now, but we suffered years of fear and hatred from their bombs. You never knew when you were going to be blown to bits, as you got into your car in an underground garage, as you did your shopping in a supermarket. Here in Castile, we don't need the Basques. Neither do we need the Catalans, always criticising us, always trying to pull away from central Spain, trying to impose their languages on us, trying to give us a complex with their ebullient industry and mercantile view of life. Similar, I suppose, to the view of many bankers, so I shouldn't criticise that feature of them. But it's true, the Catalans in particular, are more mercantile than the Castilians. If I were a politician, I would speak out loudly against anyone who criticises Madrid. I prefer Madrid to be hermetic. We don't need any outsiders here telling us what we should do with our city. Madrid is the core of Spain, the heart of the whole country and by the whole country I mean Catalonia, the Basque country, Galicia. It is for them to fit in with us. Most of us in the bank have the same ideas.

None of us, except David perhaps, could care two-pence for the Romanian beggar at the door of the bank. Let's face it, she doesn't want to work. She could move her hefty frame and try and look for a job. Anything. Cleaning out public toilets, for example. Although I think she'd dirty them rather than clean them. And I suppose that she doesn't have her papers in order. They come here, expecting us to provide them with jobs, with papers and what do they give in return? I hate them. I wish they didn't exist. I wish they would all go back to where they came from. I've already said, I don't want my children mixing with any of their kids. Those South American gangs are frightening, dangerous, a dreadful influence for young Spaniards. Things were better when I was young, under Franco; he had everything well organised, well tied down, people then didn't go off the straight and narrow, they did as they were told. We all studied hard, none of this failing and dragging your education on for years as they do today. People then were strict and religious. Franco would never have allowed all these grubby immigrants into the country. Me neither. I am Jorge.

7

Roxana the Tyrant

I see her face as plain as day. Roxana wore her hair back off her forehead in a cruel sweep. Cruel like her personality. I would sob into the mattress in my house for Simona, for Tatiana, for the father I never knew. I would sob because of my mother's cruelty. She wrenched me away from my studies. She urged me, insistently, to have the child in my womb. She said they would punish both of us if I had an abortion, and they would punish the doctor that helped me to have it. She said she was scared of the authorities. They would come to the village. They would find out about me. The neighbours would tell them. The authorities, the dictator's guards, did rounds in the villages every couple of months, asking, asking about our families, how many were we, how many children, how many students, how many living away from home, where were they living, asking, asking, forcing the neighbours to spy on each other.

They controlled our lives, those guards with cruel stupidity written all over their brutish faces. They controlled the village people because they could frighten them. They couldn't control everyone in the bigger cities. They couldn't control the clever people. At least, not to the same extent. And I whispered into my mattress at night. Why, I asked, should they control my life, why did I have to bring my foetus into Romania to add another unhappy soul to this land, why should anybody else tell me how to lead my life, why was my mother so scared of the guards, why did they poke their noses into our rations, into what we grew in our vegetable garden, why did they pry into Simona's death. So many questions in an un-free society. And I hated them and I hated my mother for bowing to their will. I considered that she was weak, despite her sturdy arms and her hard-working body. I knew that this child within me would ruin my life, Doctor.

Tatiana, you have ruined my life.

If my father, Mihaita, had been in the house, it might all have been different. But he had left before Viorica was born, when I was only two years old. He must have realised the mistake he had made marrying Roxana. She told me once, years ago, when I asked her what had happened, that one evening he had returned home from the fields and said that he was joining a group of labourers to go into Timisoara, or Bucharest, to find work. He said that they were leaving together that very night. His face was ruddy and his eyes bleary from drink. His hair was tousled and his clothing unkempt. She said that he smelt of alcohol and sweat. She said he said that he never wanted to see her again, her, or her children, or Simona, her mother. She told me he said that they could all go to hell, he didn't want any more of her charity, he couldn't live any longer in Simona's house, looking after Simona's crops and vegetables. He couldn't live any longer trapped within her sturdy washerwoman's arms. That's what he said, she said. And so I never knew him. I often wished I had known him, particularly during the festivals in our village. Then he would have danced with me, swirled me around in time with the music, laughed with me, the way Simona my old grandmother laughed with me. But perhaps the vision I had in my mind of my father was a false vision. Perhaps he would never have wanted to dance at the village festival. As for my mother, even the festivals were drudgery for her. She hated decorating the house, cleaning the house, preparing the food for anyone who joined us at the table. She was a sour woman with a sour face, a sour heart.

As I am sour now. History repeats itself you know.

And she was sour to me all through my pregnancy. She held it against me because she said that I had ruined my life, ruined her life, that I was the talk of the village. I could never have an abortion now that my figure was bloated and it was obvious to everyone that I was carrying a child. The authorities, only the authorities, would be pleased. She would receive the allowance they would give me for bringing a child into the world, into the dictator's Romania. For that she was pleased. She seemed to be so sure that I would have the baby and that we would live with her in Simona's house and she would be Simona to my child. She could never have been Simona. My beautiful old grandmother was made of another metal to her daughter, to my mother.

Meanwhile, my days were filled with longing for Petre. But I have told you, he never spoke to me again. As my pregnancy advanced, I felt certain that Petre was the father of my child. The episode with Radu had been so short. A few fateful days, that was all. If I hadn't been so honest I wouldn't have told Petre about it, but I feared that he would find out from hints made by other students. It was better to tell him. He went pale and impenetrable beneath his olive skin when I told him. We stayed together for several months after Radu, but he was never the same again. It was as though he was masticating his hatred for the other man, masticating his scorn for me. We forgot how to laugh together. He felt betrayed and nothing I could do would repair that sensation of betrayal. The more he withdrew into himself, the more I desired him and wanted to be with him. Always. So when I realised I was pregnant, the first person I told was Petre. He let all his pent-up anger loose, all his hatred and scorn came bursting out. Not a look of compassion did he have for my pain, for the agony I felt over what I had done. Petre was a straight, honest man and he believed that the whole of humanity should be straight and honest. He found it almost impossible to accept human weakness, to forgive.

Roxana went to see Petre's parents. She said that he ought to marry me. She pleaded with them as best she knew how. They replied to her with a stony expression on their faces. They retorted that Petre doubted whether he was the father of the child. Why should he marry a slut, they said? Petre would find a cleaner, nicer girl. They told Roxana to go away and never to come back to their house. When she entered our living room I could see from the expression on her face that they had not welcomed her and that night I went to my mattress and sobbed, yet again I sobbed.

*   *   *

But that was years ago. Another lifetime, perhaps. In the heat of the Madrid summer I would lie in my hut, tossing and turning through a sleepless night, sweat trickling down my body, from my armpits to my waist. I would push away the bed cover feverishly searching with my eyes, straining with them, for the first light of dawn. When the day started, my own thoughts would be pushed away by activity, by the shouts or laughter of others, by a dog barking, by the little cat *miaowing*, by the shrill shriek of a prostitute being carted off in a police van, by neighbours on both sides of me yelling at each other, chiding their children in stentorian tones. Sound carries far on the air of Madrid, this crisp, stark, waterless air. There is no humidity to quell sound and so it rises and vibrates in all its force. I awaken tired, exhausted in the morning. I get up off my mattress, take my bowl to the street tap dragging my numbed limbs after me, fill it with cool water and splash the water over my face and behind my hovel I attend to washing my intimate parts as best I can. One mustn't smell on the metro beside showered, perfumed humanity. I put on a long, loose skirt, a tee shirt over my drooping bust, I brush my hair – the greying strands that have replaced my erstwhile black locks in an exercise of slow, inexorable mutation – and tie it back off my forehead, like Roxana. Like my mother. Can I ever escape her? I heat up some water on my small gas ring and add a tea bag to it. I forgot to buy a bun or bread yesterday. I shall buy it on my way to my begging. I must eat something between morning and night, or I shall faint in the street.

Would that matter?

Perhaps today will be better than yesterday. Like people, some days are good, some are bad. My religion never talked about lives like mine. Christ never taught me anything. The Bible never taught me anything. I used to believe in all those religious teachings when Simona was by my side, until I saw what real life was about.

It is cold, so cold, in the heat of Madrid without friends.

8

Compassion

A handsome youngish woman sighed as she lay awake in her bed. Every morning I see the beggar. On my way to work, I would see her sitting pitifully on the pavement, on the side of the pavement, so as not to disturb pedestrians walking in one direction or another. She never missed a day, I will say that. She was conscientious in her begging, as though it were a job, as though her life depended on it. I thought she looked sad. She looked as though a crushing weight was forcing her downwards to grovel on the pavement at people's feet. Why? I wondered. Then I realised that was a silly question. Who, after all, wouldn't be sad living the way she was, picking at life's crumbs from the worst possible position? Don't they understand, these people, these foreigners, that we just cannot give work to everybody. My name, by the way, is Francisca. Paca, they call me at my work. I work in an office, an insurance office. There are no immigrants there.

Not that I have anything at all against these people who come to Spain from other lands. They are desperate. They accept anything offered them, anything at all is better than where they come from. Some run to escape from poverty, others from dictatorships, probably like this woman I see because I imagine that she is from Romania. She has been here for years. It is years since I have been seeing her almost every morning, so I imagine that she ran away from her country when it was in the iron grip of that dictator. Lots of people here ran away from our country to escape from Franco when he was ruling the roost here. There was no work to be had. Their ideas didn't coincide with his. They had no option but to go and sweep the floors of the well-to-do in other countries. I know this because my sister, Rafaela, went to France. She is older than me and my mother told me that she would send money home every single month earned from her floor-sweeping and nappy-changing in a rich French family. But what sort of money can this Romanian woman send back home? She barely earns enough to keep herself, let alone have any spare to send home to support her family in Romania.

There are some days when I pass by her and I see her bowed down with sadness, heavily humped into the thick long skirt that she wears, her large face slumped down onto the worn jumper that covers her breast. She seems immovable. Her waist is invisible, her neck is invisible. She is like a large sack of potatoes. But she is not a vegetable. She is a human being with her thoughts, her past and her terrible present. I often wonder why she has never made a move to improve her life. Surely she could find some cleaning work somewhere? Somewhere where they would pay her a pittance, but enough to help her to eat better, to dress better, to have a better life. I know she doesn't get much just begging like that. ... There are days when I give her a coin. I put it down on the little raffia mat she has beside her and, as I do so, I search for her eyes. I try to meet them with mine, but she never looks up at me. Is she shy perhaps, intimidated, cowering into her misery? On the few days I have put down a bag of old clothing for her, her only reaction is to nod wearily at me. She never smiles. Her eyes never meet mine. I see from that fleeting moment that her eyes are brown. Brown and sad, like a dog's eyes. They are dull from the want of laughter and happiness in her life.

Why don't I speak to her, offer her a few kind words? Maybe that is all she needs to tell me about her past. Yet I can never find the time to stop. There are even mornings when I vow to get up a little earlier to have the time to say something to her, but I don't. Obviously I don't have the will to do so. And I have to admit that I would feel a bit embarrassed to get into conversation with her, me in my smart suit and high heels, her in her rags. Also, I don't think that she speaks a word of Spanish even after living here for years and years.

*   *   *

There is so much difference between people in this world. Look at me, off to my insurance office, animated with my job, animated with my life, always grateful for what I have, enjoying the company of my office workers, their jokes, their laughter, their teasing. I have spoken to them on occasions about the Romanian beggar and they often say, Paca, how's your Romanian friend this morning? Don't tell us that you didn't take her home last night, give her a good supper and a warm bed! You disappoint us! And they laugh. I laugh too. But secretly I wonder why I feel so sorry for that woman and yet I'm not capable of offering her some positive help, help apart from those few miserable coins that I drop onto her raffia mat. We all tend to lock ourselves inside the comfortable web that we have woven around us. We might push gently out towards the edge of the web yet we fear breaking through onto the other side for what we might see or suffer. We don't really want to get involved. We think we do, but we only dream about helping others. We rarely branch out offering substantial aid or comfort to another who might need it. Of course, you can't give to everyone who needs your help, but we reduce our circle of acquaintances and friends and we limit our help to them. Anyone who happens to fall outside that circle cannot hope for much from us.

As life goes on our aims become more paltry, our dreams shrivel and we reduce our actions to minimal contact with others, to the conventional, safe contact we have always known, shaking off any more adventurous contacts. Today it is easier to satisfy any altruistic strain we may have because we can use the social networks to leave our signature in favour of this or that issue. We don't have to move outside our house or our office to offer our support to those who need it. We can do so almost anonymously and with a minimum of effort. Using the internet, we don't even have to go out marching on the streets, making our physical presence felt. Revolutions of all sorts are occurring in the virtual world today, in the Arab nations, with different issues in lands like India, China, social changes are being made merely by people pressing buttons on their computers. So easy, so clinical, so utterly divorced from the reality of human contact. ... We don't have to dirty ourselves anymore by rubbing up against the poor, by touching their grime. We leave our old clothes for them without a kind word, a bundle in a bag where they sit begging, clothing left inside the containers placed conveniently in the streets by humanitarian organisations. So easy, so anonymous, freezing cold charity without that kind word that could signify hope to a beggar, even more than a bowl of hot soup or an article of clothing.

How can I ever bring myself to talk to her?

*   *   *

It must have been towards the beginning of winter, sometime in November, I think. I remember I got out of bed with the firm intention of talking to her, of asking her about herself. I got dressed and made myself a cup of steaming coffee. Whilst I was drinking it, I imagined that she would never have a cup of steaming coffee to start her day. In the early mornings, she looked as though she had had nothing to really wake her up, no clean water, no shower, no hot coffee, nothing to eat. I couldn't envisage going off to work on an empty stomach - particularly in the cold of winter - or not having had a shower and clean clothes to put on. Reacting on an impulse of sentimentality, I put a few small cupcakes inside a Tupperware box. In a bag, I put two apples and some hot soup into another Tupperware container. At least it is something for her to start the day on, I said to myself. I hesitated. Here I was getting more and more involved with this woman, without knowing anything about her. It was inexplicable, but my heart went out to her, every morning of the week as I walked passed by her to catch my bus to work. I wanted to see her smile, nod happily at me, I wanted to see a change in her miserable disposition. I wanted to see her sadness transform to happiness, if only for a fleeting moment and I wanted to feel that I was the cause of her transformation. I wanted to give her something to look forward to every day, to imagine that someone cared about her. And that I was that someone.

It crossed my mind that my job in the insurance office wasn't really as satisfying as I had always imagined it to be. My days there were beginning to pall on me. I had never noticed boredom before amongst my papers and policies and clients, but just recently my work there was beginning to drag, the hours I spent in the office with grey filing cabinets seemed longer and longer. I even noticed that relations with my companions there were no longer fulfilling. We would be eating together, several of them chatting animatedly around me over lunch, and I would fall into long silences, imagining the Romanian beggar on her street corner, alone, all alone, all day long. 'Where are you, Paca, back in Romania!' they would tease me and laugh. And I began to retaliate, sometimes with harsh words: 'Don't be so sarcastic! How would you like to beg on the streets in a country where you can't speak the language, spend all day alone on a pavement?' They retorted, 'Well, take her home and teach her Spanish!' This jibing wasn't too serious, but I could sense that it was the beginning of a change in my life. I wanted to do something more worthwhile, more positive in the way of helping others. And the office became greyer and greyer, my work there more and more senseless. Yet what could I do? I would be useless in the pragmatic tasks of helping immigrants, making meals for them (I was a dreadful cook!), teaching them the language - I had never had experience in that, helping them to find homes or jobs. What could I do? And how could I do it? If I walked out of insurance, how would I pay off my flat? I needed a fixed salary every month. Most of the agencies for immigrants were run by charities, or NGO's, people who had sufficient to live on and could afford to devote their time to others and not be remunerated for it. I wasn't in a position to do that.

All these thoughts were in my head as I prepared to leave the house that November morning. Outside it was misty, a chilled stillness hung in the air and I caught my breath against the cold. I sank into the woollen scarf round my neck, grateful for its soft warmth. As I walked along, clutching the plastic bags with the food I had for her, it occurred to me that maybe she wouldn't be there this morning. I even considered that she would be crazy to come out of wherever she slept to sit on a freezing street corner just for a few cents. And if she was there? Why hadn't I brought something more for her, hot coffee, hot pastry filled with tuna and red peppers? How stupid I was! Quite positively deficient! As I rounded the corner of my street I caught sight of her several yards in front of me. Her heavy body ensconced in her flimsy rags, bits and pieces of patched clothing, an old worn black jacket, a long skirt made of light material more suited to summer than to winter, a pair of woollen stockings on her thick legs. Round her neck and over her head she wore a thin scarf, like many Muslim women I thought, but no, she didn't wear it in a harsh straight line across her forehead the way they seemed to, she had pushed it back off her forehead and it was only protecting her ears from the cold. Not much of a protection, I thought to myself as I hurried towards her.

I came up to her and clumsily proffered the two plastic bags and stammered stupidly, without a smile, embarrassed at what others might think of me. 'Here, this is for you', I said. She seemed to me to take an age to raise her head and grasp the bags. She was as surprised as I myself was. Yet not a sign of gratitude was there on her face, barely a look of recognition in her eyes. Merely a shrug of her shoulders, which might have meant anything – a begrudging thanks, a warning not to get too close, suspicion, fear, goodness knows. I opened my mouth to smile and say a few words to her, but they didn't come out. I felt shy. As I turned on my heel to leave, I caught sight of the scornful expression on the face of a man inside the bank. I clutched my handbag and, strangely out of breath, raced down the road to the bus stop.

9

Jorge

Just what we need! These stupid, sentimental do-gooders! Look at that young woman giving the beggar food, clothing, bags of something or another. ... And she isn't even grateful. Look at her! Jorge stared at the beggar through his bank window. She is opening up the bags, taking out the clothes, greedily, emptying out the contents onto her skirt in front of her. Yet she didn't give a word of thanks to that woman, not even a nod of thanks!

She is peering at the skirts and jumpers, holding them up against her own body, imagining herself in them, all of them far too elegant for someone like her. She doesn't deserve all that stuff. She is fingering the clothes without any sign of gratitude. Just as though we owe it all to her! Who does she think she is, coming here and accepting our droppings of charity without so much as a gesture of thanks. I know for one I wouldn't give her anything, neither food nor clothing. Let her starve. Let her go naked. Not that her fat body would be even worth looking at. She's like an old hag, an old foreign hag, not like our smart Spanish women. They're all gypsies, these Romanians. Out! Out! I say. Push them all out. They can go anywhere, except come here. I don't care if they go and dirty the streets of other countries. In France the politicians and police might be harsher with them and send them packing back to their own country. We have too many unemployed Spaniards to accept any more people, let alone people who don't speak our language. There just aren't jobs for them. On top of that, they take jobs away from our people, when they decide to work that is, because mostly they just sit around idly begging.

Look at her now, stuffing all the clothes back into one of the plastic bags. She is opening the other one. It obviously contains food. She is sniffing at the plastic boxes. She takes the lid off one of them and sticks her finger into the hot sauce. She raises the rim of the box to her lips and drinks, noisily, slurping at the contents. She rubs the remains that have dribbled down her chin with the upper end of her long sleeve. Yes, she stinks of stale food and unwashed female. She puts the empty container back inside the plastic bag and opens the other Tupperware. Obviously - I can't see in much detail - it contains something solid, perhaps a leg of chicken or meat or fish. She is staring at the food, but hurriedly replaces the lid. She's sure to keep that for her supper. How lucky can you be! Here we all are in the bank working away hours of our life, in the bank, in all the offices of the country, hours every day having to do things that don't really interest us, putting up with grumpy bosses, pay reductions, envious working companions, just to be able to buy a small flat, pay for our children's schooling, the occasional holiday, hours of our life, I say, and these wretches from abroad come and live off the clothes and food we don't want. It isn't fair. Where is the justice in that? Some of us work hard to give to others who do nothing.

I just hate her. And I know she knows I hate her.

10

Nostalgia

Mara was thinking, muttering to herself: What am I doing here? I want to go back home, to my hovel, go to work again on my street corner. Why am I here? Who are all these people? I see them coming in and out of the room through a haze. This room. Where am I? I didn't ask to come here. They stop and talk to me imagining that I understand what they say to me. Sometimes I do. Sometimes I don't. I think that I must have been on the edge of death. All those tubes draining their liquid into me, oxygen to breath and I was so weak, barely able to move a limb. The terrible pain in my head. But now I am feeling better and, although I miss my hovel, my previous life simply because it was mine, not for any other reason, perhaps I should be grateful for this clean, comfortable bed where they change my sheets every day, for all the attention I receive. Perhaps I should try to help them to help me. Perhaps I should try to help myself. I must search within myself for the reasons for my downfall. Because there has been a downfall, hasn't there?

When I was young, I was pretty, intelligent, a good student and I loved life. Something happened to make all that disappear. My youth disappeared as though blotted out by a black velvet curtain, thick and impenetrable. Somehow, somebody took my youth from me and pushed me into unhappiness and into premature old age, into depression, into misery. Living in my hovel was misery, wasn't it? Even though I would like to return to it now. It is the only identity I can remember as my own. Everyone needs an identity, a place, even a hole in the ground, that they can claim as their own. This hospital room doesn't belong to me. It is merely another stage in the lengthy

48

process of living, another stop on the way towards death. Death takes so long to come. Why didn't they let me die? Why are they keeping me alive? I don't deserve to live ... What is this here? Who has given me a pen and a notebook, a notebook whose empty white pages stare up at me crying out to be used? Do they want me to write something? Do they want me to tell them my story?

*   *   *

Rosa's eyes were wide with excitement. 'You wouldn't believe it, Manuela! When I went in with her lunch today, there she was, Mara I mean, sitting up in bed sucking the end of a pen. She had that notebook that Raimundo gave her resting on her knees in front of her. He gave it to her days ago and it's been lying by her bed all that time, untouched. As I asked her to make space for the lunch tray, I noticed that the first page was almost completely covered with writing.'

Rosa appeared to be in a better frame of mind that afternoon. She seemed to have finally recovered from Jaime reprimanding her and she was genuinely happy that Mara had taken a turn for the better. Had she not known her better, Manuela would have thought that she'd met a new man. She had to force herself to suppress a giggle at the thought of Rosa with a man.

'Yes, I know Rosa, I saw her staring at the notebook the other day as though she was waiting for it to jump into her hands, open itself up and ask her to start writing! I thought then that it wouldn't be long before she decided to write in it. The trouble is we can't read what she's written. She writes in her own language. I know that Raimundo has found someone to translate it so that he can read it. We'll see how long she sticks at it. She really seems to be much better now. Goodness me, when I think of the terrible broken mess she was when she was brought in, and to see the difference now with our care and the doctors' treatment, it seems that she might, she might just pull through'.

There was a hint of pride in Manuela's voice, not only pride in the part she'd played, but pride in the clinic where she worked, pride in the team of nurses and doctors who struggled beside her daily to heal their patients. Rosa could detect that pride and satisfaction in her voice and fleetingly wished that she could feel like that too. Life for Manuela was easier and Rosa was convinced that it was because of her open personality. Not that it was really anything to her credit because, after all, we are born with one personality or another - the nice ones and the nasty ones, the generous ones and the stingy ones. Rosa felt with a touch of envy that she herself had not been treated that well when good personalities were being handed out.

'When she first came out of the coma,' Manuela continued, 'she used to scream, don't you remember? She used to hit out at us. Jaime told me that she shrieked at him, ordering him to get away from her. I think Carlos was able to handle her better. But now she seems to be calmer with all of us. She even smiles at me every time I go into her room.'

'Yes,' Rosa admitted. 'The other day I saw that she'd left her bed and was over by the window, staring out at the landscape. She looked a bit sad then, as though she was remembering something in her past.'

'My opinion is that she lives for her past,' Manuela remarked sympathetically. 'I mean, she doesn't seem to have much of a present life, does she? No-one visits her here. Her Spanish isn't that good. She can't really communicate with people very much. So she obviously hasn't known many people here. Perhaps she has no friends at all. Imagine that, Rosa, not to have any friends! When I asked her where she was going when she is better and can leave the hospital, she looked at me with a heavy expression and just said: Home. I shall go home. And where's that, I asked her. She waved her hand and murmured something about a dusty street at the end of the metro line. Out there with the gypsies, she said. When I said that she'd be better to find a job and hire a small apartment somewhere, she began to cry. So I kept quiet. I've never mentioned her "home" to her again.'

'I don't think you should ask her so many questions, Manuela. After all, we still don't know anything about her and it's obviously easy to upset her. Maybe she'll talk to us more freely in a few days. She's still on her medication. Carlos and Jaime want to continue with that for some weeks yet to see the outcome. She's still too weak to think of leaving the hospital even if she is stronger than before. She's had such a bashing that it'll take a long time for her to get right. Raimundo's working on her mind. He says that there is still damage there. If she left here and something happened to give her a shock, or she has another fall, then all our good work would be spoilt and what on earth might happen to her then?'

'Yes, I suppose that's true. I notice that she still has some pretty turbulent nights. The other night she was muttering non-stop. Only muttering, but that makes a considerable noise in the silence of the ward at night. She went on and on about Roxana. Someone, I think, that she didn't like because her tone was hateful and full of bitterness. Roxana this, Roxana that ... on and on she went. She must have been talking for about four hours, Rosa. I went in to her and took her hand and told her to be quiet and sleep. Forget Roxana, I said. But she was obsessed with Roxana. *Cruel, cruel, mala bestia,* she muttered. Sometimes she throws in a few Spanish words amidst her Romanian. Enough so we understand if she has good or bad memories of someone.'

*   *   *

Carlos was flicking through some papers, the sun's rays penetrating through the window of the small office, lighting up his slim brown face. The papers were a few notes that Raimundo had made on the Romanian patient. Beginnings of thoughts about her, really, not much more. All of them at the clinic were swimming around in the mystery of her past life, trying to take each wave as it came and fit it in with the previous ones.

'I think that Roxana was actually her mother. Has she mentioned the name to you Jaime?'

'No, never.' Jaime was sitting on the other side of the small formica-topped table. He pushed his chair backwards carelessly scraping it against the metal leg of the table. 'I sometimes wonder if we pay too much attention to this patient.'

'Well, if it isn't to the detriment of others, does that matter?' Carlos replied. 'She needs us. I am sure that we can pull her through this if we make enough effort. This Roxana, she hated her for some reason.

Yes, I know a lot of people have problems with mothers and fathers, but Mara seems to have it worse than many! When I was on my rounds the other day, I saw that she'd written Roxana in enormous letters in that notebook Raimundo gave her. They almost filled a page and then she'd put a thick cross through the name! There's obviously a problem there. Roxana and Mihaita - written and linked by arrows and then both of them crossed out. By the way, she still seems to suffer from awful headaches. Do you think we should increase her medication?'

'I'm a bit wary of doing that Carlos. An overdose can be just as dangerous as an under-dose. Keep her on the oxygen mask for several hours a day. That will help to clear her brain. Also, I want to get her onto speech therapy as soon as possible.'

Carlos looked up, his brow furrowed in concern. 'Do you think that'll do much good? After all, her Spanish is so bad that we're not going to know if her errors are because of that or because she lacks concentration.'

'The therapist will deal with that,' Jaime replied. 'I don't think it's such a problem. It's most essential that she eats well now. Good, nourishing food, appetising food - if we can call hospital meals appetising! - but good food will do almost more than pills and other treatment. Well, everything together will help her to pull through.'

Carlos stretched and yawned, then relaxed into a more comfortable posture. 'I'm beginning to feel that she really will pull through now. She seems to be better since Raimundo has got her writing. Every couple of days I can see that she's filling more and more pages of that notebook. So soon we should have something more tangible to work on.'

'Yes, true. But it's all got to be translated.'

'That shouldn't take too long Jaime. I doubt when she's finished that it'll be another *Hundred Years of Solitude*! What I am hoping is that we'll have some inkling as to who all these people are that she goes on about.'

*   *   *

Florencia looked worried.

It was upsetting but I told Raimundo about the day Mara kept mentioning Andreea.

'Now that's a new person,' he replied. 'Thanks, Florencia. What exactly did she say about Andreea?'

'Well, I couldn't make it out very well, could I? But she talked about a van full of men who kept on and on pestering her, pulling up her skirt, getting inside her pants, all day long and Andreea was there too. It sounded like a brothel to me, but she insisted it was a journey, an endless journey in the back of a van. As she talked she started crying, quietly at first, then her sobs got worse and the tears began to flow. When I went to remove her book so it wouldn't be smothered in tears, she grabbed my wrists and looked wildly into my eyes. She said: No more! No more! I hate this. I hate you all. I hate Andreea for making me do this. I want to go back to Trieste! Where was she going, Raimundo, what was that all about?'

'Well Florencia, I imagine that she's remembering her journey from Romania,' Raimundo suggested. 'She must have done that journey in several stages. This is what I am hoping will come out in her writings. Thank you for the information. Don't forget to tell me even the smallest details about what she says. Every bit helps. We're getting there. You will see, we'll get there! The poor woman. What is your impression of her, I mean, when you go into her room to clean up. Is she tidy? Is she pleasant to you? Apart from her outbursts, does she try and talk to you?'

I felt so pleased that Raimundo asked me all this. He's really nice to confide in me. After all, I'm only a cleaner. I told him what I thought.

'She complains on a lot of days about severe headaches and that she can't see very well. Sometimes she tells me to come closer because she can't distinguish my face. She tells me I am pretty.'

'And so you are!' Raimundo winked at her.

'She asked me once if I enjoy my work. Before I could answer her, she said, I hate cleaning, I hate cleaning other people's mess. But she's fairly tidy I think. She keeps her few belongings in the drawer of her bedside table. Not that she has many things, only what the nurses have given her and, of course, the book and pen you gave her. Often I catch her combing her hair. She keeps it well and now that it's shorter, it's easier for her to brush it. And she seems to be clean - her face and hands. I know Manuela helps her to file her nails and to put some cream on her face and hands after she has washed. And she likes to have a shower too. She never smells bad, Raimundo. Oh, and she's asked me several times if I like what I do. I just say, some days yes, some days no. And she laughs. It was the first time I heard her laugh. Not exactly an open laugh, it was a chuckle, as though she was sharing a secret that I'd told her. What else can I say about her? She is starting to communicate better with the woman in the bed beside her. They say good morning to one another, but that other woman is in a pretty disastrous state, not much of a companion I'd say for Mara. In a way, I think she is happier by herself. It's as though she's used to her own company and doesn't need anyone else with her. But, yes, she is educated, well brought-up.'

'Florencia,' Raimundo said quietly, 'she is an intelligent woman, but I know that she has had a very sad life. My job is to discover what happened to make an intelligent person simply give up and not want to go on living. If I can do this then perhaps I can encourage her to make something out of the future left to her.'

11

A Plan

Mara's bed was a mess. She'd been tossing and turning and was sweating profusely. Again, she had begun to mutter to herself: I hate taking medicines, pills, liquids mixed in water. They all taste bad, leave a coating on my tongue. I don't want any more of them. I feel better now. Why do they keep on making me take medicine? I don't need it now. They make me take pills with my meals, after meals, others before meals. I don't want them. I don't know if I am better because of the medicines or if I am simply better despite them. Perhaps I don't need them anymore. I shall never know if I don't stop taking them. I could throw them down the toilet and flush them away. They wouldn't know. Yes, that's what I'll do. Because now that I can eat by myself, they don't stay beside me to see if I take the medicine or not.

Pleased with her decision, Mara turned her thoughts to the clinic staff.

My heart leapt when I saw the psychiatrist. It was as though Petre had returned. His name is Raimundo. He came and sat beside my bed and I studied his face, olive-skin, his black wavy hair, slim limbs. He has a high, honest forehead and a serious smile on his full lips. He reminds me so much of Petre. All those years ago … Petre, my beloved friend. My only friend. The friend I betrayed. The father of my only child. Raimundo is kind and gentle to me. He coaxes me to talk. Unlike the others who just fling words at me and don't even wait for me to reply – except Florencia the cleaning lady and Manuela the nurse, oh and the doctor Carlos – Raimundo takes time with me.

He is gentle, the way Petre was. He listens to me as though he really cares about me. Why? I wonder. Why would anyone care about me, and even less someone who has never been part of my life before? But, of course, he is my psychiatrist. He is interested in people's minds, in people's pasts, in their pasts that have made them what they are today. He talks to me and asks me about my youth, about my family, about my friends, about my work, about my journey from Romania to Spain. He asks me about the things I like, the things I don't like, about my fears, my joys, about my interests.

Of course, he doesn't ask me all these things at once. He takes his time. I have said that. He takes notes as I speak, just a few, but mostly his eyes are on me. His eyes are beautiful, big and brown and expressive and they penetrate my soul when he stares at me. His fingers are long and slim, like Petre's. I like him very much. If only I were younger and more attractive … And when I told him that I used to write, that I enjoyed writing, that was when he gave me the notebook and pen. Now I spend a lot of time writing each day. It has come back to me, after all these years. Now I feel that I have wasted so many, many years of my life. I could have kept a diary during all this time. The diary would have been a friend to me, something to come home to every evening, something to keep my mind working, because I have no-one I can talk to. A diary would have supplanted that void. Yes, I have wasted so many years.

*   *   *

There are days when I am unable to write, when my thoughts are too painful and on those days, I spend the hours staring out of the hospital window at the barren earth, at some hovels rather like my own and at the blue mountains on the horizon. I watch the shadows. I remember my hovel with affection. Would you believe it? That miserable hole where I live in a dusty road, miserable with its iron roofing and leaking walls. How could anyone call that a home? Perhaps I should listen to what Manuela said to me. Why, she said, don't you get yourself a job and hire a small flat? She doesn't know what it is, though, to be without legal papers, to have a broken soul because life isn't worth living, because life has pummelled me into the shape I am now. She doesn't know that. Perhaps if Raimundo

56

were to tell me to do that, I might try when I leave here. It would help my self-esteem. Manuela said that to me on the day she came to give me one of those painful injections in my hip. How it hurts! Not the jab, but it hurts as the liquid pours into me, it feels thick and heavy, like liquid concrete. Manuela is kind to me and she does the injections well, but I always say to her: no more, no more injections. And she says, we'll see about that, with a mischievous smile on her bright face.

Manuela has blonde, curly hair that frames her face. She has a hefty bosom and big, flat feet that pound the floor as she enters and leaves my room. She always has something to laugh about and she makes me feel happy, just a little bit happy, as though life really is worth living. I think she is a very good nurse. She's worked here for about ten years, she told me, and she loves her job. Not like Rosa, the other nurse who visits me. Rosa is withered and dry. She keeps herself very much to herself, perhaps like me. There is something mean about her. Her lips are thin and pursed, stuck together in a fine line. She is unsmiling and goes about her work unwillingly, although she is efficient. But she is spare with her words and she doesn't smile. With Rosa, I feel that she begrudges paying me any attention, that she really feels that I shouldn't be here, a foreigner, a parasite to the Spanish health system. Not that she's ever said anything like that to me. But I can feel it. She spurns me. I'm not stupid.

Of all the women I see here, the one I most like is Florencia, the cleaner. She breezes in in the mornings, flicking her duster, twisting her wet rags, polishing window sills, bedsteads, bedside tables, mopping the floor. She works very quickly but, unlike Rosa, Florencia always has a smile on her lips. Not only her lips. It's really her eyes that smile. She always says something nice to me: How's Mara today? How's my favourite patient? And if I am uncomfortable or unhappy, she sits by me for a minute and takes my hand in hers. She tells me not to worry, that soon I shall be better, soon I'll be able to go home. I have never told her much about my life, except something one day about Andreea and those awful men, that terrible, terrible journey we made together. And she was sympathetic, although she didn't seem to know what to say to me then. Merely the pressure of her hand on my wrist, when she takes my hand in hers, it is like having a friend. And I feel grateful to her.

What about the two doctors, Carlos and Jaime? Of course, there are other doctors, other nurses, other cleaners in the hospital, but these are the ones I see most. Jaime seems to me to be abrupt, always in a hurry. Carlos, on the other hand, always has more time for me, like Manuela and Raimundo. He seems genuinely interested in my life and often asks me about my village in Romania. He is olive-skinned too, rather like Raimundo, but smaller in height and he has thicker fingers. Jaime is a very big man, tall and fat and pale-faced. He breathes heavily and sometimes his breath smells. I don't like him when he leans over me with his stethoscope. I feel like telling him to go away. I think I screamed at him once, mixing him up with someone else, with Radu I think it was, but I can't remember very clearly. It doesn't matter much. If you don't like someone, you don't want them near you. He mentioned how I'd reacted to him the next time he came and saw me.

But Carlos was the doctor who helped me to get out of bed for the first time. He encouraged me to walk over to the window, to sit there and watch the world on the other side of the window. He said that the day would seem shorter and fuller if I did that. He said I shouldn't always be lying down in bed thinking about myself. He told me to walk out into the corridor, to go just that little bit further every day, to try and talk to other patients. They don't seem to want to talk to me and I am too shy to push myself onto them. I sometimes watch the nurses as they go about their business, changing the sheets and towels, jotting down information about the patients in their books, administering medicines. Those horrible medicines! For several days now I haven't taken any of them. I throw them down the toilet and pull the chain. And I feel just the same. They weren't doing me any good at all. Only the beastly injection that Manuela gives me every fortnight or so. I hate it, but I can't get out of it.

These people are my world now. There are others in this place. Of course, there are others, but these are the ones who mean the most to me now. I shall miss them when I leave the hospital.

12

Paca's Good Intentions

Shortly after I had left her food and clothing, that cold November morning when I had so clumsily tried to speak to her, had almost run away from her in my embarrassment, I changed my life. I found a job working with immigrants in a non-governmental organisation. As I was becoming bored with my insurance job, I began to put out feelers in the humanitarian sector. I knew that insurance was corroding my life, I had to make a change for the better. I was lucky. My new job meant fewer hours, but that afforded me more time for other activities, and of course it meant less money, but still enough to cover my expenses. Above all, I was happier. Happier amongst caring companions, people whose main purpose in life was to live out their principles about how the less fortunate should be treated. It was exactly what I had been looking for. It altered my life completely and, for that, I felt grateful to the Romanian woman who, without realising it, had jogged my conscience. However, I no longer took the bus to work. I had to go on the metro and this meant that I didn't pass by her on her pavement any more.

Working with those who need help gives me such satisfaction, watching their black faces turn from crimped sadness to generous smiles, or their hermetic Asian countenances pleading with you to keep away, keep out of their lives, turn to welcoming glints of happiness, or their cold Russian blue-eyed stares turn to fresh, red-lipped laughter, or their miserable sallow shifty looks turn to honest gazes offering warmth. All of them, hurt by life, yet offering friendship and gratitude. Gratitude for what we were teaching them, for how we were helping them with their papers, to find rooms for shelter, telling them where they could get a decent meal, in short, befriending them, making them realise that not all Spaniards were against them, that many of us were fascinated with their different stories, that we understood that they would change our nation for the better with their customs and their ideas, that we knew that they would make their own special contribution to our land, like a breath of fresh air. So many of my countrymen consider that they come here to bleed our welfare system. Those people don't understand that immigrants are forced to leave their barren lands, their miserable dusty workless villages, their countries under the whim of corrupt dictators where cruelty and torture and hunger run rife, forced to run away from all that tragedy, to run away anywhere where they can live without feeling humiliated. To run away not only once, but twice, three times, so desperate are they, making and re-making the same sordid journeys across desert lands, confronted by high impenetrable walls protected from them by the spurs and spikes of injustice. Our countries turn them back on their tracks once, twice, three times saying No to them, No, No, No. I found jobs, mostly menial tasks, for many of them. They were grateful. I accompanied them to obtain legal papers. They were grateful. I found schools for their children - their hope for the future. They were grateful. We all helped them to learn the Spanish language, with a greater or lesser degree of success. And they were grateful. We were helping them to feel part of this country, to feel that their frightening, dangerous journeys had been worthwhile and that their miserable past was well and truly past.

I was gleaning experience with all these people. One evening, reflecting on how I had come to be immersed in this world, I realised that it had all begun with my feelings for the Romanian beggar. Surely, if I was helping other immigrants, I could do the same for her? I owed her that. I would go and visit her the next day. Since my job in the insurance office, I had only seen her a couple of times lumbering along the road between the metro and her street corner, beleaguered by her long heavy skirts and the bags she always carried around with her. Tomorrow I would go and talk to her, somehow convince her to come to our office for help.

*   *   *

The spring morning was beautiful, fresh with a light breeze that made the soft clouds prance carefree in the blue sky. It had rained overnight, easy cleansing drops that had freshened the world. I walked, light of step, excited about helping the woman who had been responsible for so positive a change in my life. If she showed interest in my proposal, then she could come with me right away. It would be like pulling her up out of her doldrums into another sphere, another world where life moved forwards instead of backwards. I imagined the light in her eyes as she grasped at this straw in the ocean, as she took my hand willing me to help her, as she stuttered words of thanks in her elementary Spanish. It wouldn't take us long to help her to speak better, find some cleaning work perhaps, organise papers for her and a better place to live in. I visualised all this as I made my way along the pavement, busier now with people hurrying to their places of work. As I approached the corner, her corner, I strained my eyes anxiously because I couldn't see her. Perhaps she had moved slightly away and was sitting with her back against the bank wall. I came level with her spot only to realise that it was unoccupied. Where were her things, her meagre belongings? Had she not left them and gone off somewhere to attend to nature? Had she not yet arrived that morning? In the past, she had always been there at this hour. There was nothing to speak of her presence, either today, yesterday, or ever. I looked about me to verify that I was on the right street corner. … I felt shattered, all my hopes cascaded to the ground. Where could she have gone?

A flat disillusionment overwhelmed me for a few moments as I stood, feeling useless and bewildered, my fingers lingering gently on the battery disposal unit where she had rested her back, on the spot which had been hers for so long. As I pulled myself together and made to leave, realising that there was nothing I could do save perhaps return the next day, I caught sight through the bank window of that man again with a leering grimace on his face, directed straight at me.

13

A Glimpse of Understanding

I remember the first day in years that she wasn't there! God be praised. It was a relief for us all in the office, but particularly for me, with my desk just by the window. It was impossible for me not to see her, not to be aware of her ugly presence. Her large humped body was reflected in the window and I was obsessed with her because I would see that reflection at times even on my papers, depending on how the sun slanted its rays. It was as though she interfered with my thoughts, getting between them and my customers. The boss had even pulled me up a couple of times because of mistakes I had made in my calculations. Of course, I blamed her for that. It was her fault. Just being there. I have said I was obsessed by her. But from that day her spot was empty.

This morning I caught sight of that silly little woman who left her bags of food and clothing. I wonder why she came back because I haven't seen her for a long time, several months at least. But the beggar's place on the pavement is empty and the space she has left makes me feel free. Perhaps she'll never return. I hope that she never will return, disgracing our bank corner with her filthy belongings.

A disgrace, that was what she was! A disgrace to our decent, civilised society, to our well-dressed men and women, to our diligent workers, to the client-savers with our bank. Look at the Chinese ... you never see them badly dressed. I've never seen one of them begging on the streets like these Romanians, or Africans, or Arabs. No, not that I like the Chinese any better, but at least they are clean and if they do underhand work, they do it concealed from the rest of us, sewing in the basements of their restaurants. Not many people seem to eat in those restaurants, yet there are masses of them - every few months another couple seem to spring up in the area. At least they seem to be clean and gaily decorated. Mind you, I would never go to them for a meal. I once heard that they served up rat to their customers. They disguise it as chicken or pork and smother it in their wily vegetables and sauces. No, that sort of food isn't for me. Where there is a good plate of chickpeas or a succulent cut of Spanish veal or a piece of fish from our coast, don't offer me any strange dish from other lands! ... Yes, I really reckon that the Chinese use their restaurants to sew all the garments they sell in their smelly bazaars and even the clothing you can buy in our big stores that puts *made in China*, I bet it's made here in basements underneath their woks and saucepans full of rat or chicken or pork, or whatever it is. My companion, David, once said that he thought they brought colour to Spain - as if we need their colour, their flat sallow faces - we have our own Spanish colour. Then he said that they brought an *interesting difference* to our society. I ask you, what is there of interest in their difference? As far as I'm concerned, they can stick it, take their *difference,* interesting or not, back to their own countries.

At least now that she's gone - and let's hope that she really has gone - if we can see out the year without her there, then I shall begin to believe it. We ought to put something on her spot of pavement to prevent any more of them from coming along. Perhaps she's gone off to another place in Madrid, or perhaps to another city in Spain, or perhaps she earned enough with her begging to take the coach back to Romania, which would be the best option. Or perhaps she's sick and has stayed in bed, although I can't imagine that she has much of a bed. Where on earth do these indigents sleep anyway? My son is at school with two immigrant boys from Morocco and he told me that when their parents first came here, they occupied a grubby flat with ten others in *Lavapiés*, right in the centre of Madrid. All of them had got into the country illegally, four or five of them hiding away under fruit lorries that cross the Straits on the ferry between Spain and Africa, two others had paid money - probably stolen - to the mafia and came in a van. The others had crossed the sea in a dinghy. They had seen several deaths on that journey, one dead baby dropped overboard and the others who drowned. Why on earth do they come like that when they don't even know how to swim! I ask you!

Ten others! Imagine that! Imagine the smell of unwashed bodies, of dirty clothes. My son said he was fascinated with the stories those two Moroccan boys told him, about the way they lived in Marrakech, begging in the souk, stealing coins from tourists in the *Djema El Fna Square*, sometimes working by the hour in the town's tanneries for a pittance, about their journey to the coast, to Tangiers where they waited for a boat to bring them to Spain, to the land of plenty. In Tangiers they begged too, just enough to be able to eat once a day, always trying to avoid the police, terrified of the police, but agile and cunning as they fled. They hated the police, the way a lot of people in Spain used to hate the police when Franco lived, but his police force kept us all disciplined and hard-working. They removed the riff-raff from the streets, flung them into gaol - the way it should be. I warned my son not to get too involved with those Moroccans. They aren't like us, I told him. They aren't Christian, they have other beliefs, they eat different food. He just told me not to be silly, that they were nice boys, not that he knew their parents, they had good marks at school too. But, no, I feel uneasy about him mixing with them.

*   *   *

I had a lot of work to get through that first day she was not there and I was pleased at the end of it to realise that I could concentrate better without the Romanian presence on the pavement outside. Well, a good part of the morning my thoughts were occupied with her, but I settled well into my accounts after that. For several days, I walked towards the bank, fearing that she might have returned, but when it seemed that she really had left, I began to heave sighs of relief. ... Then David came into my office one morning and, with a suspicious look on his face when he saw me happy and relaxed for a change, blurted out in an accusing tone asking me what I had done with the beggar woman. He seemed suddenly to have realised that she was no longer there.

'What do you mean, what have *I* done with her?' I retorted.

'Well I seem to recall that you had some very strange ideas about ousting her from there, filling bags with rubbish and loads of unwanted files, making signboards and slashing them through with red crosses,' he said.

'One thing,' I said, 'is what you say and another is what you do. You know perfectly well that I never did that. It was only a threat because she annoyed me so much. I hated her.'

'I know you hated her, why I can't imagine. The poor have just as much right to the planet as we do.'

'There you go again with your do-gooder arguments! I don't know why you never helped her out, bringing her food and clothing like that silly woman I used to see. As for me, I hated her. Just to look at her made me cringe. She interfered with my work. I've told you before, I want all these foreign skins out of Spain. I want it the way it used to be - hermetic, Catholic, Spanish! They have no right to be here.'

'If you go on like that, don't count me amongst your friends, Jorge. You are cruel and hard.'

Me, Jorge, cruel and hard? Perhaps. Perhaps David is right. Perhaps my son is right. Perhaps they *are* nice. Perhaps that Romanian woman really did have a good heart. Perhaps I am the one who is wrong. … Is there really any doubt in my fascist soul? I doubt it.

Either way, she's gone and I don't care where.

14

Radu: A Mistake

It is a long ride, Doctor, going on the metro from my home to my
work, from my hovel to my begging place. And back again. I stand
alone on the train platform. On purpose, I try not to stand close to
anybody because I know that no-one wants to be beside a beggar,
that close to a beggar. They might dirty their clothes and they might
wrinkle their noses at my unwashed state and I would feel
uncomfortable. Remember, I never use soap to wash my body. And
my clothes are grubby. Sometimes I wash them when I can afford a
small box of soap powder. I have to hang them outside my dwelling
to dry and if I leave them there without watching over them they
would be stolen. There are lots of needy people in the dusty street
where I live. So I do any washing I have on a Sunday. That is my day
of rest when I sleep late in my hovel and stay there all day.

Yes, I sit on a seat in the train by myself and if anyone comes to sit
beside me, I get up, remove my hulk of a body and stand alone at the
end of the carriage. It is a long journey, seventeen stations with a
long way between some of them. I live at the end of the line and
when I get off the train and come out of the metro, I have to walk at
least fifteen to twenty minutes. This is the only exercise I have each
morning and each evening.   I drag my body along the highway,
stumbling against the stones on the gravel, the dying sun piercing my
eyes, my body still heavy from the searing heat of the afternoon; the
cars zoom past me, hooting at each other - that noise pierces my
brain and I jump visibly if they pass too close to me. Then I turn off
the main road onto an unmade pathway lined with shacks and hovels,

the homes of the poor, the destitute, the forgotten, the outcasts, the tumours of society. ...

Is this really what I have become, Doctor? A tumour?

The hovels sit in the grit, the dry burnt up crust and dirt on the outskirts of Madrid. They sit stupidly in a long row, one after another with their sheets of corrugated iron for roofs, held down with stones and bricks, their walls stuck haphazardly together with large pieces of plaster board found on a building site, more corrugated iron, some with bricks piled chaotically one on top of the other, some with long planks of wood badly nailed together. Those not lucky enough to have a real door, however old and shabby with peeling paint, hang a thick curtain across the entrance.

I have never known what luxury is. Simona's house in the village wasn't much more than a country cottage, but it was solid, it was a house made of brick walls and it had a real roof with tiles and fitted windows. No, I don't ask for luxury because I have never known what it is. My house in Madrid has only one small window, a roughly gouged hole in the wall on one side. And through that hole a street-lamp shines from the main highway. This gives me enough light at night. Sometimes it keeps me awake, but I am normally so tired that I flop down on my mattress as soon as I have eaten my supper. On most nights, the little cat comes to bed with me. She comes more and more. We are friends. I can only give her the warmth of my body, the smell of my body, and the scraps from my plate. She gives me her affection. If she were to leave me I would feel sad. Four-legged animals are better company than two-legged human animals. At least, that is how it has been for me, all my life.

None of these dwellings has sanitation. All of us have to relieve ourselves behind a bush or in a nearby ditch. Some of my neighbours have a makeshift shelter that they use. I have told you that the police come often, with their sirens, their barking, growling dogs with bristling fur. They march up and down asking questions to anyone they see outside the houses. With all their questions, they remind me of Ceausescu's guards in our village.

Will I never be free of persecution?

And they often pick up one or two of the younger men who are drugged to the eyeballs, or anyone who looks suspicious, as though he is selling drugs, or occasionally they pick up a prostitute and cart her off screaming in their police van. It is all just to make us scared, so that we don't get too comfortable living the way we do, an eyesore on the edge of the Spanish capital. It's true. We are an eyesore, our hovels, our bodies, our clothes, everything about us, but only the police come to visit us. No social workers. They leave us to our own devices. They prefer us to remain on the edge.

When I wake up in the mornings the little cat has disappeared. She goes off to attend to her daily business. I admire her independence. She needs no-one, she takes the little food I can give her - if I have nothing, she finds food elsewhere - and in return she gives me her furry warmth. Cats know how to look after themselves.

*   *   *

I didn't know how to look after myself, did I Doctor? Radu burst into my life. Just burst in. He forced himself on me. He used to sit behind me in the classroom at university and wouldn't leave me alone. He was always making sly comments, kicking me under the bench, touching my long hair, poking my back, insinuating, coaxing, pulling me, enticing me towards him, even though he knew that I was with Petre. He made certain that I felt his presence, constantly, not only during classes, but outside on the campus. When I walked home alone on the days that Petre had different hours to mine, Radu would accompany me, talking, talking about literature because he knew that was the love of my life, apart from Petre. … I resisted him for weeks and weeks, but then I began to feel the strength of his pushing and manipulating of my life, my ideas. He was very good looking. No, not my type, but really, very good looking. He wasn't sensitive like Petre. He was bombastic, sure of himself, sure that he could get whatever he wanted.

And I was what he wanted.

Nothing would stand in his way. The first time on one of our walks home was when he grasped my hand, nothing subtle, nothing tender, just a strong masculine grip, a male possessiveness that made me

68

cringe, accustomed as I was to Petre's unassertive, almost timid affection. I withdrew my hand with difficulty. His hand was clammy and large. A possessive hand. Petre's fingers were fine and gently searching. What a difference! Radu laughed at me. He was not one to take no for an answer. When, after a time, he realised that his persistence was getting him nowhere with me, he changed his tactics. He became more solemn, less talkative, taciturn as though immersed in the depth of his thoughts, slightly scornful of my comments. He knew that he would attract me more if he established a distance between us, a superiority. Occasionally, he wouldn't be there on the days I walked home without Petre. He was trying to make me miss him, make me want him. And suddenly I realised that I did miss him when he wasn't there, that I did want him. He even went to the lengths of not turning up to classes on one or two days. Then he asked me if I could fill him in with the notes I had taken. I wouldn't lend him my notes. He suggested that he come to my room to copy them. Petre had had to return to the village for several days because his father was ill. I missed him, but my curiosity for Radu was becoming more and more intense. So I said yes, he could come to my room to copy my notes. I even felt a certain fascination at the idea of being unfaithful to Petre, not because I didn't love him, it was more a curiosity about my own female guile to attract another man. And why not? Radu wanted me. And so it happened. He wheedled his way into my room, to my table and into my bed. Ours was burning passion during seven days. For seven afternoons we explored each other's bodies, crudely at times, cruelly at times, no gentle caresses, we bit, we scratched with passion. We were beside ourselves with youthful desire. Desire without any ties, totally immoral, fucking for fucking's sake. I had never known this obsessive use of desire. With Petre it had always been attached to affection, to deep feeling. There was a delicate timidity in our relationship. But with Radu, it was as if we had to exorcise some sickness within us, a scouring of the frenetic desire in our loins, as if we had to punish ourselves for this crazed passion behind Petre's back.

When Petre returned, I could barely meet his gaze. Yes, I still loved him. I wanted him. I wanted to return to his gentle loving care. I wanted to escape from the strenuous acrobats of passion I had experienced with Radu, where everything was utterly physical - and intellectual through our common interest in literature - but where nothing was warm or solid or beautiful. I told Radu never to come again, never to come back, never to accompany me home, I told him I never wanted to see him again, that I belonged to Petre, only to Petre. ... I could see that Petre could see that I had changed in those few short days. I had no option but to confess to him. My guilt was written all over my face. I have already said that he closed up on me after that, scorn and disillusionment was festering inside him.

Which of the two was Tatiana's father? I believed that I could see Petre in her on the day she was born. Or was it, Doctor, that I wanted to see Petre in her?

There are still nights when I lie awake in my hovel thinking about Radu, thinking about Petre, thinking about the young university student I used to be. All that has disappeared now. It disappeared long ago, a time when I believed Simona when she told me to make wishes as I lighted my candles. Then, I never believed that life could be so cruel, that people could be so cruel. Then I believed in a good world, even when my mother was sour. Of course, childhood is innocent. It takes most of us years to learn how to hurt, how to lie, how to be cruel, how to be corrupt, how to torture, how to be dishonest, how to sin, how to envy, how to scorn, how to be selfish. Because all this is what we are. All these negative traits are there, in every human being, just occasionally threaded through with glints of bounty, generosity, sincerity, love. That was Simona. She had more good in her than bad. Roxana, my mother, had more bad in her than good.

If Simona had been alive when my daughter was born, she would never have allowed Roxana to arrange the adoption. An adoption out of spite for me, her own daughter. Petre too had more good in him than bad, but the good in him prevented him from understanding me. Or perhaps it was his male pride that I had soiled and, for that, he could never forgive me. And so for me, his goodness turned bad. It rotted.

As for Radu, he was selfish from the start, he was only motivated by his own needs and desires. He thought nothing of the consequences.

When Petre returned, Radu went straight to another girl, to a friend of mine, to do with her what he'd done with me under my very nose, to hurt me as much as he could. When I left university I never saw him again and he might, just might, have been the father of my child.

A child who is part of me, whoever the father is.

15

Pregnant and Friendless

Those months beside my mother, waiting, waiting for the birth of the child within me, building up anguish, desolation, feeling heavier and heavier with the child that I didn't want, the child that would ruin my life, the child I was having for Ceausescu, that I was having to help him fight against his zero- population-growth. I was being *a model* within the communist regime. The authorities had seemed to realise, all of a sudden, that there would soon be no willing hands to labour in their factories, to work in their fields, to build up the Party red tape. Their answer was to have more babies, more babies, large happy families, perfect families. Just like any Catholic nation.

Maybe if Simona had still been alive, she would have encouraged me with my pregnancy. Maybe if Petre had stayed by my side, I could have put up with my mother's gruelling comments. Maybe, then, I would have wanted the child within me. For Petre's sake. But Roxana spoilt everything. She was there, always there, accusing, moaning, scolding, criticising everything I did. The worst thing for me was the look of accusation in her eyes. I used to try to avoid her gaze as I went about the chores she imposed on me. How I hated that ruinous daily routine around the house, repeating senseless activities, making the beds, sweeping the floors, washing the dishes, cleaning the windows, preparing the meals. She wouldn't allow me to read. Everything she said and made me do was aimed at obliterating my studies, my books, my desires. With spite, she wanted to wipe that era out of my life, crush my intentions to read and to write. You have betrayed all that with your fatherless pregnancy, she said accusingly. Now, I had only to concentrate on becoming a mother, a housewife.

Nor could I find respite outside the house. Walking out into the village was even worse because I was the object of recriminating stares, whisperings, even cruel comments that I was incapable of retaliating to. On many a night, when I sobbed into my mattress beside Viorica, I imagined doing harm to the baby, I dreamed of ripping myself open and grasping the foetus and casting it away from me, stifling it amongst the contents of a rubbish bin. I could fall over. I could drink a lot of *palinka* one night, behind my mother's back, in an attempt to wash all trace of this child away. I could take lots of pills to vomit and vomit. But I didn't do any of these things because I knew that they may not achieve my goal, that they might only harm the child and I would give birth to a cripple or a monster. Or they might make me very ill. No, I was a coward, Doctor.

And I am still a coward.

Very occasionally I would find peace in the early evenings, walking away from the village towards the blue hills, darkening to purple in the dying light. I would lie down in a secluded glade - that same glade where I came upon Simona in her dying hours - on the sweet summer grass and breathe in my freedom, my solitude. Away from my mother's discontent, away from the accusatory glares of our neighbours. Then I would dream of Petre and wish and wish that he would come back to me. Why was I so weak? Why did I give in to my mother time and time again? Why couldn't I stand up for myself? I have no answer to this. Even now I have no answer. Perhaps it is just that some of us are weaker than others.

Now I am overcome with weakness.

It was on one of those soft evenings as I lay on my back, my eyes squinting against the sun as it set behind the deep mauve hills, that I perceived a movement in my belly. It was at first like a vague tickle beneath the surface of my skin. I lay still, hardly daring to breath. And I listened, all my senses alert. Then again. This time I noticed that the movement was stronger, like a feeble pushing within me. Instinctively I placed my hands underneath my jumper, over my swollen belly, against my bare skin. My fingers lay inert, waiting for another movement. And it came, this time stronger. Yes, it was my baby floating around in its liquid hollow inside me. Suddenly I noticed that I was trembling, shuddering with emotion. Tears were welling up inside me. They came from deep down in my womb, pushing up, up, through my stomach, into my breast where they spoke to my heart. They oozed from my eyes and ran, salty, down my cheeks. I sat up and realised I was sobbing freely. But this sobbing wasn't like the bitter sobbing into my mattress at night because of my mother and because of my fate. These were tears of love and compassion. These tears were asking forgiveness from my child for having not wanted her - or him - to be born. They were cleansing tears and they opened the way to realisation, so that all of a sudden I saw clearly that this baby was part of me, part of my life, that she was my future, I was her future. She was my own, my very own and she would be everything to me. I would be everything to her, because I also suddenly knew that my baby was a girl. And as I sat hugging my knees in my bed of grass blades, my face towards the waning light behind the far-off hills, I realised that I wanted this child. Above everything else, I wanted her. We would make our life together. We would build a cocoon around ourselves where no-one else could harm us. Petre hadn't wanted to know, so I wouldn't let him near her. Roxana was cruel to me, so I wouldn't allow her to be a grandmother to my daughter. She would never be the way Simona had been to me. For the first time in months I felt a glow of true happiness inside me. I talked to my baby. I told her that everything would be alright for us. Yes, all of a sudden, I really wanted her.

*   *   *

Why do I always go to beg in the same place? I found this place during my early days in Madrid when I would take the metro to one point or another of the city - just to get to know the dry capital of Spain - and I sensed a certain sympathy with this long street lined with gardens and trees, with many people going about their lives, with shops and animation. I liked it, even though it was a long way from my dwelling. And so, for years now, day after day I carted myself off on the metro beside the washed and perfumed. Day after day I walked, slowly, heavily from the metro along the wide, gardened street, busy with people and cars, to my corner, the corner by the bank.

I am a human being and human beings are prisoners of routine. Some have better routines than others, of course. Mine is boring. Perhaps it allows me to dream. I still tend to dream and remember my early youth and this helps me to overcome my boredom. Perhaps it is because it allows me to watch the passers-by - them and their ankles - and, although some of them are the same day after day, there is always someone different. I carry my belongings in plastic bags: my thick piece of cardboard which serves as my cushion - I fold it to make it even thicker; my raffia mat for the coins; my small leather purse with a few coins for the metro ride and for my supper; an empty plastic bag to take home any scraps or clothing that people offer me. On some days, if I remember, I take my umbrella; in the winter to protect myself from the rain and in the summer to protect myself from the hot sunlight. My umbrella is broken. Two of its spokes stick out sideways like the antennas of a car and, between two other spokes, the nylon material is torn. I have difficulty trying to keep it up because the clasp keeps slipping. Perhaps I should buy a new one, a cheap one in the Chinese store down the road, but I hate to spend money if it isn't really necessary and my umbrella still wards off the sun and the rain. Mostly anyway.

Also I think that I always go to the same place because I no longer have the will or the desire to go elsewhere. I no longer want to seek out new experiences, new fields, new faces. The place I chose some years ago now is just right for me and it feels like my special place of work. As I said, I found it when I first arrived in this city. I had no idea where I was going. I simply jumped on the metro, sitting lulled by the movement of the train. Maybe that is why I went so far from my night residence, so far from the dusty street where I live. Sixteen stations, one after the other. When I eventually emerged from the underground, the sun shone through the trees lining the centre of a wide street, a busy street, ideal for begging I thought. I knew immediately that this would be where I would come every day. It was very different to where I had bedded down. ... Why change now? Changes are for the young and enthusiastic, for those who feel that life still lures them to live.

I no longer feel the lure of life. But I am wary of death. I admit that, Doctor.

And I am friendless. I only find communication with others in the occasional smile, the crooked, sideways smile of a passing woman, generally an old woman, the young ones are too engrossed in their own lives to worry about the scrap of humanity which is me, a disturbance at their feet. There are times when I receive a nod, a very slight acknowledgement from an old woman who passes me almost every morning. There are days when children point at me and exclaim to their mothers. They say: Look at that old woman sitting on the pavement! And their mothers retort: Let her be. Don't talk to her.

I am like a pariah, one of India's untouchables.

No friends, no. My very own solitude is my friend, my own thoughts are my friends, my silence is my friend, the night is my friend, the stars are my friends, the moon is my friend, the trees are my friends, and the sun is my friend when it isn't too hot, the birds are my friends, the dogs are my friends, and the little cat is my friend. So, Doctor, you can see that I am rich in friendship. When people talk to one another, they talk and talk and never notice the sun, the moon, the stars, the trees. Their conversation blots out these beautiful things. I can remember the trees and grass and the hills in Romania. When I was pregnant waiting for Tatiana to come, when I was so alone in the presence of my mother and of the unfriendly neighbours in our village, then I learned how to find friends in the nature around me and I found that the trees whispered and spoke to me, that the dogs would nuzzle me in warmth, that the stars twinkled their secrets to me. Simona spoke to me, often, about the gifts of nature. And so I have no human friends, but I don't need them. They would complicate my life. I haven't known what a true friend is since Petre left me. Why search for another friend now? For him or her to deceive me? And, in a sense too, this street corner where I come every day is a friend to me also. The hovel where I sleep at night, the spot on the pavement in front of the bank are my friends. They are the only life I know now. I want compassion from nobody. I want sympathy from nobody. In that, I am quite self-sufficient. No need to

76

look elsewhere for a better spot on a better pavement, to make a different journey on the metro, to search and search. For what? It is all the same. A beggar's life is all the same, whether in Madrid, in Istanbul, in Bucharest, in Timisoara. And, remember, I am Romanian. I am resigned to my lot.

Indeed, there are summer days when the sun shines down on my head, against my face, when I squint my eyes and rest the back of my head against the used battery disposal unit, I squint until the light playing on the lashes of my eyes turns them to gossamer, to the fine veined wings of a wasp, to delicate colours, before I close them completely, blocking out the light, the colour, to find peace in the darkness. At first that darkness is a heavy crimson block which gradually changes shape and colour. Finally, the crimson turns to jet black. Then I imagine death. I imagine what it would be like to die, to finish with this life of mine. I would be alone. No friend would accompany me, because I have no friends. No human friends. Death could come upon me at any moment, in the metro, as I sit on my cardboard cushion, as I drag my body homewards along the dry, gravel path towards my hut. Or in my hut. I could drop down, dead, on the floor, the little cat clawing at me, imploring me with her *miaowing* to wake up, she would be the only one to care. Or I could die in my sleep, still and calm.

I must sleep now.

16

Ceausescu and God

It is time I spoke of Ceausescu. Simona always used to tell me that death was a release from the toil of life. She said that she knew she would go up to heaven and see God. She believed that He was the Maker of all things. She had learnt that from the Bible, from the Sunday sermons of the village priest when he harangued his parishioners. She was convinced that He would forgive her for all her sins, for all her wicked thoughts. She truly believed that she would find peace beside Him and that He would treat her well, better than any other man had ever treated her.

Wide-eyed, I used to listen to her talk. For many years I listened to her, hanging onto her words as though she were an oracle. God in my mind was a benign, bearded old man, sitting up on His throne of clouds in the sky, waiting for us all to go up there to be with Him, the proud Father of an immense family. Simona talked about our souls. She said we didn't journey up there with our body. Our body stayed here, under the ground. It was only our soul that flew, spiritual and transparent, on a marvellous journey into the heavens. She believed with all her heart that she would re-find her dead husband, my benign old grandfather, benign like God, that she would meet her dead brother, her old uncles and aunts. She believed. Simona believed. Simona was lucky to believe like that. Those beliefs make life bearable. But Petre and I used to discuss religion and all Simona's beliefs and it was during that time with him that I began to disbelieve.

Perhaps it was because of Ceausescu. If there is a God, a Maker, how could He possibly wish that His children be tortured and cruelly treated by others? That didn't make sense to me, or to Petre. Because, apart from the summer village festivals, our lives in Romania were hard. Food was scarce and what there was was poor. We were an oppressed people - noble in our resignation, yes - but oppressed. Oppressed by the sly smile and the cruel lips of the dictator whose image was everywhere, all over the country, as though we should never be far from his brutal paternity, outside his control, as though we must never forget him and what we owe him. In my case, a child.

He was a tyrant who led his people to poverty and misery. He ordered his *Securitate* to keep a firm watch over us all. In Timisoara at the university we had to be careful not to say anything critical about his regime. We learned to speak a sign language so that any nearby spy wouldn't realise what we meant. No-one in Romania was allowed to disagree with the dictator; the media bowed and scraped to him. He was of God's doing. How could I, a subject of this malevolent example of humanity, believe in the bounty of God? Simona said that Ceausescu could never take her God away, that he could never bereave her of her peasant life with her little brick house and her timber church where she lit her candles and prayed to her God. She had been modelled in a world of thatched mud roofs and thick colourful woollen blankets on her bed, her wooden kitchen bench and table that harboured the secret whispers from the noble, towering trunks of the Romanian forests. Simona came from the peasant heart of Romania. She had tried to transmit its qualities to Roxana, to Mihaita my absent father, to my younger sister Viorica and, of course, to me. I shall always attribute my love of nature, of the countryside, the mountains, the birds and the soft winds, to Simona. All that, yes. But I found it very very hard to love her God.

Ceausescu destroyed many of our Transylvanian villages. He wanted to rid Romania of any trace of Hungarian influence. Simona said that he would never reach our village. He wanted his people to be urbanised and to live in ugly blocks of flats in the large towns, where it would be easier for him and his men to control them. He was our *Conducator,* our one and only leader. I thought that God wanted his people to be tolerant. No, He wanted them to be obedient. And

Ceausescu wanted an industrial, ugly Romania. He wanted us to turn away from our village roots. Yet I shall never forget going home to my village at weekends. Despite Roxana and her difficult nature, my village responded to the deepest strains in my soul. I have never forgotten it. My most vivid tragedy today is that I know I shall never go back to it. I cannot go back. I don't have the means. And now, I suppose Roxana is dead and that Viorica has left. It is years since I have heard from them. Why go back? Perhaps only to hear the wind in the tall trees blowing gently down the mountain side. No, with people in this world like Roxana, my mother, like Ceausescu, the *Conducator,* I cannot believe in God. With people like them, hell is here on this earth, not in any afterlife. Not in death. Death is oblivion.

My death will be oblivion. A relief from my daily suffering.

17

Beggars and Birth

I have said that we beggars always respect each other. In general, this is true. There is, Doctor, an underlying respect amongst us. Some might try to rob the rich, to eke money out of any passer-by, even to steal a sandwich from a supermarket, or a bottle of wine. But if I were to leave a bottle of wine on the pavement beside me and turn my face away, another beggar would never try and take it from me. He might ask if we could share it. But that is merely an example. I don't normally have a bottle of wine with me. We recognise each other's misery, each other's lack of money. And in our trudging around the streets, in our night-time hovels, in our shared dormitories, our soup kitchens, in our hideouts in the underground, on our street corners, over the months and the years and the seasons we have built up a mutual understanding, a mutual respect.

Each and every beggar has his or her own way of going about the life that has befallen him. I know of one man who lives with his victuals at the entrance to a travel agency. He is bearded and unkempt, but I have seen him reading. He takes a book from the overloaded trolley that goes everywhere with him, carting his odd ends of clothing, bottles, tin dishes. His worldly belongings are filthy or broken and ragged. He sits and sits during the day, sometimes reading, sometimes staring at the world as it passes him by, but I have passed by him at night and I see that he beds down inside a structure of cardboard boxes. He has a foldable mattress, blankets, thick socks and he crawls right inside two boxes. He chains his belongings to his wrist through a hole in the box. And there he sleeps, night after night, shielded from the wind and the keen Madrid air by his cardboard, at home in the wide entrance to the travel agency, two steps up from the pavement.

A few streets away from him near a metro station I have seen an armless man. Through winter or summer, he wears only a sleeveless vest, exposing his shoulder bones from whence the arms were once wrenched away, or perhaps he was born from thalidomide, the pills that caused physical deformity in the foetus of the mothers who took that medicine. This man exhibits his deformity and his ugliness. He is like a vision from the Middle Ages. He holds a plastic goblet in his teeth, waving it under people's noses, coaxing them to drop a coin in it. Many shun him. His armless shoulders are too ugly, too embarrassing, to look upon.

Some sit, like me, day after day in the sun, in the rain, in the heat, in the cold, hoping, hoping for benevolence from some kind soul. We have little to offer the world, no songs, no poems, no dances. Others heave their lives around on a pair of crutches, maimed, or pretending to be maimed. They play on people's sympathy imagining that their physical handicap will be enough to move the egotistical human soul. Some wait at traffic lights and when the cars stop they stare with hope at each driver, knocking on car windows, offering to clean windscreens, offering a packet of Kleenex in exchange for a few coins to a driver who might have forgotten his handkerchief. They weave their way in and out of the stationary cars, pestering drivers, waiting, waiting for the one who reluctantly gives them something.

Then there are those who shun the street. They prefer to stay underground. They jump on the trains going from carriage to carriage, either singing, if they know how to - though some of them sing without knowing how to - or they learn a passage of woe about being unemployed - that's obvious - about having to care for a family of four small children, about having to sleep out unsheltered in winter or summer. ... Forgive my interrupting your thoughts, your conversations, your day. Forgive me for annoying you. If you could just give me a couple of coins to help. ... I have seen one beggar on the metro who goes back and forth in the carriages with his terrible face, his deformed skin and nose, burnt in a work accident, he cries out in chipped tones: ... And now no-one will employ me looking like this. Look at my face. No-one wants me. Another complains that he has cancer and cannot work. His body is wasted and thin although he is quite young. His feeble voice is lost against the noise of the train, the chatting of the travellers. They don't hear him, but they know what he is saying. He doesn't lie and people feel sorry for him and they give him some money.

Once in the centre of the city, in the *Cibeles Square*, outside another bank, not a bank like the one opposite me, but the majestic Bank of Spain, I saw a crippled beggar. She was an old, old woman bent double, her nose pointing downwards towards the pavement beneath her, with one long arm stretched out pathetically, emerging from her crouched shoulder, her upturned hand waiting for coins. She was clinging onto the traffic light beside the pedestrians waiting to cross the road. She knew that many tourists go there. Instead of sitting collapsed on the pavement, as I do, she prefers to stand up, exhibiting her handicapped body to all and sundry. A beggar's life has its eccentricities.

I suppose that I too have become eccentric.

All these beggars I used to see when I first came to Madrid, when I walked the city to become familiar with it.

Today I still see the ones who work in the metro. Some sit beside a board written by another, telling of their woes. They sit in their rags and their filth, wondering why they have been born, wishing that they had never been born. Some have a small dog or a pair of kittens beside them. For company. And because animals soften peoples' hearts and they know that.

And when their time is up and death calls, they go alone because they have no-one to accompany them. They lie down in resignation and wait for the final blow. Perhaps their illness has led them to emergency wards in the hospitals and they spend their last hours between clean, white sheets, being fed through tubes, in the company of nurses and doctors. Maybe they just collapse somewhere in dire pain, their body collected up like any street offal with no-one to weep for them, no-one to miss them.

So much solitude, Doctor.

But it could all have been so different. At least for me. If I had Tatiana.

*   *   *

Tatiana ... I named you Tatiana even before your birth. You were there inside me and I knew you. I had always loved that name and I loved you, so that is why I called you Tatiana. Simona used to speak to me of the Tatiana who had devoted her life to Christianity - a saintly woman murdered in the persecutions, two centuries after Christ. It wasn't so much that — the Christianity I mean — that I liked. It was the sound of the name, its music, and the valiant way you pushed your tiny limbs against the sides of my womb. I knew you would be strong and decisive, not puny and wayward. I knew that you wanted to be born to know me, your mother, to look trustingly into my face, to cry on my breast, to wrap your little arms around me. As your mother, I knew all that. I talked to you for hours on end, during the day as I moved around the house doing the chores that Roxana forced on me, at night on my mattress in silent whisperings because I never wanted Viorica to hear me, but most of all outside the village in the fields, in the copses and glades where I used to go. There I taught you to listen to the wind in the trees, to see the snow on the mountain tops, to hear the gurgling of the stream as it wound its way down from the hills, to gaze upwards into the blue sky and to search for images in the passing clouds. In the latter months of my pregnancy, Tatiana, you became so much a part of me that my whole life revolved around you. I no longer cared about having abandoned my studies, my books. Even my household tasks seemed lighter although my body was heavier with you.

And you were born. I was rushed to a hospital in Lugoj. You came quickly, in just a few hours, pushing yourself forcefully out into the world between the grubby green stained walls of the hospital ward. You caused me hardly any pain, Tatiana, just the normal contractions. That day I thought that I would burst for joy when the midwife placed you in my arms. She had washed you, cleaning off the mucous from the placenta, and there you were, my very own baby girl. All my own, for Petre wasn't there to see you, Simona had died and neither

Roxana nor Viorica had come with me to the hospital. Just you and I together, Tatiana. If only it had stayed like that ... if only Simona hadn't died. She had fought willingly and long against her old age. She had fought alone after her husband had crumpled up beside her in his cancerous state. She had fought with strength and determination, her God by her side, watching her beloved Romania turn sourer and sourer, sadder and sadder, under the *Conducator*. She had fought beside my mother, against my mother. She had fought for me. She had fought for Viorica, my sister. But one day she could fight no more. The strength drained out of her, her vitality waned, her laughter dimmed, the flame of her candle wavered. The day before she died she called me to her side. She told me how much she had loved me. She said I must try to overcome, always to overcome. Those were her last words to me.

And I have failed her.

*   *   *

Because there is so much that I haven't overcome. Look at what I have become, Doctor, living in this shambles, creeping along the pavements of this foreign city, afraid to be seen or singled out. Living only for my memories, my memories of Romania which weren't always good. But then I had hope. Then my body was cleaner. Then, I knew how to enthuse about life. Here there is nothing for me to enthuse about.

Autumn, perhaps. As the summer sun yields its furnace to autumn's shade, to the fresh mornings, to the warm wholesome days, to the still evenings, I am happier as I sit on my pavement. Autumn brings with it relief, release from the suffocating heat of the aestival season, when life comes to a near standstill. With the autumn air comes hope, hope brought in on the balmy breeze. Although I always wish that it would remain a breeze and not turn itself into a howling gale, because when that happens, all hell is let loose, papers fly, collect in the nooks and portals of buildings in whirling eddies, empty drink cartons dance along the pavement in noisy scraping jolts and starts, skirts billow, hats fly, dust attacks my eyes, accumulating on my eyelids so that when I rub them to relieve the sore itching, my fingers are blackened. These winds can come at any time, but the worst ones are the winter winds and the summer winds. Both are ferocious and exhausting. The winds of winter pierce my ears, even though I pull my woollen bonnet over them. They come at me in sharp gushes and they cause pain, a sharp pain in my forehead. The winds of summer are like the searing lashes of a whip. They are violent and unexpected in the heat. They are burning swathes that try to wrap around me as I sit huddled on the pavement.

Yet Simona used to tell me that the wind brings us messages as it blows through the branches of the trees in the woods. You could hear it rustling through the leaves, you could hear the boughs bending as it whistled against them. She made me love those clean winds off the mountains. I used to run through the country alone, or with Viorica by my side, free and happy, listening to the words of the wind. I imagined that it was bringing me good fortune. I never imagined that it would bring me bad fortune. I listened to its soft whisperings. I turned my face to its harsher lashings and I laughed, always laughed with Simona. That was in Romania. But here the wind gets under my skin. It lifts my skirt above my knees so that I must fix the loose material in between my thighs and my cardboard sheath. I bury my face against my chest. I close my eyes to keep out the grit. I feel even more alone, more forlorn when the wind whips around me. More vulnerable, I suppose. If it is a hot summer wind, I can only shelter from it behind my hands. If it is a cold winter wind, I nestle further and further inside my coat. These colder winds come at the end of autumn. They herald the approaching winter.

But generally speaking, autumn is a kind season for a street dweller like me. It is the kindest of the four seasons. Autumn is stable and golden and warming. There is a stillness in my heart. Could I mistake this feeling for love of life? Perhaps. Perhaps it is the closest I shall ever come now to loving life, when the days are still, like my heart. And autumn transmits its goodwill even to the people in the street. I receive more coins on my raffia mat at the end of an autumn day. This must be because passers-by also feel the bounty of autumn in the air. It stimulates their generosity.   And it even stimulates my own generosity with myself. I am able to walk more easily in the autumn. I get off the metro at one stop before my own and force myself to walk further each day. I know I must exercise my body, try to fight against the thick folds of fat which have settled around my waist in all my years of begging. But I don't really worry about them because I have no-one to look at my body.

I keep my body for nobody.

18

Andrei

There was a man, for a while, an intruder in my hovel. One autumn evening he burst through my open door whilst I was eating my potato soup. He slumped down on the stool across the table from me in a haze of alcohol. I could smell his breath from where I sat, pungent whiffs of regurgitated wine. I remember that I wrinkled my nose in disgust and told him to leave. But he pleaded with me, I have nowhere else to go, he said in soft, slurred tones. His voice pleased me in a strange way. Somehow it was reminiscent of Petre. It made me nostalgic. So, for the sake of nostalgia I told him that he could bed down on the floor of my hut, but not to come near me. He immediately curled up in a grateful ball on the floor beside the box I used for a table and fell into a deep, repairing sleep, snoozing in fits and starts, snoring like an animal at times in sudden crashing jerks. I studied him in this pose. I observed that he must have been around my age. I was about forty then. The wrinkles on his forehead revealed a harsh existence. His hair was fair and hung in longish curls over his brow. It wasn't only his voice that pleased me. I regarded him as some sort of demi-god sent into my life to relieve my solitude. If only he didn't smell of sour wine. ... I lay down myself, half dressed and, for the first time in years, I imagined that a man might come to me. I was no beauty and I was grubby, but we were both grubby.

As sleep came over me I found myself dreaming about Petre and imagining that this man might take his place in my life, that I would no longer be alone. Yet when I awoke the next morning, I was alone. The man had disappeared, or had it all been a dream? I peered into the semi-light for some evidence of his passing through my life, a talisman of my past, but there was none. Not even a wisp of his fair hair had caught against the splinters of my box table. The smell of alcohol had disintegrated into the autumn breeze that entered my hovel through the cracks in my door. And I felt sad, and used, as though he had turned up uninvited, taken advantage of my floor and left without a word of gratitude. Then I remembered that I hadn't so much as offered him a bite of my supper. Had he really anything to feel gratitude for? And so, Doctor, my Spanish Petre had left, abandoning me once more to my lonely fate.

All through the next day I couldn't keep my thoughts away from my intruder. Sitting on my cardboard pedestal I stared at all the men who passed, stared at them almost seductively, wondering, wondering if he had followed me and would come and sit beside me. I rejoiced in the feeling that someone might be waiting for me, that I had someone to talk to, apart from ruminating in and around my own thoughts, muttering words and phrases to myself. I knew this muttering would get worse with the years. People alone mutter to themselves, as proof that they think, that they are alive. They mutter and they answer their own questions. I stared all day at the men, at every single man with fair curly hair, not that many Spaniards have fair curly hair. In the late afternoon I sighed heavily, collected up my mat, the few coins, I took my cardigan from the bag of belongings that always accompanies me and put it on. The evenings were turning slightly chilly then, I remember. I made my way home imagining that he might be waiting for me outside my abode, but when I reached there, I saw nobody. With a fleeting shadow of sadness, I undid the latch and let myself in.

All of a sudden, my body felt heavier, my movements slower and I caught sight of the lines on my forehead in the cracked mirror on the wall. I straightened my hair and sighed, a sigh of disappointment. Disillusioned, I set to preparing my supper as I did each evening. I went for some water to the pump in the street, I peeled a potato, I cut up some cabbage and put them on the gas ring to boil. I cut up a tomato in small chunks and added a little oil and vinegar. As I began to eat, for the first time in years, tears came to my eyes and I gulped my disappointment down with the lumps of potato. If I had had the little cat then, I would have confided in her, but she came much later.

Darkness fell, so when I saw a silhouette standing in the doorway I didn't recognise the man from the night before. Yet there he was. He had come back. To sleep. Only to sleep? I was happy to see him, pleased that he had returned. I bid him come inside. He obeyed me. He entered my hovel with a gingerly step, but he didn't teeter. He didn't smell of sour wine. He looked me straight in the eye. His eyes were light in colour, like the hair on his head. And in his voice, like Petre's voice, he said: I have come back because I wanted to see you, not just to sleep. I felt something melt inside me. In a split instant I felt all the loneliness disappear, cascade downwards around my ankles, lifting me high up in the world again. This poor, broken man had come to lift me up, out of my sadness. But why would you want to see me again, I asked him in a voice on the verge of tears. How could anyone want to see me again was what I was really saying to him. Come and share my potato supper. He was hungry. He ate noisily, slurping the soup, gulping down the potato chunks, as though he hadn't eaten in days. I fetched him water from the pump outside. Water was the only drink I could offer him. No wine, he asked. No wine, I answered. He told me that his name was Andrés. He was Spanish. Andrei, I whispered, patron saint of Romania, patron of the wolves, you have come to protect me. He barely heard me. Perhaps it was better that he didn't hear me. He was in no position to protect anybody. But his mere presence was a token of company for me, a sign that I was no longer alone.

I remembered Petre with his lithe body, the mole on his wrist, his dark hair and eyes. I took off my clothes, without a word, and lay down naked on my makeshift bed, I felt no shyness, no embarrassment at my imperfect body. Andrei had come back to me and he had come back to take me, to possess me, so that he too would feel less alone in his solitary world. I looked across the room at him in the dim light. I looked straight into his eyes, willing him to come to me. He loosened the string around his waist that held up his trousers and they fell to the floor revealing a pair of olive-skinned, emaciated thighs. He came to my bed. And we were two lonely souls striving to make momentary sense out of our existence, perhaps a little breathless, a little bewildered, a little clumsy and out of practice. But we managed our climax and we knew a fleeting sensation of something close to joy, as though stolen from the tragedy of our days. Satiated, I wept silently, tears oozing from my eyes in the darkness.

I put out a hand to touch the body beside me, to assure myself that he was truly there, that it hadn't been a dream. He was there, snoring already. No affectionate whisper or longing look. He had done what he had come to do. I knew that I could ask for no more from this man. I was glad that I had given him what he wanted, what we both needed. Yet the next morning when I awoke as the sun filtered through my dungeon window, I realised that I was alone. Andrei had left, without a sign, without a word, without promise of return. It was obvious that he wanted a bare relationship, a non-committal friendship devoid of obligation.

But Doctor, he did return.

For several nights after that he ate his supper and came to my bed. He spoke very little. I knew nothing of his past and he appeared to have no interest in mine. Both of us simply went about what we had to do and thought no further. That is a lie. I used to think further. When he pulled away from me after having sex, when he slipped effortlessly into a deep sleep, I would start to think. I wondered about him, about his life and resolved to ask him how it had all crumbled to pieces, like mine. I would tell him, too, about my problems, about Tatiana and my Romanian past. I might even suggest that we both begin again, together, try to work up and out of the hole we had fallen into. Yet with the morning light and his disappearance, all my thoughts fled and, deep down, I knew that I shouldn't be hoping for any more from Andrei, I knew I had no right to impinge on his existence, to make demands on this broken man. I steeled myself over my breakfast coffee. I steeled myself against the lonely future awaiting me, for I knew in my heart of hearts that one day he would disappear and never return.

In the end they all go, I thought ... Petre, Radu, Andrei ... Perhaps I was not built for a stable home life. Is it because I was not built to be a responsible, loving mother?

After Andrei, I would search every day for meaning in the clouds. Would they, could they tell me why he had gone? I saw pictures of loving mothers in the fleeting clouds of autumn. I saw mothers with babies and young children on their laps, the white curls of the cloud framing their hair and shoulders. I saw the children's legs dangling in the pale cotton wool that drops away from the solid circle of cloud. I saw their little arms wave upwards as the wind breaks the clouds into elongated pieces of whiteness in the deep blue sky. I saw men running away in the wind, the cloud streaming its fluffiness out behind them, propelling them along, streamlined figures their hair flowing out behind them. The clouds help my days to pass. I see all sorts of figures in the clouds. I see animals, humans, trees, insects, grotesque masks. And I see my thoughts blow far away from me as the clouds dissipate in the sky, as they mould into other cloud masses, forming new thoughts, new shapes. If the wind is strong, the clouds race past. My thoughts can barely keep pace with them. No sooner do I interpret a specific form than it changes to become another or to disappear.

The clouds accompany me during my long, endless wait. My wait? Wait for what? For the rain. The autumn rains. Sometimes they come in September, sometimes in October, sometimes in November. They aren't like the rains in monsoon lands, tropical drenching rains, the torrential rains that I read about when I studied at school. When the white clouds gather to form the greying nimbus, I know that the water will begin to fall. Here the rain is soft. Although, true, sometimes it falls with a vengeance whipping against the objects of the world in fury. But usually it falls in gentle lashes against my cheeks, my eye lids. Sometimes I lift my face gratefully to this water. It is like a gift on my skin. At others, I hide my head wrapped in a scarf covered with a plastic bag for protection. Then I hear the rain pitter-pattering against the cars. I hear the car wheels swishing against the soaked tar on the streets. I hear the people quicken their step, trying to avoid puddles as they make their way along the uneven pavement. This is when I go with my few belongings into the gardens in the middle of the street where there are trees; their generous boughs and graceful summer foliage protect me from the rain. I sit on a small wooden bench listening to the water on the leaves. This damp world reminds me of Romania.

So many things remind me of Romania.

19

Kidnapped

In the rain I go back, way back, in time. I peer through the rain drops, through the shutters of my memory, through slits in the memory of time, of my time ... At our village festivals the men used to drink palinka. Palinka is a strong brandy made from plums or cherries or apricots. I remember their bulbous noses and their cheeks aflame and their slithery lips red and seductive, their voices slurring. I remember how they would lunge out at the girls' waists as they whirled in time to the music, slap them with jolly resounding noise on their backsides, try to grasp their breasts and press them hard. I remember how Simona laughed - always her laugh. And the mere thought of it raises my spirits for just a moment. Then I remember how Roxana grimaced - always her grimace. And I think now that it is her black moods and her ever-pressing need to be sad that I have inherited. She never imagined that life was to be enjoyed. Life to her was drudgery, a long journey through dark, routine boredom. And not even the village feasting would change that.

On the days when there was no feast in the village, which were most days, we continued to forge our pathway through that boredom, Roxana and I, alone now without Simona, Viorica on the side. Only my little Tatiana – you, Tatiana – helped me to forget my sadness. With you, my life was no longer a futile journey. You gave purpose to my days and I lived for you. I kept your tiny body clean, your clothes spotless, your cradle soft and welcoming. I played with you and you responded with your gurgles and dribbling chuckles. You crinkled up your eyes in joy when you saw me leaning over you. I picked you up and kissed you, my lips ardent on your soft baby cheeks. I fluttered my eye lashes against your chubby arms and legs, against the folds of baby skin on your neck and you responded to those tickles with jubilant shrieks of happiness. You loved splashing in your bath. Life was so full to you. And full to me then too. Our fun was only curtailed when Roxana would appear in the doorway, her ample arms hanging heavily by her sides, her long face sour.

Three months of fun we were given, you and I. Just three months. At the end of each day, I would try to avoid Roxana, my mother. After working at her senseless, ceaseless cleaning in the living room, in the kitchen, in the bedrooms, the bathroom, after preparing the potatoes and vegetables for our supper, after attending to you. After all these activities were finished, I allowed time for myself, time stolen from my embittered mother. I used to take you out of the village, into the fields, into the autumn colours on the hill slopes and there, as I had done when I was pregnant when you were inside me, I would lie on my back looking up at the clouds, lost in their shapes, describing their shapes to you, my dearest child. I explained the universe to you, the sky with its clouds, with its night-time stars and black cloak. I explained the earth, the ground where we lay covered in grass and flowers and soil. I picked the tiny blades and tickled you under the chin and you cooed in delight. As many late afternoons as I could, I would take you away from my mother, away from her house, wondering how I could escape somewhere else with you. And together we would return as twilight fell gently over our world, you nestling … snug in my arms. We knew happiness then. Those three months are the only time I have known happiness in my whole life, except for the time I went to university with Petre, except for when I was a small girl, at the village festivals. Yes, we were happy then.

I recall one morning when I was cleaning the hallway, a man and a woman, both with sober faces, called at our door. Roxana was out in the backyard. They wanted to see her. They asked about my baby. They wanted to see Tatiana as well. Something in their disposition put me on guard. I said they couldn't see my baby. She was fast asleep and mustn't be disturbed. I invited them into our living space, against my will because I could sense a foreboding in their demeanour and their visit. Then I called Roxana to come and attend to them. She welcomed them, unsurprised. At that point Tatiana began to cry, a foreboding wail, and I rushed to her. She screamed loudly, frantically and as I picked her up, she sobbed uncontrollably, clutching at me with all her might. She was sweating profusely as though she had just come out of a nightmare. It took me a long time to calm her down and, although I had intended to listen to the conversation held by my mother and the man and the woman, Tatiana's screams prevented me from doing so. Why had they come to our house, why did they want to see my baby, I asked Roxana after they had left. She shrugged her shoulders indifferently. Just a routine check-up from the State, she replied. I cringed at the cold note in her voice. Now that Simona has died they want to check up on how many of us live in this house ...

Life and our days went on as normal. Roxana was harsh with me. She was harsh with the baby. Only Viorica seemed to escape her frigid attitude. I thought more and more about running away, running off in the middle of the night with Tatiana strapped to my breast and a bag containing our meagre belongings strapped to my back. Then I realised that the autumn leaves were falling, that winter would soon be upon us with its ice and snows, that the intense cold could kill my baby at only three months old. I would bide my time and wait until the spring broke through. Then we could go far together, put all this unhappiness behind us. During the summer, we could stay in huts in the mountains living off berries and fruits and milk from the cows. The farmers would feed us. And little by little we could make our way towards Bucharest where I could find a job. I knew how to sew. I could sew for people in our room and look after my child at the same time. Perhaps, later on, I could even write the story of my life, return to my books. I dreamed ... I dreamed as I pushed the broom around the house.

One day Tatiana fell ill. Her hoarse cough filled me with despair. Nothing, no home-made remedy, seemed to help her. My mother said that if she wasn't better the next morning, I should go for medicine to the chemist in the neighbouring village. After a sleepless night, I didn't think twice about leaving my baby alone in the house, although I had sworn to myself since the man and the woman had visited us that I would never leave her alone with Roxana. I didn't trust Roxana. I knew that many babies were taken off to Ceausescu's orphanages to be moulded, instructed according to his designs. The Ceausescu children. That evil personage who rampaged his way through our country, stealing our money to pay off his foreign debts, stealing our children to keep them in institutions where they would grow up into soulless robots with hatred in their hearts, where they would learn to perpetuate the *Conducator's* cruel deeds, for his heart was indeed filled with hatred. He lived with his equally evil wife, Elena, in luxury, whilst his people lived in misery and in fear. I had read a lot about Marxism, about socialism, about communism and I sensed that these were essentially good theories, caring theories to help people to live more justly, but when I saw what Ceausescu was doing to us all, I began to hate communism. I was too young, then, to understand that you shouldn't hate a political theory because it is being wrongly applied. Nearly everyone was poor in Romania. In our house we were poor.

Now I am poor, begging on the streets of a capitalist society. What is the difference?

*   *   *

I remember Tatiana's cavernous cough. Her little body shook with fever as she choked and spluttered with her coughing. No, I didn't think twice about leaving her alone in the house with Roxana as I hurried my way along the path to the next village to buy medicine at the chemist and to call a doctor. I was away for nearly two hours. It was raining and I had to skirt numerous puddles. At one point, I slipped over and hurt my knee and this beleaguered my step. When I arrived the door of the chemist was locked. I rang the bell several times. I waited in the street in the rain for endless minutes before the chemist came to open the door. He said that none of his medicines would be suitable for so tiny a baby and that he would mix one himself if I could wait a little. Almost half an hour passed as he made the potion - would it be magic - and telephoned the doctor for me. Clutching the small bottle to my breast I walked, half ran, as quickly as I could, back along the wet, muddy path, beneath louring trees which darkened my way yet protected me from the rain.

Like the trees in Madrid in the gardens in the centre of the road.

*   *   *

As I neared the long stretch of road which approached our house I felt relieved. Yes, my baby would get better now, with the medicine, with the doctor. I burst into our house, down the short passageway into the living room. I stopped short. All was silence, uncanny silence. Where was Roxana? Where was Viorica? Where was Tatiana? I ran to her cot. It was empty. I called out. There was no reply. Where were they all? Suddenly I started to panic. I recalled the sober faces of the man and the woman who had spoken to Roxana. I sensed, I knew, that something was wrong, that the inevitable had occurred. Frantic, I looked everywhere in the house, inside and outside in the yard. There was no sign of anyone. They would never have taken my child out for a walk in the rain and far less with the way she was coughing. I returned to her cot, half hoping to see her there. Was I suffering hallucinations after my long, hurried excursion into the next village? No, the cot was empty, there was no doubt about that. Then I looked nervously for the small bag that contained her belongings, her nappies, her powder, her creams, her soap. Where was the bag? It had gone.

They had taken my baby away. They had stolen her from me, Doctor. They had kidnapped her. They sent her to be adopted into another home, or to an orphanage, to one of Ceausescu's orphanages. I sat motionless by her cot. Even her blankets had gone. My fingers stumbled blindly over the wooden bars. Inside I was tense, like an iron rod. I shed no tears.

I was frozen and numb.

I remember that when Viorica appeared from nowhere, her face fraught with anxiety, I stared at her unseeingly. She came to me and put her arms around me and hugged me to her, for once a little expressive. I was stiff and unresponsive. I looked straight through her. She tried to explain what I already knew without having seen it. That couple, the man and woman with the sober faces, had come for Tatiana. Roxana had handed her over without a whimper, without a kind word to the child, like a bundle of unwashed clothes. She, Viorica, had shrieked at her mother: What are you doing? Where are

98

you sending Mara's baby? My name is Mara. Mara is my name. It means bitterness.

Like my name, my life is bitter.

The man had handed an envelope to my mother. It contained the payment for the transaction. For that is what it was, a mere transaction, to make Tatiana disappear, to bring her up as a true communist, to educate her for the Romanian State to do as it pleased with her. When Roxana came home, I got up, still tearless, and pushed violently past her through the door. I didn't give her as much as a look for I was determined never to look her in the eye again. I marched outside into the rain. I walked and walked, away from the house, away from the village, up into the nearby hills. The rain drops caressed my cheeks, my eyelids, where I could feel the tears now pricking their way through. I found the small glade on the hillside where I used to go during my pregnancy. I sank down onto the humid grass beneath the tall, proud trees. I stared upwards through their branches to the grey racing clouds in the autumn sky. My tears sprang forth, unstoppable, free, emptying my soul of its burden, emptying my being of love and tenderness, of hatred even. I cried like that for several hours, enough to bring about a metamorphosis within me. Those tears didn't sooth me, they hardened the kernel of my soul, my soul withered and became trapped inside a steel casing. My heart was broken, lost forever behind a dark shadow.

I wanted nothing any more. I desired nothing, only to leave the scene of the crime. Where to go? I had no idea. All I knew was that I had to leave, to put it all behind me and never, never see my mother again. I returned to the house, no longer my home, for supper. I ate voraciously in silence. Not once did my gaze meet that of Roxana or Viorica. I ignored all their comments. They spoke as though nothing had happened. Without a word to them, I retired to bed early, packing a small bag with my meagre belongings. I turned out the light so that the room was in darkness when Viorica came to her mattress beside mine, so that she wouldn't notice my rucksack, so that she wouldn't see that I had got into bed fully dressed. With the first glimmer of dawn, as the pale grey fingers of early light penetrated our bedroom, gently resting on Viorica's sleeping silhouette, I rose. I took my things and crept into my mother's bedroom. I knew that the envelope containing the money would be under some papers beside her bed. I found it quickly and silently withdrew it from its hideout. I wasn't stealing. It was my money. My recompense for having handed my child over to Ceausescu. I didn't stop then to think that I would never have done that of my own free will and that the active agent had been Roxana. No, Tatiana had been mine, therefore the money was mine.

I left the house of my childhood, the house of my grandmother Simona. I left my mother Roxana, my sister Viorica, never to return.

20

Loneliness

Yes, autumn in Madrid is one of the best times of year. It is my favourite season. When I return to my hovel in the evenings, after my day of begging on the city's pavements, after I have eaten my supper, I pick up my chair and take it outside my door. There I sit, listening to the sounds around me.

Further down the dry clay street, I can hear some children playing, shouting at each other in sharp tones, interjected by rowdy laughter. They must be teenagers, already forged into a harsh life, moulded into life's desperation, ugliness, belligerence. I can hear all that through the raucous tones of their voices. They will grow old before their time. Already they sniff glue, they try to escape from their reality by enmeshing themselves in a world of drugs. They know how to steal, how to frighten others. They know how to run away from police cars, police dogs. They know where to hide where no-one will catch them. They raid small shops. They terrify the shop owners. They frighten young girls, pulling them off into the bushes to rape them. And they laugh at their own misdemeanours, at their teenage behaviour, already the behaviour of young men. They don't scare me. There is nothing for them in my abode. They don't scare me, but their ugly words hurt me, *la rumana, mira la rumana, jodida vieja, vuelve a tu país...* Simona told me that sticks and stones can break your bones, but that words can never hurt you. That isn't true. Words hurt, but in a different way. They hurt inside and the hurt takes longer to come out than if they throw a stone at you and bruise your body.

When the children say *vuelve a tu país … go home to your own country,* I feel sad. I feel the weight of exile and loneliness. When the children stop their shouting and disappear, there is silence in the street for a while. I hear the far-off rumble of traffic on the motorway. I hear the barking of a dog. I hear the occasional rustling in the leaves of the trees as the birds settle for the night. I hear the anguished wailing of a baby. Then two women emerge from the hovel next but one to mine. I don't really know them. I don't really know anybody. They don't worry about me and so I leave them to get on with their lives. They chatter non-stop to each other. They are obviously complaining about something, probably about their men. Most of the men in the street drink heavily. They get money for their drink by selling drugs to youngsters who come in search of anything that will calm their need, or by selling to drug peddlers who go off in turn into the city bars and discotheques in search of easy prey for their wares.

I have never taken drugs. I used to smoke cigarettes when I went to university. I smoked with Petre after our meals, after making love with him, but I never smoked much. It didn't really appeal to me, and the idea of drugs even less. Life is hard enough without making it worse. The shrill voices of the two women tore at the silence of the evening. They were unabashed, unaware that I was listening. They went to the street tap with their buckets for water. From inside another house I could hear someone washing the dirty dishes after supper, pieces of cheap crockery clashing, glasses chinking against a metal draining board. All these sounds were part of my life now. I couldn't imagine any other sounds. I didn't really wish for any other sounds, just this modicum of human life around me so that I didn't feel quite so lonely. The two women put their buckets down near the tap. One of them placed her hands on the small of her back as if she was in pain. She straightened herself with a long, loud, resounding groan. The other one scratched at her bosom and straightened her apron. They were earthy and elemental. Their hair was long and unkempt, like mine. Although it was too dark to see, I knew that their finger nails were dirty from their daily toiling amidst the grub and filth in their homes, if they could be called "homes", those huts with boarding for walls, with sheets of corrugated iron for roofs, with dried mud flooring.

These people were my neighbours. They had been my neighbours for years now, over twenty years, perhaps nearer thirty years, I cannot remember. Some of them leave, stacking their paltry belongings into the back of a broken-down van, and off they go to another hovel, to another settlement for drug addicts, for the outcasts of society. New neighbours come, yet they are all much the same — rude, crude men with their withered wives; young women with their startling black eyes and shiny hair, proud and haughty, waiting to catch a male, flouncing themselves up and down the dusty street, defying the men with their stares; rough young teenagers, tantalizers of society; screaming babies clinging to the ample hips of their carefree mothers. They are all around me. I am simply one more of them in this gypsy environment. All our lives have been broken at some stage or another. None of us even hopes for anything different.

I sigh. How can there be a God with all this suffering? All of these people have stories to tell, stories of brutality, cruelty, desperation, fear, violence. All of them continue to live on in this quagmire of a life, what else can they do short of committing suicide? But how many have the courage to do that, however desperate they may be?

There are evenings when the police cars come. I can hear the sirens from afar closing in on us. They burst into the street with vehemence, the wheels of their vans bouncing along over the dried ruts in the road. The neighbours disappear inside their living areas, doors are closed with a bang, warning shouts can be heard. The police pull their vans to a standstill. They jump out and rap loudly on someone's door. There is an exchange of shouting, recriminating, crying, screaming from the women. They haul two men out of the house and shove them roughly into the van and off they go, back to where they came from, their sirens bleating in the dark night. These visits from the police occur in autumn, but they also occur in the summer, in the spring, in the winter, once, twice, three times a month. I have lost count. They are always searching for some down-and-out or other. That is how they justify their earnings.

I sit on, in the autumn evening, listening to all these human sounds around me. I sit on until late into the night. When the street life subsides, I sit on, enveloped in the darkness and the silence. I feel the soothing freshness on my skin, the fresh cool air of the autumn night. At times like this I remember Tatiana. I am always remembering Tatiana, although her memory dims with the years. Her memory is little more than a habit with me now. She was taken from me over twenty-five years ago. Would I know her if I passed her in the street? She wouldn't want to know me if she could see me begging on the pavement, of that I am sure. Sometimes I dream of her coming to me, recognising me, gathering me up in her arms and taking me off to a warm, secure place. I dream that she is caring for me and that all my worries are over. ... Suddenly I jump. Something soft wound its way between my bare legs. It was the little cat. She comes to me and we enter my hovel together, she and I. She is more faithful than Andrei was. Because he never came back, did he? Perhaps he found a better woman than me, someone prettier, more ready with her body, someone who cooked him tasty suppers. Or perhaps he lives now in an oblivion of drunken stupor. Or perhaps he is dead. Who knows?

Why don't I try to make friends with some of these neighbours? All those years ago, I promised myself that I would never trust anyone else again.

*   *   *

As the autumn leaves begin to fall from the trees in the centre of the wide street where I sit day after day to earn my living, I begin to feel the cold of winter penetrating my thoughts, my body. On those mornings when I raise my eyes to the heavens and I see that the sky is blotched with cobblestone clouds, wide sheets full of white cobbles, I know that the breeze will bring the rains. It is the time of year when I most hanker after company, almost any company, even the company of those whom I cannot trust. The leaves die and fall in light swirls to the ground and I suppose that it is this sensation of death that saddens me and makes me want to look to others for company. Why don't I join up with the mad people who come with their minders into the green area in the middle of the street? They would take me in as one of them. Yet I am not mad, not yet, anyway. How would I get any sense out of people whose minds fail them? ... Why don't I smile at other beggars like myself? Because there is something in me which tells me that I am not like them either. I could exchange a few words with them, but I could never build up a friendship with them. I tried, didn't I Doctor? With Andrei, but he didn't want my company. A woman constantly alone, like me, becomes obsessive, obsessed with all sorts of things and lives with her back to the world. She lives out-on-a-limb with relation to others. She lives wrapped in her cocoon, her own thoughts, her own desires, her own needs. She becomes utterly selfish, thinking only of herself and her dreams, her past, her failures, obsessed with her failures because she has no friend beside her to confide her failures to and perhaps, to laugh about them.

When there are so many leaves fallen to the ground, trampled underfoot, moist in the damp air with their faintly rotting smell, the gardeners come with their brooms, with their mechanical blowers. They blow all the leaves into large piles and then gather them up with the brooms into metal containers on wheels. They clean the pavements leaving them bereft of their autumn attire. ... A clean slate. Why don't I make a clean slate of my life? Look for a job? Get my papers in order? Forget Romania? Make friends? I could go and talk to the women in the houses in my street. Why not? They would welcome me, not like their children who tell me to go back to my own country. Or perhaps the children learn those words from their parents, more from their fathers than from their mothers. Yes, I must go back to my hovel and talk to my neighbours, before the cold winter comes when I lie shivering at night under my blankets. On the warmer autumn evenings when I sit outside on my chair, I could call to them, wave to them, beckon them to come and talk to me. I am not shy. I have simply been hurt by life and this has made me wary, always wary, wary of sharing myself with others. Then there is the language too. My Spanish isn't good. They would laugh at me. Years here and somehow I can't pick up this language. A few words, yes, enough to get by on. Yet, Doctor, I have no desire to even try.

*   *   *

But this is a harsh neighbourhood. I have already spoken about the type of people who come and settle here – so many are drunkards, so many are drug addicts, so many are drug traffickers, so many are prostitutes, so many are simple and utter down-and-outs. Most of them are Spaniards. But there are illegal immigrants like myself, black Africans, several Moroccans. And what about other Europeans, Romanians, for example? Is it possible that I am the only Romanian woman in the settlement? Others have come through, for several days, for several weeks. I remember some gypsies from Romania came by once. They were noisy and joyful with hordes of screaming, snotty-nosed children, the men were greasy and sensuous, the women fat and over-worked, but happy. They tried to camp at the far end of the street and they cleared some bushes there and made as if to stay for good. For some reason the dogs on the street objected to them. They barked incessantly around the gypsy camp. The men and young boys threw stones at them and the animals yelped in fear and anger. The dogs were rarely like this with the other neighbours. They barked and barked, day in, day out, night in, night out. One night there was a terrible scandal with those animals. Two of them were racing round, enraged. They whined and screeched as if in agony. They growled ferociously. They bled at the mouth. Everyone thought they had rabies. The following morning, they were found dead outside the gypsy camp. The youngsters came and carried them off to bury them in the undergrowth. When they came back to the street one of the young boys was carrying something in his grubby fist. He showed it to his father. It was a ball of meat pricked through with needles.

Fists were hardened, elbows poised, hairs bristled. The gypsies would pay for this. The revenge took place the next night. At two o'clock in the morning I awoke to the sounds of violent blows, shrieks, glass splintering, babies crying. There was a smell of blood on the air as it drifted towards my hovel. It was as though all hell had been let loose. Knives were sharpened, gardening hoes, trowels and spades, iron bars with hooks on the end, any utensils that the men had in their hovels were good for frightening off the Romanian gypsies. There was bloodshed. Of course there was bloodshed. There was a death, a Romanian death. There was weeping, there were sobs, there was screaming, howling in the dark night like wolves. Humans like wolves. And with their tails between their legs, the Romanians took to the road. They gathered up their cudgels, their pots and pans, their clothes drying on washing lines and the dead Romanian body to bury they knew not where.

From then on, for some two or three weeks, I sensed the menacing stares of the young adolescents in the street. There was hatred in their eyes as they glared hard at me and muttered *rumana, rumana, hija de puta,* and I was nervous for a while, imagining that they might attack me during the night. I would lie awake waiting for them to barge through the entrance to my hovel, rip off my clothes, pull me from me mattress, kick and savage me. But they didn't. They never came and the hatred gradually faded from their faces. I avoided them as best I could, but they had turned their minds to other ploys.

Perhaps it was because of the Romanian gypsies that I was hesitant to try to befriend the neighbours. I imagined that they wouldn't want to know anyone else from Romania. Besides, I was tired, tired of human relations that hadn't worked out, for I was still obsessed some twenty summers later by those young years, obsessed by Petre's harsh rejection, his beautiful dark-skinned face twisted into dislike, hatred almost, an ugly grimace, obsessed by Roxana's cold authority and evil mind, obsessed because Viorica had never learnt to stand up for me, obsessed because my father Mihaita had left me when I was so young, obsessed by Radu's selfish love-making, obsessed by Andrei's unexplained disappearance, and, lastly, the only person I had loved, loved from the depth of my heart, Simona my grandmother, had been taken from me in death. Why bother now to look around amongst the Spaniards? To me, they were foreigners, as indeed I was to them. They had their own lives to lead, their own people to care for. What had I to offer them? Nothing. Nothing at all. No, I was better off alone, looking after myself as best I could without creating links and obligations and responsibilities with anyone else. I would live alone and I would die alone. That way, no-one would have to worry about me, Doctor, and I wouldn't have to worry about anyone.

And the autumn leaves fell, fell in their swirls, swooping from the branches of the trees black and nude, twisted, agonising forms pushing out and away from their solid, life-giving trunks. In the middle of the road, sheltering from the rain, I would sit on my piece of plastic on the ground and press my back hard against the trunk of a tall plantain tree. ... Then I could almost feel the sap working within, the surge of life stilled now by the onslaught of winter, a restraining of energy, a hibernation was occurring. I would watch the leaves dance lightly to the ground. Rarely were they heavy enough, like the fig leaf, to fall in a straight line hitting the earth with a gentle thud. It was more normal for them to whirl, to float on the air, to dive at first with purpose and then to be diverted. Some which fell from great height teetered on the upper branches, caught amidst the tree's smaller twigs. They would only fall to the ground with a severe blast of wind. And on the ground the leaves made patterns, thick carpets with bare spots where people had shuffled them to one side with their boots and shoes. I stare at the leaves fallen to the ground. I stare at them the way I stare at the clouds and I see shapes, faces, countries, hills, my Romanian hills. I dream as I stare at the leaves. I am always dreaming, Doctor. I live in a dream world. It is my way of escaping from the crude reality around me.

21

Love and Romance

I look intently at Mara. She is more responsive today. Her eyes glisten with life and hope as they look at me, her psychiatrist. This is a positive reaction, a change from the dull gleam, the hazy sadness I so often found in her eyes.

'Let's talk about your love life today, Mara,' I said to her with a jovial smile.

'Love? What is love? I don't know what love is!' She seemed to shrink physically as she mentioned the word love. 'Nobody loves me.' Her voice grated in the silent ward. 'Nobody has ever loved me.'

'What about that man Petre?' I dared to ask her. I say *dared* to ask because I didn't want her to feel that I was prying. It's a difficult line to draw for a psychiatrist, the line between prying and helping. At least from the patient's point of view. They often confound the two and accuse you of prying, it's none of your business, they say, don't try to get into my life like that.

'Yes,' she said with a sad smile, 'there was a man called Petre. Was it love we knew? We went to university together and, yes, we shared the same bed. We loved and we made love in the night after our classes. But we were young, perhaps too young to be too serious and I spoilt it all. I spoilt it because another boy - that was Radu - got in the way. He was so strong-minded and he stole me from Petre. Yes, I went with him and because I went with Radu, Petre dropped me. Yet Petre was the father of my daughter. I know that. I am convinced of it. You ask Roxana, she will tell you that; that Petre was Tatiana's father.'

I asked her who Roxana was.

'I have written about her. You will find it all in my story,' she answered. But I could not yet read it, I told her.

She was craving love. I could see that. No-one had loved her for years. But that was not all.

I held back, but I knew it had to come, that prying into the journey to Spain, the prying into what happened in the van with Andreea, that Florencia had told me about. I had to make her talk about all that. It was the only way to cure her of those ills. I imagined what had happened, but she had to tell me about it herself, rid herself of the feelings of guilt, rid herself of the horror.

'You must have found other lovers?' I asked her. 'You were pretty. Men like pretty girls.'

'But not unhappy girls,' she almost spat back at me.

'There must have been others who wanted to be with you, Mara?'

'No, that no!' She looked at me pleadingly, her eyes filling with tears. 'No, that wasn't love!'

'What wasn't love?' I asked.

I knew I had to take advantage of this moment when she was receptive, emotional. If she hardened, withdrawing into her inner core, all that tragedy would never be drawn from her.

'Tell me about that, Mara. Everybody has difficult, unhappy moments in their life. If you can talk about those moments, then that is a better cure than all the pills you are taking.'

She looked away slyly. I didn't know then that she was throwing all her medicines down the toilet. First she sobbed, sobbed inconsolably into her hands.

'You are like Petre, you are a good man,' she said to me, grasping my wrists with a sudden movement. 'You won't understand. You will cast me away, just like he did.'

'I shall never, ever cast you away, Mara. You know that. I want to help you, help you to return to your old self, to the clever pretty girl who went to university in Timisoara, who wrote poems and short stories. What happened to that girl? Why did she throw away all her opportunity and go off in a van with some horrible men?'

There, I had said it, outright. She stopped crying. She breathed deeply, lifting her face to me, then to the ceiling, then back to me.

'Never, never again! Never would I let them do that again. You can't understand. They treated me like a whore. They treated me as though I was nothing but a body without feelings. That was them … ugly brutish men who only thought about sex. Sex all day with three of them. Sex all night with three of them. First Andreea, then me. They wouldn't stop. It went on for 2 days, 4 days, I don't remember. I only remember that I thought it would never end. That sex was my ticket to freedom, the price I had to pay so that they would smuggle me out of Italy and into France. You can never understand, Doctor, what it is like to be an unwanted person, to be an unwanted immigrant. But, worst of all, to be used as a woman, as a prostitute by men who are less than you are in every way; by brutes. No, it wasn't only the physical hurt, it was the mental, the emotional hurt of their actions. I hated them. I hated every second of their clumsy hands and fingers, their smelly breath, their filthy male organs, their grunting and their sweating. Never, never again! But never will I forget that. I remember that when it was over and they dropped me and Andreea on the streets of the port at Marseille, I remember then that I felt broken. I could have died then. Why did I continue on, come down here to Spain? I felt so worthless. I felt I could no longer look life and nice people in the face again. I just wanted to blot out existence, to be blotted out of existence. Before that ghastly journey, I had hope in me. After it, nothing, nothing mattered anymore. I couldn't think straight about anything after that. Life became a series of unconnected moments. No purpose, Doctor, no purpose.'

I bent forward and kissed her gently on the forehead. 'You will live again, Mara. Things will start to matter again. You will get better. I promise you. Trust me. Trust all of us here in the hospital. We are here to help you. We want to help you.'

'Perhaps I am too old now,' she said quietly.

After that conversation with her I concluded that a surfeit of uncaring sex had broken her into pieces, and that since then she seemed to have found no-one to help her out of her pit of despair, no-one to show her that sex can be good and beautiful. Her lack of sex since that time had made her build up a bitter encasement around her soul and had prevented her from turning her life into a positive existence. She had fallen more and more deeply into her tragedy. This cascading into tragedy is typical of hyper-sensitive people. I could see that she was telling me the truth, that her mind was gradually fitting the pieces of her past together. I didn't give a thought to the possibility that I was wrong. I resolved to speak to her of Roxana and Simona on my next visit.

22

Love and Family

Rosa was complaining again. Sometimes I feel she never stops complaining. If it wasn't the Romanian patient, it was some other patient, or it was because she felt over-worked, because she had no-one to go home to, no love in her life. Her life, she felt, was drudgery, just coming to this smelly hospital and attending to bodies, not people, bodies and dying bodies at that, who never showed her any gratitude. All they did was to moan and groan and cloak the ward with their dissatisfaction. She hated it. She resolved to get out of it somehow. But how? And wasn't she too old to change professions now? She had to make a living to pay off her small, ugly flat in one of the outer districts of Madrid, line upon line of grim red brick flats interspersed with a few trees poking up out of the gravel earth. Goodness knows how the trees in Madrid flourished with their roots embedded in the dry crust of earth, but they did. True, the flats were surrounded by shops of every kind, but they weren't exactly a place you could think of as home. Still, Rosa, on her nurse's salary, could ill afford anything else and she'd been led to believe when she started working that to purchase a flat, however small and dingy, was an investment in the future. Not much of a thought to start the day with, though, and so she dragged her ill humour into the hospital and around the ward with her.

'When I tried to give her her injection yesterday, she pushed me away with a shove — she's getting much stronger now that she's eating properly. She said, No, no, it had to be Manuela. Only Manuela knew how to give her the injections so they don't hurt. I tried to insist. You were off yesterday and I tried to explain that to her. Manuela,

Manuela, she said, almost screamed, hysterically. She wouldn't let me near her with the injection. She waved her big arms furiously. She screeched. She pulled at the strands of her own hair, almost trying to hurt herself. She threatened me. She wouldn't listen to me. She even said, No, no, I don't like you. You are Rosa. You're not like Manuela. Do you know, I really hated her when she said that! I know that we shouldn't show our likes and dislikes with patients, but she was so difficult that I gathered up all my instruments and marched out of the room angrily! I left her there and I thought that I would make her wait for her lunch because of the way she'd treated me. She doesn't like me, I thought. Well, I don't like her. But I was the only one in the ward who could take her her lunch tray. Difficult old bitch!'

'Don't be like that, Rosa. She isn't well and also she's entitled to have her preferences. We all do, don't we?' I was trying to be conciliatory.

'Yes. That's true. But it's not much fun being disliked by her, or anybody for that matter. Particularly when we have a job to do and that includes helping the patients.'

'Did you give her the injection in the end?' I asked.

'No, I didn't. I thought of waiting until she was asleep and doing it then, but I imagined that she might suddenly wake up with the jab and hurt me, or hurt herself with the needle.'

'I think you're losing your nerve, Rosa' I replied. 'You ought to have been firmer with her. If we get out of the rhythm that Carlos has fixed for her injections, it could have a negative effect on her health. She must have one of those injections every two weeks.'

I stared at Rosa's thin pouting lips and thought that she looked unpleasant. I could almost see why Mara didn't want her. There was something vindictive, something slightly – dare I say that - cruel about her. Mara wasn't the only patient who had had problems with Rosa.

'I think, Rosa, that you've chosen the wrong profession. You'd be better to work in an office, or a bank, or somewhere where weak or sick people don't depend on you. They just stress you.'

'Well, you know I never wanted to be a nurse. My mother forced me into this profession and I never had it in me to refuse. I should have left and trained for something else as soon as I began to earn money. But I didn't really know what I wanted to do. I liked the other nurses I've worked with and the company and I suppose, with the years, I have just adapted to it, accepted it and now I feel it's too late to turn to something else. It's not easy to make such a change in your life.' ... I started to feel a bit sorry for her.

'It's never too late! How old are you, not even 50 yet? You've got over 15 years still to work, maybe even more if they increase the years we have to work for a pension. Fifteen years is a long time, Rosa. Think about it. After all, Mara isn't the only difficult patient. There are plenty of others.' I hesitated. 'Are you sure you've not got it in for her because she isn't Spanish.'

'Don't be ridiculous, Manuela! It's not her fault that she wasn't born here. I know that. I'm not stupid. What makes you say that?'

I felt the blood begin to rise in my cheeks, but continued: 'Well I've seen you treat other Spanish patients better than you treat Mara, patients who are more difficult than Mara. To me it's obvious that there's something about her that makes you react nervously with her and I'm sure that that something is because she's Romanian. Or is it because she's obviously a beggar, hasn't ever bothered to legalise her situation here? Maybe you don't feel that she's also entitled to medical help?'

'Don't be so hard on me, Manuela.' Rosa defended herself. 'It's true that I'm not that keen on her, but it's not because she's a foreigner or a beggar, at least I don't think so. It's just that I can feel she doesn't want me near her. It's easier for you. She likes you. It isn't always a question of how we treat the patients. There's also an element of compatibility between people there.'

'Maybe you're right,' I said, ' Still, try not to upset her. The last thing we want now that she seems to be happier, is to send her back inside her shell again.'

*   *   *

The two doctors sat alone at the long table in the staff conference room. 'Do you reckon, Jaime, that she's any better? I mean the Romanian woman.'

Jaime enjoyed the fact that Carlos would ask him for advice.

'I would say that there's a definite improvement. She's more relaxed. She certainly hasn't tried to attack me again, although Rosa said that she attacked her the other day, wouldn't let her get near enough to give her the ketamine injection, the anti-depressant we've put her on.'

'But she must stick to those injections,' Carlos replied. They are much more effective than the pills she's on. I know she doesn't like them much, but I've only prescribed one every couple of weeks, so she shouldn't complain. Maybe it's that she isn't too keen on Rosa. She's a bit of a sour one! Manuela's much nicer. And patients notice that, Jaime.'

'Yes, I know they do.' Jaime looked at Carlos as if to say that Mara wasn't keen on him either. 'You get on with her better than I do. She obviously has a temperament. How long is it that she's been here now?'

'Well, first there were the 30-40 days in a complete coma, when we all kept on peering at her, checking her pulse, changing her IV feeding, etc. And since she came out of the coma, she must have had about four of those injections. So we're talking about another eight weeks there almost. That makes something like three months in all, doesn't it? We're certainly getting used to having her here. She's like a fixture in the ward. Florencia the cleaner loves her. I often catch them chatting together while she does her cleaning. I know too that Raimundo is happy with the way her writings are progressing. He's beginning to understand much more about her past. He really seems to have taken her on as a personal challenge.'

'Yes, but Raimundo does that with certain patients.' There was a slightly scathing note in his voice. 'He's a good psychiatrist in general, but I've noticed that he often takes more care and time with some patients than he does with others.'

'Don't we all? That's life. It's natural. Personally, I'm enjoying having this Romanian woman here. She makes a bit of a change from our lot. Also, I think she makes us react more strongly and she leads us - quite unwittingly, of course - away from our normal routine. We're all having to think more about the way we treat her. Emphasising what we say to her makes us actually dissect what we're saying in general to our patients. Instead, I mean, of just throwing the usual words of encouragement at them or at their families. At least I find that I'm more analytical about my attitude and treatment in general with Mara.'

'But you've always been more analytical than I have, Carlos. You tend to take your patients more to heart than I do. I consider them part of my normal day, part of my job and I rarely let them worry me outside the hours I work in the hospital. I suppose I'm rather indifferent. But that's the way I am, Carlos. I can't help it.'

'Maybe you're right, Jaime, it's better not to get too involved. Still, that boils down to individual personalities, doesn't it? I can remember when I was a student I used to get over-involved even in practice work. So that aspect of me still comes out now in my work, even after years of experience.'

'I envy you, Carlos. You really enjoy your work, even though it occasionally gives you headaches. I can't imagine you doing anything else than medicine. What would you do without your patients? How do you ever relax? Haven't you any outside hobbies?' Jaime tried to lead the conversation away from the clinic, away from their work.

'Yes, of course I have, Jaime. I play tennis well and try and have a game every weekend. Then I love listening to classical music and I also go to the cinema as often as I can if there's something on that interests me. But, it's true, I leave much of my human involvement to my work. You know I never married, never wanted to marry. I've always considered that my patients are my life, instead of taking a lover or trying to plough affection into a family. And to keep frustration at bay, I sometimes look for sex with an elegant prostitute. There are some really classy ones in certain parts of Madrid.' Carlos looked at Jaime as if searching for his reaction to

117

that. He knew that he was a family man. Perhaps he wouldn't approve of the prostitute bit. Still, why not be honest.

As Carlos expected, Jaime said: 'My family's everything to me. So perhaps that's why I regard my work as a doctor simply as a job, a job to provide for my family, but I don't want it interfering in my private time.' He shrugged his massive shoulders as if to shake off any sensation of guilt for not wanting to spend his life in the hospital.

The two doctors went down the ward in different directions to check up on their many patients. This was the routine they had every day when on duty. They were both responsible for all the patients, but they took it in turns to inspect them. That way, they had their own views about the state of their health. Jaime took longer to get his hefty body into motion. He laboured rather than walked, whereas Carlos moved more quickly, his slim body like a shadow as he went about his tasks.

23

A Job and Humiliation

Forgive me, Doctor, I hope you are not disturbed by me continually skipping back and forward between the distant past and my years in Madrid. But that is how my memories present themselves to me. ... I said that I had never worked in Madrid. That isn't true. Not so long ago, I was invited to leave my pavement in this bone-dry city. A woman who sometimes used to give me bags of clothing and the occasional coin approached me one day and asked me if I would like to do some cleaning for her. I shrugged my shoulders in response. It was my indifferent way of saying that yes, I would like to do some cleaning, not that I had ever liked cleaning. I had had enough of it in Roxana's home. It was a fruitless activity. One thing is to know how to keep one's own home organised and clean, quite another is to make a profession of it, cleaning up other people's mess, picking up their strewn belongings, sweeping the dust off their floors, washing their dirty dishes, tidying their cupboards, gathering their dirty underwear for the wash. Yet what choice did I have? Here, in this dry city, so utterly alone, without a friend or contact in the world.

Everything is relative in life and so now the prospect of cleaning seemed to open a new pathway for me. My grandmother, Simona, once told me that when life crumbles before you, dragging you to the ground, God will always pick you up. When you feel that things could never be worse, that you are at the end of your tether, when you feel the bleakness and coldness of the future, to say nothing of the present, He is there to provide a shelter, an alternative. I used to believe my grandmother, when I was very young. Now I know that she was wrong. Perhaps I could regard the woman in front of me offering me a cleaning job as one of God's shelters, one of His alternatives. But no. I just don't believe in Him anymore. How can I convince myself that He has accompanied me on my thwarted path? He might be there for others, but I have never found Him at the turn of any of my life's corners. Simona would say that it is because I don't search for Him. Now that she is dead (and one day I shall talk of her death), I don't have to worry about explaining my disillusion to her.

The woman was verging on middle-age, her hair beginning to turn grey at the roots, although she had attempted to cover the grey with a dye. There was nothing in her face that particularly appealed to me or that repulsed me. Rather, she seemed a nonentity. Yet, here she was, inviting me to go to her home the very next day. She explained how to get there. It was in the vicinity, in the same area where I did my begging. She asked me to be there at nine o'clock in the morning. It would mean that I would have to get up a little earlier than normal, but I accepted her offer all the same. How many hours would I have to be there cleaning, I asked. All morning, five hours, she answered, Until two o'clock. She would pay me every time I went, three times a week. On my way home - if I can call my hovel home - I calculated that the extra money would come in handy and that I could continue with my begging in the afternoons and on the other free days. You may laugh, but I was loathe to leave my beggar's spot to another. It had become my security in life, my identity in life, my reason for living. Maybe, though, this cleaning job would even lead to more work in other people's houses.

Maybe.

For more than a month I worked in that woman's flat. A large flat with fourth floor windows giving onto a busy road. As I moved around the living room and the kitchen I could hear the whine of the traffic mounting, the heavy exhaust from the buses as they ground along the street floating upwards towards the apartment windows, the hooting of car horns, the screaming of small children. I dragged myself around behind my duster and hoover, attempting to give some sort of a sheen to the pieces of wooden furniture, to clean up the crumbs and grubby specks on the parquet flooring. I felt no interest in what I did there. I preferred the more restful task of begging. I was lazy and indifferent at that time. Don't forget that my soul had been broken into pieces.

The worst part of that job was cleaning up the child's bedroom. For two reasons. Firstly, because it saddened me to know that I was in the precincts of a little girl who might have been my own daughter. When I first entered the room, I sat down on her unmade bed in a haze of nostalgia, of sad memories, looking around me at her scattered belongings, at the rosy-cheeked dolls and the furry animals, remembering Tatiana, my eyes pricking with tears. Tatiana had never had any toys. Secondly, because that child was so messy. She cast all her used clothing over the floor or under the bed. She never put her underwear in the wash-basket, one sock lay in a small white knot beneath the chair, another over the other side of the bed, her jumpers smelt of rubber and ink and school classroom, the sleeves were worn and stuck with chewing gum, she never made her bed, that was for me to do and her rumpled sheets and pyjamas smelt of small body and the sweets that her mother surely forbade her to eat in bed, but which she ate nevertheless. Her desk was smothered in papers, school books, bubble gum, pencil sharpening, crumpled drawings, smeared with sticky sweets, the wood ingrained with the ink from felt pens. She had scissors and pencils and rulers and rubbers and figures for cutting out, all chaotically strewn over the desk. Her wastepaper basket was always full to the brim with the bitty ends of her school life. And I had to clean up this mess every time I went. Any tidiness I managed to make on that table was completely disrupted the next day.

I only knew the child from photographs and from these remains of her days. She had long, blond hair in rat's tails, unkempt. Her nose was snub, her face flat with a bored expression, her eyes colourless, a sort of misty grey that stared at me unquestioningly, almost like the eyes of a blind person, expressionless and un-telling. In the short time I worked in that flat, we never met each other. Perhaps that was for the better, because I would have wanted to scold her for her untidiness and I would have been sad remembering my Tatiana.

Then there was the kitchen. It was always a mess and I tired of washing up dishes from supper the evening before with the remains of food stuck to them. There was no machine to help me. Often there was oil spilt on the stove and that took time and effort to clean. The kitchen was the worst part of the flat. Fortunately, I didn't have to cook. The woman and the daughter never came home for lunch. They were only at home for supper and I only had to put some ham or a piece of cold pie and salad aside for them, although the woman obviously cooked something else, some hot food because of the splodges of oil on the cooker. Of course I never asked her about her life because we rarely bumped into each other and because it wasn't my place as her cleaner to delve into her personal relations. I could only suppose that she was divorced (she seemed too young to be a widow) or that she was a single mother. All that was her business, not mine. But there were times when I felt like telling her how to educate her unsmiling daughter, that insipid, blond-haired, grey-eyed specimen of young humanity. The child would end up being a problem in her adolescence, spoilt and capricious and demanding in her early twenties, dissatisfied with life in her thirties.

Yet so was I dissatisfied with life ... I was in no situation to point my finger at anyone else.

As I moved around my chores I would turn on the television because it was a hint of luxury for me, Doctor. I had no television set in my hovel. I had never had television in Simona's house in Romania. It was a novelty for me. I couldn't understand it very well, but I could pick up a lot of the meaning from the images that flashed to and fro on the screen. I found it entertaining and so I would have one eye on my cleaning and the other on the television. If something appealed to me I would stop the hoover or stand still, duster hanging from my hand, mesmerized by what I was seeing. But mostly it was little more than company in the flat for me. Artificial company, that is true, because the people were boxed up inside the screen and I couldn't touch them, or smell them, or participate in their conversations. I could only hear their voices. Better than being alone, although I preferred to watch humanity pass by on the streets, imagining people's lives as I sat on my pavement.

For a while, however, this cleaning job was a change. I tried to do it as well as I could, frustrating as I found it and demeaning as I found it. Surely begging was more demeaning? Not necessarily, I thought. At least when you beg on the street you have no-one to answer to, no boss to push you around, no dictator hassling you. You do as you please. The third week I was there, I began to feel bored with the work and cooped up in the flat. Five hours were too long to be inside a house that wasn't my own. I began to treasure the freedom of my life in the street. In the flat I was hemmed in, suffocating. If I look into my past in search of a reason for this sensation, it might have been similar to what I felt during those long months when I was cleaning Roxana's house, my mother's house, the loneliness, the boredom of a stupid cleaning routine. Had I been more rational with my feet on the ground I might have realised that it wasn't such hard work and it gave me a little money and perhaps even a little prestige. But no, this wasn't so. I could find no prestige in cleaning up after a messy child and a slovenly woman. On the contrary, I found it humiliating. I, a beggar, was too good for that kind of work.

These were my thoughts as I tackled the dirty dishes in the sink, as I waxed the parquet flooring, as I emptied the rubbish bins, as I dusted the wooden furniture, as I pushed the hoover over the rugs, as I cleaned the windows. These were my thoughts and I started to feel embittered, against the world and against this woman and her ridiculous daughter. This was not my place in life. I couldn't go on kowtowing to an inane situation. The woman's money wasn't everything, it was hardly even anything. And I began to long for my street corner. That job wasn't the way to emerge from misery. It merely made me more miserable.

I sighed heavily and flopped down into a chair watching the television screen unseeingly. I cast my eyes around the objects in the living room, glass decanters, pieces of silver, an assortment of ornaments, porcelain dishes. It all seemed pointless and superfluous to me. I found myself getting irritated, annoyed at some people having so much and being so careless and at others having so little. When I cleaned out the bathroom I used to peer at her face and body creams. I even went to the lengths of trying some of them to see if they would eliminate the wrinkles around my eyes and across my forehead. I only took a little and I put the recipient back exactly as she had left it. She would never realise. Or so I thought. Those creams were a temptation to me. I had never had the money to pamper my skin with beauty devices. I hated bending over the bath and cleaning the scum from the child's evening bath, a rim of grubby soap clinging to its enamel sides. What am I doing, I asked myself, cleaning other people's toilets. And the sense of humiliation grew hourly.

One day I stole a bar of perfumed soap from the bathroom cupboard. One day I stole a few carrots from the fridge. I took them home and my evening soup tasted better. Another day, I stole a small packet of ham, she won't realise I told myself, without thinking that the ham was precisely what the child liked for her supper, always screeching to get her own way, I imagined, when her mother said she had to eat greens and meat, she wanted pasta and ham, when her mother said she had to eat fruit, she wanted sweet desserts. I could hear them, at each other at every supper every evening, and the little hussy stomping off into her room, banging the door in insolence and stuffing her clammy fingers into her bags of jelly babies. I imagined. No, Tatiana wouldn't have been like that, with me or with anyone else. Perhaps they had starved her in the orphanage, perhaps she was too weak to protest, perhaps she had fallen ill.

Or perhaps she had even died?

Then every day after stealing the ham, as I opened the fridge I found myself wondering what I would steal that day, butter, milk, tomatoes, left-overs, just a little, very little, no-one would miss it. As I left the building I had to pass by the porter's cubicle in the hall. He would nod indifferently at me, although I suspected that there was a hint of superiority in his gaze: These wretched Romanians, Arabs, Turks, Chinese, South Americans, all coming here, he would think, to take jobs from the Spaniards. No Spaniards wanted these tasks anymore. They had climbed up the ladder and preferred to work in offices, in banks, in universities, in schools, anywhere other than in their own homes. They would let the outsiders, always outsiders, do the dirty jobs. I could see all that in the porter's smug expression as I walked past his cubicle on the days I went to work there, in at nine in the morning, out at two in the afternoon. But one day one of my stolen tomatoes fell through a hole in my plastic bag. It rolled out onto the floor of the entrance hall, towards the porter who happened to be standing by the front door. He bent down and picked it up. Where did you buy this? he asked suspiciously. Did you buy it this morning before coming here, when all the shops are closed? What business was it of his? Instead of staring him in the eyes and ignoring him, I stammered and blushed saying I had brought it for lunch and hadn't used it, and I knew I had been caught in the act of my stealth. I knew he would tell the woman that her Romanian maid went off with her tomatoes.

And sure enough, the next day when I opened the flat door, I realised that I wasn't alone. It didn't take long, her tantrum, her accusations, her words filled with loathing for the foreign scum I represented. Of course, I was in the wrong. I don't know what came over me really. Simona would have been so disappointed in me. It wasn't so much that I'd felt like doing something underhand like stealing. It was rather that I could feel the humiliation of my life, the difference between their lives and mine. Why did she and her small daughter have so much, so much food, so many objects, things to make life easier. When I stared all this in the face and compared it with my life, with my hovel, I felt that there was a certain justice in taking a little of what she had, just a little. But of course, I was convincing myself that my stealing wasn't wrong. Society was wrong, wrong in Ceausescu's world, wrong in the capitalist world. It didn't matter where you were, the rich were rich and the poor were poor. The woman never wanted to set eyes on me again in her house, why had she ever taken in a foreigner off the street, she screamed, as if the Spaniards never stole, I thought, and I thought she looked stupid as her eyes bulged and the veins in her neck swelled in anger and her face became redder and redder. I can't even imagine what she was thinking.

Her fury over my misdemeanours was my passport to freedom once again, to my life on the street. I didn't even consider that I would have less money. When you are right down at the bottom, a few coins less or a few coins more make little difference. These memories hurt. I must sleep.

24

Ana

I actually offered her work. She came and cleaned in my flat for several weeks. But she was a robbing bitch. She stole some of my creams and perfumes. She stole tomatoes and carrots - the caretaker told me that he saw her leave one day with her bag full of food from my fridge. You can't trust her type he said and he was right. I remember that she stole ham too and even some of my daughter's jelly babies......

I am Ana and my little blonde-haired girl, my daughter, is Eva. I needed help. I work from 9 a.m. to 8 p.m. every week day. With a break for lunch, of course, but my job is demanding. I work in tourism and in the high season we never stop. The telephone never stops. The questions never stop. The bookings never stop. The complaints never stop. On the go we are, from the second we enter the office until the time we leave. My journey to and fro takes me almost an hour on the bus, so you can imagine what time I get home and how tired I feel having to prepare a meal at night. Sometimes I would ask her, Mara I think her name was, to prepare a snack for me and Eva. All she had to do was that and the cleaning and sometimes shopping when I would leave her the money to do it.

For a while it seemed to work well. I thought that she was the answer to a more relaxed life for me. She only came three mornings a week, not every day, and she cleaned the flat quite well. I had seen her often sitting aimlessly, uselessly, on the street corner and I felt sorry for her, also faintly annoyed that some of us work so hard and others just sit back waiting for money to fall from heaven! That isn't fair. Since Manuel, my husband, no, my ex-husband, walked out on us, my life has been much harder. I was mulling over all this one evening, eating supper with Eva. Eva is only ten, but she is intelligent and has an agile mind. She was the one who suggested asking the beggar woman on the street corner to come and help. She used to stare at her on her way to school. I don't think she felt sorry for her, Eva is not a compassionate child, but she was certainly fascinated that some people, women like her mother, could live on the pavement. Where does she go to sleep? she asked me. She must live somewhere. Yes, I suppose that she must live somewhere. Maybe she has friends or family here and they let her bed down with them. Maybe she goes off to a hostel for immigrants or for indigents, some residence place run by nuns. Maybe she eats in those eating houses for the poor, but I have never seen one in this district. So I don't know.

Anyway, when Eva put the idea into my mind, I decided to try her out. After all, I would be doing more for humanity, something decent for a change, by offering her a job and helping her to make a go of her life, than by giving work to a Spanish woman who perhaps had other cleaning jobs. Yet it wasn't only the fact that she stole food from our fridge, that she cunningly smeared my creams over her face. No, it wasn't only those mistakes on her part, there was something else that influenced my decision to give her the push. That something was Eva.

Perhaps I should say that Eva, clever as she is, is a highly sensitive child, temperamental and demanding. I admit to having spoilt her since Manuel left us. I can't help it. I return home tired after my work and because I need a bit of peace I tend to give in to all her whims and fancies. She is cunning enough to realise that she can get what she wants out of me. She plays on the fact that she no longer has a father and, of course, that, she gloats, is my fault. It isn't my fault, well, not entirely anyway. Manuel was proud and capricious, self-willed, always wanting his own way and Eva is like him in that. I knew that he had begun a relationship with another woman. He would fall into frustrated tantrums in the evenings, loathing me for my fatigue and depressions and complaining, in short, for my neuroses. He blamed me simply to smother his own guilt. He caused our fights so that he would have an excuse to run out on us. He said I didn't know how to bring up our daughter. I ask you! Wasn't she his responsibility too?

When Eva was younger, she would cling to me crying after hearing us fight. She said she loved me, she needed me, please don't run away Mama and leave me here with Papa, she would whisper between sobs and trembling, as I put her to bed. Of course, I would stay and calm her fears whilst her father would go out never saying where he had gone. He used to come back, creeping into bed, peeling back the bedclothes as silently as possible in the darkness of our room. But I was always awake, waiting, and I knew he had been with another woman. I could smell traces of her perfume on his neck, as he moved his body fretfully about in our bed. This must have gone on for two years or so — how forgiving can one be, how stupid can one be — the arguments, the violence, his comings and goings, the recriminations. And there was Eva in the middle of it all. Yet, to cut a long story short, when Manuel eventually left us, saying he wanted no more to do with us, we could do what we liked, he would never come back, and I never knew where he had gone — for weeks my phone calls to him were unanswered — I tired of the whole business, swearing that I would never let him into the flat again.

I changed the locks on the door and that was when Eva began to torment me by saying I was cruel to lock him out, he hadn't been so bad, it was my fault as well. She seemed, uncannily for her age, to know how to make me feel guilty. She never sees her father. She has to be with me all the time. She has, she says, had to learn how to live without a father, other children from separated parents spend time with their mother and their father. Other children have much worse family situations. At least Eva has a mother who loves her.

But she bore a grudge in her heart and it seemed to grow daily. I made the mistake of trying to repair that grudge by bowing to all her desires.

And one of her desires was that Mara should leave.

25

Eva, My Child

It had something to do with the presence of Mara in her bedroom. How weird! How could Eva, a child of only ten, imagine such a thing? She told me that the beggar woman had to leave, never mind if she was helping me with the cleaning in the flat, no matter if she prepared something for us to eat in the evenings, none of that was important to Eva. She just said that she wouldn't tolerate her bedroom, her own intimate space in life, being violated by an unfamiliar presence. Of course, she didn't put it quite like that. I hate that feeling, she told me, of walking into my room and knowing that a strange person has been in there. I don't like to think of her hands making my bed, her dirty gypsy's hands pulling up the sheets I sleep in at night. Sometimes I shiver when I am in bed because of that. Then she told me that that woman moved all her things. She is always tidying my desk. I like my rubbers and pencil sharpener and crayons and pencils to be where I leave them, she said. But Eva, you're very untidy! Maybe I am, she retorted, but I still know where I put everything. They are *my* things. Why does *she* have to touch them? One day I even saw her fingerprints on my photo-frame, as though she had been staring at my photo. I am nothing to her. She is nothing to me.

But you wanted her to come and work for us, I retaliated. … Eva said, almost in tears: Yes, but she doesn't have to clean my bedroom. Who will make your bed in the mornings? I asked her. You never do it. I don't care! She shrieked almost hysterically at me. She was such a nervous child. Anyone would think that you were hiding something from Mara, from the world, I replied. And so, what if I am, that's not your business, is it! Eva was only ten, I have said that, but she was utterly selfish, probably like most children of her age, and very highly strung. She thought only of herself, of her own whims and desires. She was obsessed with herself and her world and she obviously regarded her bedroom as a very private place. Even before the beggar came to work for us, she never liked me going into her room, opening the door and surprising her to call her for supper or in the mornings to get up for school. I can get up by myself, I know how to use the alarm clock, she protested. Indeed, on most mornings, she did rouse herself out of bed.

Knowing how self-centred my daughter was, why did I give in to her over Mara? I could have told the woman simply not to clean the child's room, to close the door on her untidiness. It would have been better if I had made her clean up all her own mess, make her own bed, grow up a bit. Yet, I have said, it wasn't only Eva. It was the way she had started to rob us of food ...

In a strange sort of a way I feared my child. That had something to do with my feeling of guilt for having deprived her of her father, although he was the one who made the decision never to see us again. Yet it meant that I was always cajoling her, trying to cure her of her tantrums, to smooth out her difficult moods. It wasn't easy. Now I can see that we were both caught up in a suffocating web that we were weaving around ourselves. It was dangerous because it was a web that excluded everyone else and everything else outside our life at home together and our work and school routine. Although employing Mara had been Eva's idea, she could never have envisaged that a third presence in our flat would interfere with our life, albeit psychologically. Because Eva's hatred of Mara was psychological, even pathological. The fascination that she had felt for her when she used to pass her on the pavement turned into intense dislike, a feverish rejection of the older woman, merely because she could sense her presence inside her bedroom, because she knew that she had touched her belongings, I know she's been into my photo album ... I saw one of her long hairs in it, she said one day. And of course, Mara made her bed, peered inside her drawers and wardrobe, touched her clothes.

130

I'm not wearing that top today, she screamed at me one morning. Mara folded it up and put it inside the drawer. I didn't want it on top of the pile. I don't like it. I'm not wearing it anymore! And nothing, absolutely nothing, would convince her to wear it again - a pretty, yellow and green top that looked so nice on her. The top, her bed, the photo-frame, the photo album, her pencils and rubbers, every day she would torment me with her growing obsession against the Romanian woman. What else could I do but tell the foreigner to leave? I was glad to have the excuse of her petty thieving, because she would never have understood that Eva, a small child, loathed her.

*   *   *

Of course, I don't know whether Eva's hatred for her was all because of her. Perhaps it was Manuel's departure, a feeling of abandonment because her father had left her, perhaps it was because she blamed me. She knew that Mara had helped me and so she, my little daughter, wanted to punish me for locking her father out of the house. It is impossible to discuss these things equably with a child, particularly with a child who has tantrums. She shrieked one evening over supper. It began because she didn't want to eat the salad on her plate. You can give it to Mara tomorrow morning - go on, I bet you won't dare to. The words tumbled from her mouth. She was taunting me, daring me to approach the beggar I had thrown out onto the street. I still hate her, she gasped between sobs.

But she's gone now. She isn't any longer part of our lives, I said trying hard to calm her down.

She may not be part of *your* life, but she is still part of *mine*. I still see her every morning. She looks away when I pass, without a nod, without a word.

But Eva, she wouldn't want to talk to us now after what happened.

Yes, but *you* still want to talk to her, don't you? You'd be happy if she came back to clean our flat again, even if she did steal a few things. You're weak! Her words were filled with recrimination. How could this ten-year-old be so full of revenge and yet have so much insight? Because she was right. I would have had Mara back again to clean for me, to help to ease the burden I had. We fell into silence, an uneasy silence. Then Eva said:

I would like to hurt her. Sometimes when I go past her in the mornings I want to chop her up into pieces and throw them to the dogs to eat. Sometimes I dream about setting fire to her dirty body, her dirty clothes, her dirty bags. Why don't I do that? I could do it, couldn't I? I stared at my daughter, aghast that she had such cruel thoughts. I explained to her that if she did any of those things, the police would take her away and put her into a school for evil children who would treat her badly and her whole life would be ruined.

It couldn't be worse than your life, she replied vindictively.

What was I hearing? Callous, cruel words inappropriate even from an adult! What was happening to Eva, to my own beloved daughter? There was a cutting hardness in her words which grated against the very core of my heart. And I felt a failure. I had failed as a wife. I had failed as a mother. I had even failed as the employer of a cleaner. I blamed myself, constantly, but it was because others blamed me. Eva was changing. I knew that. She was growing up, yet into an adolescent prematurely embittered, a person I didn't want to know, someone I would never have chosen, never have searched for to spend my time with. I couldn't believe it. Here I was admitting dislike of my own daughter. How was this possible? Was there anything I could do to alter the way she was developing? Of course, there must be ways of helping her to come around to me again, to transform her unpleasant thoughts into pleasant thoughts. No, it wasn't only the old beggar woman, it was a combination of other causes and feelings that had needled their way into her life. I couldn't just sit back and watch her bitterness grow.

I had to help her. But how? Agreeing with her wasn't the way. She was so strong-minded that she wouldn't tolerate disagreement either. So where was the middle path between the two? One thing became clearer and clearer to me: you can't go backwards and undo what's been done, what you have done or said, what someone else has done or said. You have to keep going forwards and somehow make amends. How could I bring my daughter back to me? On the other hand, what had I done to deserve this? Our lives - her life and my life - had been affected by the Romanian beggar. What a fool I had been to take that woman into our flat!

*   *   *

If Eva had been the one who had wanted her to go, a few days later she was almost hysterical when she realised that Mara was no longer sitting in her usual spot on the pavement. The beggar-woman had gone! All Eva's vituperative remarks and hatred about wanting to chop the woman up into small pieces had turned to an uncanny silence, the calm before the storm, as though she had been deprived of the figure that was the object of her hatred. And what could she do with her animosity now? She obviously wasn't going to start blaming herself for what she considered was going wrong in her life. Mara had disappeared, suddenly, without a word, leaving Eva without her object of recrimination. The woman's absence obviously meant that she would have to turn her attention to someone else to rid herself of her fears and dislikes. And I was that someone else.

It didn't take long for her uncanny silence to turn to hysteria. Every single time I crossed her she would flare up into a temper, biting, snapping, irritable and filled with a hatred that I couldn't understand. With a sigh, with many sighs, I asked myself what was happening to my child? Was it that Mara herself had actually had nothing to do with her bad temper? Eva had labelled her as a cause to her own unhappiness, dissatisfaction with life, had made her the target of her own misery. But now that the older woman had disappeared completely, she felt bereft of that target and at a loss to know where to direct her anger. Of course, it was natural that it fell on me. And how could I handle it?

My imagination reached no further than the conventional disciplinary measures, or the endeavour to divert her attention from her dislikes to something more amusing. One evening when she wouldn't eat her supper, she stomped off and locked herself into her bedroom. That was the last straw for me. There was nothing I could do from the other side of the locked door. I would have to wait until morning came and the child emerged from her room at breakfast. But breakfast time came and there was no sign of Eva. I knocked on her door and tried the handle, but it was fast shut. No sound came from inside, no answer to my calling.

If you don't get up, you'll be late for school!

I don't care! I'm never going back to school again, was her sudden response.

She was provoking me. I fell completely silent, thinking that would arouse her curiosity more than any admonition. I had my own breakfast, gulping down my coffee between chesty sobs. I showered and dressed for work. Without a word. I put on my jacket and took up my handbag and went out through the front door, banging it on purpose so that she would hear me leave. I was at a loss to know what to do. Perhaps I should speak to someone, not just working companions — several of them also had young children — but to someone professional. Where had I gone wrong with my daughter? Apart from having broken with her father, whom she had never seemed to love anyway, I couldn't find any other reason for her ruffled character. True, Manuel had been a difficult person, a man of harsh judgement, unaffectionate, at times withdrawn and unwilling to share his thoughts with me. It was logical that Eva take after him in part. He too had had an irascible nature. He always needed time to recover from any arguments we had. He was spoilt, had been spoilt by his own mother and two doting sisters. Had we also spoilt Eva?

I remembered times when I would feel guilty for working such long hours out of the house, away from her. That, surely, wasn't being a decent mother? And perhaps I gave into her more than I should have done, as a form of compensation. We should have had two children, instead of one, a brother or a sister for her. But it was too late for that now. I couldn't see anyone else on the horizon who would have replaced Manuel and I certainly didn't want him back, so that put paid to that. Anyway, I don't think that would have been the answer. I don't think that Eva would have relished having a smaller brother or sister who might have pushed her nose out of joint. She was too selfish, too used to throwing her weight around in her own space.

All these thoughts oppressed my brain as I made my way to the travel agency where I worked. But I didn't reach there. As I emerged from the metro station, in a split second, I decided to retrace my steps and return home, not to spy on Eva, but to try and comfort her. After all, she was my daughter, she was what most mattered to me in life, despite the difficult time she was going through. Somehow, I had to encourage her to forget Manuel, to forget Mara, to forget all the nastiness in her life. But, apart from these two people, what was the nastiness? What had I done to upset her so strongly? There I was, blaming myself again.

When I entered the flat I couldn't hear a sound. I called out. No response. I went gingerly towards her bedroom after assuring myself that she wasn't in the kitchen or bathroom. I called out gently to her, knocking softly on the door. No answer. I turned the handle expecting the door not to open, but it did. I went into her room. Her bed was unmade, the sheets and blankets thrown back untidily. Her slippers had been cast off, one upside down under the bed, the other flung, as though with anger, against her chest of drawers. The clothes she had worn yesterday were missing from the chair. She must have put them on hurriedly. As usual, her work table was chaotic under all the bits and pieces, papers, chewing gum, pencils and colours, sweet papers, elastic hair bands, paper clips, folded notes, school books. School books! Why were they on her desk? She should have taken them to school. Then I noticed that her satchel was on the floor beside her desk. I gulped. Hadn't she gone to school? If she hadn't gone to school, where had she gone?

I opened up the top drawer of her work table and saw a small notebook where she had jotted down her thoughts about her school mates. I flicked through the pages nervously. *I HATE her*, I read. *I HATE, HATE, HATE her! I HATE him. I HATE them all. They are all horrid and hateful - my mother, my father, the cleaning lady, the girls at school. I HATE them, all of them. I never want to see them again, NEVER.* I sat down on her bed, trembling. My first reaction was to bury my head in her pillow, in search of the trace of her smell, the smell of her hair shampoo, of her young body. Then I went quickly, the notebook in my fingers, straight to the kitchen. I noticed crumbs, breadcrumbs. I smelt the smell of the toaster, still warm. I noticed that the thermos flask was missing, pieces of fruit were missing, bread slices were missing, cheese was missing and I saw that the cupboard where I kept plastic bags was all upturned. *I never want to see them again, NEVER,* I repeated. She has left home. Her coat wasn't hanging up, some of her clothes had gone.

You don't understand me. I am going away to live like Mara, by myself on the street (I thought she'd said that she HATED her and yet, she was taking her as an example). She's gone mad. That crossed my mind as I read the note by the toaster. The child has gone mad. My daughter has gone mad. Eva has gone mad. I collapsed onto the sofa, defeated. What to do now? If I tried to go after her, she would reject me. And where to look, anyway? My only option was to ring the police and ask them to look for her. I imagined that she could be prey for any evil-doer on the streets. My head was filled with visions of her sleeping on a street corner, sitting there, just like Mara, begging for money – a little waif of a girl, vulnerable and unhappy. Someone could kidnap her, take her away, use her for prostitution. I clapped my hands over my ears and squeezed my eyes tight shut in an attempt to block out these terrible visions. In my utter confusion, the one thing I had clear was that I must retrieve my child, bring her home to me, give her love and warmth and time. I promised myself that if she was found I would give up my job and work only in the mornings when she was at school, when she grew older I could go back to full-time work. I lifted the telephone receiver and rang the police.

I have to blot out the memory of those two long days, interminable days with their sleepless nights, if I don't want to go mad myself. I have never known such agony, my self-recrimination for not having known how to help Eva was like a razor blade cutting into my skin, into my tendons, hacking away at my innards. The pain was excruciating as I sat, hour after hour, waiting for the phone to ring. If she ever comes back ... things will be different, I sobbed to myself. After nearly three days I was in a state of utter desperation and on the point of ringing the police again to ask if they had found her, when the doorbell rang. I jumped, startled, dishevelled and bleary-eyed. It took me a moment to come to my senses. The bell rang again, this time more urgently. I stumbled to the door and, fumbling with the lock and chain, opened it. There, cowering behind the sturdy frame of a policeman, was a frail waif of a child with matted hair, eyes red from crying, a deathly pallor hung over her face, her jumper was torn, her trousers were dirty. Like any little urchin off the streets. They had found her shivering with cold and fear at some crossroads ten kilometres away from our house. She was completely lost and bewildered.

At first, she was shy in my arms, halting and reticent as if she was scared that I wouldn't take her back. But I enveloped her with warmth and motherly love and utter relief and little by little she reacted and responded to that love, to a warm bath, to a hot meal, to a soft bed. No recriminations. No questions. All the hatred seemed to have drained out of her. Finally, she looked up into my eyes, *I wanted to know what it is like to be Mara*, she whispered. *Now I know that a little bit, I feel very sorry for her. I shall never run away again. Please forgive me. I promise I don't really hate you. I LOVE you!*

26

Simona's Death

Madrid is shedding her leaves. As I huddle in this my grave above ground, the winds blow down off the nearby mountains with a vengeance whipping the fallen leaves along the pavements in erratic gusts of chilly air. I draw my collar up around my chin and wish that I had brought my hand-knitted beret that morning to protect my head and bare ears from the freezing blasts. Winter was on its way and the next day I would wear a thicker coat. The only thick coat I have. Last winter a woman had dropped it down on the pavement beside me in a plastic bag. I had taken it home to my hovel and tried it on. It was too long for me everywhere, the hem, the sleeves, although it fitted me round the middle. Evidently it had been for a taller woman than myself. But I didn't care. That extra length would help to keep me warm. It was dark red in colour with large, wine-coloured buttons and a wide collar. Yes, I decided to keep it. It would protect me from the cold. And so the autumn gold and russets and reds were falling to the ground in richly coloured flurries. As they fell I watched them intently. Why, I don't know, but they reminded me of Simona, my grandmother, and of her untimely death, perhaps because it was autumn when she died.

*   *   *

Was she fearful of the advent of winter with its searing winds and snow on the mountains and in our village? She was an old woman. Exactly how old, I was never sure, indeed she was never sure. All her life she had been a happy woman, yet I had noticed when I returned for weekends from Timisoara, that a shadow of sadness tainted her expression. She moved more slowly. She seemed for the first time in her life to resent the grating words of her daughter, my mother Roxana. Before, she used to laugh them off and tell her daughter not to be so bitter. Now, she took them to heart and they weighed on her. I blamed Roxana for Simona's sadness. You make her life impossible, I said, as I watched the old woman hobble away from us out into the yard to get some logs for the hearth. She used always to be happy. Why do you make her sad? Why do you speak to her like that? Why can't you have a kind word for her? And Roxana would shrug in annoyance, as if she held the whole world's problems on her shoulders. Never, never had she laughed with Simona and now Simona had tired of laughing alone, with no-one to laugh with her, as I used to before I went to university. And each time I went home I could see the sadness growing within her, covering her face with the waxed parchment countenance of death before death came. I used to inveigle her to come out for walks with me, away from Roxana and her grumbling, and I would ask her why she was sad, but she only answered me with a distant silence. Simona, where is your laughter, I would ask her and she would retort with dark eyes cast downwards as if trying to avoid my gaze, my questions, as if she knew very, very well why she was sad but she had no intention of telling me, because she loved me and didn't want to make me sad.

One chilly autumn afternoon, she left the house without a word. For several days she had been ill, her body in the grip of a fever and racking cough. Roxana still asked her to work around the house, to go out for the logs into the cold, bleak yard, better she said than moping in bed. Simona had lost weight, she had lost weight quickly and suddenly and when she coughed it was as though her bones rattled inside her frail body. We had eaten together, the four of us, that day. Simona had eaten without uttering a word during the meal. She averted her gaze from me and from Viorica when we tried to joke with her and coax her to eat more. She averted her gaze from Roxana when her daughter chided her for falling ill and letting her body waste away. She averted her gaze from us all.

How she had changed, I sighed to myself, swallowing my discomfort with a lump of potato. She normally slept a little, dozed a little in her chair by the hearth while I would go out to wash the dishes. When I had finished, I returned to the living room to find that she wasn't there. In response to my query about Simona, Roxana just shrugged her shoulders – her answer to almost everything was a cold shrug of the shoulders. I went to my room to do some studying. Viorica had gone out with her friends in the village. Two hours later Simona had still not returned. Without a word to my mother I left the house. I took a pathway towards the nearby forest, a pathway that I had taken many a time with Simona, when we used to laugh and joke and talk together. We were kindred spirits. Today the path was cold and lonely.

I could feel the autumn leaves soggy beneath my feet, water dripped from the branches of the trees. The path was cold. The air was cold. And, most of all, I was alone. Simona wasn't with me. But I remembered her soft, round voice mouthing her joy of life, her love for me, as we walked. She never complained about Roxana. She knew her too well and she knew that her daughter would never change. She had turned out to be sour and sourness was her defence against life's blows. I felt, as I walked along the pathway, that perhaps Roxana had just gone that bit too far with her mother. I, for one, would always blame her for her ill-timed reproaches and ugly disposition. She never allowed herself to be melted into softer metal. It was as though she was afraid that a smile, a kind word, would undermine her strength.

As I walked on, I remembered that only the previous day Simona had summoned me to her room and had told me how much she loved me. She was grave and there was a finality in her words, a melancholy in her voice. The afternoon light began to dim and long shadows fell across my path. For the first time, I noticed a strange eeriness surrounding me as I walked. I began to feel nervous. And lonely. Very lonely, without Simona. I started to call out to her. I had no doubt that she had taken this same path and that soon I would find her. I would catch up with her I thought as I walked, almost ran along, further and further away from the village and deeper and deeper into the forest. I knew a glade on a slope where we used to go together, from where we could see the mountains. ... It was the same glade where I went later on to talk to Tatiana when I was carrying her inside my belly.

Yes, Simona died of melancholy, because the world was no longer the world she had known, because her husband had died so long ago, because the struggle was too great to keep everything going in her little house, because she missed my company when I was away at university (as I had missed her company when I returned to the house to have my child), and finally because she could no longer accept Roxana's bitter recriminations, her insistent chiding, her whining and dissatisfaction, when she had had more in life than many women of her condition even though her husband, my father, Mihaita, had walked out on her. That was no wonder with her sour nature, few men could have put up with that for a whole lifetime.

I came upon Simona, lying deathly still on the damp ground of our glade. I was convinced when I stared at her, unbelieving, that she had not died and then just fallen to the ground. I was convinced that she knew her end had come, that she wanted her end to come, and that she had lain down on purpose to die a calm and dignified death. She had settled her body into a graceful pose, stretched out daintily amidst the grass and the autumn leaves, she had crossed her large hands over her breast in an attitude of reverence to her God, her legs lay perfectly side by side, her feet opening outwards, relaxed, dead. A death befitting her. And she had prepared herself for this final step in life. She had combed her hair before settling down to die. The wrinkles seemed to have vanished from her forehead and around her closed eyes. She had died smiling, there was the faintest of smiles hovering over her thin grey lips. She looked beautiful, saintly. She had carried her beauty and her bounty to her grave. She would always remain thus in my memory, generous and benevolent, a profoundly good woman. I knelt down beside her and placed my head against her breast. It was still warm. Why, oh why, had I not come to her more quickly? I might have been able to dissuade her from ending her life. My words might have incited her with the desire to go on a little longer. My dear, dear grandmother, gone for ever. Would I ever accept such a loss?

141

I remember her as I sit on the street in Madrid, in the autumn sun, in the autumn wind, in the autumn rain. I can never forget her.

As I can never forget Tatiana.

They are the two people who have given me most in my lifetime. Simona gave me my youth, she brought me happiness and laughter in those early years and Tatiana brought me fulfilment and uncompromising love. The pain was excruciating when they were taken from me.

But life goes on.

27

Julia

I could sense her despondent, brown eyes studying me as I laboured, dependent on my walking stick, every day along that pavement towards her. Yet, as I approached her, she would lower her gaze and crumple down into her own body as if trying to hide, willing the ground to swallow her. As I am old and wise – my name, by the way, is Julia – I know that it is impossible to befriend someone, however kind you are, when that person constantly feels inferior, and I know she felt inferior to me and to everyone else who walked past her. I could see the inferiority in every fibre of her body, her expression, her misery. I knew that she preferred to be left alone, to get on with the bits and pieces of her life, of her sad, degraded existence.

Yes, I am old now.

You can imagine what I have seen in over eighty years of life ... To start with, I was about ten at the end of our horrendous Civil War. In those days there was poverty, real poverty, gnawing hunger, abject cruelty, utter degradation, fear and inferiority. Although if I think twice about it, the inferiority was actually on the side of the conquerors who were inferior in their aims and in the way they carried them out. Of course, I didn't realise that then. It took me some years to realise that and now, at eighty-four, I am quite convinced of it. Inferior beings who so often manage to get to the top, to force their wilful way upon others beneath them who are more intelligent, but more sensitive and less ambitious. We all hated them and hated their bloody ways, their torturing, their swaggering with guns in their belts, their hatred of culture, of the poets and artists of this land. Yet, what can you expect of military people in their short-sighted obedience to law and order, in their cringing before authority? This Romanian woman on the street has more true pride in her little finger than Franco and his parasites had. That is why she is incapable of looking me in the eye because she is proud and she feels shame for her situation.

Perhaps she too knew what it was like to live in a dictatorship. She probably left Romania when that dreadful Ceausescu was in power there. Left wing, right wing, it really doesn't matter. When a megalomaniac takes over a country, the inhabitants haven't got a chance. Those jumped-up madmen should be strung up by their private parts and carted through the streets for all to jeer at. But of course, you would call me a barbarian for even imagining such a punishment. I don't care. I lived through forty years of Franco's madness. I saw two of my uncles and my own father flung into gaol. After months of suffering, they were shot for their ideas.

And the suffering was my mother's and my aunts' as well. The women would hang about the prison entrance waiting for permission to enter, stamping their heels and rubbing their hands together to ward off the biting cold on the mornings during the Madrid winter. They would take food for their men, chorizo sausage wrapped in creased brown paper, that was later stolen from them by other desperate, hungry prisoners. They saw their male companions, their faces daily more gaunt, their features daily more distorted by torture, their eyes daily more sunken into their sockets, their complexions daily paler and their bodies daily more skeletal. That was what those women suffered, watching and waiting, impotently, for the death of their loved ones, watching and seeing tragedy unfold before their eyes.

And then they had to confront the prospect of rearing their own children alone, without the help of a male companion, a father.

I used to help my mother during those years after my father was shot. I was the eldest in a family of five children. What else could I have done? My mother was worn. After they murdered my father, yes, murdered him, she had no alternative but to find work outside the house, scrubbing the floors of offices and hospitals and sewing clothes for others into the early hours of the morning. She needed the cash to feed six hungry mouths, to clothe us and to educate us. She was worn to a frazzle and she depended on me to run the house and to care for my three younger sisters and brother. It was a lot of responsibility for a ten-year old girl, but I managed. At night, I would fall asleep sometimes over my studies. My mother and I were both determined that I should never give up my studies, however hard things became. For years that was our life. A fight against hunger and grime and fear. Yes, I have known hardship also. Those years were terrible years. This is why I can commiserate with anyone who has lived under a dictator.

*   *   *

I often take the Romanian beggar home with me in my thoughts. It is inexplicable how you can feel an affinity with someone you have never spoken to. Despite her shying away from me, from life and the little it has to offer her, I can sense that there is a tenderness, even a certain intelligence, about this woman. Some beggars are offensive with their pleas, but her way was more modest. I imagine what her past might have been. I imagine that she might even have given birth to a child who was later taken from her, captured and sent to be educated for Ceausescu and his cause. If that was the case, then she would never have seen her child again. I know that such things went on in Romania at that time, because we read about them. Here in Spain many of our children were given to the Church, or taken by the Church, the spiritual arm of Franco.

I am sure that it was something very sad that made her run away from her country, not merely the need for money because, had that been the reason for her leaving, she would have done more with her life than what she does today, merely begging. There is a solidity about her – I can only imagine this as I don't know her – which convinces me that she would never have left her land and her people and her roots to come and beg on our streets unless life had forced her to do so. There is something in her that reminds me of my own mother. A courageousness that has been crushed with life's setbacks.

145

These are women who keep on and on, obsessively, with their daily grind, with the commitments they form for themselves. They are brave, yet somehow incapable of taking a decision to improve their destiny. And so, their tragedy, their misery, simply become a habit. And, as time passes, they accept the life they have, their imagination is crushed beneath the weight of tedious routine. In the case of my own mother, I know that she placed all her hopes of change on me, her daughter, and I didn't let her down, although she died before I finished my university degree. She never saw me happily married either. She never knew her two grandchildren or her son-in-law. But life moves on and now her son-in-law has left to join her in death – not that I believe that we meet up again when we die, I believe that the end of life is the end – her son-in-law, my husband and father of my two children. I have lived alone now for fifteen years, sixty-nine I was when he died, crippled with illness and disillusion, six months of agonising suffering with a cancer that rotted his liver, three months of living between our flat and his hospital room.

I used to remember my mother during those difficult months of suffering and her memory gave me courage to bear my husband's illness. After all, her life had been much worse. And I am alone now because both my children have left Madrid to work abroad. My son lives in South Africa, in Johannesburg working as an electrical engineer in an important company there. He lives there with his wife who is a doctor and with their two children. I wish they lived closer. They return home once every two years and I have only made one trip to Johannesburg to see them. I miss them enormously. As indeed I miss my unmarried daughter. She is a musician and was chosen for a position of cellist in an orchestra in Helsinki, in snow-covered Finland. I haven't been there yet. She tells me not to come in the winter. Perhaps I shall go next summer to see the Baltic Sea. She is happy there. She never found what she wanted in Madrid. But I don't know whether she will ever return, whether I shall still be here if she does return.

Studying the Romanian beggar makes me nostalgic. There is something in her that makes me nostalgic. I must try to talk to her one day.

146

*   *   *

Yes, life is intrinsically sad. My life is sad now that my children are no longer with me, now that I know what it is to wake up and wonder how I shall fill the hours of my day, the long hours of my shortening life. I feel this and I know that the Romanian woman on our streets must feel it too, although she is younger than I am. I have never noticed this sadness before. I have talked about the difficulties of my youth, but after I got over them, my life took a much more favourable turn and I could forget all those early problems. I began to enjoy life with my studies, my travels, my job as a translator (I had worked hard with English and French, spending lengthy periods in the UK and France, in the States and Canada), my blessed marriage to my worthy husband who died so many years ago now and my family life. Unfortunately, two of my sisters have died already and Celia, the artist, lives abroad. She lives in Caracas.

After the death of my husband, Juan, I still reaped pleasure and happiness from my son and daughter and from their lives and activities. But they have been taken from me, taken because of the need to work, away to other lands far from their home and I have no option but to accept that. I know others who, at this ripe old age, are still besieged by their children and grandchildren, women who thrive on all the family links that they have created throughout their days, but who complain all the same about how their children and grandchildren impinge on their time, their money and their ceaseless efforts. They feel tired. Alone as I am now, I would like to feel those intrusions into my days. My days drag. They are too long now, when others complain that it all goes so fast. Worse than time dragging are the aches and pains. I suffer from arthritis in my fingers, which makes it hard trying to pick things up, carry out the odd jobs around my home. And severe attacks of lumbago force me to walk with a stick. I suffer too from acute indigestion, a violent flatulence that jolts my body after every meal. I eat less because of that. Eating alone isn't much fun anyway. These are all minor problems. Basically, my health is reasonable and I am lucky for that. I know people who have died ugly deaths after lengthy periods of suffering. I like to think that I shall lie down one night and never wake up again to receive the morning light. It is the easiest way out, the coward's way out, perhaps. But only a very few years ago, I never had thoughts about my end, about my sadness. I would immerse myself in a book, never worry about searching for company outside my house. I have never needed the constant company of others. Their chit-chat always bored me.

Even as a younger woman, I never hankered after clubs or associations or coffee mornings. I have always enjoyed my own company. I have always been self-sufficient. That was when my children were close to me. Now, I wonder each morning how to fill my day. I have said that. I potter around my flat. I do a few things in it. I watch a little television. The screen tires my sight more and more and the strident voices of some of the interviewers irritate me - there is so little worth watching and it is as though I have heard it all before. I take up a book. My memory isn't what it used to be and sometimes I find myself re-reading paragraphs. And there is nobody to talk to about what I have read. That is why the thread of a novel disappears into thin air. That is why I can no longer remember the titles of films, the names of actors and actresses, why the content of the film disappears also into thin air. I used to love the cinema.

Another of my activities is to walk out into the street each day. I feel that I need to move these ageing bones and muscles. It isn't always easy. I labour along the pavement now, not with the quick, lively sprint I used to have only a few years ago. My sight is failing too and so I find it hard to distinguish people and objects in any detail. But it was on my walks that I discovered the beggar. She has become an obsession with me.

She isn't there on Sundays and I miss her presence, but why shouldn't she have a day of rest, like everyone else? Yet on Mondays, I wonder if maybe she won't be there. Even as I lock my front door, make my slow way to the lift and go down to the street, I find myself thinking about her. Her solitude makes me feel less lonely. Her loneliness is company for me. In a strange way, that woman has altered my existence. I now feel an empathy with her sadness and, knowing that she too suffers, makes me less alone in my solitary life. That makes two of us. Two women, at least, who share each other's sorrows, albeit at a distance. Of course, she doesn't know that her mere presence helps me. There must be some way that I can tell her that. Surely such knowledge would make her feel better, wanted, needed, even loved? And what if I invited her to my home to spend a few hours with me each day? I would pay her for that. We could talk, she in her halting Spanish, learn about each other's past. We could give each other something to live for. Yes, I must consider doing that.

*   *   *

Only a short time has passed and my mind dwells on the beggar yet again. This woman has altered my life. In a strange way she has restored it with purpose. I have said that I notice the hole in my existence, now without my only daughter, without my engineering son and his doctor wife and their children, my grandchildren. I am separated from them all in my final years by oceans of water. I wish they would return, not so that I can interfere in their lives, simply so that I could feel their protection, their closeness. Old age is frail. I wouldn't want them to be in and out all the time. I have always said that each and every one to his own roof, to his own bed, to his own routine. Yet I would be grateful to feel their proximity. I am becoming more and more vulnerable with the years and now, because I am so old, with the months, the weeks, the days even.

But when I come across the Romanian beggar, she helps me, unwittingly, to put my life into perspective. Yes, without knowing it, she has become part of my days and I have built up a solid relationship with her, without knowing her, without even passing the time of day with her. There are days when I leave her a few coins, deposit them on a raffia mat that she has in front of her. As I walk hesitantly, with a walking stick, I prepare the coins before I come level with her. I would feel embarrassed if she were to watch me fumbling around with my purse and my arthritic fingers, searching for a coin to give her. And so I have the money ready in my hand so that I can just leave it for her on her raffia mat as I walk past. I bid her the time of day, of course I do, as I slacken my pace. She, in turn, never opens her mouth. Neither does she smile. She lifts her shoulders with a heavy sigh and presents me with a wan gaze, the gaze of a lost and lonely person. I know, however, that she feels grateful to me. And somehow I know, too, that she also understands that I am a lonely person battling with my final years. There is an unspoken complicity between us. We do not need words to confirm that.

Yes, she has put my life into perspective because when I start comparing myself to her, I can only be grateful for all that I have, for all that I have known. The simple things in life like a comfortable home, a convenient kitchen, a cosy bed, warmth and beauty around me with my plants, my paintings, my photos, sufficient money to feed myself and to treat myself occasionally, all these supposedly simple things which make my life bearable. To be bereft of them, as this poor woman must be, would be tragic. Her life is obviously a terrible, terrible tragedy. Somewhere along the way she went wrong, or things went wrong for her, and now she is suffering from the errors in her past, from her own errors or from the errors of those around her. She must have painful memories. My memories are pleasant.

Memories of my own family are enjoyable, something that is often not the case in families. I always had a good relationship with my younger siblings, although, as I say, two of them have left this world while I linger on. The other two – a brother and a sister – live far from Madrid. My sister Celia went years ago to live in Venezuela where she says that she is in love with the colours of the plants, the skies, the water and the joyous cries of the ragamuffin children who scamper around the streets and on the beaches. She has a small art gallery in Caracas. I have never been there, but we write to each other and speak in our letters. She is 78 now with her ailing body and, very sadly, her failing sight. Perhaps we shall never see each other again. When she no longer answers my letters, I shall know that the end has come. As to my brother, he lives in Málaga. He says he could never return to the harsh clime of Madrid. He has softened to a more temperate climate and he loves the sea. Widowed and childless, he lives alone in a small flat overlooking the ocean and he watches the boats come and go. He is 81. Occasionally, we speak on the telephone.

These are the bits and pieces, the fragments of my life. And this poor beggar has come with her life, whatever it may have been, to leave her imprint on my lonely days.

*   *   *

But the day came when I no longer saw her. That day, the following day, the next day, that whole week - and the week after... Her absence struck me with a sharp force. It was like a blow across my face, a black hole in my existence, a bad dream. Where was she? Had she died? Had she had an accident? Was she ill? Had the police chased her away? So many questions. I imagined her suffering all alone in some dreadful place with no-one to turn to. Each morning I went out, always with hope in my heart, with hope that she would have returned to fill the gaping hole in my life. But no. All I could feel was gratitude to her for having filled some of my days and my thoughts with her presence. She can never know how much she meant to me.

I remember once I considered talking to her, inviting her to my flat, helping to put a little warmth into her days. Now it is too late for that. And I am too old to have any more regrets. At my age, one has regretted all the mistakes over and over again, so many times, until one realises that it is pointless to fill life with regrets. Life must be filled with living and living means making mistakes. Unhappily, we only seem to realise this at the end of our journey, when it's almost too late.

28

Exodus

Yes, it really was crude my life, how I came to Spain. The horrors of that night when I joined up with five others, four men and two women we were, setting out on our adventure as illegal immigrants. I had been sitting on a street curb in Bucharest. I was dirty, exhausted, the dirt on my face streaked by the tears I had shed. I was frightened and lonely. I had walked for days around the city, half mad, searching for Tatiana, knowing that I would never find her. Disheartened each night and dishevelled, I would sit on a park bench, hugging my roughened knees, wishing I had a home to go to. But I only knew that I had to leave Romania. Tatiana gone, there was nothing left for me in that cruel land. Wouldn't it have been more logical for me to stay on there, amongst my own people, living frugally, finding some menial job and, little by little, working my way upwards towards a better life? To start with, there were no jobs, however menial, to be found. I stared unseeingly at advertisements in the newspaper kiosks. All I could see was Tatiana. I peered into prams, sure of seeing her, peering insistently, wanting her so much, until the mothers would almost run away from me. Some of them pushed at me. Hostility was written all over their faces and I shied away from them feeling unwanted, feeling an outcast. I was frantic to find Tatiana and my search had led me to Ceausescu's orphanages.

Tatiana was not an unwanted child. I was her mother and I wanted her, but most of the children inside the orphanages were the result of unwanted pregnancies, mothers who were too afraid to have an abortion, doctors who refused to act against the law. Those children lived in fear and isolation. I mean that they were cut off from normal society and were afraid of the people who looked after them. They were subject to abuse of all descriptions. Young boys and girls with beautiful faces and lithe bodies were raped by others stronger than themselves. They were threatened if they didn't want to accept what was forced on them. They were beaten and bruised. Instead of kisses and warmth, they knew only severe blows and bitter cold. Many were brought up side by side with the mentally handicapped. The tiny babies were under-nourished and some of them starved to death. The *Conducator* was ferocious and mad himself. He wanted to populate the land, our beautiful Romania, with idiots and ill-treated children who would later grow up to perpetrate similar crimes and offences against others, or form part of the cohort of young slave workers who could be easily manipulated by cruel bosses.

I tried to visit some of these orphanages in Bucharest. I toiled along endless streets, avoiding the ruts in the pavements full of rain water, tripping on jagged morsels of dried tar and uneven tiles. I dragged my unhappy body past rusty house railings, past ominous ugly blocks of grey flats, past evil-smelling taverns, past street stands selling putrid flesh and withered vegetables, past old unhappy faces fraught with nostalgia, past young unhappy faces disfigured by discontent and depression. The streets in Bucharest seemed interminably long to me after my village paths. They were noisy also. When I came to an orphanage I recognised it, looming up before me, immense and ominous, large slabs of gritted concrete, dull and sad from the outside as if telling the tale of the misery within. There were bars on the windows, on all the windows, even the higher ones, bars to prevent the orphans from climbing down the guttering to freedom, to prevent them from committing suicide by jumping to their death. Like the house railings I had walked past, the bars were rusting in places and the windows behind them were cavernous and dark showing no hint of life. The paint on the doors and the window frames was peeling off in shreds.

The orphanages were entities negating life and they were guarded at their front entrances by hostile, unhelpful officers, soulless bureaucrats who cared nothing for the lives of the children inside the walls of the institution. They would stare at me, a blank expression on their faces, unwilling to commit themselves to offering any information, shrugging their shoulders, brutal, vulgar blobs of humanity lacking in personality, in warmth. I am looking for my daughter Tatiana, I said to them, she has been taken from me, stolen from me, and brought to one of these orphanages, I know that. Are you sure, they asked disinterestedly, that it is this orphanage. When I replied that I wasn't sure, they said bleakly, indifferently, that my search was pointless, that I should go to another one, and to another one, there were plenty of them in Bucharest and outside Bucharest. They were like useless blocks these guardians of orphanages, faces without compassion, unfeeling eyes. They were the grey cloak of Romania under Ceausescu. Impenetrable and passionless, doing a job of work without interest, without soul. Never was I allowed to cross the threshold. I could hear only screams and shrieks coming from within, never laughter or giggling. The only thing they made me realize was that my search for Tatiana was pointless.

*   *   *

I sat hugging my knees on the curb of the road early one evening. I had spent the whole day occupied with my search. I had plodded over pavement after rutted pavement. I had stared at babies in prams supposedly with their mothers. I had knocked on doors with peeling paint asking where the next orphanage was. I had mounted the steps to the entrance of these ugly buildings. I had exchanged fruitless words with the guard on duty. And I had come away, time and again, bowed with sadness, my eyes sore and heavy with weeping. Now, on the curb of the street I felt gnawing pains, hunger pains, in my stomach, but I felt that life had beaten me down, that it had thrashed the will out of me, so that I no longer cared if I collapsed and died on the curb without satisfying my hunger. My search was pointless and my life without Tatiana even more pointless.

We are driven down into the pit of despair when we are sure that nothing could be worse, but many are the alternatives of pain and evil. Misfortune is wily and flexible. It adopts different guises. Like the man and woman who came to my home to take Tatiana from me, the woman standing before me was accompanied by a man. She shook my shoulders gently, coaxingly, and asked me what I was doing. I look up squinting at her as I rubbed strands of hair from my eyes. Perhaps she was thirty to forty, I don't know. Her companion looked older. They looked at me furtively, as if afraid that we might be seen by police. Did I need, did I want, to escape from Romania, they asked. Did I have money? If I had money they could help me to go abroad, to another country where I could make a new life. The woman offered me a bun with salad and mayonnaise. Her fingers were thick and ugly and her finger-nails rimmed with dirt.

I was dazed and stunned. I didn't know whether to accept her food, her offer of escape. I could only shrug my shoulders indifferently. I had no intention of confiding my sorrows to these people. The woman sat down beside me on the curb and she put her arm around my waist. Come on, you can't stay here like this, she wheedled. It's cold at night. I can find somewhere for you to sleep. You need to sleep. Look at you, you're exhausted. I drew back hesitantly, wondering at her interest. You have some money? The man interrupted again. I nodded at him stupidly. How much, he insisted. I remembered the envelope I had taken from Roxana's bedside table, the money she had received for my daughter, my money. Unthinkingly I delved my hand in my pocket and took out the crumpled envelope. I didn't know exactly how much it contained. In a flash, the man took it from me, opened the flap and began to count the notes. You want to come with us, escape from Romania, it's OK. Without waiting for me to respond, he pocketed a wad of notes and returned the rest to me. I didn't have the strength or the will to protest. And remember, I was so very young then and innocent. The woman helped me to my feet and dragged me along behind her, the man urging us to hurry. Before I could react at all, they asked me to climb into a van waiting on the side of the road, a small van with no windows, except for the driver's seat and the passenger's seat beside him. The man was the driver, the woman was the passenger.

In the semi-gloom in the rear of the van I came vaguely to my senses. I was not alone. There were other passengers. I strained my eyes but could only make out the silhouettes of three male faces, three unshaven faces, heavy with sleep, crossed with wrinkles, premature wrinkles. I withdrew with a shudder into my corner of the van trying in the dim light to erect a barrier between myself and those men. I could smell their breath, their bodies, strong and unpleasant thickening the air in the windowless van. I would have preferred to travel in the front beside the cocksure driver and his woman. At least there was air there. But no, they had stuffed us into the small, uncomfortable space at the back of the van, hidden from the world like packets of illegal produce. We were illegal, but we weren't produce.

The van jolted and swayed. I wasn't sure but I think they were taking us across country on small, uneven roads, some of them maybe even unmade roads. The men were in silence. They occasionally groaned with somnolence, but they uttered no comprehensible words. They looked tired, like me. Perhaps this strange couple, supposedly our saviours, had fished them off the pavement at Bucharest, like me, pushing them into the van in exchange for their notes, telling them that they needed rest and a new life, convincing them that they were being taken to some foreign paradise. After a couple of hours of the rough journey, I began to doze, my head fell forward onto my chest, my eyelids weighed and I couldn't keep my eyes open. I was vaguely aware of intermittent snoring coming from the opposite side of the van. I was falling asleep. But not for long. I awoke with a start. A heavy male body had fallen against my breast, unshaven stubble scratched my neck and there was a sucking sound from pasty, sleep-sodden lips, and a thick masculine hand was stroking my inner thigh. I jumped to my senses and flayed out with my arms and fists screaming. The men woke up and the one who had fallen across me began to beat out at me with harsh blows across my head and shoulders. I kicked wildly at him.

The van came to a dead stop and the man and woman opened the back door. They threatened us: Not a sound out of you, do you hear? We are almost at the border and as we cross into Hungary, not a sound must you make, otherwise you will be discovered and sent back to Bucharest, to jail in Bucharest. His voice and gestures were threatening. I was about to protest about my travelling companions when the woman put her hand over my mouth: Not a sound out of you! The next one who speaks will be thrown out onto the road to escape from Romania as best he can. They had mentioned Hungary. We must be close to Timisoara, my university town I thought with nostalgia. Why not clamour for them to let me out? In a fleeting moment, I had visions of re-making my life there, of somehow returning to university. Then I remembered Roxana, what she had done to me, and I realised that I had to go, to put a whole world between us. If I stayed in Timisoara, I would be tempted to return to my village. Never, never. That, never.

We must have been travelling for five or six hours. It was still dark and we would cross the border into Hungary in the early hours of the morning. I tried to stretch my legs. They were stiff and my arms and head were sore from the blows of the man beside me. It suddenly hit me just how hard the floor of the van was, for the four of us were sitting on the floor with its wood and metal strips. I could feel the bones in my backside, my spine ached and I had pins and needles in my legs. For at least another hour or so we jolted along and during that time my only desire was to stand up and stretch. It was hot in the van so I took off my coat, folded it and put it under me to protect my body. I noticed that two of the men sitting opposite me had also removed their jackets and were sitting on them.

Suddenly, the woman slid open the dirty window separating the driver's compartment from the back of the van. She was severe and the dim light showing through the windscreen behind her head seemed to outline her spikey head of clipped hair, her sharp features, her caustic expression. Once again, in threatening whispers, she urged us to absolute silence, telling us to lie flat on the van floor and cover ourselves with our coats and some ragged lengths of oil skins that were piled up in a corner of the van. We had then to cover them with some planks of wood and two or three bags of carpentry tools in an attempt to camouflage our presence. We weren't to move a muscle, nor utter the slightest sound until she signalled to us. Lying down on that hard flooring wasn't funny. With every jolt of the old van I felt that my bones were being cracked out of joint and I wished I had more flab on my body instead of being so thin. I tucked my oil skin tight around my body to make myself inaccessible to my lewd travelling companions. The smell of the oil skin over my face was nauseating. I had never felt discomfort like this, but I knew that my escape depended on my silence and stillness. And so I obeyed the woman and so did the three men, lying absolutely still beside me.

We hardly dared to breath. The van lurched to a stop and I could hear the muffled tones of someone outside speaking to the driver. They seemed to be on good terms. I could just make out the words carpentry job ... for a day or so ... nothing else. The man handed over some papers. The frontier guard outside yawned loudly, bored, disinterested and too tired in the early hours of the morning to carry out a thorough inspection. He waved us on. So that is how I left Romania, the land of my birth, and how I entered Hungary. Fifteen minutes later the woman told us that we could uncover ourselves and sit up again.

In another hour or so I could see the dawn breaking through the murky window which separated us from the driver. In that faint light, I could better make out the features of the men opposite me. One of them, a large fellow with black, greasy hair, thick eyebrows and sensuous lips banged on the window. He asked the woman if we could stop to relieve ourselves. She told us to wait another half an hour. The man retorted that he was in a hurry, that if they didn't stop he would do what he had to do right there in the van. You wait, said the woman cruelly and authoritatively. And the big fellow shrank back into the shadows as if he had been struck violently. We waited in silence. With every jolt and sway of the van I felt as if my body were stuck to the hard floor of the vehicle and that I would never be able to move again of my own accord.

At last we stopped, the van kangaroo-hopping to a standstill over what seemed to be soft, turfy ground. The driver opened his door violently, jumped out and came around the back to let us out. We half tumbled, half climbed to the damp Hungarian ground, looking around us in the grey, milky light with stiff, wry expressions on our faces where sleep and discomfort and fear had left their imprint. Ten minutes for a pee and a walk the driver told us, no more, if you don't come back on time we'll leave you behind. I set off for some nearby bushes to relieve my bladder, steaming hot urine in the cold morning air. Then I jumped to get my limbs into motion. I had five minutes to study the people I was travelling with. Yet before doing that I studied the strange notion that had hit me, of no longer being in Romania.

How is it possible, you might ask, that one can have such a notion only an hour or so after crossing the border? I looked around me and could see no apparent differences in the countryside where we had stopped, yet the sensation of change was strong and pressing. On the one hand, I felt that I had shaken off an immense weight and I was pervaded by relief that Romania was behind me, for ever, perhaps for ever; on the other, I felt a mixture of nostalgia for my past, for things familiar, even for my young life's tragedy and all this was mingled with a certain apprehension of an unknown future, fear for what would become of me, for what might become of me travelling with these unknown people. It was these sensations that I felt, more than any geographical or physical difference in the land. As far as the eye could see there were fields, harvested crops, bushes and trees, like Romania, there was early morning dew on the grass blades, like Romania, there was the creeping dawn sky before the sun rises, its faint eerie hue that makes me tremble, shiver, shudder, like I used to in Romania. There was virtually no difference in any of these things, but I knew, I unmistakeably knew, that I was no longer in Romania. I was in Hungary.

We were hustled back into the van. It would be another two or three hours before we could stop for food, they told us. What sort of food? With a grimace, I remembered the bun with mayonnaise oozing out of the sides that the woman had given me last night and I longed for something hot, hot, spicy stew that would warm my body and my innards, warm my broken heart. Back inside the foul-smelling van with the oil skins and three unwashed males, I closed my eyes to try and blot out my life as it now was, to blot out their unpleasant faces, to blot out a world that I didn't understand. But the men began to mutter to one another, in low, uncultured tones. There was a hostility about them that frightened me. The one who had fallen against me a few hours earlier was thick-set. His lips were red, voluptuous, the lower lip drooping over towards his determined chin. He must have been about thirty. Unlike the dark, greasy-haired man opposite me, this one had a head of blonde, tousled hair, a mass of tangles and knots that it would be impossible to run your fingers through without pulling at the stray hairs. In contrast to the darker man, his legs were short and his fingers were stubby and dirty and he gave off a faint stench, whether it was his body or his clothing, I couldn't make out.

All three of these individuals seemed to me to smell nasty. Perhaps because I was so close to them in the airless van. The last man was older, slightly better shaven than the other two and his hair was orderly, plastered down against a large scalp. His skin was finer too. With a stretch of imagination, I thought that there was even something nice about him. He looked kinder and must have been around fifty. It was he who had started up a conversation with his dark neighbour, but I couldn't make out what they were saying because of the noise of the engine and also because I was beginning to doze again. Yet only doze. I realised that I was on my guard, feeling vulnerable as the only woman in the van. I felt nervous too. I was weak against any possible attack from the man beside me. I tried to give a watery smile to the older man, hoping that he might act as an accomplice if I were to fall into difficulty. He nodded indifferently in response. Fragments of thoughts about them and about my new situation drifted in and out of my mind with the jolting of the van and two or three more hours passed before we came to a stop.

Hopefully this time we would be fed. The money we had paid for this journey was more than enough to cover food. I found myself shying away from the idea of sandwiches or buns, I found myself imagining hot broth with lumps of juicy meat and potato. Again, the man jumped out of the van and came around to open our door. He warned us not to get involved with people nor to enter the cafeteria I could see several metres away on the other side of the road from where we were parked. We could use the toilets and his wife would bring us some food. Then we could exercise our legs for half an hour. My dreams of hot broth were almost satisfied. The woman came over to give us cartons of hot tomato soup and sandwiches which we gulped down hungrily, the men noisily.

They didn't try to speak to me and I had nothing to tell them. They murmured amongst each other in male complicity and I was left alone on the edge of their murmurings. I didn't mind, in fact I preferred it that way. In the stronger light of day their faces didn't look quite as threatening as they had inside the van. I moved away

160

from the small group towards the field and bushes behind us. I stared back towards Romania and for the first time I felt a traitor, my own mother had betrayed me and now I was betraying my own daughter, running away from her. Yes, for the first time, I felt the gaping distance between myself and Tatiana. Tears welled up in my eyes and I could only quell them by promising myself that I would make money in my new land and return later to find her.

I have never kept that promise, Doctor, have I?

The driver came towards us. He had a loping gait under his heavy body. I noticed his double chin and two or three ugly moles on his thick neck, his bulldog neck. He might have been fifty odd and he already had a paunch that protruded out over his trouser belt. His hands were thick and ugly, not Petre's fine fingers I can remember thinking. His wife, or his woman, had a crueller disposition. She was neat and small-limbed, shrewish like a weasel, determined and outspoken. He was the driver, the physical motivator, but she was his mentor, his leader. And, for the time being anyway, our leader. If we wanted this couple's help, we had no alternative but to obey their commands. She stared at me, at my tear-stained face oozing nostalgia and in her matter-of-fact tone, she said to me authoritatively that there was no going back now. Another few hours and we would approach the Austrian border. We would stop close by so as to cross the border at night.

Back in the van again, jolting along the Hungarian highways, we might as well have been on horseback for the van advanced slowly in stops and starts. There was traffic on the road they told us. Later, we noticed the road winding upwards, the van was spitting and spluttering as if out of breath. I calculated that we must be passing through a hilly region. My companions, if I can call them that, slumbered untidily around the van. I could see the bare flab emerging from the shirt of the blonde, tousled-haired one. I shuddered in repulsion and tried to close my eyes, blocking them out again. They meant nothing to me these men. Our lives had come together transitorily, but the moment I could be free of them, I would run hard and get away.

This part of the journey took longer than anticipated, four or five hours and I noticed that the autumn light was glowing less brightly, heralding the end of the day, of that traumatic day. Soon darkness would fall, smothering our unhappiness and the prints of our refugee feet. The next time we stopped I heard the woman say to the man that she was going for more food. When she returned, she handed each of us a pack of food and a bottle of water. Don't eat it yet, she warned. It will have to do you until you can find somewhere to eat in Austria. What was this? Were they leaving us to our own devices? They could not accompany us outside the communist region, they said. They knew of a place where we could ease our way under the border fence and not be discovered. After that we had to run, disappear as quickly as possible. They could do no more for us.

So this was their game? I had visions of police dogs running after us, of losing my way, of starving in an Austrian ditch, of drowning in an Austrian river. And how could I speak to the Austrian people? I only knew Romanian, no German. I would be better to return to Romania with them. I pleaded and wept, but they took no notice of me. They had no intention of carting us back to Bucharest, or even Timisoara, they said. I snivelled miserably. The older man tried to comfort me: You'll be much better off in Austria, all of us will, but it'll be easier for you than me, you're younger than I am, you're a woman, you'll find work he said looking slyly at the other two. What sort of work? I retorted. Well, what do women like you normally do? Cleaning, cooking, sleeping with men. I cringed away from his words, away into my own thoughts. Was it possible that I had once been a university student? I felt pitiful through and through. At that point, the man and woman told us to jump out, to put all our belongings into our bags and to follow them. There was deathly silence all around us. We could only hear the movement of our legs inside trousers, brushing against damp grasses. They told us to walk stealthily, as quietly as possible. I could just make out a high wire fence in the darkness. Now you get the hell out of here, all of you. Separate on the other side. I thought of all the money the driver had taken from me in Bucharest and I asked him to give me some of it back. I had paid too much for this journey for it to end in danger. He grimaced and shook his head, his eyes glinting evilly in the moonlight. In response, he indicated a hole under the fence where the wiring was loose, just about big enough for a man to fit through.

I was suddenly overtaken by a sense of urgency. I knew that there was no going back and the quicker the deed was done, the better, the quicker I could escape, the sooner would I emerge from this nightmare. Without a word to any of them I clasped my belongings and pushed them under the fence and then down on my tummy I wriggled my way underneath, my nose touching clods of damp earth, the soil dark against my skin, a rich smell of primeval nature, my hands and face scratched by briars. At one point my jumper caught against a spoke in the fence, but I managed to disentangle myself and wriggle out from under the barrier. On the other side, I stood up, listened carefully into the Austrian air for any tell-tale sound and, without so much as a look behind me, gathered my coat and bag and, as quietly as I could, I stumbled my way through the clump of bushes. All I could hear from the communist side was a gruff: Now you, hurry up!

No time to think now, I had to put distance between me and the border before the light of day, between me and those hostile men. They were the typical product of Ceausescu's regime - dull, brutish, insensitive, like heavy machines that can only grind on and on with a pre-established routine, incapable of understanding the lights and darks of life, of sensing difference, of displaying bursts of deep emotion. The only emotion they knew was that which surged from time to time within their loins. I remembered the thick slobbery lips of the tousled-haired man and I walked faster to get right away in case he was chasing behind me. We had been told to separate from each other, less chance of getting caught, but you never know what designs he had on me, a lone young female, easy prey. I picked up a thick stick as I marched on amidst the grasses. I might need it for defence against him, against any other man, against an animal. But I tried not to dwell on horrible thoughts. My whole being was propelled towards escaping into a better future, escaping into the Austrian dawn.

29

Austria

Fortunately Doctor, I never saw those men, the men who had accompanied me in the van from Bucharest to Austria, ever again. The blond curly-haired one didn't follow me. I never knew whether they had separated, or whether they had decided to go against the advice of the driver and stick together to look for their fortune. I only knew, several hours after I had walked away from them at the Hungarian border, that I was in one of the most beautiful parts of the world.

I walked fast along stony paths that wound round hill slopes where the grass looked as though it had been washed and brushed and combed. This was a soft, clean world, softer than Romania, cleaner than Romania, more exhilarating than Hungary. There were small villages with large sloping-roofed houses built of wood, masses of coloured geraniums tumbling down the walls of the houses from their balconies. I could smell the hay in the fields, I could smell animal dung, I could smell milk in the barns and the people who crossed my path had jovial faces, an expression of satisfaction smoothed out the wrinkles in their ruddy farmer complexions. In Austria there was a sensation of well-being and for the first time in months I experienced something inside myself akin to happiness. I sat on the banks of an enormous lake where pure crystal water lapped at my feet, clear and green, and I ate part of the food that the driver and his woman had given me, food bought with my money. On the other side of the lake the mountains were high and blue, penetrating the clear blue sky with their sharp peaks not yet covered in snow, for it was autumn and although the air was chilly, the sun was still warm. Yes, I felt almost happy. I drank water from the lake and lay flat on the grass, as I used to do in Romania outside my village when I had been pregnant with Tatiana.

And I dreamed.

Not for long because I knew that I had to find shelter for the night. The days were closing in and the twilight fell early in the evening like a vast cape smothering the world in darkness. I walked on to the next village. I had felt safe all day on my march but as the darkness began to close itself around me I became nervous. A little way ahead I saw a barn. It was on the outskirts of a village. I entered through a creaking wooden door and peered gingerly into the dim light. All I could make out were walls and walls of straw and hay. The barn seemed to be empty of life, either animals or humans, but it was warm. And like an animal, a dog circling round and round before he slumps down in the spot he has chosen, a cat padding with her paws to feel her ground, I too went around and around my chosen spot before laying my weary body on the straw mattress. It was warm and comfortable and it wasn't long before I fell into a deep sleep.

And again I dreamed.

The next morning dawned chill and fresh and clear. I had slept deeply and I felt refreshed. I emerged, tousled, from the barn, bits of straw peeping out of my long hair. It was too cold to wash in the lake, so I rubbed the sleep from my eyes, pinched my cheeks, moved my jaws, breathed deeply gulping in the fresh air, and brushed my hair. That would do for now.   Later as the sun warmed the day I could wash. Strangely enough I wasn't hungry. I had to keep walking and I could postpone eating until my stomach rebelled and clamoured for food. The less money I spent, the better. Money? Only then did it occur to me that all the money I had were Romanian *lei*. Outside Romania no-one would accept my *lei*. I was young and innocent in financial affairs, not only in financial affairs.   Where could I change this money? I had no documents, no passport to say when I had entered Austria. No-one would change my *lei*. And the envelope containing my wad of Romanian notes weighed like pebbles in my pocket.

Only the previous day I had felt excited, free, almost happy. Today I felt nervous, tense and scared. If I approached the wrong person, I might be flung into gaol or sent back to Romania. That alternative appealed to me, to return to Timisoara and to live somehow there without contacting my family. Why not? The alternative was tempting and I was on the verge of retracing my steps, going backwards towards my own people, when a small van approached, bumping along the stony road. A woman was driving it and she pulled up just in front of me. I was about to run off and hide in the bushes when I saw that she was smiling. She spoke to me. I shrugged my shoulders in response, not understanding a word. She wasn't put off. She made signs to me that I interpreted as the offer of a lift to a nearby town. In return, I smiled also and climbed willingly into the van beside her.

That lift might have been a risk, but again, Simona would have said that it was God picking me up, saving me, putting me on the right track. That woman was kind and generous. She offered me a hunk of bread and salami sausage that I devoured hungrily, suddenly aware of the gaping hole in the pit of my stomach. She stopped on the roadside and took a thermos of coffee. Take it, take it, she insisted. I took it, shyly. I felt revived. Where are you going, I imagined that she asked me. Again I shrugged my shoulders in reply. After repeating her words fruitlessly, she took out a map, spreading it open on a large stone table raised above the grass. She pointed at some place in the south of Austria, then pointed to herself and her van and again at the map. She placed her finger on a town called Trieste. She pointed at me, at herself and again at Trieste questioningly. I nodded. The world seemed to open up to me. Italy, Italy she laughed and I laughed with her. How rarely since then have I laughed, Doctor.

How different she was from the terrible Romanian couple who had dropped me at the border, and I no longer wanted to return to the grim faces and the poverty in my country. Through the bumping van window, I could see the lofty crags of the Austrian Alps, some of the peaks disappeared into cloud, others rose proudly, sharply into a blue sky. Yes, I was almost happy. Youth is nonchalant and moves easily, to and fro, from tears to laughter. From time to time I glanced at the woman beside me. She was large and capable, her strong hands manoeuvring the wheel of the van with expertise, her eyes glinting joyfully tucked away into her rosy cheeks. She oozed warmth and kindness. This time, she was my saviour, not the mean-faced Romanian weasel of a woman. She seemed to understand my predicament even though I couldn't explain it to her and for that I felt grateful and I felt that I could trust her. She looked at me also, when she could take her eyes from the road. She continued to speak her words and although I was at a loss to know what she was saying, those words enveloped me in a warm, protective cocoon. Then she pointed to her watch. It was three o'clock in the afternoon. She pointed to the six. At six o'clock, Trieste, she informed me. Italy ... Italy ... and she laughed again and burst into song and her music vibrated comfortingly in my body and I hummed in tune with her.

The next three hours passed quickly. I dozed from time to time and whenever I opened my eyes I was regaled by stunning boulders, high peaks, green glades and the company of my driver with her staunch body and positive vibrations. And suddenly I realised that I would miss her. When she stopped the car in a side street in Trieste I knew my journey with her had come to an end and I was afraid. But I overcame my apprehension because I was grateful that she had brought me this far, far away from Bucharest and from my hateful past. I took a note from the bunch stuffed away in my underwear for safety. She looked at it and laughed and I knew she said to me in her German tongue that what could she do with a few *lei*. It wasn't that it was too little money for her pains. It was that she couldn't change them anywhere. Gesturing, she made me understand that I must search for other Romanian people. There were plenty in Trieste, she gestured. They seemed to be thousands from the way she waved her arms. We were standing on the pavement beside the car. I could say nothing. I merely looked deep into her eyes and thanked her from the bottom of my heart for what she had done and for the way she had done it. This, I said to her in Romanian and she understood, comprehending not one of my words. We locked in a warm embrace and as the tears welled up in my eyes, I smiled at her and walked rapidly away. I felt that I had no right to steal more of her time. I had to work my own life out for myself. But she had made me see that there was some good in the world, that not everyone had ulterior motives. She had given me a piece of paper with the name of a Romanian hostel.

*   *   *

I was twenty and I had never seen the sea. Can you believe that, Doctor? Well, it's true. Of course, I knew from my studies that the seas and oceans of the world were immense volumes of salt water - unimaginably immense — separating countries from one another. I knew that the sea adopted the colour of the sky, either blue or grey or metallic white. I knew that it was a lighter green colour, turquoise, in the shallows and that it could be a darker blue or metal grey in the deep. I knew that some seas were mostly fierce, where large often dangerous fish swam rapidly amidst the swift currents, and that other seas were mostly calm. I knew that some of them had higher tides than others. I knew that there were parts of the ocean that delved down, way down, into the entrails of the earth, that there were mountains beneath all that water, hills, hillocks and coral crevices in the warmer waters where tropical fish joisted and played and bred. I knew that the sea bed was uneven in part, like the land. That it had caverns and reefs and platforms, a whole topography just like the topography of dry land. I knew all this about the sea, but when I saw it for the first time, on the morning after the first night I spent in the poor Romanian hostel at Trieste, I was breath-taken, stunned. Nothing in the world could have been more beautiful, I thought.

I sat on a bench in a green park overlooking the port, the islands, the whole expanse of water that washed the shores of Croatia and Italy — the Adriatic — and in my imagination, down, down to the heel of Italy, down to Corfu and the Greek Peloponnese where it flows into the Aegean. I was aghast and overcome at so much splendour, so much beauty. I could hear the voices of the port workers as they pulled at their ropes, clanged and hammered their utensils against the steel helm of a cargo boat, hanging in mid-air against the white hull of a passenger liner, their cries and shouts rose up to me on the breeze as I sat transfixed in the park watching their activity, watching the gulls swoop down towards the masts of the boats, paddling in the pools of water on the wharf, pecking at crumbs dropped from the stevedores' bread, hearing them cry out in tune to the workers' songs, their strong wings flapping, or stretched out, gliding on the air currents, watching the water shimmer in the sun, the wavelets push and flop, jostling against one another, backwards, forwards, backwards, forwards, moved by the breeze and the swirling green depths beneath them. And watching all this I felt an immense breath of freedom, I felt the freedom of the ocean, the enormity of its solitude. I imagined being alone, a tiny human form, in the middle of all that water and I knew that I would only last a short time being lulled in its bosom, it would only be minutes before the water would penetrate my eyes, my ears, my nose, seeping greedily into all my orifices, pulling at me, sucking at me, cajoling me downwards into its dark, heaving kingdom. I shuddered and clutched stupidly at the wooden bench I was sitting on. I felt dizzy with my thoughts and after my long journey from Romania. I found myself wondering what the sea that bathed the shores of Romania was like.

I dreamed of taking Tatiana to that sea. To the Black Sea. But would I ever return?

At the hostel, I changed my Romanian *lei* to Italian *lira*. I could speak my own language and no-one asked me any questions, where had I come from, where was I going, how long would I be staying at the hostel. It was obvious that all the Romanians had escaped from the *Conducator* and had entered Italy illegally. The less said, the better. The place was run by two Romanian men, young men obviously friends, perhaps even lovers. I didn't know and I didn't care. For very little money I was given a room, a tiny room with a dirty window looking out onto a back alley with cobblestones, street cats *miaowing* all night long, a narrow, sinister alleyway, a cul-de-sac that led nowhere, only to dark doorways and evil-smelling portals, culminating at the end in an ugly high brick wall smothered in garish drawings, rubbish piled high into overflowing containers, spilling out onto the cobblestones around them. The unpleasant smell wafted up to me on my third storey as I tried to settle at night.

I locked myself inside the room which was virtually bare of furniture, a creaking bed with a minimum of bed linen, darned sheets and pillow slip with a thin blanket threadbare in parts, an old wooden chair and a wooden slab which served as a table, no wardrobe or drawers, just a few metal hooks on the wall and a couple of shelves. Not only the bed creaked but the wooden flooring creaked as well. There was a wash basin in one corner and a toilet with cracks in the sides of its bowl.   The wash basin had only one tap from which a thread of cold water dribbled when I turned it on. Above the basin there was a mirror smeared with marks that could have been anything from semen to blood.   That mirror had never been cleaned and I could see from the black smudges where the mercury had worn off that it was obviously years old. When I stared at my face in it, I had to move it round and in between two or three black spots, otherwise I had a black mark over one eye and another one on my nose.   In short, the place was grotty and unwelcoming, but it was cheap. I couldn't afford anything better. I flopped down on the bed and wondered what to do next. If I wanted to stay in Trieste I would have to earn some money. If not, I would have to keep travelling until I found a town where I could work. I decided to talk to one of the Romanian women in the hostel next morning.

Would this be my future?

30

A Coffee Factory in Italy

I could have stayed at the Romanian hostel in Trieste as long as I paid the rent for my room there and that I could do with the money I earned amongst the army of cleaners at a large coffee factory. There I pushed my broom and mop over the vast flooring of the factory, I cleaned the machinery for crushing the coffee beans, always, always that smell of coffee beans, from five-thirty until nearly ten o'clock in the morning when we had to finish to make way for the factory workers, to make way for them but not to get in their way, or under their feet with our cleaning utensils.

We worked hard and during the first mornings I felt exhausted when we had finished. I remembered pushing a broom around Roxana's house and cleaning her kitchen and I remembered that that had been much easier than this enormous factory with its glistening machines, the never-ending surfaces where the workers lined up to execute their repetitive tasks. I supposed that it was preferable in a way just to be cleaning instead of having to bear the noise of machinery, to repeat the same movements hour after hour as the beans were washed and crushed and the packets of coffee prepared and sealed. The same worker did the same task day in day out. I was also doing the same task, day in day out, but I wasn't controlled by the speed of a machine. And so I preferred my mop and broom and dusters.

In the four and a half hours each day that I worked there, I rubbed up against the other cleaners, some with a smile, some with a grimace, but we were controlled and the only time we could really communicate was if we left the building in the company of someone else. Yet it was amazing how quickly the mass of workers dissipated on reaching the other side of the factory gates, as if into thin air. No-one seemed to want to befriend anyone else. They marched away down different streets, like a great octopus waving straggly tentacles. I was wary about people – all those illegal people were wary – about striking up friendships that might betray me later on, or, that might hurt me the way I had been hurt by Petre, by Radu, by Roxana my mother. Perhaps it was better to keep away, keep to myself. Also, I had no legal papers to cover my stay in Italy and I knew that my job at the factory couldn't last long. They took advantage of illegal workers then. They could pay them less and we were happy to have anything to bring in a bit of money.

And so I had hours every day to wander in the city of Trieste. I liked it. It is a pretty city. There are some beautiful squares and monuments and gardens and, most of all, I loved being so close to the sea. I used to go to my park bench above the port and stare out into the ocean, following its whims and waves, its incessant movement. It seemed to induce me to relax, to feel free of my unhappiness. Yet at the same time, when I stared out into that great expanse of heaving water, I felt desolately lonely. I searched for Tatiana, her little face and figure in the troughs of deep blue liquid, in the glistening foam-tipped waves. And when my mood became too hard to bear, I would rise from my bench with a profound sigh and slowly make my way to another part of the city to watch the passers-by, to listen to their Italian language which I was gradually beginning to understand, to gaze with envy at the expensive shops, at the gay bars on the terraces and pavements.

But even then, I was unable to shed my sadness. It was there, inside me, like a stone, a cold unfeeling stone, that was dragging me down like a weight, further and further into some sort of a hole. I just couldn't rid myself of it. When the sensation of tragedy became almost too strong a burden, I used to retire to my ugly little room at the hostel where I lived. It was only there that I could give vent to my misery, to the loss of my baby daughter. It was there that I realised that she would pursue me wherever I went, pointing a tiny finger of recrimination at me. I had run away from her. I had run away from

Romania, but Romania had me in her clutches, Tatiana and Romania and all that I had ever known there. I knew at such moments that I could never, never forget my Romanian past. Why didn't I return instead of fiddling aimlessly with a new life that could never replace my old life? It would have been easy to pack a bag with my few meagre belongings, find someone to take me back through Austria, through Hungary, back to Timisoara. I had done it once. I could do it again in the opposite direction.

Though I knew, if I retraced my steps that I would find Viorica, perhaps even Roxana, and I would have to resume the fruitless search through Ceausescu's orphanages. I shuddered. No. That, no. My soul was wilting and I didn't have the courage for that.

31

Viorica, Drugs in Trieste

Viorica, my sister, was a strange girl. I used to wonder sometimes if she had a streak of our mother's cruelty in her, or was it merely indifference? All these years later, Doctor, she comes to my mind occasionally, very occasionally, as a phantasmal figure from my past. She floats in on me as I am settling for the night, she approaches me walking along the street where I sit each day begging and I imagine our reunion. It would be tearless, with few explanations, few questions. She would be older, as indeed I am older, her face more lined, her hair also greying. We would stare at each other, into the past reflected in each other's eyes and I know that there would be no wish to continue in her company. Remember, she had betrayed me. She had known of Roxana's intentions with Tatiana and she never mentioned them to me. She had sided with our mother. She had been an accomplice to my bereavement. Her embrace when she saw me after they had taken Tatiana away was false. She hugged me to smother her insincerity. Not that I thought that at the time. It is only now as I dwell on her personality that I remember her faults and I have no wish to see her again, no wish for her to share my life.

If I can call it a life, here in Madrid.

A strange person, yes. Many was the time when she would shy away from company, from conversation. Her eyes would turn opaque as you talked to her, hiding away behind a sort of blank mist. It was a way she had of cutting short, of cutting you out of her life and thoughts. Sometimes you would say something to her, something serious, and she would burst out into a sudden peal of laughter, a senseless mirth. When Simona chided her, she would clam up, staring hard at the wall or into the flames of the fire.

There were days when she wouldn't speak at all, when she would turn her back on anyone who tried to speak to her. When we were younger, she would always try and get out of the tasks Roxana imposed on us, making sure that I took the lion's share of the work because, she protested, I was older. She was dishonest, always keeping a few *lei* for herself if our mother had sent her out on an errand to buy food at the grocer's. She lied a lot, mostly to save her face, if she realised she had done something wrong.

I could never confide in her. If young sisters have to sleep in the same room, as we had done for years, they generally confide in each other, talking about their parents, their school friends, their boyfriends, they giggle and unconsciously build up the strongest of bonds, of sisterly love. I felt no sisterly love for Viorica. She never spoke to me of her aspirations and I soon realised that nothing that interested me was of interest to her. She attended school in an aura of indifference. She did her homework quickly and quietly, but there was a flatness in her activities, as though she could find no spark of animation in anyone or in anything and, least of all, in herself.

All these years later I could only imagine that she had remained in the village, had tended Roxana in her old age, tended her with indifference, with a sense of obligation, and had taken on the tasks of Simona's home as being her own. I could never imagine her married to a man or bringing children into the world. There was no tenderness in her makeup.

Yet, I know that Roxana preferred her to me. Why? Perhaps because the older woman sensed that I hid behind a veil of criticism. There were moments when I despised her and she must have felt that. She had wanted me to study and when I did, she forced me to help out in the house. She burdened me with tasks saying that Viorica was too young. There were only a couple of years between us. Ostensibly Viorica was more difficult than I was, but her tantrums were more direct, her outbursts were easier for Roxana to cope with than my silent mistrust. Mother and younger daughter had a bond between them, an invisible bond that held them together, both together in their unpleasantness, in their spite, in their dislike of Simona and of me. I sensed that for some reason they were jealous of me.

Jealous of this bundle of begging humanity.

But of course, then I had been studying and going through my pregnancy and that made me different to them.

I have spoken of Roxana before, but one day I will speak again of her and try to delve into her relationship with me.

*   *   *

Now, I remember the trees in Madrid being bare of leaves, most of them anyway. The pines and cedars cling to their green attire all through the winter and push out their new fresh needles in the springtime. This is the end of autumn, the tail end that pushes inexorably towards winter. I may have said already, Doctor, that I love the autumn, at least in its early phases. Towards the end, it is indistinguishable from winter. The days are damp and cold, often grey under steel grey skies, mournful skies.

They are mournful, like me.

Then my mind would easily turn to Trieste, where for a brief time I was happy.

*   *   *

Trieste was a good place to be. If I look back on my past I think it is the place where I was happiest, except for my constant dwelling on Tatiana. Was I relatively happy there because I was young and innocent, because the waves of the sea were willing to listen to my woes, to carry them far away, because I had a job, however demeaning it was, because it was the first town I could compare with my miserable life in Romania? Trieste represented a certain freedom for me.

Perhaps I would have stayed there if events had not taken the turn they did. Every day I went obediently to my job at the coffee factory. I did my cleaning there as best I could and no-one ever complained to me or about me, although, as I have said, I never had much contact with the other workers. Then one day they rounded up about twenty of us, twenty of the cleaners. They shouted at us. They shook some plastic bags full of white powder in front of our noses. They questioned us intimidatingly. I understood enough Italian to realise that they had found these drugs stuffed away, concealed in a corner under one of the coffee machines. A coffee bean selector had found them when he went to work. He had unwittingly kicked them with his toes. That was how they were discovered and he took them, all ten or twelve bags of them, to the director of the department. Somebody – one of us, one of the Romanian cleaners – was involved in drug peddling. That would not be tolerated, they told us, never tolerated inside the coffee factory.

Who was the cleaner responsible for this? Who was the filthy rat who had left drugs on the floor as if trying to put blame on one of the Italian workers? They had been wrong to trust the Romanians. We were dishonest, corrupt people, they said. There were three of these directors screaming at us, threatening us. We stood quaking in our shoes as they marched up and down the line of workers, gesticulating, ugly grimaces on their faces, and out of their minds. Out! All of you are out! No more work here for you. One Romanian woman who had been at the factory longer than most of us and who spoke Italian, protested vehemently. They took no notice of her. They threatened her, raising their fists. They asked her to leave in no uncertain terms. The rest of us stared after her loping, defeated figure, her long black hair, her thick arms and legs. I remember feeling grateful to her for trying to save our jobs.

But our jobs were lost. The culprit was never discovered. We never knew if the drug-meddler-peddler was a Romanian like us, or whether he or she was Italian. That didn't matter. What mattered was that they had thrown us out of the coffee factory without paying us the ten days we had worked that month – was it May or June? I can't remember. We were discarded, like any bits of rubbish, out on the street. Why, though? Why, I asked myself so often, did the culprit leave the drugs in a place where they would be discovered? What did that person have in mind? Was he trying to incriminate someone? Was he looking for a place to hide his merchandise when he was suddenly surprised by someone else walking into the factory and so he just left the stuff in the quickest and nearest hideout he could find? It was a mystery and, to this day, I have never discovered what really happened.

And so I was out on the streets of Trieste once again, with no job to go to, with little money to go on paying the hostel. But worst of all, was the fear. One morning one of the Romanian receptionists at the hostel, a disagreeable man with unshaven bristle framing his stubborn chin and an evil-smelling, hirsute body, muscled arms, thick fingers and grubby fingernails, pointed slyly to a photograph in the crumpled newspaper he was waving at me. I stopped short to catch my breath. There was I in the photograph, standing in the line of nineteen others, the cleaners who had been called up at the factory, chastised, and thrown out onto the street. Who had taken that photo? How appropriate for our bosses that the press had been there just at the right moment, at the time of our expulsion from the factory. Yes, it was me, sure enough. It was unmistakeably me, there was no doubt. I asked him to tell me what the article said. He leered unpleasantly. So you are in trouble? He grinned menacingly. You stupid people, messing around with drugs. I opened my mouth to protest, but he took no notice of me. The Italians are complaining about you. You come here doing stupid things and you make my life harder. I work hard with this hostel to try and help refugees from our country and this is the thanks you give me.

He wouldn't listen to my explanation when I tried to tell him that I had nothing to do with the drugs, it was an error, none of us in that line had anything to do with the drugs, we weren't bad, we just went every day and did our cleaning and left the factory. We didn't know who had done it. With a surreptitious laugh, he said that it might even have been one of the Italian bosses. It might have been a way of getting rid of a group of us so that they could take new people on and pay them even less. It wouldn't be the first time. But now they know you. They have your photo. You ought to leave Trieste, get away before they find you, he said menacingly. I stared at him and was bold enough to say that he didn't work so hard in his hostel. It was a filthy, grimy hole of a place and I'd only put up with it because it was cheap. I told him not to worry, I would leave as soon as possible.

Out on the street I hurried to my bench in the gardens overlooking the sea. It was where I used to go when I needed to think. Now I wished I hadn't insulted the man in the hostel, he might throw my things out of my room and not let me go back that night. It suddenly occurred to me that he might be trying to get rid of me so that he could hire out my room to someone else for more money. I was young, but I was beginning to realise that people often acted with an ulterior motive. Solidarity between humans was a chimaera, well, between most humans anyway. Friendship was based on self-interest, on money, on what you could get out of someone else.

I sat for more than an hour, watching the waves bash against the rocks on the coast, tantalizing the land with their relentless forceful blows, absorbing the restless movement of the water, it seemed in tune with the restlessness that was needling its way into my own body, into my mind. It became more and more evident to me that I had to leave Trieste if I didn't want to be in trouble with the police. The receptionist at the hostel had told me several months ago about the time the police had turned up there and ousted all the inmates, asking for the documents they didn't have, threatening them with gaol if they didn't leave Italy. When he told me that, I recall that I had shivered in fear, but I soon forgot about it and continued to go to the coffee factory where, in some strange way, I felt protected. Yet now, with my photo in the press, with all the noise that the drug trafficker had caused – was it a Romanian, one of us, or was it some Italian wanting us out? – it had become dangerous for me to continue in Italy. No point either in making my way down to Venice or Florence or Rome or Naples, or even Sicily.

We were all of us, all the cleaners in that factory photo, on the Italian police records now. No, I had to escape. I wasn't sure how to get out of the country, but as I sat on my bench in the morning sunlight, I felt confidence in my destiny, I remembered Simona with her beliefs that someone would always be there to force a change in events. Confident that this would be the case, I rose from the bench. I had, almost unconsciously, made a tentative decision. I returned to the hostel and packed my bag with the few belongings I owned. I'm leaving, I said to the receptionist with the dirty fingernails. You won't have to worry about me causing you any problems. I paid him what I owed for my rent, not a *lira* more, not a *lira* less, and left without a word. I turned my back on his dubious hospitality, I was turning my back on Trieste where, yes, I had known a short period of happiness.

Or something like happiness.

As I emerged from the hostel door my eyes alighted on a woman a few metres in front of me. She had long, black hair, thick arms and legs and a loping gait. She was also carrying a bag. I recognised the Romanian woman in the factory who had tried to stand her ground in front of the managers. I quickened my pace and caught up with her. We immediately recognised each other and each other's intent and purpose. We smiled and agreed to somehow leave Italy together. Somehow. But how? If only we could fly, soar above man-made frontiers like migrating birds. But no. We were not birds, though birds now fascinate me. We were two refugees amidst the jostling Italian masses on the pavement. So once again, I thought, she was Simona's guide who was to help me to the next stage in my life. Could I depend on her? At least it was a relief being with someone whom I could understand. She was older than I was and had been in Trieste for longer. She too had escaped from Bucharest with some others in a van. It was pretty well the only way we could leave the country. There were too many controls on the trains or coaches and it was impossible to get across the borders if you didn't do it clandestinely. So her experience had been similar to mine, although her life in Romania had been even worse.

She - her name was Andreea - was an orphan. She never knew her parents. She had been reared in one of those terrible orphanages that I had visited to search for Tatiana. She had been strong enough not to fall ill, not to go mad like many of the inmates beside her, strong and clever enough to avoid the beatings, she had somehow managed to steal more food than her daily ration. Her sense of humour had helped her through a lot of complicated situations. Of course, there had been days when she'd hated life, hated the miserable, sick children who were her companions, but she tried not to fall into the grip of depression, she always knew that there would be a light at the end of the tunnel but that the light was outside the orphanage.

Because she was physically stronger and mentally more alert than the others, the warders chose her to carry out a lot of tasks and she learnt how to get around them. She despised them. She hated the greyness of the building, the smell in the dining hall, the filth around her, the whole stench of poverty and infirmity and sadness that had been her lot since she could remember. She had fought against extreme cold in winter, against extreme heat in summer, against hard boards for a bed. She had slept beside children wailing and snivelling because they were sick or they had been beaten for nothing at all, or wailing because they were out of their minds, and one day when they asked her to run an errand outside in the street, she decided that it was her only chance to break away from all that tragedy, all that misery and unhappiness. She was sixteen and old enough to look after herself on the streets. Or so she thought.

32

Birds

As the years pass, I notice that I am more and more conscious of the birds around me. As I sit on my cardboard seat at the corner of two roads, I listen to the birds singing in the nearby trees. I have learnt to block out the noise of the traffic and to only hear bird song. I can distinguish which birds are singing. In the springtime the purest song is sung by the blackbird before he has mated, more than likely to attract his partner, and after he has mated and his companion has nursed her eggs to life, after they have both worked hard to feed their young, he sits in the branches singing for all his worth. I listen to his song and it seems to me full of plenitude, of joy, of beauty, of exultation.

How I would love to be able to sing like that.

There are many other birds apart from the blackbird. The magpie is raucous and strident. His feathering is magnificent, his plump lustrous body gleams with jet black and iridescent blue and white. He is a proud bird and when he lands in a tree, the branches sway and the smaller birds fly off. Are they scared of him? He is certainly large enough to be the lord and master. In the fields and the mountains, outside the cities, it is the vulture, the eagle, that subjugate all other bird life, but in the cities, it is the magpie. During the early weeks of spring, the magpie comes and goes carrying long flimsy sticks of wood or pieces of debris or grasses in his beak. He works ceaselessly to build his nest, flying back and forth several times a day and when he isn't flying he is weaving the material he has gathered to furnish his companion and offspring with protection. All the birds do this, but some of them are more visible than others. I have already said that I watch the sparrows, minute birds chirping and fluttering around the crumbs on the pavement, sometimes right in front of me. If I watch them on the branches of trees they look grubby brown in colour, but when they come close to me I see that the males have black and white stripes on their wings with truffle-coloured fluff on their tiny breasts. They aren't scared of me, even though they may be scared of the magpie.

Oh, and only recently, there are lots of immigrant birds in Madrid – immigrants like me – without papers, without a real home, the only difference is that they have more friends than I do because they fly across the sky, swiftly, exchanging joyous shrieks to each other. They fly between cedar tree and cedar tree. They are small parrots, the parrot family with their curved beaks and rounded heads, their flinty green feathers. They breed quickly and each year I notice that there are more and more of them. Yes, they are immigrants too and I revel in their company. They sing to me of other far-off lands. From my lookout on the ground, I hear some people complain about these birds. They complain that they are taking over, that they are pushing the Spanish birds out of their nests and branches, away from their natural habitat. These same people complain about the human immigrants as well, that we are pushing them out of their jobs and their homes. I hardly think I could be accused of pushing any Spaniard out of his home. My hovel has never belonged to a Spaniard. I don't know who lived in it before the old woman in the dry, dusty road showed it to me and persuaded me to rest there. That was a long, long time ago now. But I am convinced that the previous *owner* of my hovel wouldn't have been a Spaniard.

Of course, there are many other sorts of bird flying around the Madrid sky, but I don't know them all. I have spoken of the ones that I can identify, the magpie, the sparrow, the blackbird and the austral parrot. Yet I shouldn't forget the pigeons, the cumbersome low-fliers, with their brooding cooing, sounding as though they are gargling, gurgling in their throat; plump pale grey birds they are, waddling between crumb and crumb, always hungry, always shitting everywhere, the males always pestering the female birds for sex. All these birds seem to have partners.

Unlike me who has no partner.

The cranes are another feature of Madrid bird life. They are large stork-like birds with glistening white bodies and black feathers on their wings. They are strong, strong fliers and in the autumn and the spring I watch them fly over me in formation, in "V"-formation. There are hundreds and hundreds of them in the group, one group after another, all following on their leader. In the autumn, they fly southwards to spend the winter months in warmer climes. In the spring, they fly northwards to the wetlands in the softer, greener pastures. They seem able to fly for hours, gliding on the air currents, flapping their wings to progress when out of the range of the currents. As they fly, they call to each other. Are they conversing in their urgent guttural tones? Are they happy?

I like to think that they are announcing their arrival to me. I sit with my head back squinting into the bright light of the blue expanse above me and I am mesmerised by the beauty and valour of these courageous birds who emigrate so far, far away from their home in search of warmth or coolness. They herald the autumn. They herald the spring. They are the bearers of unknown tidings. They are a prayer to life, to the good things in life. They belong to a universe – the feathered universe – where life is just and right and good. They lead their lives according to a set of unquestioned rules and they know that it is what they have to do. They have no doubts. They have no choices to make. They are attuned to their animal intuition. They don't complicate their existence as humans do. True, there are a few stragglers who drop behind the "V"-formation. Perhaps the others slow down and hover for them. Is this kindness or something else? They live in communities and community life demands solidarity. They know no loneliness.

Unlike me, lonely and selfish, absorbed by my own small life.

33

Andreea and her Past

Andreea endured her harsh street existence with a certain pride. She was proud of herself for having escaped from the orphanage, for having tricked them into letting her out to run an errand, into believing that she would be faithful to them. She ran fast and far, as far away from that building as she could. She didn't want any of the warders to discover her on the streets. She had very little money and only a small bag of clothing and a couple of crusts of bread that she had stuffed into the shopping bag they had given her. She told me that the first nights out in the open on a park bench were terrible. She would awaken in the morning cold and stiff and drag herself to a tap in the park to wash. I said that she was proud. She brushed her hair, more to raise her morale than to try and look attractive. She was indifferent to people's stares.

It was obvious that she was an orphan, that she had no home to go to, no job to go to. She sat each day on the pavement, in a different spot, and was given a few coins. She lived on a diet of buns and pasties for days on end. She kept away from the soup kitchens for fear of being detected. She watched people with a rapacious eye in an attempt to distinguish who would betray her, who might help her, and her intuition served her well. She was sixteen then, old enough to do a job of work. She didn't care what she did, anything, anything, was preferable than returning to the dreaded orphanage.

She found a menial job in a street market, sweeping up around the stalls, laying out the pieces of fruit on the trestle tables, helping to put up the canvas protection against sun and rain. They didn't allow her to serve, but the ugly old lady whose stall it was gave her a pittance of the day's earnings and two pieces of fruit. She went there, day after day for several weeks until one morning she caught sight of one of the warders from the orphanage snooping around the stall. She rapidly bent over some boxes busying herself with the fruit in them. She swung her hair right over one cheek and then unhurriedly walked away as if involved in a task. She hid herself behind the tradesmen on other stalls, her eyes glued to the orphanage guard, her heart beating fast. She knew that if he saw her she could only make a run for it and he would yell out and other people would catch her. It was a tense few moments, but then, relieved, she saw him buy a bag of fruit without exchanging so much as a word with the vendor, and then he disappeared. Obviously, he was more interested in his fruit than in searching for Andreea.

One evening, as she walked to her park bench, she was followed. He was a young man from the fruit market who had had his eyes on her for several days. As she settled down to sleep she saw his thick, male figure standing high beside her. She knew immediately what he wanted. It wasn't the first time. In the orphanage she had had to put up with the adolescent inmates, half crazed with desire, opening up their fly buttons, rubbing themselves up and down in front of her, pushing her into corners, getting up inside her pants. If she screamed nobody heard, if she swiped out at them they were always stronger and there had been whole weeks in that place when she had become the orphanage whore.

She didn't like those boys, but she quite liked what they did to her, so she let them drool and dribble with their rubbery lips, pushing their rods up inside her, panting like animals. One day, in the corner of a deserted corridor, one of the warders caught her at it. He brutally pulled the culprit off her, kicked him where it hurt and sent him howling. The warder had his own designs. He too was brutal, but he was expert and Andreea realised that the life of a woman could be good if she was made to feel desirable. The warder did it to her whenever he could, protecting her in exchange from the lusty young louts. She didn't like him particularly, she was indifferent to his strong, male caresses, but she was at an age when she needed to assert her sexual prowess and this was one way of satisfying it.

And so she knew what was expected of her, when the man came to her in the park. They did it behind some bushes. As she was buttoning her blouse afterwards, he threw some *lei* on the ground beside her and disappeared quickly. It was more money than the fruit vendor gave her. The next day she decided not to go to the market, she decided to wash herself very well and put on her shortest skirt, push her breasts high under her tight top, she combed her hair for a long time until it was silky and soft and, aware of her charms, she waited that evening on a street corner.

Her days as a prostitute, however, came to an abrupt end. One man told her he could get her out of Romania and take her to Italy where her life would be different, better. She never tired of having sex with him in the back of his van on that journey. He was gentle, he fed her well and he helped her to emigrate in exchange for her sex. He even taught her some Italian, so that you can defend yourself when I leave you in Trieste, he said.

Andreea looked at me surreptitiously, as if asking what I would be prepared to do, would I sell my body to anyone who could take me out of Italy into France?

No, I never wanted it that way. But did I have a choice?

*   *   *

I was nearly hysterical after that journey and the sticky, humid heat of Marseille only added to my frustration. I was incapable of separating sex from love, and love certainly wasn't what I had felt for those men in the van that took us from Trieste. Three of them, at night, sometimes during the day … it was the price I had to pay, Andreea had to pay, for this interminable journey from Trieste to Marseille. Andreea didn't mind, one after another they entered her. She was insatiable. She was relaxed and let them do what they wanted to her. … I was tense, half pushing them away. That made it worse. It was like a battle where every blow hurt, every thrust, every scratching caress. I squealed, I pinched at them, I turned my lips away from their hot, panting waves of breath that almost suffocated me. After it was over, the first one, the second one, the third one, I would push open the van door and limp away into the darkness, broken and hurt and whimpering from self-pity. This wasn't love, it wasn't a job, it wasn't even decent sex. It was violence. Was there no other way I could leave Italy and reach France?

For the first time in my young life I was beginning to realise that I was a used object, that my intrinsic value as a person was under attack. My pride was gradually being undermined. I was beginning to think of myself as valueless. My self-esteem was dangerously toppling. I was becoming more and more vulnerable to life's blows, to the whims and ugly desires of men. And the more I clamped up, the harsher were the men's reactions towards me. The final day and night of the journey were unbearable. Andreea told me that the men were annoyed with me. If you don't do it better, she said, they'll throw you out in the country and you can walk the rest of the way, you don't speak French, you have no francs, what will you do? I was desperate but I controlled myself. If I had had to put up with all this raping for two days, I calculated that I could put up with it for another day. Think about other things while they were at me. These men seemed to be in no hurry to reach their destination. They were enjoying the journey – at least with Andreea.

*   *   *

As I sat alone in a gutter of Marseille, in the filthy port area, I felt defeated. I heard passers-by talking French. I couldn't understand them. Andreea and I had changed our money, the little money we had, and the men had told us to get lost. They even spurned Andreea. And I also spurned her. The moment we changed our money, I knew it was the moment to separate from this woman who seemed to have no other thought in her mind but to go on working as a prostitute. She suggested we work together and live somewhere together near the port, there were lots of sailors in Marseille, she said with a gay laugh. There was money to be made. I gave her a long, penetrating stare and without so much as a word, I turned on my heel and walked quickly away. I could never forgive her for having made me go through the hell of the last couple of days. I never wanted to see her again.

So many times, as I sit ensconced on my Madrid pavement, as I watch the passers-by without seeing them, I ask myself why I embarked on that torrid journey from Trieste to Marseille with those terrible men. Didn't I have any pride then? Was I so utterly innocent? Was I weak without any marrow in my bones, allowing those bastards to do what they did to me. Why didn't I leave them, run away and find my own path towards Marseille? I got not an ounce of pleasure from them. Surely by then I had lost faith in Andreea observing the way she behaved? Didn't I have enough guts to walk out on them all? I paid well and truly for my weakness. I reflected that she might have been the way she was as a consequence of her tragic upbringing in the orphanage, that those sick, crippled minds had influenced her and shown her that women were on this earth to be used by men, not to be loved by men. What I couldn't understand was that she simply seemed to accept that as a fact of life and, worse still, that she even seemed to enjoy having her body mauled by ugly, evil-smelling males.

Marseille, for me, didn't hold the enchantment of Trieste. I felt suffocated by the hot humidity there. I bedded down in a stuffy little room on the fifth floor of a *pension*, the fifth floor without a lift. It was grimy and depressing. I had to share a dripping tap and a hole in the floor for a toilet, the only washing facilities in a bare corridor peopled with a medley of illegal immigrants, mostly from Arab countries and Africa.   All this grovelling around because I was an illegal immigrant, I had no documents, worse still, I had no desire to obtain any documents, no desire to search for a decent job.

What did all that matter to me when I could feel my life falling apart? And where was the will to mend it? I didn't have any will. I was bruised by life, by my mother who had arranged for my baby to be stolen, by my journeying away from Romania in the company of detestable people. Only the woman in Austria had been kind to me and I nostalgically remembered her wide face and generous smile. In this frame of mind, what could Marseille hold for me as a city, as a prospect for a decent future? I have already said that I was beginning to understand the Italian language, but faced now with French, it was like listening to a mass of gargling birds chirping stupidly together as they busied themselves in the streets with their purchases. I felt very much an outsider. And I was conscious of their disdainful looks, as if they were saying: Not another foreigner!

Yet I couldn't return to Italy. The police would end up finding me, even if I went down to Sicily. My photo had been in the paper. Where to look for a job in this hostile French environment? My money wouldn't last forever. The *pension* was too expensive for what it was, far too expensive for the uncomfortable bed, the grubbiness in all the corners of the building. After only a few days, I knew that I had to leave. I knew this place, this country, wasn't right for me. It wasn't even worth trying there. At the same time, I was determined not to depend on unknown people anymore.

Somehow, I would go alone. But where?

Something told me that I should go south, south to the warmth and to people who were more like my people. If I couldn't go back to Italy, I could go down to Spain. I remembered in my school studies learning a little about that country and, for some unspoken reason, I felt an affinity with it. Perhaps it was that both countries knew what it was to survive under a dictator, though oppression of the people knew no bounds in Romania. In Marseille the people were either too well-dressed and snooty, or down and out like me, but arrogant and unfriendly, all of them. At least, so they seemed during those few days I spent there. Yet I know it's true to say that a city is beautiful or ugly depending on whether you are in a good or bad frame of mind and of course Marseille could have been very beautiful if my circumstances had been different. But, in the intense heat, surrounded by aggressive people whose faces looked hostile to me, all I could think about was my own personal tragedy.

My loneliness was exaggerated unbearably. I was on the point of going to the coach station when I realised that I had no passport to cross the border into Spain. I groaned pathetically to myself imagining yet another torrid journey in the company of vile men. My only option was to try to find a lift in a private car. I could thumb a lift if I walked out of Marseille on the main road towards the Spanish frontier. But would anyone accept me in my illegal state? That was doubtful. No decent person could be expected to endanger his own integrity by trying to help an illegal immigrant. It was my fate to travel under cover.

34

Dictators

Of course, Ceausescu was a monster. There was no doubt about that. He made himself exceedingly rich, yet he impoverished his people, his whole nation. And we were all terrified of him, Doctor, or perhaps more terrified of his secret police and of his not-so-secret police, the guards who sniffed in and out of our lives. They were at every street corner. They were on the trains, on the coaches between Timisoara and my village, between Timisoara and Bucharest, knocking on people's doors, wandering up and down roads, everywhere, intimidating us. We used to feel that we had to speak to each other in whispers. They were outside public buildings and banks and cinemas. They supervised our every movement and, had they been cleverer, our every thought and conversation. But they were blunt, obtuse, insensitive idiots, obedient to the whims of the *Conducator* and his sycophants. I don't know whether they were typical examples of what communism does to man. I am sure that there are many like them in the capitalist world – ugly police with guns and truncheons who attack street demonstrators everywhere. I have seen pictures of them in countries outside Romania.

But for the Romanian people, Ceausescu was the problem. He created a State of frightened, cowering citizens and those who were valiant enough to stand up against him were flung into prisons and tortured. It was madness, all that. Then there was his terrible wife, Elena, who had struggled through her university studies, yet even with her mediocre academic ability she rose to positions of power and ended up as vice-Prime Minister of our country, just because her husband was who he was. She was as cruel and ruthless as he was. They ruined Romania between them and for their own benefit.

All these thoughts flashed through my mind as I sat in the back of a truck full of crates of fruit. The driver had seen me waiting around like the lost waif I was outside a coffee bar near the lorries parked there. He must have taken pity on me. He had a pleasant face and his dark eyes gleamed with comprehension and even a certain tenderness and sympathy. At least, that is what I read in them. I forgot the fear I had felt, the hateful experience I had been through with those other men. My desire to leave Marseille was so pressing that I felt I could put my next journey into his hands. He told me to hop onto the back of the lorry and to cover myself with canvas as we crossed the frontier, or at least that is what I understood. I took out the few francs I had and offered some to him, but he refused. Intuitively I trusted him. I could see he was a Spanish family man without any ulterior motive. He would drop me off somewhere near Barcelona he explained and I understood as best I could. *Barthelona* he said, the way the Spaniards pronounce it. I nodded. It was enough. The floor of the lorry was hard, but I was used to that by now. I was much smaller than the crates and there were plenty of canvasses to hide under. I felt a keen sense of anticipation as the lorry jolted along the highway. Was I at long last on my way to something better, to somewhere better?

At least I was further and further away from my homeland. I was so optimistic about the idea of Spain, which had recently escaped its own dictator, that I could no longer imagine returning to Romania with its depressed society, people living on next to nothing with food rationed, with their movements and journeys restricted, with lighting and heating cut in the middle of winter when they were most needed, with the queues of livid faces outside employment offices and shop stalls. Their drunkenness. Many of our villages were routed and spoiled and the inhabitants sent away, their lives ruined, to live in communal agrarian-industrial centres where they were utterly disoriented, most of them incapable of making a success of this new life. There was an air of mistrust everywhere.

The country was poverty-stricken and Ceausescu had moulded us all into the pattern of poverty. We thought poverty, we breathed poverty, we spoke poverty, we smelled poverty, we dreamed poverty because it was all we knew. But Ceausescu and his wife Elena lived in the lap of luxury. At university, I knew that the radio and television programmes were controlled by the State. No-one could say what they thought and if they made even the mildest suggestions, they were tagged as a danger to the State. Petre and I used to talk in whispers about this as we shared our small bed. We were told that communism was the fairest system in the world. Twenty-one years inhaling a system monitored by the *Securitate*.

The *Conducator* really had no respect for life. He asked his people to save their newly-born babies for his State, and then he took their babies away and put them inside inhumane residences, beside the ill and insane, to grow up under-nourished, without love and proper care, to be converted into savage, broken, embittered adults trailing their fear and remorse and hatred through the land, changing Simona's wholesome, happy Romania, into a vast prison of crippled souls. No, Ceausescu had no respect for human life and no respect for animal life.

I knew that Spain, the country I was going to, had a monarchy and I knew that the Spanish monarch had on occasions been the guest of our dictator. Together they hunted in the wild Transylvanian slopes and valleys. They hunted big game. They hunted deer, eagles – kingly birds like themselves, yet nobler – foxes, wild boar, wolves, lynxes and bears. Particularly bears. Ceausescu ensured that his forests and mountain slopes teemed with a large, healthy bear population. He needed them to practise his prowess at killing, at shooting them down. He was an obsessive, maniacal killer of these magnificent flat-pawed, pigeon-toed, shaggy-haired beasts. So that there would be more of them for him to kill, his own finger on the trigger of his own gun, he made it illegal for any of his citizens to hunt them down. Anyone found hunting them was fined. Thus, there were more for him, to satisfy his crazed desire for beautiful bear skins. His men would hang lumps of raw meat high in the branches making the bears easy prey as they reached up on their hind legs to satisfy their appetites.

I think that was a cowardly way to shoot them. Perhaps he was more interested in possessing their skins than in the excitement of the shoot. Ceausescu was a mad man, a cruel man. And I suppose that he invited his kingly friends and regal acquaintances so that they could admire Romania's population of wild animals, so that they could quell their royal desire to rule over all things on this earth, men and animals. I hate people who hunt for pleasure and excitement. Hunting should only be for sustenance. Yet what could one expect of a villainous character like Ceausescu? If he could do what he did with his nation's children, it is logical that he had no qualms about killing our beautiful animals. Yes, I know that the Spanish King was one of his guests.

*   *   *

The lorry braked suddenly causing me to bang my forehead against one of the crates. I stifled a squeal, stiffened and automatically hid in a corner under the canvasses, quite invisible to any rapid glances from border police. It would be a different story if they were to ask the driver to unload his crates of fruit. ... I froze, my heart beating, thumping loudly in my breast, yet only in my breast. Please God, if You exist ... I whispered to myself under the canvas with its pungent smell of melons and oranges. It could be worse I remembered, comparing the pleasant smell of fruit to the smell of oilskins and unwashed males on my first journey from Bucharest. I heard voices, *España! Vale!, ¿Sólo fruta? Alé, buen viaje!* terse phrases uttered in jarring tones, but which I could more or less understand.

The lorry accelerated and I heard the driver singing a forceful, melodious tune. He relaxed and banged his strong hand against the back of the driver's compartment. Half an hour later, he stopped and jumped out. *Venga!* he motioned to me to jump down and pointed to the pine woods where I could relieve myself behind some bushes. When I returned to the van he was smiling. He pointed to the expanse of ocean glinting under the strong sunlight and to the road: *España, España bonita, bella!* He smiled and laughed, patting me on the shoulder. *Dos horas más ... Barthelona*, he said. I managed a smile and laugh as well. Then he broke a piece of his bread and cheese and offered it to me, pressing the meagre fare into my hands, a*gua … agua,* he pointed to a crystal-clear stream at the edge of the woods and I drank freely from my cupped hand. *Vamos, vamos,* he urged pointing at his watch.

*   *   *

I was too young then to make comparisons between communism and capitalism. Now, as I sit on the pavement thinking and dreaming and remembering, I realise that communism is the fairer of the two systems. It tries to help the under-dog, whereas capitalism crushes him. In theory, communism is preferable, although not the way it was run by Ceausescu and his men. They took hold of an idea, of the idea of a more equal world, but they smashed it to smithereens. Instead of raising the poor and miserable to even a medium level, they smashed the ordinary man down to grovel to an over-powerful State. They made us all equal, but equally poor. That was the mistake. Their theory was good. Marx was right, yet none of his followers knew how to put his theories into practice, or they preferred not to do so, they preferred to enrich themselves at the expense of their citizens. But now all that has crumbled and capitalism has taken over the world, bearing abreast the flag of freedom, yet it pushes us all into a melting pot of envy and harsh competition … and those of us who are weaker,

weaker like me,

get pushed down to the bottom of the pot and find it impossible to scramble up out of the whirling frenzy of money and competition.

All I can do is to sit outside a bank, never to go inside it. The capitalists lie as well. They promise us many good things, yet only the stronger characters survive. The rest jog along in a massive wheel of senseless routine, desperately trying to make money to buy their houses, their cars, their luxury clothing, their meals in restaurants, to buy what society tells them to buy. I think that all they do is to create obligations and useless necessities for themselves. That way they imagine that they are happy. True it is, that the inhabitants of capitalist nations are free to move around, to leave their country, to return without questions being asked. They consider themselves free. They have the liberty to speak out and criticise their politicians, to express their disagreement.

That was impossible for us in Romania. Yet freedom is a complicated question. We are only free to the point where we do not curtail the freedom of another person. No-one is entirely free. Still, let's not get involved in discussion on philosophical ideas about freedom. I refer in the main to normal freedom in a normal society where the police take second place in the background, there only to curb crime and disturbance, not to be constantly spying on the citizens. Surely these hovels in the street where I live are proof that capitalism has its flaws. Communism is hateful, but so is capitalism. One system or another, Doctor, it all boils down to what man makes of it. And the same goes for religion too. Man has made a mess of the religious messages and he has used religious dogma as an excuse to control, to plunder, to assassinate, to crucify, to mould people into his own way. Religion, as I see it, is a personal sensation, a belief to help you over the rough moments. The trouble is when you don't believe, then it doesn't help you at all. So often I wished that I could believe like Simona had.

*   *   *

I live in a hovel, Doctor. Or perhaps I should say I lived there, as it may even now be occupied by another in my absence. ... I would use some old blankets I found on a rubbish heap to keep the cold out of my hovel. They cover the slits in the wooden door, the holes in the crumbling bits of cement and the cracks where the plastic sheeting has split. The slits and the holes and the cracks are welcome in the summer because the night air penetrates my room and freshens it. But the winter in Madrid brings a harsh cold. So I am grateful for those blankets. One of them has a few moth-holes and another is frayed at the edges, but they are better than nothing. I have no electricity for heating. At night, I use the old-fashioned hot-water bottle which I put between the bed clothes wrapped in my pyjamas. If the little cat comes at night, as she normally does, she sleeps in the crook of my knees and I am grateful, too, for her animal warmth, as indeed she is grateful for my human warmth. I reward her in the mornings with a tin bowl of milk.

197

I always try to eat and drink something hot at night to stave off the hunger cramps and to warm the blood in my body. It is a trial to get my limbs to work in the winter months now I am older. I notice that my legs and arms are stiff when I get out of bed, my back aches, my fingers are swollen and deformed from arthritis, my ankles don't move freely. In short, life is an effort in the cold and in the dusty street where I live, all the inhabitants feel the winter. Some of them light fires, but I am scared that the flames could catch onto the blankets and the wooden boxes that I use for a chair and table. I prefer to eat my supper and breakfast shivering beneath a thick jumper and the blanket from my bed than to run the risk of my hovel going up in flames. I remember feeling cold in Timisoara also, a bitter, searing cold, and I remember the thick snowfalls in my village, but I was younger then and I had the company of Simona, of my family, I lived in a family house where we used to burn wood in the hearth and warm ourselves near the kitchen stove.

Here, I am alone with no-one to warm me with human laughter or smiles.

The cold on the streets in Madrid is far worse than I could ever have imagined. I told you that I had always thought of Spain as being a hot country. That is true, in part, but not all the year round and at least two or three months in Madrid, the freezing winds blow off the nearby mountains, sometimes bringing with them snow flurries or hail storms or icicles and frost. I watch the women hurrying past me on the pavement, many of them protected with luxury fur coats, others with thick woollen scarves wound around their necks, covering their chins and mouths, their faces grimacing against the cold blasts. I sit with a thick beret on my head and a scarf that I pull down over my ears and wrap around my chin and neck. I also wear two pairs of knitted leggings. I put some old boots on my feet. They are lined with sheep's wool and they keep me warm until the cold penetrates them to reach my toes.

As I move so little, the cold attacks me, invading my body, numbing my limbs and freezing my soul. I wear two thick jumpers, a lined vest and a long, woollen skirt almost down to my ankles. And I wear mittens on my hands. All this clothing has been left here for me, sometimes when I am here a woman places a bag of stuff beside me with a reticent smile and bids me the time of day, sometimes I find it on arriving at my spot. I make use of it all and I am grateful to whoever has been kind enough to leave it for me. So you see, not everyone is mean and unkind in this world. There are people, passers-by, who know me now. That is why I always come to the same place every day. People are familiar with my begging hump of a body. Some, most of them, ignore me, but there are others who are kind.

*   *   *

I remember it was December when they killed Ceausescu and his wife, the twenty-fifth of December, Christmas Day. I remember that I was walking past a bar and I saw their crimped faces on a television screen. I stopped and stared. They were like a pair of animals hunted down, like the bears and game that the *Conducator* had hunted all his life, cornered and shot, like the thousands and thousands of Romanians he had tormented and finally killed. Now it was his turn and his wife, Elena's, turn. There they were, sitting at a bare table with a tribunal of military men firing questions at them. I couldn't understand because I couldn't hear the Romanian and I couldn't understand the Spanish interpretation of their words. I realised from the way they spoke and gesticulated that they were protesting. Those men were accusing them.

From snatches of the television I could just make out that they held them responsible for genocide, for having accumulated excessive wealth for themselves, for having pauperised the country and the inhabitants of Romania. Deafened by the passing cars, I could just about hear that Ceausescu retaliated that he didn't recognise this National Salvation Front, that he was only responsible to the Parliament of Romania. He said that the accusations of the Tribunal were false. He didn't accept that he had been deposed as President of the country. That, I could hear. He kept on repeating that he was President. Elena chipped in from time to time in her birdlike voice. There seemed to be no public at the hearing. It had been quickly arranged. The man had to be got rid of. He had been a danger to his

199

people and to have imprisoned him and had him awaiting a proper trial would only have complicated the transition in Romania.

I was proud to know that the rebellion had begun in Timisoara, my old university town, near my home. The Tribunal told him that his entire fortune would be confiscated and that they were condemning him and his wife to death. I stiffened. I watched the men approach the Ceausescu couple with ropes. Elena protested with her nervous, bird-like movements and remonstrance: How can you young men tie me up? The next thing I saw was that they were lying dead, shot down by a firing squad against a wall in a courtyard. Two soldiers threw a tarpaulin over each of the bodies after a doctor had verified their death. I felt a subversive sensation of joy. I looked around me, but no-one on the Spanish street showed any interest. I looked inside the bar. There were men at tables playing cards, others standing at the bar engrossed in conversation. Only a table of four women displayed interest in what they had seen on the television and I could see from their gestures and the expression on their faces that they were at once shocked and relieved. I too was shocked and relieved. That night, back in my hovel,

I remember thinking that perhaps I could return to Romania.

35

Barcelona and Some Regrets

It was Roxana, my mother, who put an end to any thought of my returning to Romania. Not Roxana directly, but my recollection of her and of my relationship with her. When Tatiana was born I recalled that she, my daughter, was everything to me, absolutely everything. How could Roxana have been so bitter towards her own daughter? What had I done? It wasn't only my unwanted pregnancy that had turned her against me. I remember even before that, we only put up with each other. Any sentiment or affection we displayed the one for the other was false, superficial. How could a mother and daughter live like that?

I have said that she was embittered because her life fell apart when Mihaita, my father, left her. Yet I don't think that even his leaving was the reason for her sour sarcasm. Had my pregnancy gone against her stringent view of life? She was a harsh battler. She hit out at life giving blows all around her. Yet she wasn't religious. She used to laugh at Simona for bending on her knees in church and beside her bed and for talking about God's bounty. She scorned all that. Really, I suppose, she was against all of us and against the neighbours in the village. She had a chip on her shoulder. Life grated against her and thus she dealt her blows to all and sundry. That freedom with the palms of her hands was, I suppose, a way of relieving the inner frustration she felt. I have often reflected on the fact that she should never have had children. She was a woman cut out for her own self alone, her own needs. Utterly selfish. She had borne us into the world, but she wanted us to look after ourselves.

Viorica, I have said, seemed to tolerate her better than I did. My sister tolerated everything behind her opaque stare. I only know that, over the years, during my adolescence, Roxana's grudge against me grew. I was relieved to go off to university in Timisoara. Of course, I never really recognized any of these doubts about us then. It didn't occur to me to do so. Before she committed the crime of selling Tatiana, I merely accepted her with her peculiar personality. She was my mother, unquestionably my mother. That was all. It only came to a head when she got rid of my baby. That was the most evil action she could have taken against me, and it was a premeditated action. There was nothing spontaneous about what she did. She is a criminal and if I were to return to Romania, I would hound her down and have her sent to gaol. This is why I can never go back, anyway I no longer have the will to do anything which requires strength of purpose, let alone forcing imprisonment on my mother.

I am a broken piece of humanity.

Why, oh why? Was she jealous of me with my baby girl? But she herself had had two baby girls. No, it can't have been that. Was she envious because I had a better mind? Was that why she tried to push me down, make me grovel around the dirt in her house, sweeping it up instead of allowing me time to study and do something worthwhile with my life? She took advantage of my weaker personality. … She hated me.

Ah! Now I remember, Doctor, that she had her reasons for hating me. Because I was the fruit of one fleeting night in a barn. There was a neighbour in our village, and I learned that he had seduced Roxana. I had forgotten about this up until now. It came out one day in a conversation I had had with the man's wife. Or ex-wife. She had divorced him long ago. She told me that he had been with a lot of the village women. He used to disappear at night from his bed beside her and meet up in the barn with whoever would have him. And my own mother had him, she said surreptitiously - on one night, on two nights, who knows? Roxana herself never spoke of that, but she knew when I was born that Mihaita was not my father. She knew intuitively and probably from her own silent calculations that I was the fruit of another seed. And she hated me for it. I was the consequence of her guilty action, her hidden night of passion, her frustration because she no longer loved Mihaita and had turned briefly to another for consolation. Yes, although it mattered not to me, this must have been why she had to get rid of Tatiana, because, for her, the child was history repeating itself. She could never have supported the idea of another fatherless child in the family. She had arranged Tatiana's adoption to spite me.

*   *   *

And as I sit here on this concrete slab of pavement in Madrid, I tell myself, over and over I tell myself, that it is pointless to ruminate over my pathetic past.

So why do I do this? I do this because I have no future. I am drained of the desire to improve, to search, to love, to befriend... And meanwhile the winter passes, each cold day upon another cold day, shattering my weakened body with cold. What is the point of spring coming, I thought, if the freezing blasts of winter return. I fear that each winter takes years off my life.

*   *   *

In Barcelona, the winters weren't as harsh. There were strong winds blowing in from the sea, there were thick grey clouds mounting up one upon another, whirling, swirling in the sky, and there were days of thick drizzle, and of thin drizzle, but when the sun came out, the day became warmer, even in winter. In Madrid, the temperature goes right down to zero and below. In Barcelona, never. Yet the dampness of that city, both in winter and in summer – even more unbearable in the summer months – depressed me. I found it suffocating. I found it hard to breath. It reminded me of the few hours I had spent in Marseille. Stifling with sweat!

I was a year in Barcelona, more or less, after the kind man dropped me off in a central street of the city. I moved away from the impressive buildings, the cathedral, the wide tree-lined Ramblas with their attractive flats and offices. I felt out of place amongst the rushing pace of well-dressed humanity, amongst people who seemed as though they had no time for anyone but themselves, busy, busy, always busy. I felt that there was a certain antagonism in those

203

people. I felt like an intruder. I moved away from the centre, making my way down towards the port, towards the ocean whose breeze caressed the skin on my face.

I found a nook on a beach between some shiny black rocks at Barceloneta, and this nook I made my home for the first two or three days in Barcelona. I preferred to be there rather than to immerse myself in the dirty streets of the red light district frequented as they were by sailors and down-and-outs. I sat on a boulevard during the daytime, putting my hand out almost mechanically waiting for someone to put something into it. One woman gave me a thick bread roll with a strong salami sausage filling. It tasted good and I washed it down with water from a nearby street tap. One man put a few small coins in my hand to add to the pesetas that the kind lorry driver had given me in exchange for my French francs. Had he cheated me, I don't think so? Looking at his eyes, I thought that he had probably given me more than my francs were worth. I don't know. It doesn't matter. Another woman placed more coins in my hand and when I went to buy a sandwich to take to my nook on the beach for the night, I realised that I had more than enough money.

I sat eating the food and watching the waves beat ceaselessly, one after another, onto the sand. I put my bare feet in the water and was fascinated by the surging froth that sucked at them. If it had been warmer I would have doused my whole body in that water, but night was falling and I would never have been able to dry myself. I returned to my nook between the rocks and stood for long minutes listening to the water, to the waves coming, going, coming, going, swishing their liquid against the sand and the rocks. As night fell, I realised that I was quite alone on the small beach, secluded, alone with the water and the wind, the rocks and the sand and I felt happy for this.

When I awoke the next morning, sandy grit stuck to my tousled hair and the sea's salt dried to my ankles, when I awoke I noticed that the waves had come almost to my doorstep. Now they were receding but there was a line where the sand was damp very close to where I had been sleeping. How stupid of me, I thought. The next night I would have to move further away from the water, up the beach towards the boulevard. I knew that the sea with its capricious yet rhythmic tides could be dangerous. Yet I was happy there in my beach hideout. Nobody molested me, I didn't feel lonely because the sea spoke to me with its restless groans and sighs. I would surely have stayed longer living that way, but the next morning I awoke soaked to the skin, not with sea water, but with rainwater. The rains had come to stay, or so it seemed. The sea heaved itself in vast troughs and massive walls of greyness with white capped waves bashing against the land and the rocks. It was grey and full, a seething mass of liquid fury and it frightened me. Its groans and sighs had turned into an intimidating roar as though at any moment it might engulf me and all the buildings on the boulevard. I shivered with fear and cold. I could have dried myself just by walking in the air had it been windy and fresh, but the rain fell in sheaths around me, whipping against my legs and my face. I had to find protection.

Because I had so little money, because I had no change of clothes, because I couldn't speak Spanish, in short, because I looked a mess, I had no option but to take shelter in yet another miserable hostel in the back streets of this immense city.

I suppose that it was Barcelona where I learnt to beg, to beg seriously, even to subconsciously decide that begging would be my future.

I could sense that my spirit was crumbling. Each day I was feeling weaker with what life threw back at me. I knew I could no longer entertain the idea of selling my physical wares. My body was my own and in the future, I would only give it to the man I wanted to, not to anyone in exchange for a few coins. I had had enough of that abuse during the journey from Trieste to Marseille. Because I had no papers I was too scared to go to the police and ask for permission to stay in Spain, to work my way up little by little, learn the language, search for some sort of menial job, instead of scrounging around for people's left-overs. Yes, left-overs, for apart from begging, I also learnt to search inside the rubbish bins.

In the hostel I had chosen, no questions were asked. As in Trieste and in Marseille, it was a depressing, damp building with paint peeling off the doors, plaster off the outer wall, broken panes of glass in the windows. The neon light outside blinked the word *Hostal* in a wishy-washy green; it blinked day and night and I had to use my clothes to cover the window at night to blot out the blinking green light. As you will imagine, Doctor, there were no curtains in the room. The floor-boards were splintering in parts and dirty with ugly spots – remnants of previous occupants – and dust. The bed creaked every time I moved. I laughed silently to myself imagining the noise it would make under two active bodies! On occasions, I could hear the couple at it in the next room and I could hear their somnolent sighs and groans, their arguments, although I couldn't determine what they were saying but I knew they were arguing from the tone of their voices.

People didn't stay long in the place and after the young couple there came a single man. He used to sing and hum to himself in the evenings, deep resonant tones weighty with rounded sounds and once I poked my head out of the window to see more of the street and came face to face with a wide black visage framed in tight curls, the widest nose and the thickest lips imaginable. This negro was also staring out into the street. His was the harmonious voice that I used to hear. I withdrew quickly, fearing any closer contact.

The sheets had holes in them, they were sewn in part, badly sewn with lumpy seams and the only blanket on the bed was spare. To keep warm in the damp Barcelona nights, I used to wrap it tightly round me twice. The street below was extremely narrow and across the road I could see the inhabitants of the flats in their lighted windows. Concealed by the darkness in my room, I used to watch them kissing or quarrelling, men and women with each other, some hitting out at each other, some violently throwing objects around the room, some women screaming and crying, others sitting despondently staring at the flickering images on television. ... Had I had a television set I might have felt less lonely, but the few coins I earned each day simply weren't enough for luxuries like that.

At night, that street came alive. I used to see the prostitutes luring clients down on the corner. I felt sorry for them because, from a cluster of five girls, I could see only one who appeared to enjoy her job. The other four were bored, strained, hurt by life, nervous, I could see that from my second-floor room. I watched the men approach them, some surreptitiously, peering around as if scared to be seen, others taking control of the prostitute immediately as if she were their private property. Sometimes the men would stand half-hidden in a doorway exciting themselves as they watched the girls from a distance, too poor or too shy to broach them. The street was also the nocturnal playground for youngsters in rowdy hordes, on motorbikes with tarty girls, or engaged in homosexual embraces with another in the group. All this went on night after night after night. I considered that it was really just as good as any television programme! But it was hard to sleep, particularly hard to sleep during the stuffy summer nights, but also hard in the damp cold of winter. In the morning, the street fell silent, as if sleeping. The small shops and coffee bars didn't open until quite late.

I put up with Barcelona for over a year, I think. Yes, it must have been over a year because I had arrived in the autumn, I stayed through the winter, the spring, the summer, the following autumn and winter and left in late spring. I was only young, I suppose in my mid to late twenties, but already I was beginning to notice rheumatic pain in my back and my fingers and I knew that that was the dampness. It was the heavy moisture of the coastal city that pushed me towards the dry interior, towards Madrid, which has been my home ever since.

*   *   *

In the Madrid winter, many nights are cold and frosty and clear. The sky is so clear that, when I reach my hovel, I take a last look upwards before going inside to get warm. The stars glisten and twinkle at me from their home on high, set like a myriad of jewels and gems in a dark velvet sky. They gleam so brightly and cleanly on these crisp nights. I remember the stars in my Romanian village and I remember missing them when I went to Timisoara. They are never as visible in the sky over a big city because of the reflection of all the lights from the buildings. It is in the country areas with small villages or empty pathways that they can be better seen. Nevertheless, on the outskirts of Madrid, they can be seen and enjoyed.

On the summer nights too, I would sit outside my hut, my head turned upwards towards the heavens, staring at the stars. In winter, it's impossible to spend so much time outside because of the cold, but I love the clarity in the immense dark dome above me, even though my body is freezing! I find a strange sort of company in the stars, in these heavenly bodies. Not that I believe that there is anyone up there looking down on me. It isn't that. It is merely that they are proof of more life in the universe, silent life, distant and beautiful. There is a sense, a structural sense in their existence, a geometry, a pattern and this appeals to me. It makes me think that, although often hard to believe, there is a true destiny in this world of unhappy souls.

When I was at school and later on at university I learned that the inhabitants of under-developed countries lived far worse than we did in Romania. I have told you that we lived badly, cold from lack of heating, under-nourished, corseted within a strict diagram of senseless rules established to the glory and satisfaction of a megalomaniac. But when I saw photographs of the millions of disinherited in India, the millions of hungry refugees in Africa, the millions of under-nourished infants in those vast over-populated lands, all of them subsisting in putrid alleyways or blistering deserts, where infection ran free, gouging holes in their health and their lives, stealing their babies and debilitating the parents and old people, when I saw all that tragedy before my eyes, I was aghast. When I learned that most of the women in those areas of the world lived under the stringent rule of their men, that most of the young girls underwent ablation to stifle their sexual pleasure, to supposedly render them pure for marriage, that the women's role in society was a sub-role, a role of phantasmal presence only, smothered as they were in some countries from head to toe beneath their robes, not permitted to walk the streets uncovered, to emerge from their homes without the company of a male and when I learned about all this and that many of those people prayed five times a day, I wondered how any religion could allow more than half the society to go unnoticed.

There were countries where female babies were done away with at birth, where only the male children were pampered and appreciated.

All this I thought about, in particular about the outcasts in India, the *untouchables, pariahs, dalits* they are called, people born into the lowest of low castes not allowed to struggle up and improve, even mingle with those of a higher caste.

There were days when I felt like an untouchable in Madrid. Yes, a pariah, an outcast.

Many of those societies were capitalist societies, some were communist, but I realised that the people's lives were ruled by social morals and it didn't matter what political colour they were.

I think I have made it clear why I never returned to university. There is no point in insisting on that. It is one of my life's failures, amongst so many others. I never had the strength of purpose, the will, to mend myself, my intellect, to gather up my cudgels as it were, and re-organise myself on a more fruitful path. All my aspirations to study literature, to become a writer, fell by the wayside, they disintegrated into the muck around me, into the grime on my body, into the uselessness of everything, into my negative contacts with the neighbours, with people in general, into my idleness, my indifference to life and, yes too, into my sadness, my utter inability to recuperate a sense of purpose, a feeling of love and the desire to live. What was the point of a university degree in this quagmire of unhappiness?

And, of course, nothing, nothing could improve for me in this foreign land, in Spain, if I did nothing about making myself legal. I have spent my whole life here feeling scared, scared of the police, scared of being sent back to Romania, scared of trying to learn the language – although I must say that I have picked up quite a lot by ear, by listening to people chatting in the street, repeating the same expressions over and over. I have been scared also of declaring myself even as a human being with the natural rights that should go with that. I am scared of officials, of going to bureaucratic offices where I would be eyed scathingly up and down or merely shunned. How would I express myself to any official? How could I ask for help? I would be sent immediately to the police. And I am scared of talking to the neighbours in my street. I am scared that they might denounce me as an illegal immigrant. I fear entering their lives. They too live on the edge of society. They come and go.

Almost every month or so they change; from gypsy women to drug addicts to drunkards to prostitutes to louts to men who frighten me just to look at them. They hold nothing for me.   Really, I have forgotten about the university at Timisoara now. It is simply no longer a part of my life. Another chapter. I dropped it by the wayside, perhaps on my way across to Trieste, down to Barcelona, across to Madrid. I don't know. I can't remember. All I know is that my life would have taken another turn if I had finished my degree. I blame myself. Of course, I blame myself first and foremost. But I also blame the society that has pushed me out to its fringe. Perhaps above all, I blame Roxana, my mother. She turned me away from the university on purpose to satisfy that infirm strain within her.

I wish I could write about pleasant people. I would have done so had it been my lot to encounter them along my life's path, but as I have spent my days on the edge of decent society I can only talk about those who have intervened in my existence, the few who have blotted my days with their scum, their misery, their depression, their petty crime, their alcoholic hazes, their drug addiction. I refuse to admit that I am one of them. True, I live beside them, but they aren't like me. I am not like them. It is my economic condition, my paltry income, those few coins a day that I earn sitting on the pavement, that has relegated me to this pathetic state,

to the pathetic being that I am.

Perhaps the only thing I can be grateful for at this stage in my life is that I have never been controlled by any mafia. I am free. No-one controls me, no-one tells me when and where and how I should beg, no-one forces me to live in dreadful conditions with groups of other miserable souls, no-one exploits me, no-one takes the few coins I earn each day away from me. In short, no-one dictates to me the way Ceausescu dictated to his citizens. No-one is cruel to me. I know that the beggars and prostitutes who work in the clutches of mafias are responsible to them all their lives. They can never run away. If they try, they are followed, re-captured, kidnapped, perhaps even shot. They live in a perpetual state of fear and violence. No, for that I am lucky. I consider myself fortunate in my solitude, however much it weighs on me at times.

36

Arrival in Madrid

The life on the streets of Madrid goes on. It mills around me, indifferent to my story, to my unhappiness. There are days when I tire of sitting, begging, when I heave myself to my feet, pick up my few belongings that I stuff inside a plastic bag, and I begin to walk. To walk along, anywhere, in any direction. At first my limbs are stiff, unoiled, they seem to grate against the organs of my body as I stumble along the path in the shoes that are a size too big for me. Then I unfold and I realise that the mere action of walking helps me to loosen up, to feel that my ungainly body is lighter. Walking also helps to warm me when the autumn days are crude with cold. I walk along the pavement trying to avoid the other pedestrians who march quickly, purposefully, as though their lives depended on their rapid, jerky movements. I tend to avoid their eyes – or they avoid mine, even if I dare to stare directly at them. They make me feel inferior, an uncomfortable embarrassment on the edge of society.

Look at my clothes, all second-hand stuff, my stockings wrinkle around my ankles, my skirts are too long, my jumpers and blouses are too tight or too baggy or darned and sewn quaveringly at the seams and they simply don't suit me. If I had money, I would never buy jumpers like the ones I wear. My coat is too big, but the long sleeves keep my hands warm and even the material that flaps round my legs is warming. I don't have a handbag. I don't need a handbag. I keep any money I am given from my begging in a small red purse inside my plastic bag, hidden inside the folds of a scarf and the only bank notes that I bring with me, I keep tight inside a small cotton bag that I attach to my brassiere, the way I always have done since I left Romania so long ago. I remember how I offered a few *lei* to the Austrian woman who drove me to Trieste and had to take them out of my underwear. I prefer to keep my scant savings on me all the time because I fear their being stolen if I were to leave them in my hovel.

How did I find that hovel? When I first arrived at Madrid with a lorry driver who had picked me up on the road where I was hitch-hiking, as we approached the outskirts of the city, he pulled up his lorry and signalled to me to get out. He mumbled something about: You foreigners all live in those huts on the roadside. I jumped down from the passenger seat and stared imploringly at his impassive face. He was impenetrable and unfriendly, even though he had driven me a couple of hundred kilometres. I could see his unshaven chin jutting out over his hairy chest, jogging along, jolting along all those kilometres, his strong arms smothered in black hairs skilfully controlling the wheel of the vehicle. I had stared at him during the journey for long moments out of the corner of my eye, wondering, if he was so silent and unfriendly, why he had bothered to pick me up at all. He just waved his arm at me and pointed at the hovels behind some dried bushes and jammed his foot onto the accelerator as if to say that he wasn't going to put up with me wasting any more of his day. Or maybe he was embarrassed.

His lorry disappeared in a haze of exhaust and dry gravel. Cars lashed past me on the motorway in fierce gusts of noise and virulence. I felt small, so small there on the side of the road. And vulnerable. I recall that the afternoon was dying away, it was still very hot but the horizon was darkening, a purple heavy sinister hue against the massive scarlet sinking sun, and so I thought that the best thing would be to approach the row of hovels and see if I could find help. By now, I was used to dealing with whatever situation presented itself to me. Remember, I had found my way to Madrid from Bucharest, with many stops and starts. Forgive me, Doctor, you will remember, I have already spoken about all that.

The hovel where I finally went was the first one on the right-hand side of that gravel road. I walked all along the road peering from a distance into people's doorways. There were children, scantily dressed, barefooted and some of them even naked, children screaming, playing with each other, fighting with each other, fumbling around in their mothers' skirts, their mothers cooking over small camping gas stoves, frying in dirty frying pans; the smell of sardines wafted towards me and I realised how hungry I was, but I could see no shops in the road to purchase any supper. The women laughed, screeched out to their neighbours, to their children. At that hour, there were few men around, just a couple of drunkards lolling stupidly against the tin walls of a hovel warmed by the daytime sun. They lurched around precariously, they even tried to reach out at me as I passed, but they were too befuddled to get their limbs into any sort of coherent movement. Their lurches were accompanied by ludicrous noises from their mouths - burps, slurred utterances.

It seemed at a first glance that all the hovels were occupied. In one, I could see a couple of prostitutes readying themselves for their night activity, the tightest of skirts with the hem right at the top of their thighs, their buttocks and leg muscles crudely blatant, the skimpiest of tops over copious breasts which flowered in two enormous protuberances just below their chests, sensuous vividly painted lips, eye lashes heavy with mascara, a lion's mane of jet black hair falling suggestively around their bare shoulders, a strong pungent whiff of cheap perfume floated towards my nostrils. Their feet were clad in long, white boots with silver trimmings. They were putting the final touches to their wares, to the bodies they would sell that evening to any male needing to empty his vital sap urgently. For some reason these girls reminded me of Radu and the way he had taken me violently and sensually, that fucking for fucking's sake, and the sap within my own loins stirred vigorously.

But no, I was tired, exhausted, and I had no intention of joining up with prostitutes, no desire to sell my body. I had always had other ideas about sex, ideas that didn't fit in with purely physical sex. Besides, the thought of doing it with any man at all who might have a grimy penis, a smelly arse, filthy fingers, grubby nails, dirty hair and evil-smelling breath, turned my stomach over. I would have to find another sort of work. I even preferred the idea of cleaning than of having sex with any lout or drunkard off the street.   My experience in that direction hadn't been the best.

I laboured on along that gravel road, kicking up dust and feeling lonelier and lonelier, on the edge of those people's lives. Anyway, I couldn't understand what they were saying to each other, that I could only guess, calling their children to supper, complaining, laughing about nothing, probably about their men. They were all noisy and I felt very quiet, withdrawn inside myself. Fatigue was beleaguering my step, I walked more and more slowly. I felt tears of depression and exhaustion pricking at my eyes. What could I do? Where could I sleep? There seemed to be no place for me here, and away from the hovels there was only the motorway and burnt, hostile, parched land - the crusty surrounds of the Spanish capital.

I sat down on the side of the road in desperation, as I had done so long ago on the pavement in Bucharest and, just as that unpleasant couple had picked me up helping me to take the next step in my life, an old woman with a kind, gypsy-like face, bent over me. Her voice was rasping and croaky and when she realised that I couldn't understand a word she said, she gestured to a hovel, she put both her hands to one cheek and closed her eyes, her head on one side, in an attitude of sleeping, she pointed her finger at me, she beckoned me to follow her. I did so. She made me understand that the unwelcoming room with its gash in the wall for a window was free for me to take possession of it. She laughed and poked me again and again put her hands to her cheek making little snores through her nose, bidding me to sleep there. I smiled wanly at her, put my bag down on the earthen floor and flopped into a corner, too tired even to get my bearings. She disappeared as suddenly as she had come upon me, out into the night, a ragged, dishevelled, ungainly silhouette, waving her arm with a cackle of laughter. When I awoke on the hard floor the next morning, I saw that someone, probably the old woman, had put some bread and cheese on the floor beside me. I hungrily ate my breakfast.

That was the start of my life in Madrid, perhaps twenty years ago now, yet that hovel is still my life today. You will realise, Doctor, that in all this time I have felt no hope, no desire, to better my lot, to rouse myself up and out of this senseless routine that I have imposed on myself.

You see, I am dead inside myself.

37

Dreams

And yet, I am haunted in my dreams. I am always running away, running fast, breathless down long, dark passageways, through a medley of dirty, narrow streets, running out of breath, with two figures chasing me. One is a man. He is tall and he seems to grow taller as he runs after me, his long limbs waving threateningly at me, his large feet tripping occasionally over obstacles, the obstacles that I have jumped over or avoided, puddles of putrid water, holes in the pavement, rubbish bins, dog shit. He takes enormous strides with his long legs that bend like jelly. He is flexible and rubbery in his sagging grey suit and he comes, comes at me, following me relentlessly. I look back to see him gaining ground on me and I run into a telegraph pole hitting my head. My head spins round and around in circles and blood flies from my nose. A great big lump pushes out of my forehead, red like a beacon, swelling out of all proportion. Don't stop running Mara! Never stop running, if you do, they will catch you, Ceausescu will catch you. He has arisen from his grave in Romania. He has run all the way down to Spain to catch you, to fling you into prison, because you have stolen Tatiana from one of his orphanages.

I am holding a small, warm parcel in my arms as I run. The parcel is Tatiana, my baby daughter. She wriggles in my arms, her little hands lunge out towards the world around her, the world that is racing past her, tall buildings, doorways, shops, hovels, always hovels in a long dusty road, she cries out: No, no, no! to the tall man on our heels. He is getting closer and closer. He cries out: Thief! Thief, Tatiana is my child, my child, not yours. You had her for me, for me! His voice resounds, echoing along the passageways, reverberating against the doors and the walls of the ugly buildings. I am sweating with fear and exhaustion; my legs are trembling as I run. Suddenly I come to a wide lake and I jump. As I jump, I grow a pair of wings and fly with my baby parcel up and over the water to freedom.

As I land on the other side of the lake I see Roxana, she was the other person running after me, shrieking at me for her money, for the money I stole from her bedside table so long ago. She didn't want my baby, she wanted her money. She was an old hag in my dream with long, greying locks that fell menacingly around her shrivelled face. She was smaller than I remember, withered like Simona, when Simona was ill before she lay down to die. She is poking an ugly finger at me, at my baby, with one hand and in the other she has a long stick which she is waving at us. Ceausescu has fallen into the lake, but all of a sudden, he emerges, an immense dripping figure, a ridiculous giant, almost choking with the water he has swallowed and with the fury he feels because I flew away from him, out of reach. But there he is again, about to jump onto me, about to grab Tatiana from my arms. She screams, writhing, she shrieks with panic and fear.

I continue to run, running non-stop, but my legs don't move any more, up and down, up and down on the same spot. I shrink down and collapse onto the ground making a hole in the soil, a hole where Tatiana and I sit shivering with terror, panting from the chase, from where we see Ceausescu leap over the hole and disappear into some woods. As I peer out of the hole I see Roxana struggling in the water where she has fallen, frantically waving her arms, sinking further and further down until her struggles weaken, her voice becomes a croak, a water-logged croak, a desperate gasp and there is silence and the water ripples like a small millpond. Roxana has drowned. I relax and Ceausescu returns from the woods. He picks us both up in his enormous arms, folding his rubber arms around us like octopus's tentacles. The tentacles tighten and tighten until Tatiana stops her screaming and crying. She is limp in my arms as I feel the tentacles taut around my neck strangling me. I awaken gasping for breath, my whole body in a sweat and trembling feverishly.

I always awaken in a mess from these dreams. I am always the victim in my dreams, whatever happens to any of the other characters. They leave me shaking and nervous, longing for more sleep yet unable to sleep. I can feel my nerves frayed at the edges. The dreams make me scared of life, scared to confront the day before me, scared even to take the metro and go to my begging, scared in case I relive the dream during the day. Never, never have I dreamt about anything beautiful, say about Petre, about Simona, my dear grandmother, about the nice Spanish man who drove me in his fruit lorry from Marseille to Barcelona. My dreams are always a mixture of terrible events, in part, bits and pieces from my miserable past, occasionally mingled with incomprehensible occurrences. It is as though I have never come to grips with my past, with the mistakes I have made throughout my lifetime. Now I feel that it is too late to begin to dream about nice things. This is my lot, my destiny and I know I shall never do anything to change it at this stage,

I am too old, too tired, too disillusioned.

*   *   *

Just one more dream I would speak of. You understand, Doctor, I find it cathartic to talk of my dreams. I know they are obsessive and persistent and I remember many of them clearly. They are an extension, the emotional extension of my life, of my reality. If my days were fuller, packed with activity, with a job, with hope, with close human contact, then I would possibly forget my dreams and forget the depressing pall that they cast over my days. It is because I am lonely and inactive, because I lack friendship and love, that they come upon me. A car flashes past, an old woman walks towards me, a dog looms up on the pavement at my level sniffing his smells, any of these occurrences jolt my mind back to the dream that has been part of my night. Dreams are the life I lead at night. It is like having a dual life, a life during the day, a life during the night, yet, as I say, the dreams are but an extension of my daytime personality,

of my doldrums, of my ruminations.

The other dream I want to talk about is perhaps the most terrifying because it is the most realistic. It haunts me so often. Again, of course, Tatiana is the centre of this dream. This time, however, we are not running away, flying across ponds, hiding in holes in the ground. This last dream is about Tatiana in the orphanage. I am there, inside the orphanage. The warder at the entrance has told me that he knows of no Tatiana, that no child in the building answers to the description I have given him, but I refuse to believe him. He is a crusty old man with evil-smelling breath, a balding pate, a nose in flower with florid, bulbous excrescences caused by too much alcohol. He limps and his grubby trousers tied at the waist with a thin piece of rope are ill-fitting, he wears sports shoes on his limping feet. They are thin at the sole and I notice as he opens the door that the little toe of his left foot is protruding through the torn canvas of the shoe, showing a filthy toenail. He is not a pleasant sight this warder of the orphanage. Is he there to ward off inquisitive souls like me who go there to search for their children? Maybe so, but I am fearless in my dream and I push past him. He crumples uselessly to the ground, blubbering for his drink.

I penetrate into a long, dark corridor. What light there is is provided by gloomy lamps at intervals above some of the doors. They are bare bulbs and they are dirty covered with dust and dead smutty flies stuck to the glass. The light is dim and it casts eerie shadows onto the walls. The walls have been painted in a grubby, hospital green giving the place a depressing air. The paint is peeling off in parts, scribbled on in other parts, faded elsewhere. My steps resound on the wooden floor that creaks here and there under the weight of my body. There is a draught coming from one end of the corridor. The corridor is empty. As I look behind me I can still see the heap of human frame collapsed to the ground, the drunken warder, but he is getting smaller and smaller. I walk faster. I hear no sound from behind the closed doors. There is deathly silence all round me. Yet I continue fearlessly along the corridor in my quest for Tatiana. Why all this silence, this silence that weighs upon me? Take courage I thought to myself, soon you will find a nurse. Suddenly I heard a blood-curdling shriek that seemed to come from the floor above me, menacing voices, steps running clumsily along wooden flooring, bangs as though someone were heaving himself against metal bars, a fumbling with a bunch of keys and then the sounds subsided, merging into the silence. But there was somebody there. I must find that person. I must ask him where Tatiana is.

I came upon a flight of stairs, wooden stairs rotting in parts and with some of the steps missing. I imagined children tumbling and falling down these stairs. But where were the children in this orphanage? Where were the warders, the nurses? There was nobody, or so it seemed. But who had made that terrible noise a minute ago? I climbed the stairs with the greatest care making sure that the wood was firm under my step. The stairway went on and on, up and up seeming to lead nowhere. There were no landings, no exits to other passageways. I tired of climbing and I began to fear falling. I felt dizzy when I looked down the stair shaft. Tatiana, I called out and was surprised to hear that my voice was trembling, broken and phantasmal in the silence around me. Tatiana, Tatiana....! There was no answer, no sound, no smell of cooking.

I was alone in this ghost-like building with a drunken warder. Suddenly I saw a shaft of light above me, a shaft of daylight. I went on climbing towards it and eventually reached a small landing that lead onto another corridor. As I began to walk along the corridor I heard sounds and voices. I was overjoyed. So I was not alone in this cavernous place. I quickened my pace towards the sounds I could hear. As I approached them some of them turned into piercing shrieks, others into frenzied bursts of laughter, others into a low, monotonous murmuring, insistent and fanatical. There were steps, blows, the sound of metallic bars being beaten against the legs of hospital beds, the swish of leather straps being whipped against bare skin, more shrieks of protest, convulsive tears. An overall sentiment of hatred and fear hung in the air. I stopped short in my dream. I couldn't bear the thought of setting eyes on the people making all that noise. Yet I couldn't restrain myself. I had to search for Tatiana in amongst this hideous medley of humanity.

For that is what it was. I stood aghast as I pushed open one of the doors. The room was dimly lit and it took me a while to adjust my sight. It would have been better if I had stayed half blind on the threshold. At least thirty heads of mangy hair turned towards me, mouths open, dribbling, flabby lips, lolling tongues, eyes fraught with anxiety, crazed with tragedy, unseeing with loneliness and isolation. One little boy got to his feet and walked, bare-footed, towards me. He must have been about eight years old, his skinny arms and bony fingers outstretched, his knees knocked together, his feet were pigeon-toed. He had rickets and could hardly walk properly. He stumbled towards me and grabbed my hands, his dirty nails dug into my palms drawing blood and I screamed. They all screamed. My scream had set off a whole orchestra of screams, high-pitched, low-pitched, grumbles, piercing shouts. There was madness in the air. All these children had been abandoned, left alone to find their own way out of the orphanage, to search for food, to clean themselves. The large room with bare floorboards stank of filth. There were human excrements all over the floor, there were immense patches of darkened wood smelling of urine, there were parts of plaster scraped from the wall where the children had tried to extract nourishment with their nails and their teeth.

My one and only thought was to find Tatiana, grab her and run away from all this tragedy. Where was she? How would I recognise her? Had they given her another name? How old was she now? Was she ugly? Was she beautiful? So many questions. I peered into the faces of all the children, one by one. One by one I took their hands in mine, I stared penetratingly into their eyes, Tatiana, Tatiana, is that your name, are you Tatiana, I insisted. Some of them shook their heads, others looked beyond me with a stupid drooling expression, others - even two of the boys - said yes, they were Tatiana. All of a sudden, a chorus of children's voices chanted Tatiana, Tatiana, Tatiana ... I could feel the rising frenzy in the atmosphere.

It was like being in the midst of a war dance. The children sprang to their feet and stamped round and round closing in on me, making a circle around me. I was in the middle, imprisoned amidst their tiny stamping feet, their shaking bodies, their waving arms, their gnashing teeth and rubbery lips, their snotty noses and glazed eyes. Their frenzy grew in crescendo, their screams became louder and louder. The war dance continued, on and on. They were closer and closer to me, their smelly bodies almost touching mine, hemming me in tightly. I struck out with my arms, pleading with them to stop their noise and stamping, to let me go. Tatiana, Tatiana they shrieked, goading, laughing, crying. They were mad. One child took my hand and bit my finger, another pinched my thighs, another dug his fist into my ribs, they were pulling at my clothing, grabbing at my long hair, pummelling at my buttocks. Why had I come in here? Why had I exposed myself to these crazed infants? I could feel tears piercing my smarting eyes, I was trembling all over, sweating and terrified. As the war dance rose to a frantic pitch, I felt myself swooning, I fell against the bodies that were closest to me. They dragged me to the ground and as I opened my eyes I saw their goading faces, their mad expressions, their broken teeth, their runny noses, their matted hair, like baby hags tormenting me, they were jumping on me with their bare feet, bruising my breasts, my bones, my arms.

Suddenly one little girl emerged from the mass and stood before me. Silence, she ordered. Silence. Exhausted, extenuated, the children fell to silence, one by one they collapsed on the floor. One by one they fainted, all trace of life drained from their bodies. One by one they died. I am Tatiana she said staring at me with glassy, accusing eyes. I am the baby girl who you gave away, who you abandoned, the way you abandoned your own mother Roxana and your own sister Viorica. I rubbed my eyes. What was she saying, this child? I stared hard at her. I stared deep into her eyes, searching for the baby I had known and I saw that baby, the likeness in those eyes. She was a grown child now, but I knew intuitively that it was her. She studied me with spite, with hatred in her gaze. Tatiana, I muttered, rising with difficulty from the filthy floor. I put my arms around her. She was my own blood. She was mine.

But instead of staying fast in my embrace, she pushed me away with vehemence. She laughed cruelly at me, a laugh like Roxana's laugh. You are not my mother, you abandoned me, you left me in this place. These dead children are my friends. This is my home, she shouted. You don't belong here. Go away! Get out of here quickly before I kill you. As I looked at her I saw her fingernails growing into sharp claws that she brandished in front of my face. Out! Out! she shrieked. Never come here for me again.

I took to my heels, my body excruciatingly painful, I picked my way out of that room, jumping over dead bodies, some of them already stinking of the putrid odour of death. I looked behind me and I saw Tatiana coming after me, intent on hurting me. I went hurtling down the long flight of steps which lead to the ground floor. I almost flew down the interminable corridor, Tatiana after me, closer and closer she came with her claws sharpened and poised. Just as I reached the door where the drunken warder was still snoring, I felt her claws scraping down my back, needling their way through my clothing to my skin, scratching my skin, drawing blood. I felt poison surging through my veins. I collapsed to the ground, at the entrance to the orphanage, an inert mass of bleeding skin and broken bones. My last vision was Tatiana bending over me, gloating with scorn and hatred.

Again, I was the victim, feverish and trembling.

38

Spring Fever

With the springtime come allergies. For weeks on end I sneeze, loud outbursts that rise up from the depths of my body making me shudder all over. Perhaps it is the pollen floating on the air, the vital sap surging up through the trunks and into the branches of the thousands of trees that line the streets of this city. Sometimes, in Madrid, the pollen is visible. It comes from the poplar trees, there are so many of them, small white, buoyant bundles of cotton wool, almost iridescent in the spring light, it floats aimlessly, landing here on the pram of a child, there on the thinning hair of an old lady, it floats past my itchy nostrils, past my eyes and I squint to protect them.

I notice that I have become more and more sensitive to the springtime with the years. When I was younger I never used to notice this medley of annoying factors. The bees hum and fly busily from one plant to another, suddenly the cracks in the pavement come alive with long lines of ants racing from one hole to another carting minute pieces of bread or any leftovers they can manage on their sturdy little backs, they work tirelessly, they undermine this earth, it is riddled with interminable passageways, a veritable underground system connecting the holes to the exterior, corridors of insect activity where the sick are cared for, where the queen is revered, where the workers never stop their labour, yes, like the bees with their intricately structured society. ... Perhaps we could learn from them, Doctor, from their existence that revolves uniquely around subsistence, closed to any frivolity or unnecessary element.

224

Man is their only danger, treading them down with his great feet before they can hurry away to take refuge in their subterranean hideout, squirting them with abrasive liquids and sprays. If they were large enough and clever enough to take over the world, they would subject man to their insect will, control him by their sheer numbers. I would think about this on the spring evenings when I returned to my hut, as I sit outside on a small box watching the light yield to the darkness and I think that if in my hut there are hundreds of ants visible to my eyes and even more hundreds, indeed thousands, invisible, that all these ants live beside just one person - for one human being thousands of ants - imagine how many there are infesting the houses, the gardens, the streets and drains of our towns, the countryside. No, it doesn't bear thinking about. My mind boggles at uncontrolled numbers. During the winter these insects hibernate. It is in the springtime that they come forth in their armies.

When I lie down at night inside my hovel I can feel the itchiness begin. First I scratch my arms, just a little, then I am attacked on my stomach, next under my chin, then my fingers find their way to my hair. The obsession grows as I fight against my sleeplessness. I spend at least an hour or more, scratching feverishly at various parts of my body. It is as though the mattress has come alive with midges of all descriptions. My flesh creeps. I scratch and scratch but when I peer at my body in the morning I see no sign at all of this aggressive activity, yet when I am scratching it feels as though I am creating lumps and sores all over. I am convinced that it will all begin to suppurate. But this irritation doesn't occur during the day. It comes at night, tantalizingly, to prevent me falling asleep. And it only occurs for a week or so during the spring, so I put it down to the quickening and livening of the world after winter. It is like my sneezing.

One day is hot, the next is chilly, one day dry, one day damp with the pregnant drops of soft spring rain. As I sit listlessly on my piece of pavement I watch the long processions of caterpillars. They crawl down the pine trunks where they have been growing inside large balls of white floss, parasites to the tree, they feed off the tree, weakening the branch where they hang. They swarm round and round their mass of floss until one day they break from it and crawl in Indian-file down the trunk to the ground. They are yellow and black in colour, with spindly fur which, when released, floats in the air causing irritation to people's and animals' throats and noses and skin. I detest them, yet I know they grow into butterflies, moth-like butterflies, but butterflies all the same. And butterflies are beautiful.

The best aspect of spring, I have already said this, are the birds. They chirp and chirp joyfully, inviting all and sundry to join in their feasting. I notice the passers-by seem to lighten and quicken their step as they shed their overcoats and thick jackets, their scarves and gloves. They are lighter of spirit. They are frivolous, less serious, they laugh easily. I too have shed some of my layers of clothing and feel lighter of spirit. The days are longer, coaxing people to life after the months of fighting against the harsh cold of winter. Perhaps you won't believe it, but there are moments when I feel joy too, when I shed those heavy winter garments like a snake shedding its skin, like dogs and cats moulting. I suppose that I look better too in lighter clothing. Not that I'm any beauty – I never was and certainly never will be. I always imagine myself as a bundle of clothes in the cold weather, a shapeless bundle that anyone could pick up and pile into a used garment container. Still, I'd be too heavy, wouldn't I, for that? ... And here I am, chuckling away at this grotesque image of myself, Doctor. ... Am I mad?

With the spring, my desire returns to search for my daughter, to search for her despite my recurrent dreams about the orphanage. Will I never be rid of the persistent thought that one day I shall return to Romania? Humans are strange beings, always wanting to return to the places of their past suffering, perhaps because they imagine that they can start all over again, do it properly, make no mistakes, find warmth and kindness in those whom they left behind. Yet if we lived our lives again, we would be sure to make the same mistakes. We live as though we are programmed, tied down to an unchangeable routine. And the years have disappeared in the runnels of time, like water trickling away down a damp hillside. It is too late for me now to go backwards, backwards to a different Romania, to a different village, to a different Timisoara, to a different Bucharest. Yet what if I were to find Tatiana exactly as she was in my orphanage dream? No, better to leave things as they are. A mess.

My life is a mess.

*   *   *

I must tell you, Doctor, about my fevers, my sweating, my shuddering. It was like a pall hanging over our street, the street with all the hovels. Suddenly there were no more screams and shouts. The people, the children were laid low, hiding away from life in their miserable abodes, incapable of carrying out their usual activity. I can remember the uncanny silence. It was like that for three nights when I went home in the evening. It was eerie. I felt afraid. They always say that there is calm before a storm. But what storm was building up? ... I have told you that I didn't know anyone in that street, so there was no-one I could ask about the silence.

In the middle of the night, however, I heard groans coming from the hovel next to mine, a woman crying out to her god, a child whimpering, a grown man spluttering oaths and agony. I got up. Perhaps I could help them, but when I went outside in the darkness, their door was barred, the splintered plastic shutters had been lowered as if attempting to shut out life. I shivered. My curiosity got the better of me and I made my way along the street, avoiding the dried mud ruts in the road, peering hard at the humps of make-shift buildings, painful humps of sadness containing broken lives. All were in complete darkness. Only groaning and stifled weeping came from some of them. What had happened to all those people?

I didn't have to wait long to find out. In the early hours of the morning, just as the sky is streaked with shreds of pale grey that push the black cloak of night away, pale grey waiting to welcome the pink warmth of the day's first rays of sunlight, I began to feel griping pains in my stomach. I clutched at my midriff in anguish and I noticed that I was trembling, my whole body racked now with pain. I put a hand to my forehead and realised how hot it was. I was sweating profusely, but freezing cold with my teeth chattering. It was the fever. It was the start of my illness. For there was an epidemic in our street. It had come on us out of the blue and no-one escaped it. Some died of it. Others got over it. Others, like me, were picked up and taken to hospital. Epidemics like this only rage through poverty and filth. They are brought on by the grime on our bodies, the flies on our food, the rats in our sewage, the flees in our hair, the germs on our clothing, our rags. Where I go to beg, in that nice street lined with well-to-do homes and flats and shops and banks, no-one falls victim to an epidemic. It is because they are clean.

But I never managed to get back there, did I? I tried. Of course I tried. But the effort was too much for me. As I dragged my body to the metro, my limbs were shaking, dark patches danced before my eyes, my head swirled and I collapsed into an unspeakable heap of human rubbish at the top of the steps to the metro.

39

Clues

I caught Raimundo just as he was entering his office the other day while I was on my cleaning rounds. I told him that Mara had started telling me things about someone called Viorica.

'She was mean and sly,' she said. I asked her who she was talking about. She just repeated, 'Viorica, Viorica, you know, Florencia.'

'No, I don't know. I haven't any idea who Viorica is.' I answered her firmly.

'Well, you must have seen her when we were young.'

I noticed that she seemed to be talking in fits and starts, saying things in a disjointed way. 'Viorica did a very dreadful thing,' she said. 'Don't you remember?' As if I was there with her when she was young. She is obviously mixing me up with someone else in her life.

'Where did Viorica live?' I asked her. She shrugged her shoulders. Then she stared very hard out through the window as if trying to pinpoint a place out there, or a place lost in her memories.

'You must remember her!' She spoke vehemently.

'Come over here,' she commanded. She pointed way out to the horizon. 'See those mountains,' she said. 'Well, Viorica lives on the other side of those mountains.'

'Do you mean in Romania?' I hazarded.

'I don't know,' she replied, suddenly seeming very tired.

'Raimundo, she seemed to be so confused. Then she changed the subject. Viorica doesn't take any pills, she said out of the blue. Her eyes looked lazy, slightly glassy. She told me that her head was aching. Then she said that my face was blurred and that she couldn't hear me properly. When she got up from her bed to go over to the window, she stumbled, unsure on her feet, rather like a drunken person. But I know she doesn't drink. And of course, she can't drink alcohol here in hospital.

Viorica, she muttered in thick tones, never liked Tatiana. She was jealous of her, jealous, jealous, jealous ... I hate her for that. One day I'll get my own back on her.

I had never seen Mara so unpleasant, as though she was out of sorts with the world, with everyone, even with me. And with herself. She's been so nice recently, so much better since she started writing all those pages in that book you gave her. But that day she seemed to have changed. She was very confused, hiding away again in her own very personal world.'

Raimundo looked concerned. 'Any information at all, Florencia, I told you that. Thank you very much' he said. 'I shall bear in mind everything that you've mentioned to me.' As usual, he was in a hurry, but he gave me a warm pat on her shoulder. He said half teasingly: 'Perhaps you should be a nurse, or a doctor, not a cleaner!'

'I wish I had the brains for that,' I replied with a wry laugh.

Raimundo smiled at me. That made my day.

I returned happily to Mara's room to finish cleaning. She was nervous again and irritable, perhaps irritable with her own thoughts. As I cleaned the bathroom, I could hear her. She was muttering under her breath.

*   *   *

All those unfinished questions and answers that flicker through my mind. I feel ill. My mind isn't working any more. I can feel it slipping away from me. I can't remember things any more. I try, try to write, but I can't remember. Who were all those people that I knew in my past? Who are all these people who visit me in this bed? What am I doing here? Everything is confused. I must sleep. At night I lie awake, thinking about nothing. I see shadows. Some of them approach me. Some are laughing at me. They scorn me. They frighten me. Who are they? I don't know anybody. I have forgotten who I am. I have forgotten who everybody is. Yes, I just want to sleep. Sleep forever. Forget…..

*   *   *

I continued my cleaning rounds but I was troubled. I had to tell someone what I'd found. 'Manuela, Manuela! Wait! I must tell you this. I think I know why the Romanian patient, Mara, seems to be getting worse again. This morning I was cleaning her room and inside the toilet before I flushed it, there were several pills floating in the water. Do you think they're Mara's pills, the ones she is meant to be taking and she is throwing them down the toilet? Doesn't someone stay with her when she has to take them?'

The nurse looked worried. 'Ah, thank you so much for telling me that, Florencia. That must be what has happened. I'll get someone to supervise her when she is eating. And I must tell Carlos and Jaime. They might want to give her something stronger to get her back on her feet again. We should also let Raimundo know because he was already worried about her after seeing her yesterday. He came and asked me if we'd altered her medication or diet and, of course, I told him that we'd changed nothing. But he is clever. He knew there was something wrong. … She's a clever one, too. Because she's managed to flush them away without anyone noticing. But it's obvious that she is worse now, her mind I mean, if she's forgetting to flush the toilet properly. What on earth had happened to Mara for her to start throwing her tablets away. She had been so much better recently and now we'd have to start all over again.'

Manuela went off in the direction of the doctors' offices, her heavy nurse's shoes beating against the linoleum flooring, her arms full of documents and her face flushed with urgency. She was an understanding soul, normally calm and pleasant to everybody around her, but she was thorough and didn't like things like this upsetting her daily routine.

231

40

Dreams and Reality

Mara is muttering angrily to herself: My dreams have returned. I toss and turn all night long. I can't sleep properly. Then when I fall asleep, I have nightmares. Of Tatiana and the orphanage. And more. Now, they come, someone comes   …   and takes Raimundo away. They are like policemen. They drag him by the arms, pull him away from my bedside. He strains against them but he is powerless, four arms encage him and chain his wrists together.

I like Raimundo. He reminds me of Petre. In one of my dreams I saw Petre's mother. She was tall, slim and dark-skinned, like her son. She was pleasant, the sort of woman you could talk to, confide in, not like Roxana with all her bitterness. When Petre was my friend, when we were very young even before we began to love each other, I used to spend long hours in his house in the school holidays, playing together the two of us, and I used to go to their kitchen and watch his mother making cakes, or pasties, or something for supper. She would work fast and efficiently. She used to let me help her roll out the pastry, cut it into different shapes.   She had a pretty face framed by a mass of straight black hair; hair that shone from the glow of the light bulb hanging from the ceiling or from the sun penetrating through the kitchen window. She would laugh and joke with us. She used to tickle me under my armpits when I was little. She even came on walks with us occasionally, taking us through the narrow lanes, out into the fields and across to the nearby woods. She would talk to us about gnomes and goblins and fairies that lived under the leaves and in the hollows of the tree trunks, she said. I was fascinated by what she told us. I would spend long minutes searching and searching for fairies, lifting the blown leaves off the ground, peering into the holes in the bark of the trees, squinting up at the branches to see if a gnome was looking at me. ... And every year Petre and I used to help his mother prepare for the village festival. I remember they owned a donkey and she would let us thread vine leaves through his tail and hang flowers around his ears so that he could walk in the procession. I thought that he was such a proud donkey! We helped her carry the baskets of food she had prepared to the long trestle tables and place it all along the centre of the tables, ready for the feast. I always felt happy when I was with her. Those were the good times in Romania, in Ceausescu's Romania. Sometimes, at night, I would go home to my bed and wish that my own mother was like Petre's mother. My own mother, Roxana, was sour-faced and always grumpy about one thing or another.

Then there was Petre's father. Viorica's father, Mihaita, had left us. He went away from Roxana because he wasn't happy with her. Who would be happy with her? We were so young, Viorica and I, to be without a father. So in some ways, Petre's father replaced him for me. He was a big man, very tall and stout, not as good-looking as his wife and son, but with a red, jovial face. He was always telling us jokes and laughing. There were days when I returned to the glacial atmosphere in my own house and back yard, and I longed to be able to live with Petre's family. Once I even said this to my mother and she rose up and slapped me across the cheek with the back of her hand — a hard, sharp swipe that sent my twelve-year-old body sprawling on the ground. My cheek stung, smarted for long minutes and then I knew I hated my own mother. I would have run away then if it hadn't been for Simona. Simona was a beautiful grandmother and I loved her more than anyone else in the world. She loved me too. We understood each other.

But when Tatiana was on the way, Petre's mother and father didn't want to know me. They said that I was dirty, that I was not the right girl for their son. They changed their attitude towards me. They abandoned me to my destiny. When I remember that, I cannot understand it. Surely they must have realised that Petre and I were fond of each other and that our friendship and fondness might grow into love. And with love comes sex. My life would have been so different if they had taken me in at that time, after the birth of my baby girl, of Petre's baby girl.

In my nightmare, I scream when I see the guards coming for Raimundo. They put a gag around his mouth so that he cannot call for help. They pull his shoulders back and I see his lips twist in agony and they chain his wrists so that he cannot move. Then they tie his ankles together with rope and drag him away from me. I call out to him as he disappears with them down the corridor. I try to get out of bed to follow him, to help him, to find someone to release him from the guards. But my limbs won't move. I strain and strain against the bed clothes and the bedstead, but it is useless. I cannot move at all. My legs and arms are so heavy, my head is swimming around and around in circles and all I can hear are the steps of the guards, further and further away down the corridor. Soon they will be outside in the cold of the night I thought. Raimundo will catch cold. He will be ill. They may fling him into a cold cell and leave him there and nobody knows where he is. They may even kill him. Then he would never come back to me, never come back to talk to me, to help me to get better.

My life is one long series of goodbyes, of people coming and going. Nobody ever stays with me. Nobody wants me. That must have been why the guards came for him, because he was good to me, and I am not a good person.

*   *   *

Carlos came in from his rounds and told Jaime of his conversation with Mara: 'What is this I've been hearing, Mara? Someone told me that you are throwing your pills away down the toilet! ... If you could have seen her, Jaime. She looked at me with guilt written all over her face and stared at me through hazy eyes. I didn't tell her that Florencia had told us she'd found the pills in the toilet. She likes Florencia and I didn't want her to think that Florencia had come running to us, or that she was spying on her. ... Then she muttered something under the sheets. What was that? I asked her. I don't like pills, she answered. They make me feel sick. I don't need them. Doctors all love pills, but they aren't any good. Only Manuela's injection. No, I don't like that either, but it does me more good than the pills. No more. No more pills, please Doctor Carlos.

I tried to make her see that if she stopped taking them, then she'd get worse. I said, 'Can't you see Mara, that you are worse now? Don't you realise that your mind isn't working the way it used to when you were writing your story. Raimundo is waiting for you to finish it so that he can help you with your problems. It is several days since you've written anything. What will Raimundo say?' I know that she likes him, so I thought that maybe I could persuade her to take the pills again by making her feel ashamed.

'But Raimundo has gone,' she exclaimed. I was really taken aback. 'No he hasn't,' I said. 'Yes he has,' she answered. 'The guards came to take him away because he was talking to me and I am evil!' 'You have some very strange things in your head, Mara.' I said. 'That's because you're not taking your pills anymore.'

'She's so obstinate at times,' Jaime remarked quietly. 'Still, if it's true that those tablets were making her feel sick, let's change them, put her onto a milder pill.'

'Fine.' I said, 'But perhaps we'd better consult Raimundo first before prescribing anything new for her. You know that it often takes a while before a patient adapts to medicine. I agree that she is obstinate, but this isn't the first time we've had negative reactions with those tablets. I mean, she isn't the only patient to reject them.'

Carlos had his doubts about certain drugs and was always cautious with his prescriptions.

'Yes, but no-one ever saw her being sick,' Jaime retorted. 'No-one ever said that she complained about them while she was taking them. And they certainly helped to get her mind working again... She was much more alert when she was on them. I think, for the time being anyway, that we should keep her on the same ones, Carlos, but make sure that she takes them. We must get Manuela or Rosa, or the other nurses, to watch over her until she gets them down her. They are only six a day - two with each meal. Then, if we see in a week or so that they aren't working, we can ask Raimundo to put her onto something different.'

*   *   *

'Good morning Mara,' I said. 'Where are you up to with the story of your life?' I spoke softly, looking into her eyes with kindness.

She stared back blankly, as if to say: Who are you? What is the story of my life? I hadn't seen her like this since the early days after the coma. I can't accept that we are going to lose her again, that she is going to sink back into inertia and indifference; that I am failing in my job.

'It's me, Raimundo. I want you to tell me more about two people in your life,' I said, 'Simona and Roxana. You have mentioned them both in your book.' I had now read the translation of the first half of her story – I was awaiting the rest – and wanted her to distinguish between the good influence of her grandmother and the bad influence of her mother. I knew it was important, particularly in relation to Roxana, for her to exorcise all the bitterness there, to come to terms with the relationship she and her mother had had. Until she faced that without flinching, as it were, she would never overcome her inferiority, her feelings of guilt, although I realised that, if she were to come to grips with her guilt, there was a lot of work to be done where her daughter, Tatiana, was concerned. We can only go step by step. First of all, deal with the bad influences, then introduce the good.

These were my thoughts as I stared at her. She had averted her gaze from me, turning her face towards the wall. She had pulled up the bed covers, bundling them around her neck. She was humped and heavy in her bed, stubborn and un-giving. When I placed my hand on her arm beneath the blanket, I could feel her wince. It was a sign that she wanted to be alone, that she was not willing at that moment to share her life, her thoughts, with anyone, not even with her psychiatrist. She had clammed up, pushing me away. This was a problem, as in the past she had been more forthcoming with me and with Florencia the cleaner, than with anyone else. If she clammed up on us, there was little we could do to help her. Was it the pills that she hadn't been taking? Had she had enough of digging up her demons for the hospital staff? Was she simply tired of living? When the will breaks, it is almost impossible to pull a patient back. I couldn't let that happen. I knew that she had more to tell me, that she was capable of overcoming her problems much more than she had up to now. But I also knew that it is important to work during the more receptive moments, that when a patient falls into silence, little can be done to work positively. Forcing a situation never gets you anywhere. It is counter-productive. Perhaps the best thing I could do at these times was to read gently to her, read her some poetry, good literature, slowly and caringly, coaxing her out of her shell. ... Also, I must tell Manuela and Florencia to be cheerful and communicative with her, more than normal, give her lots of affection and as much company as they can. She needs the company of other women. Women have a natural ability to communicate, to relax and break down barriers. They confide in each other.

I thought I would give it one more try, by raising some good memories: 'Mara,' I said, 'tell me how you helped your mother at the village festivals in Romania.'

She pulled her blanket further up over her ears and head. She was obviously aware of my presence, yet determined not to cooperate. I would leave her for today, return in a couple of days after they had administered her pills. I sighed to myself as I walked out of her room. I was beginning to feel defeated.

*   *   *

The two nurses were seated at the cheap formica table in their staff room. They'd just about finished drinking their coffee and were thinking about going back to work.

'Raimundo says we must make sure that she is taking her pills, Rosa.'

'I know, I know Manuela, but we don't have much time to spend by the bedside of just one patient waiting for her to take her pills.' Rosa twisted her pursed lips into a grimace. She was thoroughly sick of all her patients' problems.

'But it's our duty. We must find the time. You know that she has no visitors, no relations who could do it for us.'

'Manuela, I'm not paid enough – neither are you – to get so involved. We're here to give injections, to make beds, to supervise IV feeding and oxygen...'

'And, Rosa, to administer pills and any other medicine a patient needs. And if we don't do this, Raimundo will be furious and we'll have Carlos and Jaime on our backs as well. All I'm asking is that you help me with this very small task. When I'm on duty, I'll do it. It isn't as though I'm asking you to take the whole weight of Mara on your shoulders. All we have to do is to pass by her bed at mealtimes, give her one of the pills before the food and the other one after. Pop them into her mouth and make her wash them down with some water.'

'Yes, but you know what she's like with me! She's got it in for me. She won't do anything I ask her to do. When I tell her to get out of bed so I can change her sheets, she just stays put and covers herself up with the blankets and sheets from tip to toe. She clutches the sheets and blanket for all she's worth. The only thing I can do is to pull the bed covers off her and call the assistant nurse on duty to help me lift her to the chair by the window. Since she's been off her medication, she weighs a ton and doesn't move a limb to help herself. And then if you could see the looks she gives me!'

I was beginning to feel irritated by Rosa. 'Oh, don't be ridiculous. That's your imagination!'

Rosa flared up: 'My imagination? Just you come with me the next time and you'll see what I mean.'

I spoke more softly. 'Well, it's one thing to lift her out of bed and quite another to pop a pill into her mouth and make sure she takes it. Be firm with her. I don't know ... tell her she'll never get better without the pills, that she only has to take them for another few days or weeks, until Raimundo says she doesn't need them. Yes, you could mention Raimundo because I know she likes him and respects him.'

Rosa pursed her thin lips almost stapling them together, as though this Romanian patient was the biggest problem she'd ever had to deal with.

'Cheer up, Rosa!' I said. 'She won't be here with us forever. One of two things will happen: she'll get better and leave, or she'll die. But while she's with us, we have to do everything we can for her, the way we do for all the patients.'

'Alright, but that's just it. She's not like all our patients Manuela!' Rosa got up to leave. Reluctantly, I joined her.

*   *   *

Florencia entered Mara's room quietly, without speaking and began to do her cleaning.

It's never that dirty, I thought to myself. Sometimes the toilet's a bit grubby - bits of paper in the wash basin, hairs on the floor, body cream left open without the lid on, the toothpaste tube squeezed into a thousand creases and angles as though she fights with it every time she uses it, dirty panties on the side of the bathtub. Things like that. Nothing very drastic. Other patients are worse. All the same, there are days when I feel fed up with my job.

But I want to live alone instead of at home with my parents, so I have no option but to work. Also, if I want to study computer sciences, I need the money to pay for my courses. Let's face it, we all need money to live. But there are times when I get sick of the smell in the hospital, when I tire of pushing a broom and mop around the floor, emptying patients slops down the toilet, the long hours. And some of the patients are revolting, poor old broken down things without a hope in life and that's depressing to me, not to have a hope in life, I mean. That's why I shall leave the hospital the moment I've finished my secretarial training and have found another job. ... I want to buy my own flat, not just hire one like I do now, sharing with another girl. It isn't really like a home to me. My flat-mate doesn't always co-operate with the cleaning and cooking. There are evenings when we barely speak to each other. She's a bit sour. She reminds me of Rosa, the older nurse here, thin-lipped and grim. So I disappear into my own room and close the door, turn on my tele or do a bit of studying. I suppose I ought to try and learn English as well. Everyone today speaks other languages. But I don't have the time. Perhaps I will when I finish my computer training. Only one more year to go.

There was a sound from Mara's bed, a groan, a semi-sob. Florencia moved quickly to her bedside.

'What is it, what do you want, Mara?'

She turned her head away in reply. I took her hand in mine.

'Only to die,' she said in a broken voice.

'Now, now, I don't want to hear that from you.' I wanted to comfort her. Older patients often said things like that. 'You're not going to die now. You're almost better. I'm not going to let you die. I'll go and call Raimundo. He'll cheer you up. He loves you, you know.'

Mara said nothing, so after a moment, I thought I'd better get back to my work. I knew she was fond of Raimundo. Weren't we all? Really, he was so nice to me, just a cleaner, asking me my opinion about Mara. And he's such a good-looker too. Mara said to me once that Raimundo was just like Petre. Good-looking like Petre, she said. She sighed, I remember. And I sigh too when I think about Raimundo. I feel, well, sort of up-lifted when he talks to me, when I catch a glimpse of him and when I go into his office to clean. But of course, he's married. Aren't all the best ones married? There is a photo of his wife and three small children on his desk in a silver frame. She's pretty, standing beside him and the children – a pair of twin girls and a smaller boy. The twins are fair-haired like their mother and the little boy is dark-haired, just like his father. I often pick up that photo, dust it and linger over it, imagining what sort of a home life they have.   Wouldn't it be perfect to be married to someone like Raimundo? I can see them all laughing together in the evenings. I can see him helping his children with their homework, or helping his wife with the supper. And after the children have gone to bed, he and his wife would sit and talk to each other, or watch television holding hands, then go to bed and make love. He seems as though he'd be so affectionate, the sort of man that any woman would like to have sharing her bed.

But an empty bed isn't always that bad. After I broke off with Federico a few months ago now, there's been no-one else in my life. Haven't you got a boyfriend Florencia? Mara asked me one day. When I said No, she looked hard at me and said, I haven't either! She laughed - I was so surprised - and for an instant there was a sparkle in her eyes.

Life's not the same when you're by yourself, but still, I am glad I broke off with him. He had a nasty side to him. Used to sneer at me because I go to classes, because I want to better myself. He was a garage mechanic, happy with his car engines, happy to be dirty all day long. But it got to a point when I couldn't stand his jeering at me. He didn't want me to go. I told him why, I told him why several times, but he never improved. He just laughed at me, said I was silly, sentimental. You're like all girls today, he said, thinking you can climb the professional ladder and do it all better than we men. You're stupid. He accused me of being stupid. So one day when he phoned to ask me out, I said I couldn't go. I said I couldn't go on that day or on any other day. I said I never wanted to see him again. He lost his temper, so I just cut him off. I remember I burst into tears after that. I was shaking. It was a Saturday morning. I stayed in bed the whole weekend without talking to anyone. I cried for hours and then fell asleep. I fell into a deep sleep and when I woke up, I felt better. For the first time in ages I felt free, as though I had done something to make myself grow up. I'm nearly 30, mind you, but when I was with Federico he used to make me feel young and inexperienced. I never answered the phone when he rang. He tried several times. Then he gave up. Fortunately, he never came to my flat or to the hospital. I've never seen him since. That was five months ago and, although I feel lonely at times, I never want him back.

I heard another groan from Mara's bed as I was wiping the window sill clean. I stopped my work and went to her bed again. I sat down beside her lumpy body and put my hand on her cheek. She clutched my hand and her eyes filled with tears. I bent over and kissed her.

'Tell me, tell me what's wrong,' I begged her. 'Don't bottle it all up inside, Mara.'

'I want to go. I will never get better here.' Her Spanish was halting. Her voice came jerkily to my ears.

'Of course you will. But you must be patient. You must take all your pills and eat your meals properly. Then you'll get better. I promise you. Look who has come to see you!'

Raimundo walked through the door and smiled at us both. It flashed through my mind that I could fall in love with him. But of course, I'm only a cleaner, aren't I? Imagine if I were a beggar! I got to my feet and went to retrieve my duster by the window.

'No, don't go away, Florencia,' he said, 'finish what you're doing. ... How is our patient today?' He was always so calm, always so controlled, always so nice ... he seems so well-brought-up ... 'She is sad,' I said.

41

Raimundo's Loss

I took Mara's wrist in my hands and asked her to look at me. I felt for her pulse. Its beat was barely perceptible. Yes, her eyes were filled with tears. The grooves in her forehead spoke of pain. Her hair was a tangled mess, as though she had tossed and turned for hours. She let her hand lie in mine. She didn't wince today. She let out a deep sigh, a tremor almost, and tried to blink away her tears. They persisted and so she wiped at them with her other hand. She sniffed, gulping down all that unwanted fluid that kept coming and coming, that she couldn't control.

'Talk to me, Mara,' I said gently. 'About anything at all, anything you want to.'

She moved her head from side to side in negation, fighting back her tears. She withdrew her hand from mine.

'I am waiting for you to finish your story. It is beautifully written, but you haven't finished it, have you? There is more that you want to talk about. What happened after you left the flat you were cleaning?'

I wanted to say: You realise that if you'd stayed on there you would have more money now and perhaps a better life, a better place to live in, but I didn't. Recrimination isn't what she needs. Nor would I mention the things that she had stolen. That would only have made her feel guilty, worse than she was already feeling today. Manuela had told me that she was taking her pills again regularly, but that she was always depressed. Depression seemed to hang over her like a mist, clouding her mind, her thoughts, subduing her into a state of inertia. But I didn't want to start her on another course of anti-depressants. Too many pills can be counter-productive. The other pills were clearing her mind, yet obviously not enough. I must talk to Carlos and we can decide together on how to proceed. There's no point in broaching Jaime. He doesn't seem to want to get any more involved than he is already with her. He isn't one of our best doctors. He has no empathy with his patients.

There was no further response from Mara. She'd fallen into a state of indifference, of near numbness. No more tears, but neither did she react in any way to my words and coaxing. Florencia was cleaning in the passage outside her door.

'What did she say to you this morning, Florencia?'

'She said she just wanted to die. Only to die, she said.'

I didn't know what to say. I pressed Florencia's arm in gratitude. As I turned away, I saw her place her hand on the spot on her arm that I had touched. I thought no more of it, I was unaware of her wanting to get closer, almost willing me to do it again. Without another word, I returned to my patient. Mara wouldn't open her eyes, but she seemed calmer.

I walked slowly over to the window and leant my elbow on the windowsill that Florencia had just wiped clean, resting my chin in a cupped hand and reflecting. How do I deal with this pain? For it was pain that she was suffering, pain more than neurosis. I had seen this sort of pain before. It was the pain of longing, of longing for someone or for something that you cannot have, someone who has left you, who has died or gone elsewhere.

*   *   *

His mind fled back to his youth, to his mother's suffering. And he relived it, not as the boy he was, but as if it was someone else's story. ... When he was only in his teens his father had been killed - the arbitrary victim of a terrorist attack. Raimundo heard the bomb explode inside the shopping centre where his father had gone to buy some wine for visitors who were coming to supper. He could hear the bomb now, as he had heard it then. Bodies - or rather bits of bodies - flying everywhere, their clothes rent from their limbs, flames, the smell of burning flesh, objects of all description from the shattered shop windows cascading through the air, flying at the dead bodies, jagged pieces of metal, bits of hot burning rubber, CDs, paper torn from books, wooden door frames, broken and collapsed into phantasmal figures, spread across the marble flooring, now scarred and stained with tragedy... A wreckage. A holocaust. All hell let loose. His mother said she thought that she'd heard the explosion, but she only thought about that when he didn't come home. Why was he taking so long to buy a bottle of wine? The visitors were due to arrive and still he didn't come. She asked Raimundo to run out down the street towards the supermarket, just to see if he was on his way.

Raimundo would never forget what he saw that evening - corpses and loose limbs and blood and guts, gouged objects all around him, screaming and the smell of burning, the smell of flesh burning, of human bodies burning. It was a horrendous nightmare. He could remember shaking all over, trembling while an outrageous force held him in its grip. It was anger, fury, the fever of impotence. The shrill shriek of police sirens surged forward out of nowhere, screeching their message of tragedy to all and sundry. He tried to walk home, to run away from the holocaust, but his legs wouldn't respond. He was rooted to the spot. He cried out to a policeman. He was deathly pale. The policeman took him home telling him to stay put beside his mother, until the bodies had been cleared and could be identified. Beside his mother.

She sat like a stone, motionless. Raimundo felt clumsy, useless. What could a boy of thirteen do in this situation? He remembered that he had made his mother some hot tea. But she could only stare blankly, her eyes like glass. She wouldn't drink. She wouldn't eat. She wouldn't move. Raimundo had to tell the visitors to leave, try to explain in halting tones what had happened. They'd wanted to stay, but he wouldn't allow them to. His mother needed to be still and calm, he said. Hours later he and his mother were called to identify his father's body, the bits of his father's body. Half a blackened face, the socket of his left eye empty, his left hand hanging from a shred of tendon to his wrist, his hair and forehead severely burnt, the skin shrivelled and drying purple on the half of his skull. But it was enough to identify him. There was no doubt.

Raimundo remembered his mother's pain. He remembered his own pain, but he also remembered that it was over more quickly because his mother's pain was greater and he had to attend to her, forget himself. For a while he bore a grudge, a grudge against the terrorists, against the police who had been thorough yet unfeeling, a grudge against life, even against his father for having gone to the supermarket at the wrong time. How to deal with his mother's pain? Long days of sitting motionless, except to go to the bathroom and to the kitchen where he tried to get her to eat. After that she would trail back to her chair in the lounge, the same chair where she had received the news of his death, and sit. He tried to get her to bed at night, but when he awoke in the morning, she was still sitting in the chair, staring unseeingly at the wall, the pale pink wall in front of her. Long days spent completely immobile. Life drained from her.

Then, the next phase of suffering came. The tears began to flow, sometimes noisily, sometimes silently. Her eyes were constantly filled with tears. There were whole moments when she would shriek in piercing tones that made Raimundo shiver with fear. It was like a hysteria. She would stop shrieking and the mumbling would set in, mumbling Rogelio, his father's name, Rogelio this, Rogelio that, recriminating phrases because he had left her alone in this world. Pain, pain, all the time pain. Not just pain, agony, pure agony. He no longer recognised his mother, the competent, good-looking woman who had run her affairs and his father's affairs and his, Raimundo's affairs with style and alacrity. She had been the mainstay in the household, working as a history teacher in a nearby secondary school. He thought wryly how history had caught up with her, twisting her present into an unrecognizable fragment of life.

She had been the one to organise their holidays to other parts of Spain, away from the Basque country where life was complicated. She had taught Raimundo to swim when he was only a little boy of six during a holiday in Alicante. His father, the lawyer, was always too busy. A good man, yes, but a busy man consumed by his own problems and a job that was too big for any one person, too cumbersome for one pair of shoulders. His mother had now faded to a shadow of her previous self. She lost weight, so much weight that her clothes hung shapelessly around her wasted bust and hips. Her face became riddled with lines, deep grooves of pain, like the grooves on Mara's forehead. He couldn't help making the comparison. That terrible pain of longing, of all-consuming loss, of no longer believing that life can be lived.

After the tragedy, their personal tragedy, his mother never returned to her school. He had to return to his. And each afternoon he would come home to confront one facet of his mother's pain or another. He never wilted under the weight of her pain. He was quick to stop asking the inevitable questions, why had this happened, why had it happened to him and to his mother, why had his good father been a victim to terrorism, why wasn't his mother capable of emerging from her misery, etc., etc. He realised, in only his early teens, that there were no answers to all those questions. It had merely happened and the only way to cope with it was to accept it and to overcome it. Two years must have passed in this way. Two years living beside a woman he no longer recognised as his mother, but whom he knew that he had to help. He developed in kindness, tenderness, caring, understanding and he developed in pragmatic assistance. He now was the father of the broken household. He now was its mainstay. He learnt to deal with everyday matters, with telephone calls, with bank and administration affairs. He learnt all these things well before his time. He took the brunt of it on his young shoulders which were broadening with strength and experience. But, above all, he learnt how to care for his shattered mother. While he was out of the house he arranged for an older cousin to come and be with his mother. She helped him, too, in many other ways.

His mother had taken to wandering around the flat at night. Sleep was denied her. She seemed only to sleep during the day, in her chair with her eyes wide open. But at night she wandered, she paced round and round the lounge, picking objects up, staring bewildered at them, muttering under her breath, often talking in normal tones and occasionally screaming. Then Raimundo would awaken and be there beside her in a second. He never complained, he never chided her. He knew in his young wisdom that she had been hurt, very badly hurt. Raimundo dwelt on this for hours on end. How do you help someone who has fallen into the pit of estrangement to return to normality? The question obsessed him. He spoke to one of his teachers about it, a teacher who talked about the psyche of human beings, of brain damage, of the million causes of the ways neurons could be damaged and behaviour altered. Raimundo hung on his words, fascinated. That teacher guided him. In response to the young man's interest, he suggested that he study medicine when he left school. He was good at the sciences and would easily obtain a place at university as a medical student. You have it in your veins, the teacher said. And the young man knew without any doubt at all that medicine, psychiatry would be his career, his purpose in life.

His mother never recovered from her loss. Her days were filled with glassy stares, with strange utterances, with obsessions, although she never mentioned her husband Rogelio again. It was as though she had pushed him away, out of her mind, because he had been responsible for her pain. Her pain that one day became too great for her to bear. He returned home from school one afternoon to her corpse lying in a pool of blood on the kitchen floor. His cousin was not to be seen. His mother had the kitchen knife between the stiffened fingers of her blood-stained hand. She had plunged it, through tissue, gristle, cartilage, bone, through to her heart, to her own heart. When his cousin returned, he asked her why, oh why had she left his mother alone. She said that his mother had pleaded with her to go and buy a packet of her favourite biscuits. Was it merely an excuse to get the woman out of the house so that she could put an end to her suffering?

Raimundo withdrew, too, into his pain. Now he was alone in the world, alone to forge his future, to make something of his life. For long weeks he was desolate. Nothing would relieve his suffering. He wouldn't eat properly. His aunt, the cousin's mother, tried and tried. She had taken him under her wing. But it was as if he was living out his mother's agony, as if, by imitating her, he could touch the very fibres of the pain that he would later on learn how to cure.

*   *   *

Mara groaned again and sniffed back her tears, that uncontrollable liquid welling up in her eyes. It woke me from my reveries, from my past. I was even more determined to help this poor, broken soul. I hadn't been able to help my mother, but now it was different, I had the training, the skills, the knowledge at my fingertips. But I had to react quickly.

Carlos popped his head round the door.

'Just wanted to know if you're free for a game of tennis, Raimundo, on Saturday afternoon?'

'Yes, I think so, but first come here and let's decide on what to give our patient. Something to draw her out of her depression, Carlos. Something gentle, not too abrasive. What can you suggest?'

'Why aren't the pills she was on before helping her now? They were sufficient before she started chucking them away.'

'Well, it's obvious', Raimundo replied, 'that she's moved into a different phase of her condition. It's not quantity she needs, but quality, a remedy given by just one or two pills. Couldn't we take her off what she's been having up to now and replace all that with a good anti-depressant? You know that it can be complicated, even dangerous, to administer these with other drugs.'

'What about Bupropion?' Carlos suggested.

'That's a stimulant, isn't it? It might help her low energy levels. But let's be cautious. Start her off on a small dose, increasing it only if it has no effect. You know that this drug can have negative side effects, such as suicidal thoughts, so she will have to be properly supervised and at the slightest sign of stronger depression, taken off it. I want her mind and her optimism back in place again, as it was before when she was writing. Her writings are the only way I can see what has happened to her, pretty well the only way I have of helping her, of eking out the traumas in her past and all the pain that has gone with it. It's obvious that she's completely lost the habit of communication. During all those years of begging on the streets, she doesn't seem to have made any friends.'

249

'But some people don't seem to need friends, do they? You know that Raimundo.'

'True. But it's been years and years with Mara, years without her having a decent conversation with anybody. Even all her contacts have been superficial and demeaning. That is enough to lower anyone's self-esteem. She wasn't even writing then. Had she kept a diary it would have helped her to keep her thoughts in order, chip away some of the resentment she has against life and people. In one part of her story, she talks about her only friends being the birds, her cat, the trees, the sky, in short, nature. Never people.' Raimundo sighed.

Carlos spoke softly. 'I don't really think that any of us has any idea what poverty is, what it can do to a person, how it can break a soul and a will. It isn't only the hunger either, it's the dirt, the filth, living the life of an outcast, way out on the margin of even a modicum of normality. No, we have no idea, Raimundo, sitting in our cosy homes, going to our cushy jobs, enjoying a film, a party, an exhibition, a game of tennis even. It's impossible for us to have any notion of their cold nights, the hunger pains in their stomachs, the unpleasant smell of their clothing and unwashed skin, the temptation to give up completely or to go on the bottle just to forget, the utter desolation of wanting and not being able to have.

Did I say, a game of tennis?' he said with a grin.

I looked again at Mara. She still seemed near comatose, except for her tears.

'Ok, I'll see you at the tennis courts around five on Saturday, Carlos. Thanks.'

I'm keenly aware of the importance of keeping in shape. *Mens sana in corpore sano* I thought, and a smile came involuntarily to my face. Apart from the occasional game of tennis, with Carlos or with other friends, I walk to and from the hospital. Why not? I live only three quarters of an hour's walk away. It's preferable to walk than to take the car and add to the pollution in Madrid and anyway, it's preferable to walk than wait around for buses or go down the metro. Walking gives me time to put my thoughts in order, clear my mind after the onslaught of all my patients' problems. I make sure I swim at least once a fortnight at the local swimming pool. I feel better for all this and I'm sure I look better.

*   *   *

Rosa had been having a bad week but all of a sudden she was smiling. 'You wouldn't believe it, Manuela. I went in this morning with Mara's breakfast pill. Do you know, she looked me straight in the eye and said, I want to tell you that I am sorry. Sorry! Why? I asked her. Because I have hit you, because I have ignored you, I haven't done what you ask me to do. I am sorry. I am very, very sorry, she said. She wasn't crying or humiliated. She was strong and direct with me, almost as if she were putting me in my place, demanding that I accept her apology. And of course, I did. That's alright, I said to her. Many patients go through bad times like that. They even try and hit us occasionally. Some scream at us and don't let us give them injections. You're not the only one. We're all used to it. ... Do you like being a nurse, Rosa, she asked me. Not always, I answered her, not when patients are difficult and rude to me. Then I feel as though I could run away and I wish that I had chosen another career, something different where people don't abuse me. But it's a bit late now to change. ... Yes, she said quietly, too late now. But I think she was talking about herself, not about me.'

'Take heart, Rosa! She'll come around to you eventually and you'll see how you'll feel better and even begin to like her. Did she take her medicine alright? No fuss and bother?' I asked.

'Perfectly alright. Down it slid with a sip of water and she's eaten all her breakfast. She's definitely looking better since Carlos put her onto these new anti-depressants.' For once in her life Rosa looked optimistic. She actually seemed convinced that things were easier now with Mara and that in the future her life at the hospital might even take a turn for the better.

I now felt able to tell Rosa what had happened the previous day. Had Rosa been her usual sour self, I would never have told her anything for fear of making her jealous. I continued: 'The other day I went in and she was sitting by the window humming. I said to her: That's a pretty tune Mara and she smiled at me. She raised her arms and waved them around in the air. We used to dance to that music at my village festival, she confided in me. Then I asked her if she could teach me the dance. She got up out of the chair and slowly, a bit uncertain and wobbly on her thick legs, started to move her heavy body around in circles, waving her arms above her head. Round and round she went. Then she stamped her feet at the finale and collapsed into her chair, laughing and happy. I clapped enthusiastically. Even the old lady in the other bed clapped softly. I asked her then what the people ate at the feasts. She described the meat dishes to me, the soups, a strong alcoholic drink they call palinka made from cherries, she said. And the men smoke long cigars and the women wear traditional costumes, she explained. Everybody is happy, Manuela. Everybody dances. The donkeys bring all the food in their baskets covered with white napkins, to be set out on the tables. We dress up the donkeys with ivy leaves threaded through their tails and flowers wound round their ears. The donkeys feel very important like that. All the children dance too and they play with the dogs and chase each other under the long tables. It is such a happy time.'

Rosa looked at me in disbelief: 'Did she explain all that to you in Spanish, Manuela?'

'Yes,' I replied, 'a bit halting, but I could understand her perfectly well. Raimundo says she hasn't really had a decent conversation with anyone for years, but Spanish must have been seeping into her sub-conscious all that time, so now she can manage to explain simple things.'

'I think she just needs re-oiling,' Rosa suggested with a wink and an uncustomary giggle.

'It's good to see you happier, anyway, Rosa.' How easy it is to be happy, I thought.

42

The Psychiatrist's Office

I was sitting in the patient's chair in Raimundo's office. It was another step forward. With his encouragement over the last few weeks, I had walked on my own from my bed, down the passage-way, knocked on the door of his office at a given time and sat there in front of him as though I had been invited. I felt that I was becoming part of the day-to-day life of the hospital. I would even smile at the nurses as I walk down the corridor and say hello to Manuela or Rosa. The staff know me well and I truly appreciate their attention.

Raimundo turned towards me. He has such kind eyes and a calm brow. I thought that when I am with him it's as though I'm the only person in the world who matters to him. At these moments, I even feel love for him.

'These people you speak of in your book, Mara,' he said kindly, 'I have to get them straight in my mind. Shall we take them one by one?'

'If you tell me first about the people in this photo,' I smiled teasingly at him, indicating the framed family photograph on his desk.

'Ok, of course!' Raimundo replied playfully. He understood that I would respond well to his enthusiasm.

'The pretty woman. Is she your wife?'

He nodded in response. 'She is my wife and she's the only wife I have ever had. She is a wonderful woman. She is a gym teacher at a school. And she is the mother to my three children, to these three. We are a very happy family, Mara.'

My eyes began cloud over, with what? Nostalgia, envy, emotion? I pulled myself together, smiled through the cloud and whispered, 'You are a lucky man. I could have been happy too with Petre and with Tatiana, but they didn't let me. I have written in my book that he wouldn't have me when I became pregnant. You know that, Doctor. I was a silly girl then. I went with another boy, just for fun. When we are young, we don't think about the consequences of our actions. Petre was too strict to understand that and, although he knew that I still loved him and although he still loved me, he couldn't bear what I had done to him. ... He must have suffered almost as much as I did. So he left me alone. He left his daughter Tatiana alone. We were abandoned by him. I think that the price I have had to pay for doing what I did is far too high. My life has been so hard, my whole life. Never, never again have I been able to love. I look at men and I hate them. I think they are there to harm me, only to harm me. They have harmed me, haven't they, with their insensitive cruelty. You have read what happened to me when I left Bucharest, when I left Italy?'

Raimundo nodded. His eyes pleaded with me to continue.

'I say I look at men and I hate them. That is not true when I look at you, or Carlos. You are both kind and good to me. But you have shown me that. It is the men I don't know whom I fear. Sometimes I feel glad that I am old and ugly now, so the men don't look at me anymore. They don't pester me to do things I don't want to do with them. I suppose there is a sort of freedom from that point of view in growing old.' I felt that I was drawing on years of experience, as though I had thought long and hard over my life's condition.

I felt sadness flooding back into me so I tried to change the subject. I retuned my gaze to the photograph again.

'What do your three children do?'

Raimundo seemed happy to answer my questions though is eyes looked sad, perhaps in response to the pervasive sadness I was fighting to overcome.

'They are still at school. The twin girls are two years older than the little boy. All are good students. My boy says that one day he will be a doctor, like his father. But perhaps one of the twins will study medicine. It's a good career, helping to cure people.'

I think I now felt able to bring the conversation back to myself, and asked: 'Am I very ill, Doctor? Will I ever get better, strong enough to go out into the world again?'

He nodded affirmatively and smiled.

'When you forget about certain people in your past, people like Roxana and Ceausescu. You must remember, Mara, that you aren't the only woman who lost her baby in the Ceausescu regime. There were thousands and thousands of babies taken like that from their mothers. That happened here in Spain too after our Civil War, and in Ireland also with their stringent Catholic beliefs – thousands of babies taken away to grow up as recluses. That sort of thing happens where people are cruel and don't understand when a young girl gets herself pregnant. Too much religion or too much State control, in your case. But it was never your fault. You must rid yourself of the feeling of guilt. You are an intelligent woman. There are many like you who made their lives anew, who didn't go out to beg in the streets, who didn't run away to another country.' … He had gone too far.

'You don't really understand me.' There was a crisp edge to my voice. 'I thought you understood me,' I said reproachfully. 'How can you know what it was like to live in Romania at that time? How can you, a man, know what it is like for a woman to bring a baby into the world, how can you ever understand what it is to be torn apart from that baby by your own mother?' There was a terseness in my voice, an attempt at recrimination. Strangely, I could see that he was glad that I seemed to be reacting strongly to his words.

He replied: 'I can know and understand through my own imagination and intelligence, but also because of what you have told me in your writings, Mara. I am not accusing you. Please understand that. I am not saying it was easy for you. I am not telling you that you've gone wrong.'

'But I have gone wrong, haven't I?'

'But not because of your own fault.' He said. 'Life is sometimes just too hard for us to bear. Thousands of people take the wrong turnings, make the wrong decisions, and not only once in their lives, many times. That is part of the human condition, making errors. What you mustn't do from now on is to keep blaming yourself. You did what you did because there was no option for you. How could you have stayed on in Romania knowing that your little daughter was held in one of those orphanages, knowing that Roxana whom you hated was so close to you? No, you did the right thing to come away. But you must not blame yourself. And if you want to get better more quickly, you must also stop blaming other people too. Forget the bad ones. Remember the good ones. Remember Simona, your grandmother.'

'My grandmother was the most beautiful person I have ever known.' I said wistfully. 'If she had been alive, none of this would have happened. She would have saved Tatiana for me that day I went out to buy her medicine. She would never have allowed Roxana to hand her over to that man and woman and accept money in exchange for my baby.'

We sat for several long seconds staring into each other's eyes. Finally, Raimundo spoke. 'You must return to your room now Mara. I must see another patient. You're not the only one I have, but you are my favourite one.' and he smiled warmly.

'You can tell me about Simona another day. It will do you good to remember her.'

43

Simona's Wisdom

I was again seated opposite Raimundo. 'Ah, Simona. She was above everybody I have ever known in my whole life. Even above you, Doctor,' I said, grinning mischievously at him.

I was beginning to enjoy these sessions with Raimundo and all the attention. I hadn't felt like this for years, if ever. I even felt a little important, sitting in front of my psychiatrist, just separated by his mahogany table, the beautiful family photograph in its silver frame. Nobody had ever treated me with such respect as this man was doing. In the depths of my soul I felt that I owed him something, I owed it to him to improve, to get better, to cast off the shackles of illness and depression. I would continue to take my pills. I would finish my story, for him. For this good-looking man with his kind smile.

'Yes, Simona was a guiding light to me,' I said with authority.

'But only when she was alive,' Raimundo hinted. 'In your story you seem to consider that you have let her down.'

A shadow of profound sadness fell across my brow. 'But I have, haven't I? If I had taken her advice and remembered it all through these years, I wouldn't have fallen so low, would I? Simona was a wise woman, even though she had no academic culture. There was meaning, sense, behind everything she said and did. She lived in tune with the seasons of the year, with the fruits and products of her tiny orchard. She always tried to understand people, even her own daughter. How is it possible, Doctor, that such a good person could have had such a nasty daughter? I don't understand.'

Raimundo answered in a professional manner, as if he wanted me to fully understand his words: 'Human beings are made up of many different facets, not only genes. Much depends on one's upbringing, but it also depends on our patience and tolerance levels, it depends on who we come across during our life. Some are stronger, surer than others, more confident and not so influenced by the people they meet. Others are weaker and unable to stand strong in the face of adversity.'

'That's me!' I reflected, looking almost ashamed.

'You have not been lucky, Mara. I agree that you have paid far too much, with pain, for that small slip-up in your youth. It isn't only the fault of the person himself or herself, life's options are not always positive, and in your case, they certainly weren't. Tell me how you feel most influenced by Simona.'

A wide smile spread across my face as I thought of Simona. Then I spoke. 'She taught me to love nature, to feel at one with its changes. And I still think that is important. She taught me respect for all things and for all people, however poor and ugly they may be. But she also taught me not to be tolerant of injustice or cruelty. So often I feel that I have sold my soul to cruelty and injustice, sold my dignity. And that is what has broken me into pieces. I feel humiliated with what people have done to me, but I also feel humiliated by the way I have reacted. I know I could have done better.'

I paused. I felt a growing sadness and it reflected in my face.

'Mara, I repeat that you must stop reproaching yourself. One thing is to understand why and how your life is the way it is, but it is quite another to let yourself wallow in that understanding. It is time now to put it away behind a closed door. Remember it, but coldly, calculatingly, a chapter passed, so that it can't hurt you anymore. You still have a future to live. You are a middle-aged woman and that is not old in this day and age.'

'I think I fear recovering because then I shall have to return to my hovel and my begging. I shall be dirty again, lonely again, without purpose in my life,' I replied softly.

'You are well on the way to recovery, but, don't worry, I shall not allow you to leave the hospital and my care until you have something better to go to. We shall help you to find something. But you must be willing to change your attitude, to make an effort too. People will make an effort for you if you make it for them.'

'Simona always said that too.'

Well, she was right, wasn't she?

He continued: 'Everything in life, Mara, has good and bad sides to it. You were in the middle of a balance. You had Simona one side, coaxing you towards what was good, and Roxana the other side, pulling you towards what was bad. That wasn't easy for you to cope with. It would have created a conflict in your mind when you were only a youngster and young people require more categorical answers to the things in life.'

'But I tried to fight that. I hated Roxana. I hated what she made me do. You know that from my writing. Why wasn't I stronger?'

Raimundo adopted a softer, more encouraging tone. 'I certainly don't want you to feel that I am chiding you' he said. 'It wasn't that you weren't stronger. You had plans to leave home with your baby, but you delayed that for a good purpose. You were afraid of your daughter suffering in the cold of winter and being unable to protect her adequately. So, what happened? Roxana got in first, so to speak, with her malevolence by taking Tatiana away from you, by selling her for a few coins, before you had the opportunity to run away. But you had good intentions. You would have had the strength to leave home. Indeed, you *did* leave home to search for your baby in the orphanages. But that, Mara, is like searching for a needle in a haystack, particularly in a country where legality and justice had been turned upside down. Can't you see what I am saying to you? It wasn't all your fault. The tide of events was against you. You would have been a wonderful mother if you had lived in a more favourable place at a more favourable time. You must, you must assimilate that fact and stop bemoaning your past and the way you dealt with it. Think of that guiding light, the love you had for your grandmother. It can still help you.' He paused and looked intently at me. 'I shall see you again in a few days. In the meantime, see if you can finish your story for me. Try to write it as well as you can. Stick to your pills too and soon we'll see if we can get you off them.'

He was matter-of-fact, yet warm, as he ended the session. And I warmed to his words of encouragement. I always left his office feeling emotionally lifted.

*   *   *

It was the kindness, his kindness and caring … I hadn't known kindness in years. I had forgotten the meaning of the words; just how much it means to a human being. We all need kindness and I had lived without it for year upon long year. We all need to be observed during our life's journey by someone who cares for us, but nobody had observed me as I wandered through life, traipsing through one city after another, trudging from one street corner to another, from hovel to city centre and back again. Was Raimundo sent to me for a purpose? I like to think so. I like to think that he will always be with me, watching over me, as it were. Because, if he goes, if he leaves me to my own devices, I fear that I shall fall back into the mud and grime of my previous life. I must be strong. I must understand that he can't strike up personal relationships with all his patients. He is here now to protect me until I can manage my life alone … life alone … I cringe at the thought of that again. Here in the hospital ward I have Raimundo, I have Florencia, I have Manuela and I have Carlos. And there are others, too. All of them are helping me.

What's that? A fly and it's buzzing around my forehead. It must have entered through the open window in my room. It's alighting on the rim of my water glass. 'Shooo, go away!' It's gone, up to the neon light strip on the ceiling where it stands rubbing its feet together, its clammy, spindly feet. Again it's off, this time onto the sheet covering my toes. I couldn't keep my eyes off it, this stupid, flighty insect that can't keep still, jumping inanely – or so it seems – from one thing to another. It reminds me of my own life. I too have jumped inanely from one place to another, gathering nothing; nothing at all. Not even moss, just wrinkles and grime and bitterness. At least the fly is gathering more with every jump it makes. What, I'm not sure, but obviously something it needs. Yet I have nothing to call my own and I'm over fifty. I am inferior to this fly. I don't mean in material objects. I mean someone to love, someone who loves me, children of my own, a house however small, but a place where I feel comfortable, relaxed, happy. Some people build up a good life around themselves. Others attract misery and ugliness. That is what I have done. Remember Simona, Mara; that's what Raimundo said. I must think of her, every day I must think of her. She will guide me. Now I am reaching the end of my story. I hope that my writings will help Raimundo to help me. He said that they would.

How much longer? How much longer do I have to go on taking these pills? I am sure that my mind is working much better now. I can recall memories, dreams. I can remember people and events. Surely if I can do that, I don't need to go on consuming tablets. There are days when they make me feel ill. I'm convinced that the nausea is caused by the tablets. But I must keep taking them. They were all cross with me when I threw them down the toilet. If I don't take the pills, they won't bother about me anymore and they might make me leave the hospital. I must ask Carlos how much longer I need to take medicine. Some people take medicine all their lives, but I don't want to do that. Pills cure you of one ailment, yet they bring on another. Like this nausea that I feel every day. I shall talk to Carlos about it.

The other day Florencia, the cleaner, brought me a book. She put it by my bed and with a shy giggle said that she hoped I would like it, that I would be able to read the Spanish. I nodded my thanks to her, saying I would try my best. Now I feel like reading. If I don't understand anything, I can ask you, I suggested to her. She bent forward and gave me a gentle kiss on my forehead. This girl has a heart. She is warm and willing. How I hope that she manages to find a better job than all the cleaning she does. She is wasted doing cleaning. Such an attractive young woman with a quick brain. When she finishes her studies, I am sure she will find something better as a profession. … The book is a simple story, a love story. I am reading it slowly, but gradually the words become more natural to me and I can

261

understand more or less what it is about. Reading keeps my mind off myself, my problems, my illness.

*   *   *

Carlos burst into my room with a laugh and a jovial greeting.

'You are looking better today, Mara! It's good to see you sitting up reading in the chair instead of sleeping in your bed. Obviously those pills are helping you.'

He said he needed to finish his rounds with the patients quickly that morning because he had some administrative matters to attend to and didn't fancy spending the whole afternoon boxed up in his office.

It was a beautiful day – one of those splendid days in Madrid when the sky is a clean, clear blue, utterly cloudless, an unbroken expanse of azure beauty, when the sun sends its slanting rays lighting up the needles of the many pine trees that line the streets of the metropolis, glinting off the roofs of cars, shining through people's windows imbuing them with its warmth and brightness, with the promise of a long, hot summer implicit in its rays.

'I love the summer heat,' Carlos said. He loved that dryness, the fresh mornings, the intense midday heat that spills over into the long afternoons, even into the evenings until the sun mellows, bowing its glow to the horizon, giving way to the deep indigo twilight. He knew that many people found the summer heat tedious, but he found it exhilarating, life-giving. He was physically and mentally more active during those months of intense heat and, however brutally high the temperatures, he preferred them to the mid-winter days below zero. Such were the thoughts at the back of Carlos' mind.

'Carlos, I wanted to ask you about the pills ...' I said. 'How long do I have to go on taking them? You realise that they make me feel sick, don't you? No, I'm not actually sick, but after I have eaten, the food goes around and around in my stomach and I feel that I want to bring it all up, although I don't. I'm sure that's caused by the pills. Couldn't you take me off them for a few days and see what happens?'

'I think what I'll do is to reduce your dose – two pills a day instead of four – and let's see how that works out, Mara.'

262

He examined my mouth, my eyes and throat. He took my pulse, pressing my wrist gently. He nodded approvingly and patted me on the arm. I smiled at him, a wide, generous smile. It was my way of thanking him for his attention and genuine care.

'Thank you, Carlos. You are a good doctor. You and Raimundo are so kind to me.'

'We want to make you better, Mara. That's what we are here for. It won't be long now before you can take the reins of your own life again, but in a better way than before.'

My smile waned a little and my lips trembled slightly.

'Do you really think I can make my life better than before?'

'I know you can,' Carlos said convincingly. 'But you have to try hard too, not just wait for everyone else to do it for you. I must be off now. I have a busy day ahead of me. You just keep positive Mara and you'll be fine.'

*   *   *

Mara's thoughts raced backwards and forwards trying to recall the milestones of her past, to put it all into some sort of perspective.

When did my mind begin to go? Was it my mind or my strength of purpose, my will? I must think back to the different stages of my escape from Bucharest. I hated escaping from Romania in that van with those evil-smelling men, but my mind was fresh and agile then, even though I was sad. I was on the defensive, but I was alert. After that frightening journey, I was glad to escape, however scared I was as I wriggled under the fence between Hungary and Austria. I felt free from the men as I ran through those crisp fields smothered in glistening drops of dew in search of some sort of a pathway and a direction that would lead me to a new life. It was as though I was on the brink of an adventure, a better future. I barely gave a thought to the fact that I couldn't speak German, that I had no money but my Romanian lei. I don't think I even thought that the police might catch me and fling me into jail or send me back to Romania. I associate Austria with a certain optimism, a happiness even, except that I had left Tatiana. That, I shall never forget. She impregnates my thoughts, my days and my desires.

I can remember the smell of the sweet blades of grass as I trudged through the early light. I remember how tall and dark the fir trees looked, silhouetted against the pale dawn. I remember the silence in that beautiful grey world. I felt that I was the only human being on earth, alone but free. It wasn't only the smell of the grass. Later in the day there was the taste of the fresh, cold water taken from the Austrian mountain lake, the sunlight penetrating its shimmering surface, making moving patterns and shapes right down to its green depths. Then there was the smell of my straw bed in that barn. All of this I can recall perfectly, even today, so my brain must have been intact at that time. And it was, because there was the pleasant Austrian woman who drove me into Italy. I can remember how we communicated without a common language. She was my saviour at that moment.

My next stage was Trieste. There again, there is very little that doesn't flit through my mind - the grim hostel where I stayed, my work in the coffee factory, my first sight of the sea, my bench in the park overlooking the waves. I was almost happy in Trieste, again except for Tatiana. But my mind was well and truly awake and I had the will to go on living, to better myself, although I never enjoyed cleaning the factory floors.

What happened after that? Ah, yes. My co-worker, Andreea. It was with Andreea that I developed a crust around my soul. I hated her methods, the way she used men to her own ends, the way she induced me to accompany her on that journey into France. Again men, at me day in, day out, for hours. It was after that time in the second van when I felt hatred gnawing at my soul, hatred for what life was doing to me. Those men and Andreea were tearing my sensibility to shreds. My defences were weakening, my will to live in a world that I didn't understand, a world where I no longer fitted in. My desires for a better existence started fading then. An indifference set in. So I suppose I could say that it was between Italy and France that my mind started to go, certainly my strength of purpose faded out of all recognition. ... Because I was indifferent, I no longer cared about anything. I was alone, but I didn't feel lonely. I saw myself as a victim and regarded people as cruel and self-interested. I was determined to keep away from them. I was ageing rapidly in my youthful body, but ageing in the wrong sort of way. I was piling up bad experiences, bad memories and all of that embittered me. It turned me sour. Yes, that was when the real change came in my life, and since then, everything I have done has been to spite myself. ... I really hated myself.

I have had to pay for what I have done to Tatiana.

Mara felt satisfied with what she had written. It hurt her. Of course, it did, but she knew it to be true.

*   *   *

'You write well, Mara', Raimundo said. 'Your story is sad, very sad, but I know an editor who might publish it for you after having it translated professionally from Romanian.'

Mara shrugged her shoulders.

'I don't think it's good enough for publication, Raimundo.'

'It is the story of so many lives, Mara. Not obviously all the same in detail, but with many parallels. You know too that hundreds of people live on the streets in this city, not to speak of the millions all over the world who don't have a roof over their heads. You are doing them a favour by bringing your story to those who can help, by letting them know what it feels like to be begging on a street corner, to live in a hovel.'

'But they don't have the pain I have for a lost daughter,' she said, and Raimundo was surprised by what seemed like a lack of empathy for others who found themselves in bad circumstances.

'You don't know that. Some of them may well have that. And if they haven't abandoned a daughter, they have lost contact with their original family for whatever reason. ... I am going to try to get your story published. It isn't easy, you know that. But if it works, then you might earn some money from it. ... It would encourage you to try to write something else, a novel perhaps, a product of your imagination instead of the awful reality of your own life. A story that might help you to forget all your own unhappiness. Why don't you begin to write something else now, even before your autobiography is published? If you wait for publication before starting, that may never come. The important thing is to keep on writing, keep on being active. You must cultivate that side of you. You've left it abandoned for far too long now.'

'But I wrote my story for you, Doctor, not for anyone else. Not that I mind if you try and get it published. But I don't think anyone else would be interested in all that sadness.'

'That sadness is part of life, but it is over now, Mara. I have spoken to my cousin. She runs a nursing home for old people and she would be happy for you to go there to help out. She says she will pay you and that you can live in a room there and have your meals there. No, you won't have to return to your begging. Shall I arrange for you to have an interview with her next week? You are better now. You don't need to take pills anymore. You are strong and healthy. It's time you started to live again, but outside the walls of this hospital. It's time you gave some of yourself to other people.'

'Yes, I think … I think I might like that,' she said with a glimmer of hope in her voice. 'I shall miss you all here though.'

'But you can come and visit us. You've been here a long time and you'll always be welcome here. We are your friends, Mara.'

'Yes, I would like to know what happens to Florencia, the cleaner. And to Manuela. She is my favourite nurse. And to Carlos. He is my favourite doctor. And,' softening her voice, 'to Raimundo. He is my favourite psychiatrist…' She blushed. He put his arms round her and gave her an affectionate hug. She was stunned and a little embarrassed.

'No-one has done that to me since Petre, since Simona,' she stammered. 'I have forgotten that sort of kindness.'

Raimundo smiled his generous smile. It filled the entire room with warmth. It filled Mara's heart with hope.

44

The Nursing Home

Mara could see the mountains from the window of her bedroom at the nursing home. She loved those mountains, although she had never been to visit them. They reminded her of the Transylvanian hills of her youth, although perhaps more barren. One day I shall take the train and go and walk in these Spanish mountains, she would say to herself as she watched the evening sun setting behind the purple peaks.

*   *   *

It would do me good to walk up and down the mountain paths, breathe in the fresher air, feel closer to the heavens and far from human sorrow. There is a lot of sorrow around me in this place. If I say that I am happy here, that is a lie. I am only happy because I feel closer to Raimundo, although he doesn't come here. But this home is run by his cousin, Emilia, and she is a nice woman, like my kind Raimundo.

Yes, Emilia has a pleasant disposition, not only with all of us who work with her, but also with her patients. Yet, she is extremely efficient and tolerates no nonsense. She inspires a good working atmosphere, ensuring that we all help each other, all get on together. And, by and large, we do and the place functions perfectly, as perfectly, that is, as any residence can where there are so many sick, ailing people.

I suppose I can say that my days are pleasant enough, although some of my tasks are irksome, like emptying the old patients' bed pans or the pots from underneath their beds. Sometimes I must help the nurses to hold their emaciated bodies while they are washed or showered. I am strong. I have a sturdy frame, strong bones and muscles – like my mother, Roxana, my forgotten mother, though that is something to thank her for – and so I can help them to hold up these old bodies, bodies of men and women who can no longer help themselves. Even if they are thin, they are heavy because they are immobile and their limbs hang uselessly by their sides, their skin withers on their bones drooping in misshapen crepe-like folds, their eyes are clouded, their hair is ratty and thinning. It isn't easy for one person to wash them and this is why I help out. Manuela once told me that she had to wash me when I was taken in off the street and she said what a battle it was! Also, I comb their hair and help to dress them. I am willing to do whatever tasks the nurses want because I am grateful to Raimundo for having found me this job.

The work fills my daytime hours. In the evenings, I occasionally watch television in the main lounge in the company of some of the patients. I eat my meals with the other members of the staff. The food is very good and for the first time in years I feel that my body is well-nourished. Now I have very little difficulty with my Spanish. I can communicate with everyone who speaks to me. We laugh together and chat together. They ask me about Romania and that brings back my memories, good and bad. I ask them about their Spanish villages and they tell me about the countryside, about their families. They are all pleasant people, comforting to be with. Not that I could pick out one or two special friends from them. But that doesn't matter. I have had difficulty all my life making friends. At least they are company for me, after so many years of solitude.

It is three or four months now since I left the hospital where I was a patient. Yes, I returned there after only a fortnight. I wanted to thank Raimundo for having found this job for me, to thank him for all his kindness and attention to me. He said he was very happy to see me again looking so well and that he wanted me to return to visit him at least once a month. He spoke of his interview with the editor about my book, but that is something that will take time, even if they finally decide to publish it, which I doubt. But I continue to write. I told Raimundo and he was so pleased. I spend an hour or two in my room in the evening before sleeping. It is a good time for me to gather my thoughts and to concentrate. For the first time in my life I feel that I have some purpose, instead of the endless trailing to and from my place on the pavement. Begging is so humiliating. Now I am paid some money for the work I do here. I have sufficient cash to look round the shops on my free day, on Saturdays. I have even been able to buy a few pieces of clothing for myself.

I feel so much happier within myself. And the patients like me too. They dribble and coo when I pass, they wave at me and try to force a smile onto their twisted lips. The ones who cannot see very well think that I am one of the nurses and they call to me with their feeble voices, cracked and aged. Most of them have been simply abandoned in this place. Few are visited by relatives or friends. Theirs is a sad end, but better than what mine would have been, had I died of the epidemic in my hovel or had I lived there until I was an old woman. At least here they are cared for. Their bodies are kept clean.

I realise now how important cleanliness is after all those years of living unwashed, beneath layers of street grime and dust blown up from my unmade road and sweat in the height of the summer. Having a clean body is the first step to believing in yourself. When you are dirty, you know that people will run from you, want to ignore you.

Even here the uglier parts of life can be seen. There is one man here who acts like a dictator, just another patient, although I smile to myself when I compare him to Ceausescu. Of course, he isn't nearly as cruel as the Romanian President was. He orders the others around, telling them what they can watch on television. None of them protests. They fear his stentorian voice, his strong flaying arms, his heavy stance, his ugly red face. In short, they fear his cruelty and dominant nature. No-one complains about him to the nurses and so the nurses don't realise that he orders the inmates around. Some patients leave the room the moment he enters. His name is Marciano. As for me, I try to keep out of his way. He is like a a strong boar going at life as if everybody owes him something.

No, I prefer Lola. Lola is a gentle frail old lady. She tells me that her name is short for Dolores, but we all call her Lola which is easier. She has been well brought up with exquisite manners and a winning smile. She is physically weak, but she has a strong will. She is dignified and determined. Yet nobody visits her. I sit with her in the afternoons if my other duties allow me to. I know that she understands me. She knows what occurred in the Romania of my youth. I only had to say to her that my daughter was taken from me and she released a heavy sigh, so heavy that it was almost a heart-rending moan. I know all about dictatorships, she whispered and she clutched my hands with warmth and complicity, as though both of us together could will away the evil of dictators, of the Romanian dictator, of the Spanish dictator.

Lola told me that her father had been a university professor and that her mother had had a degree in Science. Both highly intelligent people, freedom lovers who had worked for a better, fairer society – neither a communist society, nor a capitalist society – but who had been forced into exile during the final months of the Spanish Republic, forced to tramp their way up to France in a line of miserable refugees, filled with fear for their lives, for her, Lola's, life, who followed on behind them, dragging her little feet over the rutted pathway, clinging on to her mother's skirts, fearful of the gunshots, of the gutted faces of her exiled companions, of the grimaces of the guards. A line of hungry, debilitated human beings walking away from their land. She told me about the hunger pains, how she missed her aunt and uncle who had been imprisoned. But, lastly, she told me, close to the French border, how one of the gunshots had reached her father. Her memory was of a handsome, bearded man collapsed in a heap on the ground, his high forehead creased with lines of anxiety, dribbling blood from his mouth into the dust, of her beautiful mother weeping silently over his corpse, of her own little fingers touching his arm, saying goodbye, both of them being pushed forward impatiently, inexorably, away from her father, by the line of decrepit souls following in their wake, by the butt end of the guards' rifles jabbed against their ribs.

'Why do I tell you all this?' Lola said to me. 'I want you to know that others have suffered too. No, no, it doesn't make your own suffering less, but I wish to confide in someone who can understand me. And you, Mara, can understand me because so great a suffering never leaves you. You can run away, you can move from one house to another, from one country to another, even from one husband to another, as I did. You can study. You can work. You can fill your time with exciting journeys, with interesting books and music. But your suffering remains. It is not at all true that time heals all wounds. Time helps them not to fester constantly, but underneath the scar, the wound never really heals.'

I would hug her and draw her frail and noble visage towards me. I would search in her eyes for her dignity and strength.

'Yes, I can understand your suffering, and you can help me in mine, Lola.'

Not all our afternoons together were bathed in painful memories. There were days when we laughed, when I would push her round the garden of the residence in her wheelchair, looking at the plants and the trees, commenting on this and that. She had a wonderful sense of humour. We even chatted with other patients, but she always used to draw me close to her afterwards and say that she preferred to be with me alone, unaccompanied by others who understand nothing, she said. They are dolts, all dolts who talk rubbish incessantly and watch stupid programmes on television.

*   *   *

After spending time with Lola I was often overcome by the desire to return to Romania. Then I was immediately besieged by doubts. Why leave Spain now that things were better for me? I was at long last beginning to defend myself, with the help of others. Why throw all that away? To find a daughter who is lost to me for ever? To return to the village of my childhood and perhaps to find my hated mother wasted away into old age? Or my sister, Viorica, embittered. Romania is an enigma for me now, after all these years. I would return to a place I no longer recognise, to people who no longer belong to me. I must be practical. It would be pointless to return. I vehemently pushed the idea to the back of my mind, but it was there, always there, like an unwanted shadow across my world — like the suffering that Lola spoke of, the suffering that can never be obliterated.

No, my life is here now, here in this home for old people, here in Madrid, here in Spain. I was almost beginning to feel Spanish. I had been many years on the edge, on the fringe of this country, many years when I hadn't been involved, hadn't dared to be involved with the comings and goings of the Spaniards. But now things were different. Emilia, Raimundo's cousin, the Director of this home, has helped me to obtain legal papers and before long I will be able to apply for Spanish nationality. How could I leave these people who had given me the only kindness I had ever known? I was indebted to them. How could I run back to Romania? I didn't even have my Romanian passport. No, it was obvious that I had to think about my future in this country, not my past in the land of my birth. In Spain, there is a saying that the important thing in your life is where you make a living – where you graze – not where you are born. And now, I can say that there is truth in that.

And so my days in the old people's nursing home pass by, some of them more slowly than others.

*   *   *

Emilia is a tall, good-looking woman in her fifties. She is kind but authoritative and her staff obey her. We are all treated well and are obliged to treat the patients well. She is constantly vigilant and knows what goes on from one side of her establishment to the other. She doesn't tolerate any unkindness to the patients or any arguments between members of her staff. The whole place works like a well-oiled machine, a series of cogs fitting perfectly together the one against the other.

Recently, Emilia called me to her office. A new patient, she said, was about to be admitted, a youngish woman with multiple sclerosis. She was no longer able to control her own life and needed permanent help. Emilia wanted me to greet her, take her to her room and make her feel at home. I would be joined by two other nurses later on, but could I stay with this new patient – Marta was her name – until they came. She didn't want her to be alone during her first hours here. When I heard the doorbell ring I went down immediately to open it.

272

The ambulance driver, aided by his male nurse, rigged up the platform they used to lower handicapped people from the ambulance to the ground. I was intrigued, watching their efficient, practised movements as they wheeled the chair onto the platform and gently lowered it to ground level. Then my eyes fell upon on the woman sitting in the chair. It was a cold day and she was covered in a thick blanket, her head and neck wrapped in a scarf. I could only distinguish a bundle, a human bundle. Suddenly she let out a piercing shriek to the attendants and waved her arms frenetically in protest. They were used to this sort of behaviour and simply wheeled her towards me. She gyrated her body with ungrateful lunges, pushing disjointedly, this way and that and crying out in hair-raising tones. Marta, Marta, I coaxed, Come inside your new home. You will see how you'll like it. Calm down now. I had barely caught sight of her face and I was pushing her along the corridor towards the room that had been allotted to her. She was a human mess and she was going to be a challenge for us all.

I wheeled her, with some difficulty because she wouldn't keep still, through the door of her bedroom. It was warm in there. I started to remove her head scarf, the scarf she had wrapped around her neck. I caught a glimpse of her in the mirror and as I did so I caught my breath. Who was this woman? She was the image of Roxana, my own mother, as I remember her. No, it couldn't be possible. She was calling things out in Spanish, not in Romanian. I peered more closely at the vision in the mirror and then turned and looked at her. I couldn't keep my eyes off her face. If she wasn't Roxana, and she wasn't, then she was her double. I shuddered – a long, cold shudder of pent-up fear. I stood rooted to the spot just staring, staring into those eyes that were my mother's eyes, at her hair pulled back severely into a bun, at her nose and mean pursed lips, that sour unsmiling mouth, the hefty shoulders and thick arms. I took in all this in only seconds. And again I shuddered. She stared back at me, unfriendly and accusing, or at least so I imagined. I ran quickly out of the room and took refuge in my own room. I threw myself down on my bed and pinched myself hard. Was this a dream? How had this woman – Marta, yes, Marta was her name, not Roxana – come to confront me in the nursing home? Why had she come to disturb my peace in this place? I began to tremble with fear and rejection.

Of course, Emilia found out about how I had left Marta to her own devices. She called me in quickly. She questioned me kindly. I could barely answer her. I couldn't stop trembling. I remember she looked concerned. Never again, never again, I murmured. I cannot see that woman ever again. She is the image of my mother. She has been sent here to torment me.

'Don't worry Mara,' Emilia said. ' I will see that you don't have to look after her.'

But my fears augmented. Each night I had nightmares, bad dreams that seemed to mingle with my thoughts in my waking hours, so that when I got up I didn't know if I had been dreaming all night long or thinking tangled thoughts. Each day I feared coming across her in the corridor, in the television lounge, in the garden. I was terrified of having to speak to her, that she would attack me for having abandoned her.

I searched for Lola. She was nowhere to be found. She had fallen, I was told, into a coma. Where, oh where is she? I insisted. When they took me to her bedside, she was completely unconscious. I stared unseeingly at her dignified face, wasted now to a tiny bony frame. Lola, Lola, please listen to me. She was a wall of silence. I sobbed. I couldn't work anymore with the other patients. I was drifting into a state of insanity. I could feel all the old fears coming back, the old indifference to life. All that was coming back too fast. In only a month after Marta's arrival I had returned to being the useless beggar I had been nearly all my life. Out of my mind, I saw Marta sitting in the garden one afternoon. Unaware of the nurses and other patients nearby, I walked straight over to her and hit her hard, a sharp swipe, across her face, then I pulled her from her chair to the ground where she lay sprawling and screaming for help.

Of course, that action meant the end of my job at the nursing home.

45

Return to the Clinic

'You must understand me, Raimundo – of course, I know you will – but I couldn't allow her to continue helping out with the patients', Emilia explained. 'In only a few weeks, she had become one of them. She had fallen back into the black hole of her past. Suddenly.... Well, no, not quite. I could see it coming on. It was the new patient Marta that sparked it all off. Mara seemed to think that Marta was her own mother. She was convinced that her mother had returned to destroy her life.

At first, she would stare at Marta with a horrified expression on her face, her lips twisted into an agonised grimace filled with hatred. Then she began to pester her physically. She would go right up to Marta, half closing her eyes quizzically, then prodding her in the ribs, prodding at her breasts, her stomach. Marta would scream, although sometimes she laughed hysterically the moment Mara appeared. They seemed to hate each other. It was as though they were nourishing each other's madness. This went on for about a week after Marta's arrival at the nursing home. Then Mara started going up to her and pulling at her, as though she wanted to tip her out of her wheelchair. She became obnoxious, not only with the patient, but with the other nurses who tried to pull her away. She had crying fits, screaming about Roxana and Tatiana. The crying eventually subsided into silences, long sessions of utter muteness, when nothing or no-one could arouse her to respond. It was as though she froze. She started pushing her food away, staring through us into the distance, at the wall of the dining room, beyond the wall, into her own world, her past. Then she started sitting propped up against the garden wall, holding out her hand as though she was begging. She won't eat properly. She refuses to shower. We have to force her to do so, with all that that entails. She is very strong and she lunges out at the nurses. She wears any old clothes. She doesn't brush her hair and won't let us do it. She is worse than many of the patients here whom she once used to help. And the worst thing is that she won't accept help from anyone. She has become totally obstreperous if someone tries to interfere with her. She won't speak to anyone. We've all tried to talk to her, tried to encourage her. She stares at us. She doesn't recognise us. She stares through us, into another world. We can look after her here, but she needs your help again Raimundo.'

Emilia put the phone down. The conversation with Raimundo had been a long one. She had barely drawn breath as though she wouldn't tolerate him interrupting her. She had to get it all out; she had put her thoughts in order, as indeed she put most things in her life in order, and her only immediate need was to convey them to her cousin. He had to understand that she and the other members of the staff at the nursing home had welcomed Mara, done all they could to make her feel at home with them, that for a long time she had been happy there and it was only the sight of the new patient who resembled her own mother that had turned the tables of her life, thrown her backwards, as it were.

*   *   *

I felt taken aback after my conversation with Emilia. I could taste the bitterness of failure in my mouth. How could I have been so innocent as to imagine that all Mara's problems were over? Well, of course, I had known that they weren't. When she left me, I realised that she still had a long way to go to get back to normality, yet I had felt that she was on the right road, on her way to a normal, moderately acceptable existence. I was wrong, wasn't I? Psychiatrists make mistakes. All human beings make mistakes, but no-one wants to forgive a professional for making a mistake. It was obvious that I hadn't worked hard enough on Mara's relationship with her mother. I hadn't helped her to overcome those antagonistic feelings. All I had done was to eke out of her what that relationship consisted of. I should have forced her to see it in a variety of lights to be able to come to terms with it. I should have concentrated on building up her self-esteem where her mother was concerned. ... She kept on blaming herself for having kowtowed to Roxana, for having been weak in the face of the older woman's severity.

Roxana was Mara's ghost, her bad dream. As her psychiatrist, it was my job to crush that evil influence, eliminate it from her life, if not altogether, then at least help her to put it all into perspective. I should have been able to show her how to build up a protective wall against this person who had harmed her so. Instead, all she had managed to do while we were having the sessions was to suppress the pain her mother had caused her, tucking it away at the back of her brain. I remember one day she smiled at me – a generous open smile – saying that she had forgotten all about her mother. Yet her mother was there, still there, waiting to jump forth at the smallest provocation. And Marta, the patient in the wheelchair at Emilia's nursing home, was the provocation, unwitting of course, but she brought Roxana back to the front of Mara's mind. Now it is as though we must begin all over again. Where? How?

For the time being she is back in her hospital bed. At least she's not in a coma again. This time she is awake, but absent. The nurses tell me that she seems to come to at night, singing Romanian songs from her youth in a raucous, cracked voice. When they ask her to be quiet she bursts into tears, into wheezy, chesty sobs that make the darkness of the night shudder. In the morning, with the break of day, she falls into sepulchral silence. She is fed through a tube. The nurses wash her on her bed. They are adept at moving heavy bodies this way and that, in order to clean the nooks and crannies and folds of human skins. She lies there, expressionless, her arms inert by her sides, her open eyes staring up at the ceiling, barely blinking, like a blind person. Taking nothing in, or so it seems.

I go to her bedside. I take her hand, her thick-fingered, heavy hand. She doesn't withdraw it. It is as though she doesn't even feel my hand against hers. I speak to her in gentle tones. There is no reaction. Her eyes remain fixed on the ceiling. Her breathing is regular, inexorable almost. But there seems to be no tension. ... Yet neither is there any response. I ask her her name. She replies with silence. I ask her about the people of her youth, all those she mentioned in her writings. Still, she replies with silence.

Then, almost certain that she will turn on me fiercely, I ask her about Roxana. Does she remember Roxana? Who was Roxana? Was she her mother? A series of questions all around that same person. At first I ask her gently, then I gradually raise my tone of voice, my insistence, stimulating her to react. Nothing. Nothing except her glassy eyes fixed on the ceiling, on a specific point on the ceiling near the neon light strip, nothing except the faintly wheezy sound of her regular breathing. I spend nearly an hour with her, an hour every two days. This has been going on now for a month. I talk to her about myself, Raimundo, her psychiatrist, the one with the nice family. I talk to her about Emilia, about the inmates at the home where she had worked. And then, again pushing the conversation to a limit, I mentioned the patient Marta. But Marta had faded from her consciousness. We had all faded from her consciousness. This therapy wasn't working and I knew that she could continue in this state for weeks more, for months, even for years. She was on IV medication, the drugs being filtered slowly into her without her having to swallow tablets. I remembered the session with the tablets when she had thrown them down the toilet. But now, not even the drugs seemed to have any effect, except that of drugging her, annihilating her will, but they were not improving her physical or mental state. Or was it simply that she had turned her back to the world?

46

Mara's End

It was as though she didn't want to live and I dwelt on the theme of forcing someone to live on against their own will. Ethically, we doctors have no option but to take advantage of everything available to us to try and save human lives. Yet what sort of ethics are these? Saving a life that wants to die? Of course, she couldn't express her feelings to us. She was in no condition to speak about what she did or didn't want. But all the same I felt, by this very life-saving action of pumping drugs into her, that I was being cruel. Wouldn't it be kinder to take her off the drugs and end her suffering? There was no quality in her life. There hardly ever had been and it was now highly doubtful that there ever would be, even if we were able to pull her through this crisis.

I felt as though I was meddling, interfering with this poor woman who had been too sensitive all her life to bear the setbacks that had befallen her. She had been a misfit everywhere. Her tragedy is that of a sensitive, intelligent person who has simply never found her place in society. I gleaned that from her story, the story that she herself had put together. She is a perfect example of a keen mind unable to defend itself, a mind that crumbled into pieces, too sensitive to cope with personal tragedy in a cruel and blunt world, and befuddled now with a lack of self-esteem. Would it not be kinder if her tragedy could be alleviated by death?

I surprised myself at having such thoughts, thoughts that dwelt on the question of a dignified end to human sorrow and pain and illness, a dignified end that would entail, not exactly euthanasia, but withdrawing all artificial methods of maintaining life. Yes, I surprised myself that I could be thinking in this way after years and years of medical training and experience all dedicated to the protection of life, whatever state it was in.

I considered, if not taking her off the drugs completely, at least reducing her intake. Somehow I had to break down this deadly calm inside her if I were to help her. ... I say deadly calm. Manuela told me that her nights were chaotic, frightening. She would twist and turn between the sheets, calling out into the night, sometimes singing, sometimes shrieking, disturbing the silence of the ward, the dreams of other patients. It was as though the calm and stillness of her days was her way of gathering energy for her night-time antics. I had to take a decision on this, otherwise the rhythm of her sick life could go on for months without her making any improvement or getting any worse. I felt that I was solely responsible for taking this decision. She had liked me. I was the only person she had trusted in the latter part of her life, the only person she had confided in. She had nobody else. I have said that no-one ever visited her. Yet how could I live with such a decision on my conscience? I felt uneasy. I would lie in bed at night, sleepless, sweating with guilt and unhappiness. I had grown fond of Mara. Remember, she had been a challenge for me. I would miss her. Yet I couldn't bear her suffering the way she was now. Oh, the senselessness of it all! Pumping ersatz life into a dying body.

Several days later, before I had told the doctors to reduce her medication, Mara made her own decision. Florencia was cleaning her room. It was her final week of working in the hospital. She had found another job, her dream of working with computers in an office, not with mops and dusters in a hospital.

She told me, as she moved around the room with her dusting, that she had been chatting in a friendly way to Mara, although she said she knew Mara couldn't understand her.

*   *   *

As I approached the patient's bed, I noticed with a shock that Mara's eyes had taken on a cold, glassy sheen, that her skin had turned to parchment, that her breast no longer moved to the subtle ebb and flow of life. I took Mara's hand in my own. Mara was as cold as a block of ice. Her pulse had stopped. It was eleven o'clock in the morning. She must have been dead for two or three hours. The nurses hadn't noticed that she was close to the end when they had passed by to take her temperature and change her food and drugs earlier on. I bent over the corpse and tenderly brushed Mara's forehead, an ice-cold forehead, with my lips. 'Maybe you will be happy now, happy at long last,' I whispered over the frozen face. I wiped a tear from my own cheek.

After Mara's demise, I was relieved that I had such little time left at the hospital. It was all too emotional. True, I had seen other patients pass away, but-had never felt the same sort of attachment to them as I had to Mara. I knew that I didn't really want that sort of unhappiness in my life. I was too young. I had my entire life ahead of me to be lived, not marred by sadness.

*   *   *

Mara had gone so suddenly, almost surreptitiously, as though she didn't want any of them to notice she was in the process of dying. Florencia knew that she had spent many nights screaming, hysterical, but when she had approached her corpse, she could see only calm, relief on the Romanian woman's lifeless expression. And she was glad to have seen that calmness on the face of a woman who had experienced so much suffering. She didn't really believe in God or in afterlife or in angels or the Virgin Mary. She understood in an elemental sort of way that Christ's message was a good message to help people through their difficulties and she wondered if He had helped Mara through hers. Florencia doubted that. But the peace on her waxen countenance held a beauty that Florencia would remember for a long time.

*   *   *

281

That very morning, the morning of Mara's death, I received a mail from my editor friend. He said he was prepared to accept Mara's tale for publication. His only concern was sales. It wouldn't have a wide market, but he said that he had liked her story for its unlikely content. Not many beggars, he said, would have had a university education. He liked the way she had told her tale. Yes, he said, it was worth giving it a chance. How many beggars live inside a cocoon of extreme sensitivity like Mara? Possibly more of them than we imagine.

I remember that at first she could hardly hold the pen. She had difficulty finding her words. But I knew that it was lack of practice. I knew that there'd been a time when it had been natural to her. The tale of her life, so bleak and senseless to her, would now see the light of day and others would know how she had lived. I was sad, of course I was sad to have lost her, but I was relieved at not having had to make that decision. To this day, I still don't know if I could have done it.
